Denene Millner and **Nick Chiles**

Authors of the Blackboard Bestseller **Love Don't Live Here Anymore**

In
Love
and
War

"Funny and real...bring[s]
alive the dynamic that intense
attraction can create."—Honey

Also by Denene Millner and Nick Chiles

A Love Story

Love Don't Live Here Anymore

Money, Power, Respect:
What Brothers Think, What Sistahs Know

What Brothers Think, What Sistahs Know About Sex:
The Real Deal on Passion, Loving, and Intimacy

What Brothers Think, What Sistahs Know:
The Real Deal on Love and Relationships

Also by Denene Millner

The Sistahs' Rules:
Secrets for Meeting, Getting, and Keeping a Good Black Man

The Angry Black Woman's Guide to Life

In
Love
and
War

DENENE MILLNER
and
NICK CHILES

NEW AMERICAN LIBRARY

New American Library
Published by New American Library, a division of
Penguin Group (USA) Inc., 375 Hudson Street, New York, New York 10014, U.S.A.
Penguin Books Ltd, 80 Strand, London WC2R 0RL, England
Penguin Books Australia Ltd, 250 Camberwell Road,
Camberwell, Victoria 3124, Australia
Penguin Books Canada Ltd, 10 Alcorn Avenue, Toronto, Ontario, Canada M4V 3B2
Penguin Books (NZ), cnr Airborne and Rosedale Roads,
Albany, Auckland 1310, New Zealand

Penguin Books Ltd, Registered Offices: 80 Strand, London WC2R 0RL, England

Published by New American Library, a division of Penguin Group (USA) Inc.
Previously published in a Dutton edition.

First New American Library Printing, June 2004
10 9 8 7 6 5 4 3 2 1

 REGISTERED TRADEMARK—MARCA REGISTRADA

New American Library Trade Paperback ISBN: 0-451-21115-4

The Library of Congress has catalogued the hardcover edition of this title as follows:

Millner, Denene.
In love and war : a novel / by Denene Millner and Nick Chiles.
p. cm.
ISBN 0-525-94709-4
1. African Americans—Fiction. 2. Junior high school teachers—Fiction.
3. Mothers and sons—Fiction. 4. Single mothers—Fiction. I. Chiles, Nick. II. Title.
PS3613.I565 I5 2003
813'.54—dc21   2002037904

Printed in the United States of America

PUBLISHER'S NOTE
This is a work of fiction. Names, characters, places, and incidents either are the product
of the authors' imagination or are used fictitiously, and any resemblance to actual per-
sons, living or dead, business establishments, events, or locales is entirely coincidental.

BOOKS ARE AVAILABLE AT QUANTITY DISCOUNTS WHEN USED TO PROMOTE PRODUCTS OR SERV-
ICES. FOR INFORMATION PLEASE WRITE TO PREMIUM MARKETING DIVISION, PENGUIN GROUP
(USA) INC., 375 HUDSON STREET, NEW YORK, NEW YORK 10014.

And, lo, the angel of the Lord came upon them, and the glory of the Lord shone round about them: and they were sore afraid. And the angel said unto them, Fear not: for, behold, I bring you good tidings of great joy, which shall be to all people.

LUKE 2:9–10

*For Lila Elisabeth Chiles, whom we happily welcome
And Bettye Millner, whom we dearly miss*

Acknowledgments

All honor, glory and praise to our Savior, whose blessings come in abundance, even when we falter. Without Him, surely, we are nothing.

Our family continues to provide us with all the love, strength, warmth, and support that we need and cherish. James Millner and Troy Millner; Chikuyu and Migozo Chiles; James, Angelou, Miles, and Cole Ezeilo; Jameelah and Zenzele Thornton; and Maia and Imani Cogen—thanks so much for all that you do.

We added another child to the brood this year. When they aren't running us ragged, they bring us never-ending joy as we watch them grow and prosper. Mazi, Mari, and Lila, we hope you find in your lives at least half the bliss that you bring us each and every day.

To our agent extraordinaire, Victoria Sanders, we feel extremely safe and protected in your hands. Thanks for looking out.

Once again we wrap our arms around the talented folks at Dutton/Penguin Putnam, who make this all feel very easy—Laurie Chittenden, Stephanie Bowe, Seta Bedrossian, Audrey LaFehr, and Robert Kempe.

He

Okay, now that I think about it, maybe I did go a little too far.

I had pledged to be more honest with the mothers and look what it got me—the harshest attack that I had ever suffered from a parent. Zaria Chance had strolled into my classroom and torched the place. She actually had suggested that I couldn't control my class, that maybe I didn't know what I was doing. I was so stunned that I was almost speechless—which is a rarity, believe me.

As with so much in life, it was all about the timing. In fact, that's a lesson I often push with both my seventh graders and with my basketball team. Timing. Knowing when to make a move.

Zaria Chance walked into my classroom at the wrong time. I had been getting angry, thinking to myself that right there on the sheet of paper in front of me was the problem with the public education system. According to my class register, thus far I had seen parents for sixteen students. All were the parents of my better students. The difficult kids, the knuckleheads? Their parents were missing in action. So in effect most of my evening at the parent-teacher conference was spent preaching to the choir, so to speak. The ones I really needed to convert, the mothers and fathers who were failing to do their jobs, couldn't find the time to come down to the school and talk to their child's teacher. As if whatever they were doing this evening was more important than that.

Yes, I could get self-righteous about it when pushed. I considered what I did to be on the level of missionary work in its importance. After twelve years in the classroom, I had seen plenty of evidence that a teacher could pull off miracles. Okay, maybe "miracle" was too strong. Work magic. But I needed help from the parents. At least backup, the appearance that the parents cared and would smack the kid upside the head—they didn't literally have to hit the kid, of course, but at least put the fear of God into him, as my grandmother used to say—for messing up in my classroom.

Back to Zaria Chance. As I said, her first mistake was walking into my classroom just after I was getting pissed that I wasn't seeing any of the parents I wanted to see. I'm not saying Zaria's son, James, was a knucklehead, but he definitely had his knucklehead moments. I could tell the kid was smart—he had "potential," a term we teachers definitely overused (don't they all have potential?)—but there was something missing in the discipline department. My guess was that there was no man in the house. I had become quite skilled at picking up on that one over the years. Especially with the boys. That's why Principal Bell tried putting as many of the male students in my class as she could get away with without attracting too much attention.

When Miss Chance walked into my class, I was a bit surprised by how pretty she was. It's not that I never saw any pretty moms, but by seventh grade most of the suburban mothers in Teaneck had been overtaken by resignation. They had given up on pretty—they seemed to be settling for awake. But Zaria Chance looked different, fresher, carrying a hint of sensuality that I had assumed didn't even exist in these comfortable split levels and colonials. Her skin was a rich caramel, her face so smooth and flawless that you instantly knew she was a woman who took care of herself.

Right away, as I watched her settle into the small chair, I braced myself. I didn't want to let her attractiveness distract me. It had happened before and I was still embarrassed. I had been doing a stint in fifth grade three years earlier and the sexy, kittenish mother of a top-shelf knucklehead had talked me out of a suspension with her clearly calculated sexual codes. I had kept looking down at the glimpse of chocolatey thigh gleaming at me and I totally forgot the point of her visit. Never again.

"So, how's my James doing?" she said, presenting a polite smile. She had dimples. Nice.

Her James was getting on my nerves. That's really what I wanted to say. But that was much too frank. You had to ease into it with the mothers. I had gotten the sense over the seven weeks that he had been in my class that James didn't have much interaction with adult males. It was something about his needy, attention-grabbing swagger—he was calling out for me to give him extra time. These were the kind of observations that Principal Bell counted on me to make. I hadn't thought about how I would get to it, but I suddenly got a flash of inspiration. Why not just come out with a simple question?

"Does James have a father figure in the house?" I asked, smiling warmly, kindly. Or so I thought.

Right away I knew the question had been wrong. The bulging of Zaria's eyeballs told me this, as did her snort of disgust.

"Excuuuse me!" she said. "What kind of question is that? Aren't we here to talk about his academic performance?"

Her eyebrows arched so drastically that I thought they were going to merge with her hairline. She was wearing a conservatively cut business suit, light brown, and I noticed that her nails were not decorated with any brightly colored polish. Like she didn't have time for all that adornment. Right now her hands were clenched tightly, angrily. And of course there was no wedding ring, which I had noted early on. No rings of any type.

"Well, there's a good reason I asked you that," I said, trying not to let her reaction rattle me. "James has acted up quite a bit in my class. He spends too much time in homeroom out of his seat, and he often seems distracted. Sometimes he seems to be, uh, kind of searching for attention. In my experience, males frequently do that with male teachers if there's a lack of a, uh, male figure in the house."

She stared at me coldly, not responding right away. I tried to return her stare, but not very successfully. Her glare made me look away, at a spot above her head and to the left. I wanted my statement to sound strong, convincing, but I knew I had been a bit too hesitant, unsure of what I was saying. With parents, particularly mothers, uncertainty was lethal. They picked up on the scent of it like bloodhounds.

"He has plenty of male figures, thank you," she said crossly. "He's never had any problems in other classes with his, um, discipline."

I waited for more. I got the never-had-this-problem-before defense all the time. Frankly, it was not at all convincing. Most of the time, the student in fact *did* have the same problem in other classes, but the other teachers just never bothered to complain. But I believed I was doing the parents a favor by giving them as much info as possible, even if it was negative.

"Uh, well, that doesn't really concern me," I said. "I'm much more interested in what's going on with him right now."

Right away I knew it sounded too cold, a little heartless. I wanted to take it back, but it was out there, like a finger in her eye.

"That doesn't *concern* you?" she said. "Is that your way of saying you don't care what he was like in his previous classes? That would seem to be totally relevant, if you ask me. 'Cause what it would be telling me is that the problem with James might not be with James at all."

She sat back and crossed her arms in a huff. I waited for more, but she was waiting for *me* to respond. She was telling me that the trouble with her son was his teacher. I took a deep breath, told myself not to overreact. This, in fact, was the other problem with the public education system—parents unwilling to take responsibility for their children's behavior. It was always someone else's fault—usually the teacher. Sometimes when they were called to school because of their youngster's wild antics, they'd actually wind up confronting the teacher right there in front of the child. Obviously, I had one of those single mothers in front of me who thought her child could do no wrong. Boy, I was sick and tired of the Zaria Chances of the public school world. I wanted to gather them all together, scream until my voice was gone, then teach Parenting 101. No, my daughter Lane had never lived with me, but I still knew a thing about parenting—enough to teach all these blameless single moms, that's for sure.

"You know," I began, "it would be a lot more helpful to your child if you could listen to what I'm saying. James doesn't need you trying to put the blame on somebody else for his actions. He's in seventh grade, starting to become a young man. Frankly, he needs somebody to crack down on him *more*, not to give him excuses. He won't—"

"No!" she interrupted loudly. Her exclamation made me draw back, away from her, as if she had swung.

"*No*, sir. I will *not* sit here and listen to you lecture me on how to raise *my* son! That's what's wrong with the public schools—teachers always wanting to blame the parents for their own shortcomings. If you can't figure out how to reach my son, then maybe you're not a very good teacher. Maybe he needs to be in a different social studies class. If you could control your class, I *know* you wouldn't be having any problems with my James. He doesn't have any discipline problems."

I think I gasped audibly. I noticed a nasty glint in her eye; she had enjoyed her little speech. She had actually accused me of not knowing how to teach. I was so stunned that I almost wanted to laugh. This was by far the worst confrontation I had ever had with a parent because never before had any of the angry ones made it so personal, so quickly accused me of not knowing what I was doing. That was astounding. She wasn't nearly as pretty to me anymore. I glared at her, trying to gather my thoughts, trying to craft the perfect response to her unprovoked attack. Here I was, dragging myself up to Teaneck every morning, pouring my heart and soul into the classroom, trying to keep these knuckleheads still long enough to stuff something into their heads that might prove useful one of these days. It was the most thankless job in our thankless society because we were always getting ganged up on, used as a handy scapegoat by every politician from the White House down to the town council. Test the teachers, monitor the teachers, mentor the teachers, punish the teachers, blame the teachers. So they pay us peanuts, kick us in the teeth at every opportunity, then place their children in our care for the majority of their days. It made absolutely no sense to me. I mean, would your average mother hire a nanny to watch her baby after the mother had spent the previous year smacking the nanny upside the head every five minutes? I don't think so. But we come in every morning and do our job like professionals, knowing that each child who's not paying attention, who is too depressed or distracted or excited or aggressive or uncaring, is still our responsibility, even if it's clear that he has no intention of learning anything.

These are the messages I wanted to shout at this woman who had the nerve to blast my teaching abilities. I wanted to invite her to follow me around for a day, to watch me in action as the students grinned and laughed and squealed and applauded and listened—that one was key—on my cue as I did my thing every day in this classroom. I couldn't control my class? Sheeeit.

"You know, Miss Chance, I sit here all night hoping that the parents I really need to talk to find just a little bit of time in their busy schedules to come out and hear the things their kids need to work on.

But usually the parents I talk to are the ones I don't really need to see. I'm still not sure why that is, but I've come to accept it. But every once in a while I'll get a parent—and I'm going to be honest here, usually a single mother—who seems unable to hear what I'm saying. For whatever reason, she doesn't want to believe me, as if it's impossible that her little boy could be anything but perfect. And that's a problem. James doesn't need you to blame me or anybody else for his difficulties. That's not going to do him any good. If more parents took responsibility, we would all be a—"

"Oh, *hell* no!" she said, bolting up from the chair and grabbing for her pocketbook. "I'm not going to sit here and listen to this." She started toward the door. Then she turned on her heels and pointed a long finger at me.

"You need to take a good look at yourself, Mr. Roman! You seem to think you are God's gift to teaching, that you can do no wrong, but you need to think again!" And then she was gone. Just like that.

The rest of the conversations with parents over the next half hour zipped by in a blur. Right after she left the classroom, I was literally shaking. I had to run to the bathroom so that a parent wouldn't see me so flustered. I stared into the bathroom mirror, looking myself in the eyes. What had just happened? I turned over the entire conversation with Zaria Chance, pinpointing the places where I had erred. Surely the opening was all wrong. I should have suspected that she would be sensitive about a grown man asking her if she had a man. In this age of multiplying single mothers, that was a question loaded with tons of baggage. Some single mothers were frank and unashamed about their single status and the lack of positive role models for their sons and were often engaged in campaigns to find role models wherever they could—but those were usually the parents whose sons weren't knuckleheads. Again, Zaria's son wasn't a knucklehead, but he did have some knucklehead tendencies.

Once the conversation between me and Zaria started off wrong, I didn't know how to make it right again. So I made it worse, it seemed. Telling her I didn't care what he acted like in his other classes had been a mistake—even if it was true. What was wrong with me? I needed to go somewhere and have a tact transplant, I thought, as I splashed cold water on my face. Now the question was, do I reach out to her and apologize—or just let it go? Surely I was a big enough man to construct an affecting apology—right? Maybe I could send a letter home with James. I nodded to myself. That was what I'd do, sit down over the next few days and write a strong apology letter—warm but not too apologetic—perhaps even invite her out for a cup of coffee. But she might misconstrue a coffee invitation, thinking it was an attempt at a pickup. I certainly didn't want that evil woman thinking I had any interest in her other than professional. I preferred my women to be a bit funkier and a whole lot sweeter. Not that sweet is enough to make a relationship work, as I discovered about six months earlier with a woman from Queens named Cynthia. Long story, but it's enough to say that surface sweetness doesn't necessarily mean a woman won't eventually try to cut out your heart and feed it to her dog. Actually, Cynthia had a cat, but he was a mean little bastard who might as well have been a dog.

Being an unmarried, reasonably attractive male teacher in an elementary or middle school was like tossing a hunk of chum into the middle of a pool of sharks—they all tried to devour you whole, and they didn't care who got nipped in the process. The ones who were married themselves were trying to fix me up with their single friends—inside and outside of the school—and the single ones were trying to send me as many loud and clear signals as possible without appearing too desperate. A challenge at which they usually failed. I had tried to mess around with a few teachers in my earlier years—had even had a couple of brief but deliciously scandalous sexual relationships with two different married teachers (one of whom transferred out of the district after we mutually decided to end it because she felt she was on the verge of getting caught)—but it typically ended badly and messily. Nothing worse than breaking up with a fellow teacher—not only did every female in the building know all your business by the first lunch period, but you instantly became archenemy number one of the entire staff. (Though that only lasted long enough for another single teacher to decide that she now felt kindly enough toward you to invite you over to her place for dinner.) I'm not even trying to brag here—two other male teachers in the school who I had grown fairly close to over the years got just as much attention as I did, and one of them was rocking the sunnyside up, balding-pate-with-a-circular-fringe-of-hair look. Well, he didn't get quite as much attention, but he did all right. In fact, he was dating a sixth-grade English teacher.

When my classroom clock hit 9 P.M., I quickly gathered my things and practically sprinted for my car. I didn't want to linger and do the post-conference debriefings that the other teachers loved to engage in while they were sucking down leftover donuts. I really liked my job, but I had a hard time stomaching the social scene that pulsated around me in South End Middle School. Teachers were just too damn nosy for their own good, which is why it was so difficult trying to have a relationship with a teacher in the same school—or even the same district (I had tried that once, too).

As I pulled out from the parking lot, I decided to make a few detours on the way home to my Jersey City apartment. I had to cancel basketball practice on parent-teacher night, but that didn't mean I stopped thinking basketball. This would give me a chance to drive down a few choice blocks to check on a couple of players who liked to sample the Jersey City street life way too much for their own good. I worried about Jermaine and Tariq probably as much as their mothers did. Both of them were immensely talented, but I feared they both seemed to have a knack for getting into trouble. Stupid, avoidable trouble. They were both seniors, both had been All-State the previous year, and they both were being recruited by nearly every major college program in the country, pursuing them with the passion of starry-eyed lovers. If they could just stay out of trouble for the rest of the year, both of these boys could sign on at the college of their choice—and they could lead me to my first state championship. We had lost in the semifinal game just nine months earlier and I desperately wanted to get to the championship this time and win it. My team, St. Paul's, had never won a state championship and I knew if I could deliver I could probably double my annual salary. We all had a lot of big things on the line.

Which is why my heart fell into my shoes when I turned onto Tariq's block and immediately was confronted by the swirling lights and amped-up excitement of at least four Jersey City police cruisers parked haphazardly—as if they had parked in a hurry—outside of Tariq's building. Lord, please don't let it be Tariq involved in some foolishness, I whispered to myself as my SUV slowly floated down the block. As I got closer, I heard excited voices and shouts. I couldn't worry about trying to find a parking space—I double-parked and bolted from the truck, intent on finding Tariq. I saw two police officers, one black and one white, walking alongside a young man in handcuffs headed toward the squad cars while a woman who could have been his mother pointed and cursed at the officers every step of the way. When I turned to look to my right, I saw exactly what I had prayed I wouldn't—and the sight made my knees buckle. Two white officers had Tariq up against the wall and they were excitedly talking to him right up in his face—well, he's 6-6, so as close to his face as they could get. I saw one of them pointing his scary cop finger right at Tariq's chest. I couldn't see the boy's face clearly enough to read his expression, but every bit of my coaching instincts kicked in and I raced over to the trio.

"Uh, is there a problem here, officers?" I said too loudly as I approached the officers from behind.

They swung their entire bodies around simultaneously, both already wearing scowls. Oh, this was not going to be pretty.

"Hey, Coach!" Tariq said cheerily. Why was he sounding so happy?

"Tariq, what happened?" I asked. I avoided looking at the cops because I just knew they'd be sending me those cold, blue-eyed cop stares.

"Are you the coach over at St. Paul's?" one of them asked.

I was stunned to see what almost appeared to be awe on his face. It was the last thing I had expected to see.

"Yes, I am," I said, still not sure where this was leading.

"Coach Roman, so nice to meet you," his partner said, extending a hand. Wow, he knew my name?

I looked down at the hand and quickly enclosed it in mine, though I was still a little off-guard.

"We were just talking to Tariq here about that game he had against St. Anthony's last year in the playoffs," the first cop said. "My nephew goes to St. Anthony's, so I was rooting for them. But Tariq was unbelievable in that game."

The cop reached up and patted Tariq on the shoulder. My player—who had once scared me half to death telling me he hated cops so much that he dreamed about getting one alone without his gun and badge—was grinning like a little boy on Christmas morning.

"What did you have, like thirty-five points and sixteen rebounds, or something like that?" the second cop said. Tariq shrugged happily.

"Yeah, something like that," he said, his long handsome face still stretched in a grin.

"Actually, it was thirty-six points and fifteen rebounds, plus six blocks and seven assists," I said.

Both of the cops shook their heads simultaneously. I could feel the tension—no, the fear—start slipping from my body. Boy, this certainly was unexpected.

"You think you can beat St. Anthony's this year, Coach?" the first cop said.

I looked at him again. He wore that slightly excited little-boy look that men got when they talked sports. He was no longer a white cop— he was now a fan pulling up a stool in the bar.

"Well, I certainly hope so," I said. "We got Tariq and Jermaine coming back, of course. Our point guard, who was only a freshman last year, has improved dramatically, which will be a big help. If we stay healthy and focused, we should have a good shot to win it all this year."

"Yeah, that kid Jermaine is terrific, too," the second cop said. He looked toward Tariq. "It's been a long time since I saw two kids as good as you and him on the same high school team. How'd you pull that one off, Coach?"

"I just got lucky, I guess," I said, grinning. "The fathers at St. Paul's must have sent a prayer up to the basketball gods 'cause I walked into practice one day and they both were standing there, both of them already towering over me as fourteen-year-olds. I knew the next four years were going to be interesting."

The cops grinned back at me, happy to be getting an inside story on one of New Jersey's most talked-about teams. Actually, the story wasn't entirely true—I had been trying to woo both boys to St. Paul's since they were in sixth grade, and had been tipped off to Jermaine's talents by a friend, the director of a popular community center—but this was the story that I had been telling reporters for the past three years, ever since Tariq and Jermaine had combined for forty-seven points and twenty-three rebounds in their first high school game.

"Well, we gotta get going, Coach," the first cop said after he looked around and realized there was only one squad car left, which I assumed was theirs. "My name is Mike Palumbo and this is Kyle Minervini. I'm sure we'll be seeing you at the games."

He turned toward Tariq and stuck out a hand. "And you have a great season, big guy."

Tariq took the cop's hand and nodded vigorously.

"Make sure you give us your autograph when you're starting for the Knicks," the second cop said as he, too, shook Tariq's hand.

Tariq and I watched the cops walk back to their squad car.

"What in the world was that all about, Tariq?" I asked.

Tariq shrugged again. He did that a lot. "I don't know, Coach. I was upstairs watching TV with my moms and we heard all this screaming coming from somewhere in the building. When I looked out the window, I already saw the cop cars so I decided to come down. My mother wanted me to stay inside, but I thought the noise was coming from my boy Raja's crib. He's been having a lot of beef with his girl Tina's baby daddy. This big dude named Antwan. So I just wanted to see if, like, Raja needed some help."

I shook my head. "Tariq, how many times—"

"I know, I know, Coach. Why I always gotta go looking for trouble. Yeah, you tell me that shit, um, sorry, Coach—you tell me that all the time. But it was my boy, so I couldn't just leave him hangin' if he needed me. He's had my back enough times, you know? Remember that time when I had beef with those kids from Bayonne, them white boys, when I was trying to catch the bus after the game? Well, Raja was the one who punched that kid in the face just before the bus took off. So I had to see what was happening."

"So, what was happening? Was that Raja in the handcuffs just now?" I asked. Tariq looked at me with wide eyes, as if he were trying to get out of a whupping. He shook his head.

"Nah, that wasn't no Raja. Raj wasn't even home, I don't think. I don't even remember that kid's name, actually. It's like Teddy or something like that. I'm not sure what he did. I think he's a dealer or something."

I shook my head again. Tariq and his mother needed to get out of this building and neighborhood before it ate him alive. Tariq wasn't a bad kid—he just liked to be out in the street. In this neighborhood, no good could come of that particular hobby. In the meantime, I had taken it upon myself to keep a watchful eye trained on Tariq. I knew the more I kept him busy with basketball and schoolwork, the less time he had to find trouble. But I still worried over him like an anxious dad, like he was my child. His partner Jermaine also had a nose for trouble, but Jermaine had a father in his house and thus had less need for me to come sniffing around all the time—though I worried about Jermaine, too.

I walked Tariq back upstairs so I could have a word with his mother. As we approached the building, she waved and yelled at us from the window.

"Hi, Coach!" she bellowed, waving coquettishly. As I watched her little flirtatious wave, I wondered if she realized that screaming from a seventh-floor window at 9 P.M. wasn't exactly ladylike behavior. But I waved back at her so she wouldn't yell at me again.

When we reached their apartment, Tariq's mom, who always insisted that I call her Ronnie—short for Veronica, I believe—was standing in the doorway, waiting. While I liked the woman, her efforts to flirt with me were sometimes too painfully over-the-top. Curiously, Tariq never seemed bothered by them, as if he didn't even notice. But Tariq didn't notice much—the boy was forever lost in his own world.

I decided not to go inside—I knew she was about to invite me in. Best to just get on home and prepare for tomorrow's classes. The thought of classes brought me back suddenly to the encounter with Zaria Chance and my stomach did a slow burn. I still couldn't believe the nerve of that woman, to suggest that I couldn't teach. I had a few things to show her.

"Would you like to come inside for a bite to eat, Coach Roman? I made some macaroni and cheese and roast beef."

My stomach stopped burning and growled conspicuously as she described dinner. It was so loud I feared she must have heard it.

"Uh, no, that's okay. I already ate," I lied.

A frown crossed Ronnie's face. She was not an unattractive woman—her heart-shaped face and large eyes carried a permanently innocent look that was, frankly, a rare find in these parts. She was getting a bit pudgy, but I'm sure she was still considered quite the looker among her peers. She had an enormous chest that I couldn't have missed even if I'd wanted to. It might even be too big, if that was possible. I'm not an elitist by any stretch, but I knew there was no good that could come from spending any intimate time with Ronnie Spencer.

"What you talking about, Ma? You didn't make no roast beef!" Tariq said, shooting his mother a startled look.

Now her frown turned into a full-blown scowl. "Boy, how you

know what I made?! You don't stay in the house long enough for your behind to meet a chair at the dinner table. Now you tellin' me what I made?"

Tariq's shoulders slumped a bit. "Well, how come I ain't have no roast beef for dinner then?" he mumbled, more to himself than to his mother. Ronnie ignored him and turned her attention back to me.

"Well, Coach, I'm sorry I can't feed you tonight. I hope you can come back and eat some of my cookin' another time. I'm a great cook, if I say so myself."

"Yeah, Ma can burn!" Tariq confirmed, nodding vigorously and smiling at her.

Ronnie now smiled, too. Not wanting to be left out, I also smiled. Maybe there'd be no harm in sitting down at the woman's table one of these days.

"That would be great, Ronnie. I'd like that," I said.

She smiled more broadly. I needed to run.

"Uh, well, Tariq. See you at practice tomorrow. You know we got that tournament this weekend to kick off the season. We got a lot of work." Tariq probably hadn't even looked at the schedule yet. He just showed up when I told him to (usually) and put the ball in the basket, didn't really matter to him who we were playing.

I waved to them and scampered back to my car. On the way to my apartment, I started thinking about the lesson I had planned out for the next day. I was supremely confident in my teaching abilities, but I convinced myself to take it up even another notch. I wasn't responding to Zaria Chance's criticism, not directly. I just wanted to prove to everyone that I was the best teacher in that damn school. Actually, I wanted to prove it to myself. I didn't really care what everybody else thought. Especially some angry, single mother who probably had just moved to Teaneck from some godforsaken ghetto and had long ago given up on trying to control her misbehaving man-child. I didn't care what that woman thought of me. Everything I did, I did for me.

As I parked my car, I knew that was a damn lie.

She

See, what kills me is Negroes who think that just because they don't see a diamond on my left ring finger means that (a) I'm some desperate woman who hasn't seen any parts of a man since she last got knocked up; (b) I'm some ghetto hootch looking for somebody—anybody—to help me control my wild-ass kids; and (c) I'm some loser who needs lecturing on how to raise my child—particularly my son. Well let me tell you something: I'm none of the above, thank you very much. Okay, so I don't have a man, and my kids haven't seen their father in more than a year. But he's a trifling idiot who I don't want around my James and Jasmine anyway, and I don't have the time, patience, or inclination to deal with men right now, because, just like Mr. Roman, they're always trying to walk into my house and fix stuff—as if I, a single mother of two, can't handle my business as a mother/head-of-household/career woman/breadwinner. Well guess what? I don't need that madness in my life. And I sure as hell don't need fixing. And neither do my kids. Now, I'll admit they're no angels—but whose kids are? James is a boy knocking on his teens, and yes, he needs attention—but so does every other little boy growing into a man-child. That's what they do, they get into messes. And do zany things that make you want to snatch them by the scruff of the neck, smack them over the nose with a wet newspaper, and tie them to a tree in the backyard until you're sure they're housebroken. I'm sure it's no different in school. The trick is to keep their little behinds preoccupied. And interested. And intrigued. James has had plenty of teachers who were capable of doing this—good ones who recognized potential and treated the kids as individuals, not some little numbers who mechanically memorized their lessons, spewed the facts back onto test papers, and waited quietly for the next workbook assignment, like little Stepford children. James is full of life, and smart and creative and engaging. I will not have some teacher tell me two months into classes that my son is some badass child who needs a backhand slap from a "male role model"—whatever that is—in order to be a better student.

James is a good kid. And he's a good kid because he has a good mother. A role-model mother. I may not be perfect, I may have had two children out of wedlock, I may not have finished college, and I may not have a "male figure in the household," but dammit, I'm doing something right. I've got my own house, in a neighborhood safe enough to raise children, with enough bedrooms for each of us to have our own space, and a backyard to play in. There's food in the refrigerator. I'm no dummy. And my kids want for nothing. Because their mother has a good job and works her behind off to give them what they need and even what they want sometimes. If James and Jasmine fail to graduate from college—and they are going to college—it won't be because their mother didn't tell them that a college degree is one of the most important things they could ever get for themselves. If James and Jasmine don't get themselves careers in their lifetimes, it won't be because their mother didn't drill into their heads the importance of being productive. If James and Jasmine turn out to be somebody's sad news story—which they won't—it won't be because their mother never told them that they are special and loved. Or because she didn't set a good example for them.

Sure, I've made some mistakes along the way. Nobody told me to have two babies by age twenty-three, but I thought I was in love with their daddy. And I was young and foolish and stubborn and unwilling to listen to my parents, who, in retrospect, knew this was going to happen. And I dropped out of college—not because I didn't respect the institution, but because I couldn't do my studies well and take good care of my children. And since they're the most treasured things I have in my life, my decision to leave college was an easy one. I decided the day Jazzy was born that I would live my life like a woman who had a college degree—even if I didn't have one. Just so that people like Mr. Roman wouldn't mistake me for all those other trifling single mothers who make gangs of snot-nosed babies, let them run wild while they're busy watching *Ricki Lake* and eating bonbons paid for with my hard-earned taxpayer dollars, and then sit back and blame everybody but themselves when their crumbsnatchers do something wrong.

Of course, people like Mr. Roman don't distinguish women like them from the leagues of women like me. We're all the same, huh? Ghetto welfare queens full of nothing but excuses, right? Funny how people like him are so quick to blame the mothers. If he's so damn concerned about male role models in James's life, why not track down his daddy and ask him why he's not doing what he's supposed to be doing? Ask him why he's not being a man. Ask him why he hasn't been around to see his kids in so long they barely remember what he looks like—and, for the most part, don't even bother to ask for him anymore. In fact, why doesn't Mr. Roman, if he's so interested in getting into my personal business and figuring out how I run my household, go find their daddy and collect on the piles of child support he owes me? Or ask the courts why, after I spent all that time trying to get the law to make him be a responsible father, they've still only collected exactly $2,343.13 in support from his behind in the eight years since I first took action? Nobody ever gets into that. Oh no, they're too busy blaming all the ills of society on the single mother. Crime is rising? It's the single mother's fault. Test scores are dropping? Blame the single mothers. O.J. killed another white woman? You guessed it: single mother.

I'm not going to sit here and pretend like I don't have my faults. I work too hard, I don't spend enough time with my kids, I don't really have a life. But people have done worse by their kids. My children's father certainly has. And I refuse to sit back and let anybody—particularly some bubblehead junior high school teacher who's known my child for about sixty days and me for less than five minutes—tell this thirty-two-year-old woman that I'm doing wrong by my kid because I don't have some man lying up in my bed.

"Mom? You home?" That's James now, slamming my front door

and yelling from the foyer like he has absolutely no home training. Keep telling that boy he doesn't live in a barn on the farm. "Mom?"

"James?" I call back. "Come here." I'm sure he can tell by my voice that this conversation won't be pretty. What? You didn't think I was going to let him get away with whatever it was he was doing in Mr. Roman's class, did you? Goodness, what was it that James did in Mr. Roman's class anyway? He was so busy trying to determine my marital status and I was so busy laying him out that we never actually hashed out what James's offense was. No matter; I'm about to get to the bottom of it. James bounded into the kitchen and headed straight for the refrigerator. His windbreaker was practically hanging off his shoulders, as was his knapsack. And that dirty basketball was exactly where it always is, under his right armpit. I swear, sometimes I have to wonder if it has attachments. Or if it's simply stuck there.

"So tell me, Mr. James Chance, why I went to the parent-teacher conference today and got thoroughly embarrassed by my son."

"Ma, I didn't—"

"Don't you even fix your mouth to tell me you didn't do anything. Mr. Roman tells me you had an incident." Well, he didn't, but I was on a fishing expedition, and James didn't really need to know that, now did he? "What did you do?"

"I didn't do anything, Ma—honest."

"Well, that's not what Mr. Roman is telling me. He seems to think that you're having problems paying attention. Why is that?"

"It's just homeroom, Mommy." Aw, here we go. That boy only calls me "Mommy" when he's trying to con his way out of a situation. Which means that we *have* a situation. Perhaps there's something to Mr. Roman's charges. Aw, bump that—he still didn't have any right to tell me I'm not a good mother.

"Just homeroom, huh? You have him for more than homeroom. And what, exactly, were you doing in homeroom that your teacher had to call you out to your mother?"

"See, what had happened was, Joseph was passing this letter to this girl Kathy, and Kathy didn't want to read it because she's mad at him. They're girlfriend/boyfriend—or at least they were until Kathy found out that this other girl was interested—"

"James? What the hell does this have to do with you acting up in Mr. Roman's class?" He started to explain, but I threw up my hand. Not in the mood for long, drawn-out stories. "Let me tell you this: I don't give a damn about any Kathy or any Joseph. The only person I care about is James Michael Chance because he is the only little boy I'm responsible for. And I'm sure that that little boy knows that his mother is not trying to hear that her child is doing anything in school but what he's supposed to be doing: learning and listening. Now, if you weren't doing either of those things at the point and time when you got in trouble in Mr. Roman's class, then you were doing something you weren't supposed to be doing." James was silent. He knew he was about to get it; his eyes were as wide as saucers and his mouth was hanging open. Lord, he sure is a handsome little bugger—just as cute as his daddy. In fact, he looks just like him—from those big, light brown sandy eyes, to those thick, shiny eyebrows and those juicy lips. True-and-tried lady-killers—the both of them. Or at least once-and-future lady-killers. But I'm not raising a boy to be the kind of man his father is, which is why he won't be acting a fool in any class he's attending—not on my watch. "So, here's what's going to happen: since you have such a hard time paying attention in class, how about starting Friday night after school, you write one thousand times, 'I will pay attention.' If you are not finished by the time Saturday afternoon rolls around, you will not be going to Billy's birthday party. If you do not finish by Saturday evening, you will be writing an additional five hundred 'I will pay attention,' all of which I will expect to have waiting for me on my desk before we go to church on Sunday. Do you understand your punishment?"

"But Mommy, if I'm writing that punishment, I won't be able to go to Teaneck's basketball scrimmage game on Friday night."

"And your point would be?"

"It's almost the beginning of the season and everybody's going to be there."

"And your point would be?"

"It's going to be a great game and I really wanted to be there for my future school, you know, to give support to the team."

"Oh, you want to be there for your future school, huh? Well you should have thought about that before you decided not to listen to your teacher and embarrassed yourself—and me, might I add—in his classroom. Tell you what: I'd like you to be there for your school, too—so maybe you should also write 'I'm sorry' five hundred times and give it to Mr. Roman when you see him in homeroom on Monday, and then promise him you'll act like the human being and student your mother raised you to be."

"But . . ."

"I'm sorry—did you want something else to write?"

James shut his mouth and looked down dejectedly. He knew not to say another word; his mama is no joke. I don't beat their behinds anymore; the boy is practically as big as me, and his sister? Well, she doesn't really get into enough trouble to warrant spankings. Besides, a good friend of mine at the college where I work as an administrator in the bursar's office is a child psychology professor, and she's told me over and over again that beating children really doesn't do anything but teach them how to be violent and afraid of the parents they love. "If you want to get them to change their habits, you have to make them see that what they've done is wrong," Julia told me on more occasions than I cared to have heard it. "Well, I'll tell you this much," I'd shoot right back at her. "A few smacks on the butt never hurt anybody that badly. I had my fair share and I turned out just fine, thank you very much."

"Yes, you did. But did those smacks make you change your ways?"

She'd always get me with that one. Truth be told, I waited for those beatings when I got in trouble with my parents because I knew that a five-minute beating was just that: a five-minute punishment. They got to feel better about their parenting and, after the sting wore off my legs, I got to go right back to whatever it was that I was doing before being rudely interrupted by my ass whupping. The 'rents caught on pretty quickly, though, to the fact that I was much happier to get a beating than I was to be punished. Shoot, punishments lasted for what seemed like a lifetime. No bikes, no television, no phone, no after-school events—that was my personal definition of child torture. I was like, beat me, but please, I'm begging you, don't take away my freedom.

Eventually, I admitted to my friend Julia that punishment was the way to go and tried it out on James. My first punishments were no bicycle for a week, no television for two, no roller skating—you know, the obvious. Soon, though, after I realized some of the punishments weren't really affecting his behavior, I started to get quite creative. Like, once, when he got busted cursing in front of a bunch of old ladies on the bus (one of them, Ms. Smallwood, is a deaconess at our church), I made him spend a month's worth of weekends reading and singing to the elderly down at the local nursing home. He missed all kinds of school activities with that one, but ended up liking the nursing home and the people living there so much that he still goes by there from time to time to visit with the residents. Some of those little old ladies write me and tell me that I have the sweetest, most respectful child in the world—"he's so well-behaved and mannerable," one letter said, praising both my son and my mothering. I do know this much: I've never heard tell of my son cursing or disrespecting an elder since that one.

I don't know whether his having to write "I will pay attention," and "I'm sorry" hundreds of times will change his behavior in class, but this much I know is true: it sure will make him think twice before he cuts a fool again. "Is there anything else I can do for you before you go upstairs and do your homework?" I asked James.

"No," he said, turning around slowly, that basketball still connected to his right arm.

"Okay, well, when you're done, come on back downstairs and eat your dinner. I'm ordering pizza," I said, turning to the phone to dial the number of the local Italian spot. "Oh, before you go upstairs, go and get your sister next door, will you?"

James turned on his heel, dropped his knapsack, and pushed through the screen door. I listened to his basketball hit the pavement on the sidewalk until I couldn't hear it anymore.

My child.

Now, about this Mr. Roman. I'm going to have to have a talk with him—but he's not going to like what I have to say. Well, not like he liked what I had to say the last time, but whatever. I want to sit down with this man and have him tell me about my child and his schoolwork, not his assumptions about my personal business. And I'll tell him that if he can't handle that, then perhaps he can arrange for my son to be put into a classroom with a teacher who can. And if he can't do that, then perhaps the principal can get the job right. Yeah, I got something for him, all right. See how he likes that.

"Zaria? You home?"

"No. I just keep the back door open so that strangers can walk in whenever they please and help themselves to my riches."

"Girl, what riches you got? You trying to tell me I'm friends with the millionaire next door?"

"You didn't know I had it like that, huh? I'd give you the details, but then I'd have to kill you."

April cracked up, pushed the sliding door open, and hopped into my kitchen. That's my next-door neighbor and best friend—or at least the person I've been closest to since I moved to Teaneck five years ago. She's got three kids—the eldest, JJ, is thirteen, a year older than my James; Pammy is a year older than my Jasmine, who is almost ten; and she's got a little one, Summer, who's just as cute as a five-year-old can be. April and I met through the kids: I was in the middle of cussing out the movers, who had just come too close to dropping my antique headboard onto the hot asphalt, when out of the corner of my eye I saw James in some boy's face, challenging him to a game of basketball. "I bet you can't ball as good as me, though," he said, cockiness rimming his words.

"I bet you I can," JJ shot back.

"No you can't," James said, getting in the boy's face.

Now, we hadn't even sat our behinds in a chair in our new house yet and here was James, bragging and boasting and about to get his ass kicked right there on the front lawn by this great big ol' boy—solid and sturdy and tall, too. James had his chest puffed out and his chin hiked up in the air while he was talking all that smack, but he was still a good four inches and at least ten pounds lighter than that boy. I thought he was a teenager until his mother told me better over coffee later that day. In fact, she told me a whole lot about everything before the sun even set. "First off, don't pay any attention to the people on this block," April said, placing her elbows firmly on her Formica kitchenette counter and conspiratorially leaning into me. Her breath smelled like cheap coffee beans and kinda turned my stomach, but I knew I'd better pay attention because there might be some good information somewhere in the conversation. "The Hadleys—over at 274? They hate kids, so keep yours away from there. They won't hesitate to yell at your boy in the middle of the street like he's some hoodlum, and I swear they got 911 on speed dial just for Mikey's ass down the street, but he's so bad that only people with nightsticks can control his ass anyway, so maybe that speed dial is a good thing." She stopped to take a gulp of her coffee, but I know she couldn't have swallowed the entire mouthful of liquid before she'd started in on the Eisenbergs, over at 258. "Now the Eisenbergs, nice couple—but don't get into any conversations with them about race, because they'll be the first ones to start telling you about their involvement with today's poor, destitute black youth and how young black kids don't look up to all the positive role models in the community like Dr. Martin Luther King and Colin Powell and Condoleeza Rice, and how they're personally trying to save as many black boys from jail and drugs and worse as they can, but they need the help of the black community and they're not interested in helping their own and yadda, yadda, yadda."

"Well, there *are* some trifling black folks in this world," I said, shaking my head.

"You got that right," she shot back quickly. "But I don't need some old, crotchety white folks to tell me that."

"I know that's right," I said just as quickly.

After two hours, dozens of stories shared, three cups of coffee, and several promises to have each other over for dinner "real soon," April Finney and I became fast friends, as did our children. She, too, is a single mom—a widow. I'd come much later to find out that her husband, a barber who'd owned several shops in northern New Jersey, had been shot dead in his Hackensack shop by a woman with a broken heart and extremely bad aim. She was there to kill one of the barbers who worked in Al Finney's shop—apparently, the barber had been cheating on his wife with one of her close friends—but when the wife fired the gun, she shot the owner, who had been standing clean across the other side of the room from where her intended target was. By the time they wrestled the gun out of her hand, she'd shot up the place and three other people in it—none of them her boyfriend. Al caught his bullet right in the heart—died almost instantly. April was four months' pregnant with her youngest baby when it happened.

Luckily for April, he'd been smart enough to show his wife how to run his businesses and make sure his managers weren't dipping into the till way before he met his untimely demise. April had managed to keep all five shops running at a profit with the help of two good, honest, hardworking employees, and so just sat back and collected her money from the businesses and Albert's pension and life insurance to keep her and the kids happy, well-dressed, and fed.

The day she'd told me that story, I knew she was opening up to me—and that she counted me as dear a friend as I did her. Everyone knew that if they went looking for April at her house and she wasn't there, they might as well check mine—and vice versa—because we practically lived together, as much time as we spent with one another.

"What you know, no good?" she said, twirling herself into my chair, still laughing at me for calling myself a millionaire.

"I know this much: I'm about to get all in James's social studies teacher's ass," I said, my smile instantly removed at the mere thought of His Rudeness.

"Who? Mr. Roman?"

"That's the one."

"Um, um, um—with his fine self. I hope you're going to get in his ass in the right way."

"I sure am. I'm about two seconds off of calling the principal and lodging a complaint against him for insulting me and my intelligence at the teacher's conference this evening."

"The principal? You're going to call the principal on Roman? For what?"

"Well, I'm sitting there trying to get some information on how my child is doing in school, and this fool can't think of anything to ask me except if my child has a male role model at home. Can you believe that?" I asked, incredulous. "This Negro didn't know me but two minutes and there he was, asking me about my damn personal business and who I'm sleeping with, instead of telling me about my child."

"Hmm. If I were you, I would have told him my marital situation quick, fast, and in a hurry—and then asked him if he was interested in filling the position."

"Huh? April?" I paused for a second, but I still was only half paying attention to her. Then I continued. "The only thing he could tell me about James was that he had an attitude. But he was so busy accusing me of being a bad mother that he never once actually told me exactly what it was that James did wrong. I laid him out and promptly left him standing there with his mouth wide open. I hope he got some flies in it."

April laughed. "Zaria, you are too silly for words. I know you didn't curse that man out for real, did you? Fine as he is? You obviously didn't check the ring finger, did you?"

"Why on earth would I be looking at his ring finger?"

"By the time you walked into the room, you should have noticed a lot more about him than his ring finger. Like that beard, and those big eyes, and those thick lips, and his perfectly shaped head. All the mothers want him; he's fine and single. No ring," April said, practically without taking a breath.

"You know what, love? I didn't see one attractive thing on his body because his attitude was so damn ugly."

"Okay, but be careful," April warned. "That man is well liked by a lot of the parents and loved at that school, not only because he's fine but because he's an extremely good teacher. And he's the coach at one of those private schools, where the basketball team is one of the best in the state."

"I don't care who likes him, I don't care who wants to screw him, I don't care whose baseball team he coaches," I said.

April cut me off. "Basketball. He coaches basketball."

"Baseball, basketball, foosball, I don't give a damn. If he ever gets me back in a teacher's conference again and starts getting into my business, there's going to be some problems up in that school—and they'll all be his, trust."

Later that evening, while I was putting away the laundry, I saw James lying on his bed, a heap of papers littering his floor. Apparently he'd started writing out his punishment, probably in hopes of making it to the game and the party and whatever else he thought he'd be doing this weekend.

"Um, don't think you can rush through the 'I will pay attentions,' because if they're not neat or there's one misspelling or one missing sentence or anything else is wrong with it, guess what? You'll be writing five hundred more. Don't think I won't check," I said. "And did you do your homework?"

"Yes, I did my homework."

"Oh, I'm sorry—do I hear a hint of attitude in your voice? Because we could add five hundred more to your assignment right now, if you'd like. I've got nothing but time to wait for it."

He thought better of answering me back fast, and instead paused, then said simply, "I did my homework, Mommy. It's right here."

"Let me see it." Now, I'm no dummy, but half the stuff this boy was working on was already over my head. To keep up with him, I was going to have to attend some classes myself; we didn't do half the stuff he did when I was his age. In my hand I held some kind of math he was working on—the early stages of algebra. I was always good at math, so this I had a lock on. But the Spanish lessons, the English literature and all the dead white men he read, and some of the history he was studying was definitely beyond my reach. Like, here, he was working on South African apartheid. I never had time for all this when I was in school, and half the time, I didn't understand it anyway. I'm not sure if the teachers sucked, or if I was just bored with it all. But James seemed to be kinda interested in this stuff.

"You sure had a lot to read for social studies," I said to James as I shuffled through the rest of his homework. "That Mr. Roman seems tough."

"He's not that bad," James said, matter-of-factly. "I like his class. He makes it really interesting and we learn a lot."

"You like him, huh? Well if you like him so much, why are you acting up in his class?" I genuinely wanted to know what the problem was because this didn't make any sense. "Usually, if you like someone, you go out of your way to act right for them. So help me understand: What's your problem?"

"I don't have a problem, Mommy."

"No problem, huh? Then explain to me why that teacher thinks you're such a bad student."

James shrugged and looked back down at his punishment papers. "I don't know. Sometimes he gets on my nerves and a lot of times he's really cool—he makes class interesting," James said thoughtfully. Then he added excitedly, "Besides, he's the basketball coach at St. Paul's High School and he knows everything there is to know about basketball!"

"Basketball, huh?"

"Yeah," he said, looking over at his basketball next to the bed. It was never too far away from his hands. "His team is no joke."

"Well, I'll tell you what's no joke," I said sternly. "I'm not trying to hear anything else about you acting up in Mr. Roman's class, you hear me? I'm not having it. Your job is to go to school and work hard and bring home the best grades possible—and you can't do that if you're too busy acting up in class. Straighten it up, okay?"

"Yes, ma'am," James said, a guilty look crossing his face.

"And don't think you're going to sit up here all night trying to finish your punishment. And don't think I didn't notice that you started it earlier than you were supposed to. I said you were supposed to start Friday night. I'll excuse it this time. It's almost time for bed. You got ten minutes," I said, turning on my heels and heading out of his room. I closed the door behind me.

He

It was times like this that made all the craziness worthwhile. I was deep into a lesson on apartheid in South Africa, trying to make it live in their minds and imaginations. I was in a groove, cruising at a pleasing clip. I could see the interest on their faces. In some cases I might even describe the looks as fascination. The key to teaching social studies to seventh graders was to make them feel acutely the hardships and joys of historical periods, to make them relate as personally as possible. It was vastly different from the way I had been taught the subject, I was proud to say. My teachers had thrown dates and facts at us, asked us to commit them to memory for the test, then moved on to the next big historical moment. No effort to dig beneath the surface, to get us to imagine what our lives would be like if we had been alive during that period. Just drill and kill, as one of my colleagues called that old-school approach.

It was startling to realize that South African apartheid in their minds was just another distant period of history, like the American Civil Rights movement or the Vietnam War. Yet apartheid had ended during their lifetimes, in the early 1990s. I can still recall the full-throttled buzz I got from watching Nelson Mandela ride through Brooklyn in a boisterous, joyful parade after he was freed from a South African prison. I had organized protests and teach-ins at St. Peter's College in Jersey City, where I was something of a firebrand as a student. In fact, one of the school administrators actually told me they were glad to see me go during our graduation week.

"Okay, so blacks in South Africa were denied basic human rights, they weren't allowed to vote, they didn't really get educations, and their movement and where they could live were severely restricted. Does that remind you of any period in United States history?"

I looked around the room, waiting to see a light come on somewhere in the twenty-three faces in front of me. I was surprised that the connection wasn't immediate for them, particularly for the black kids. In the previous class, which was the more advanced students, they were almost insulted by the rudimentary question. But fifth period was another story.

"Come on, now. What's wrong—y'all thinking about lunch already?" I asked, getting a few chuckles out of them.

I couldn't help stealing another glance at James, who was paying attention, but was not interested in answering the question. I was tempted to put him on the spot, to poke and prod the answer out of him. I was good at that. Any teacher worth his chalk had to be good at that particular exercise.

I saw a hand go up tentatively. It was a white girl who sat near the back, Sherri. She was one of the more thoughtful students in the class. I could tell that she had conversations at home that served her well, about things like politics and human rights and injustice—things most of these kids never spoke about with their parents. I was constantly disgusted by how little they seemed to talk to their parents about the world around them. Most would be at a loss to tell you how their parents felt about the most controversial questions of our time, like abortion or affirmative action. Basic stuff that the kids would pick up just by listening to a few minutes of adult conversation. It just wasn't happening, not in the suburbs, not in the cities.

"Sherri? You're going to enlighten us?"

The girl flushed slightly at the word "enlighten." "I don't know about all that, Mr. Roman," she said. She looked down at her desk to collect her thoughts.

"Well, it's not exactly the same, but the conditions for black people in apartheid sound the same as what it was like for blacks in the South before the Civil Rights movement."

I heard a couple of muttered "Oh yeah"s around the room as the obviousness of the answer smacked them upside the head.

"Very good, Sherri," I said, nodding. "And I'm glad that you also noted that they weren't exactly the same." I looked up at the clock and saw that there were only about two minutes until the period ended. Just enough time to explain the homework. Once again, the script had been perfectly synchronized. I loved when that happened.

"Okay, that brings me to your homework assignment for the weekend." There were the obligatory groans. I heard an especially loud groan coming from James's direction. I was tempted to call him out on it, to explore the reason he felt the need to make such a rude, immature gesture in my class. But I let it go—for now.

"You heard Sherri mention the similarity between South African apartheid and segregation in the American South. And she said they weren't exactly the same. Well, I want you all to explore that further. Give me three ways that apartheid in South Africa and segregation in the Jim Crow South were different. Write it in essay form—and it should be at least two pages. It's Thursday now, so I'm giving you an extra day."

I heard James suck his teeth at the mention of the word "essay." I was tempted again to make an example out of him. But I held back for some reason. I think the reason was Zaria Chance. The woman had messed me up a little, made me question my judgment. I didn't like that. I promised myself that the next time the boy acted up, I was going to treat him like I always did—like I would anybody else. The worst thing I could do is give him different treatment just because his mother yelled at me. What kind of teacher would I be if I let that happen?

I liked the way the student body parted when I walked through the halls at St. Paul's. Winning games will do that, will make you an important person in the eyes of even teenagers. Our season was about to start the next day in a short, invitation-only tournament that would be featuring some of the best teams in the area. A couple of years ago I was honored to be invited, but now it amounted to a pain in the ass. You couldn't turn it down—that would look too suspiciously weak. But I wasn't entirely comfortable putting my boys out there against top-flight competition so early in the season. Accordingly, I had been kinda brutal to them all week in practice and they weren't in the most jovial of moods. There was a little bit too much tension in practice, too many mistakes, too much nerves. I knew it was my fault, that they were just picking it up from me. Players could sense a coach's mood in a heartbeat. Now, the afternoon before the game, I had figured out exactly what I could do to break the tension. A three-point shooting contest. Against the girls' team. From my perspective—not to be confused with the team's—it was practically no-lose. If my boys put the girls away, well, that's what was supposed to happen. But if the girls managed to win—or even come close? Oh my goodness, that would be coaching fodder for much of the season.

The team was messing around in the gym when I swung open the doors. They noticed my arrival, but tried to pretend they hadn't. But when they saw the members of the girls' team trailing behind me, I got their full attention. They all stopped dribbling and shooting and laughing and just stared. The girls were excited, giggly, and more than a little scared, but they couldn't let the boys see that. As soon as the door opened, I saw their mood change instantly. This was going to be fun.

"What's up, Coach, we gonna work on our dance steps?" Jermaine said. The team chuckled at that one. Jermaine always had jokes. He fancied himself a comedian and I had to admit that his wit could sometimes be deadly. But I was in no mood for it now.

"I thought you already did that with Tariq," I said. The team hooted at this one. I saw a look flash across Jermaine's face, perhaps anger or surprise. I don't think he had expected me to kick him so hard. I regretted it for about a half second.

"All right, men, we're going to have a little competition today. I believe you are all familiar with the three-point shot." I glanced at Derrick, the point guard. "Well, some of you don't seem to remember how to actually shoot the three-point shot, but I assume you know what it is."

Derrick dipped his head, embarrassed. He was a little sensitive, and he was only a sophomore—a brand-new sophomore—so I had to be careful with his pride. I didn't want to poke at him too much and crush his confidence. The boy was precociously skilled, especially with his ballhandling and passing. His dribbling ability had broken down many tough defenses last year, opening things up for the big boys, Tariq and Jermaine.

"We're having a three-point contest today."

"Against the girls?" Tariq asked, ready to be aghast.

I glanced at him. "Why, you scared?" I heard the girls giggling behind me. The door swung open again. I looked over to see Vicky Clark, the girls' coach, walking toward us. She was a brittle, strident woman, but she was a good coach. The girls' team had improved immensely in the last two years. They had easily won the county championship the previous season and had gone quite far in the state tournament—not as far as we had, but still it had been a breakthrough season for them.

"Nah, Coach. I'm not scared," Tariq said, grinning.

"Well, that's good Tariq," I said, grinning back at him. "I'm glad you're not scared."

I looked around at the whole group, the girls and the boys. "Okay, let's get this started."

I had considered dividing up the squads and having half the boys' team combine with half the girls' team to make up one side, competing against the other half of the boys' team combined with the other half of the girls' team. But Coach Clark had convinced me that we wouldn't get the full benefit of the competition that way. She said not to worry about her girls' feelings. She wanted the girls to compete against the boys, straight-up, with no handicaps and no efforts to shield them from the potential harshness of a gender skirmish. As the contest proceeded, I quickly saw that she had been right. The girls were more than holding their own, and it was easy to see the boys start pressing and getting a little scared the more shots the girls made. They were truly in a no-win position. I was confident that, in the end, they would prevail—primarily because the girls would get tired, even the best shooters—so they would get a little boost in their confidence from performing when there was a lot on the line. They had to go to school with these girls, and they had to be able to walk the halls the next day. There was no way they could lose.

Everytime Sondra Whitfield started stroking shots, the whole gym stopped to watch, even more than they did for Jermaine, who was our deadliest shooter. The girl was smooth, confident, clearly a star in the making. She, too, was a sophomore. And she also happened to be beautiful, a fact that I'm sure wasn't lost on my players.

I heard Ceasar, a big, goofy, junior center, whisper to Tariq,

"Damn, I ain't never seen a girl that fine who could ball like that." Tariq nodded his agreement.

We had won eight of the twelve shooting matchups—Sondra had won both of her rounds, plus our two poor-shooting centers had been beaten. The last round put Sondra up against Jermaine. A clashing of the stars. Battle of the titans. Sondra went first—ladies first—and she calmly moved around the three-point arc, banging the ball through the net at least half the time. She made eight of her fifteen shots, putting all the pressure on Jermaine.

"Yo, Jermaine, man. I think she gonna beat you," Ceasar called out. "Anybody wanna put some money down?"

"You givin' odds?" Derrick said, laughing.

"Y'all can kiss my ass," Jermaine said. But he, too, was grinning. I looked around and saw a lot of grins among the boys and the girls. This was working exactly as I had planned. The girls were happy to be having this time with the storied St. Paul's boys' team, and the boys had been loosened considerably. Now they were having fun. And putting up Jermaine in the final round was ideal because he had the least fragile ego on the team. Probably because of all the success he had enjoyed, he would be the least likely to internalize a loss to Sondra.

And lose he did. Jermaine missed his first three shots and he tightened up and lost his stroke. Balls clanked off the rim, one got no rim at all, and a few resonated ugliness as they hit backboard.

"Damn, Jermaine!" Tariq said after he had missed his fourth or fifth shot in a row.

"Shut up, Tariq!" Jermaine said, but he was starting to laugh at his ineptitude. He had made as many as ten of fifteen shots in one of the earlier rounds, but that shooter was gone now, replaced by a loud impostor.

"Coach!"

I turned toward the voice, coming from the direction of the door. I noticed that Vicky Clark turned, too.

"Coach Roman. Telephone!" It was a male student who did a lot of work in the school office.

Annoyed, I took a few steps toward him. Who would be calling me in the middle of practice?

"Can you take a message?" I said, walking toward him.

He shook his head. "I tried to tell her you were in practice, but she said it was important. She said her name was Miss Simmons."

Damn. The last thing I needed was drama from her. I turned to Coach Clark. "Uh, I'll be right back. Make the boys practice free throws." I caught her nod as I started jogging toward the door. I was going to make this quick.

"I need you to take Lane this weekend. It's important, otherwise you know I wouldn't ask." She didn't even give me a chance to catch my breath.

I clutched the phone a little tighter. "Nah, Sheila. I have a big tournament this weekend. That's not possible."

"Basketball? Damn, the season started already? Well, I know nothing in the world is more important than your basketball! Certainly not your daughter."

Oh boy, here we go again. Sheila was expert at the guilt trip, and she was fast with it, too. She'd fire it off with the speed of a quick-draw gunslinger, trying to lodge a shell in my hide. My job was to ignore the fire, or to take immediate cover from it. But I wasn't as good at my job.

"Sheila, I'm not even gonna argue with you about this because you know that's ridiculous. This is not my weekend. It's yours. You know why I set it up that way, Sheila? Because I knew I had a basketball tournament this weekend. I knew it months ago. So don't even try to pull no guilt stuff with me."

There was a momentary pause. If I knew Sheila, she was trying to think of another salvo. We had played this game many times before.

"I have to go out of town, Kenny. It's important. It's a gig down in Atlantic City. This could be a big break for me. I just need this favor. Jackie can't help me and there's no one else I can go to. Please, Kenny."

Damn, she's actually begging. She must be quite desperate. Sheila didn't often let herself sound so vulnerable and needy. But there was no way I could swing it. Not unless my mother could help.

"Maybe you could ask your mother to help?" Sheila said, her voice rising hopefully on the last word.

I let out a deep sigh. We might be playing three games in three days, starting on Friday night. I really wanted to concentrate all my energies on the games without being distracted by worries about my daughter's well-being. Not that my mother wasn't capable, but Ma wasn't the most patient woman in the world. Laney was more than a handful. I tried to limit their interactions to a couple of hours at a time. Not an entire weekend.

"I don't know, Sheila." I looked down at my watch. I looked around the office. I had to make a decision.

"Well, when will you be back?"

"I have to do a set Sunday night, too. So you'd have to bring her to school on Monday morning."

Damn, the Monday morning circus. Getting a five-year-old up and dressed on a Monday morning was not a task for the weak. Lane would fight me every step of the way.

"If you say 'No,' I'll have to call your mother myself," Sheila said.

Was that supposed to be a threat? My mother would have no problem smacking Sheila around over the phone. She didn't appreciate the woman's second career as an aspiring singer; she felt that Laney was seeing more of baby-sitters than her own mother. She had told me this on quite a few occasions. I'd actually enjoy watching Sheila try to call my mother without warning and enlist her services.

"If that's supposed to be a threat, it's not a very good one, Sheila. But you can stop now—I'll take the girl."

I got no thanks, no joyful yell, no gratitude or heartfelt appreciation. Nearly four years after our relationship had ended, Sheila still carried around a great deal of bitterness toward me, like every bit of her unhappiness was my fault. Why did women hold on to their anger so long after a relationship ended? It wasn't like she had caught me in bed with another woman. I'm not saying there hadn't been a few other women after things had turned sour between us—but she had never caught me. That counted for something, didn't it? And I'm pretty certain she had had the company of other men anyway. She had come home from more than one singing gig after the sun had risen, talking about how she had crashed at the drummer's place, or she had been practicing with the piano player. But at that point I didn't care anymore anyway. Dating a gorgeous singer required you to suspend your belief in the sanctity of your relationship. I wasn't very good at belief suspension.

Sheila was also still bitter that I had pushed her quite forcefully to get an abortion when she was pregnant with Laney. Now that my beautiful little girl is the sun that I revolve around, those days are a hazy irrelevancy to me. But Sheila is still trying to keep that alive, as if I'd still be interested in killing my little girl. And it was exactly those kinds of heartless instincts in Sheila that made me glad I had gotten the hell away from her when I did. Certainly it doesn't please me that Lane is yet another child in a single-parent home, but I am committed to being a strong presence in her life until the day I pass. She will not be one of these little girls growing up with a scant degree of self-confidence, vulnerable to the treacherous charms of every smooth-talking Lothario in the neighborhood. Not my girl.

Back at practice, I was already distracted by my daughter's impending presence in my realm and she hadn't even been dropped off yet. This weekend was not going to be fun. I watched my players shoot free throws and was pleased to note the laughter and the relaxed postures. The three-point shooting contest had been a rousing success. The boys were loose and confident. At least there was that.

Fridays were the days when a teacher had to use all of his skill to keep a class engaged. Especially fifth period, which was right before lunch, when they were hungry and could smell their weekend right around the corner. For some reason, it was even worse than eighth period, which was the final period in the day. Of course, eighth was bad, too, but not as bad as fifth. I was still on apartheid, trying to make them understand why blacks had been forced to live in homelands. They were not fully comprehending the connection between geography and power and I was getting frustrated. I hadn't expected this roadblock. I usually could predict what would make them stumble, but I hadn't called this one.

I saw movement in the corner of my eye. It was James Chance. He sat near the back and he was trying to grab the attention of Todd Sullivan, a white kid who was often James's partner in mischief. Todd didn't want to turn around. (Todd's parents were red-faced when I told them about the child's classroom misdeeds during the parent-teacher conference. His father, a large, imposing man with a booming voice, had given me the clear impression that he was going straight home and tearing off a large chunk of Todd's hide.) Todd kept shaking his head, telling James "No," trying to get his buddy to back off. This seemed to me like a perfect time to probe James's knowledge of apartheid.

"Mr. Chance!" I called out, purposely saying his name a little too loud to scare him a bit. I saw him jump in his seat like a startled deer.

"Are you with us, Mr. Chance?"

James, wide-eyed, nodded his head hesitantly. He knew he was anywhere but *with* the lesson.

"Well, perhaps you can answer the question then. Grace us with your brilliance."

I couldn't help but throw out a little nasty sarcasm. It produced snickers from the class and made James's shoulders droop slightly. I knew I shouldn't go too far with the ridicule, but I found it was an effective way of getting a child's attention—particularly misbehaving boys. But it had to be used carefully because you didn't want to make the child into an enemy.

James stared at me with a mixture of fear and what appeared to be anger. I hadn't expected the anger. At least not yet, not until I was through with him. Did I want him to be mad at me? I wasn't sure.

"Do you know what the question is, James?" I asked him. More snickers from his classmates.

He shook his head slowly. He was glaring at me now. I wasn't entirely comfortable with a glare from one of my students. It was a bit brazen, I thought, almost as if the child considered me an equal, a peer who could be moved or affected by the angry stare of a seventh grader.

"Well, James, I wonder why you don't know what the question is. I wonder why we have to go through this every week. I guess I'm wondering a lot of things about you, James." More snickers.

"What's the question?" James said nastily. He had crossed the line into disrespectful now, which I didn't appreciate at all. I would give him a little slack because, in effect, I had started it. But it was the last time I wanted to hear that tone from a student.

"The *question*," I said in an even more sarcastic tone than before, "was what benefit the South African government got out of consigning blacks to homelands."

James stared some more. If he thought about it for a moment, he could easily reason out the answer to such a question. He was a smart kid, despite his behavior problems. But he obviously was not thinking clearly right now. He didn't speak for what seemed like a long time to me. I was almost starting to fidget. What was this kid up to?

"Uh, Mr. Chance, is there a problem?" I said, wanting to keep a little edge in my voice, but not too much. I wanted to bring the confrontational aspect of this encounter down a few notches.

"Why are you always picking on me?!" James said in a demanding tone. There was a gasp from his classmates.

Now it was my turn to stare at him. He had smashed through all layers of classroom etiquette and had suddenly made this into a personal altercation. Frankly, I was stunned by his boldness. This was not the kind of conversation a teacher wanted to have in front of a full classroom. Not at all. I needed to put an immediate halt to it.

"Mr. Chance, this is a social studies class. We are not out on the street. I'm asking you to answer a social studies question. Simple as that." I said it calmly, as if my insides were not roiling about in a sudden tempest. I winced slightly at the reference to the "street," knowing a black child might be a little sensitive to that word. I probably would have gotten a little offended if somebody said that to me. But James didn't seem to react to that particular word.

"Yeah, okay. Whatever." He said this in a near mumble, but I'm sure the whole class heard it. He was attempting to get out of the skirmish. He probably saw that it was one he could never win—I said he was a smart kid. He looked away from me, down at his desk, out toward the window. Anywhere but to the front of the classroom. But he was clearly still very angry. Maybe I'd pull him aside after class and have a little talk with him. As I let my gaze linger on him for a few more seconds, trying to decide whether I would say something else or just move on, I saw the obvious resemblance to his mother. I hadn't noticed it until that moment. It was the anger that set it off. I saw the way his brow furrowed just like his mother's had earlier in the week. He was an attractive boy, with large eyes set wide on a longish face. His mother's face was rounder, but her eyes were also large and set wide.

"Sally, can you help us?" I said, calling on a white girl who I knew would have an answer for me.

Throughout the last fifteen minutes or so of the class, I kept glancing in James's direction on the sly, trying to see whether he had emerged from his funk. He hadn't. He just sat there most of the time, staring glumly down at the desk, not even trying to follow the lesson. Had I gone too far with the boy or was he just being overly sensitive? When the bell rang, I was quickly distracted by two girls standing in front of my desk and asking questions about the homework assignment for the weekend, the two-page paper they had to write comparing apartheid to the Civil Rights movement. I looked over their heads and saw James slip from the classroom through the rear door before I had a chance to call out to him. Damn. I didn't want to let his anger have a chance to fester over the weekend. Maybe I could call him later on the telephone or something.

But as I walked toward my car a few hours later, my mind was already fixed on the basketball game that night. The plight of James Chance was far, far away from my focus. Just that fast. There was little chance I would remember to call him. I was stepping into coach mode, about to leave South End Middle School well behind. But like a buzzing fly, something else plagued me, something I couldn't quite grab. Suddenly, I had it—I had to go get my little girl first. I actually halted my steps as Laney came to mind. Wow, I had almost forgotten. That was unnerving. As I started my car, I sighed deeply. This weekend had the potential to kick me in the teeth.

As I neared Jersey City, I started to get the familiar butterflies in my stomach that usually came when I was about to pick up my daughter. It wasn't nervousness, exactly—more like anxiety. I just wanted things to go well when we were going to be together—no drama from her mother, no glitch in the logistics. Being a part-time parent was all about logistics—where and when was the pickup occurring, where was the check, who was going to get Thanksgiving and Christmas? I had had last Christmas—I think Sheila had agreed to it because apparently she hadn't bought the girl any presents. She said she had used all her money trying to finish up a demo tape. I don't know what ever happened with the demo—I never heard any more about it. But I do know that Christmas with a four-year-old serves witness to so much unadulterated joy that you suddenly understand what it feels like when a heart sings. I know that I will remember for the rest of my days the glee that spread across her face when she walked into my living room and beheld the bicycle under the tree, surrounded by a bounty of glistening treasures. Her elation quickly became my own. I wanted to feel that every year, but Sheila had already made it clear that this Christmas belonged to her—she said she had already put money aside so there wouldn't be a chance that she'd be broke again. I gave Sheila $500 a month in child support. We had never gone to court, so I'm not even sure whether that's enough or too much—I think I had purposely avoided doing the research because I want to retain the self-perception that my generosity was rare and extreme. I'm sure psychologists had some sort of pithy name for it. Sainthood complex would work. I mean, I had never even been married to the woman. I know of all too many brothers who sent nothing—and some of them had even worn the ring. I just *knew* my $500 was ensuring my entrance through the pearly gates—St. Peter would glance at my record of child-support payments and personally escort me to the fanciest suite heaven had available that weekend.

I called Sheila on my cell phone to alert her that I was a few blocks from her building, which was located in Jersey City's thriving business district on the water, across the Hudson from lower Manhattan. It wasn't far from my apartment building. They were building skyscrapers so fast in Jersey City that New Yorkers could now gaze across the river and see a New Jersey skyline. Ha, maybe one day it'd compete with the view we got from our side of the river.

On a normal day Sheila left Lane in her school's aftercare program, but she had picked her up early this afternoon and brought her to the office. I had told her on more than one occasion that I was capable of picking the girl up from aftercare, but she said she liked to say good-bye before I took her away for the weekend. So she'd rather have a five-year-old bouncing around her office like a pinball than let me get her from the school. I shook my head as I wheeled my truck into a parking space. The motivations of my baby's mama I would never understand. At times, they seemed primarily aimed at inflicting some type of pain on me, but when I slipped into one of my noble moods I would conclude that that thinking was too self-centered.

Sheila was a secretary at a large architecture and real estate development firm, one of the state's largest. She claimed that she had been interested in a career in architecture at some point, but she had never bothered to finish college. She worked directly for the company's CEO, which she liked to say meant she was actually the most powerful person in the company because she controlled the man's schedule. I wondered how Mr. CEO felt about having his office invaded by an un-shy five-year-old. The receptionist at the front desk greeted me with a smile.

"Are you Laney's daddy?" she asked warmly.

I nodded. "Yes, that would be me."

"What a sweet little angel she is," the woman said, beaming at me like we were old friends. "We've been having a great time." She appeared to be about twenty-five, blond and blue-eyed, very pretty in a synthetic Barbie kind of way. I wondered if this Stepford wife would have been so warm if there was no Lane. My experience told me no—resoundingly. I would have gotten all curtness and chill.

The woman picked up her phone.

"Sheila? He's here . . . Okay, I will."

She looked up at me again, still smiling. I was close enough to wade into the smelling area of her perfume. It was far too loud and unsubtle for a receptionist. But as I gazed down at the two insistent and creamy white globes pushing vehemently out of her low-cut blouse, I figured that subtlety was a trait she had never been introduced to.

"She says she'll be out in a minute," the woman said. I tried to lift my eyes from her chest, which almost appeared to be resting on her desk like a trophy, but I don't think I was quick enough. She caught me, I was quite certain. But all she did was smile again. Like me looking at them was a good thing. I smiled back. I guess if she didn't want men looking, she wouldn't have them served up on a platter.

The next sentence that fell from my mouth stunned even me. It was one of those moments when you hear yourself saying the words, but it almost feels like someone else put them there. I wouldn't soon forget my lovely indiscretion—and her equally memorable response.

"Do you have names for them?" I asked. And then my mouth dropped open.

Her eyes widened and her mouth gaped, too. I felt my stomach start to tighten and I immediately considered how unpleasant it would be for me if the receptionist told my baby mama that I had sexually harassed her. There was a second or two of startled silence between us, then she did something that brought me joy. She started laughing.

"I cannot believe you asked me that!" she said, her mouth agape. Then she leaned forward conspiratorially, pressing the twins against the top of the desk. I moved a step closer so that I was only a few feet away. I stared down into her face, too close to see anything but the blotches of dark mascara around her eyes and the hint of red lipstick lingering on her front teeth.

"My ex-boyfriend called them Mount Malena," she said, giggling. "My name is Malena."

40

I was speechless. A thousand clever one-liners bounced around my head, but nothing came out.

"He used to say he wanted to climb Mount Malena," she continued. "That was his way of saying he wanted to have sex."

Again I had nothing to say. This was far more information than I wanted. But I wasn't bothered by this stranger sharing intimacies with me. It was thrilling, in a voyeuristic way, like I was being allowed to watch her and her ex-boyfriend go at it. I wondered if she did this all the time, inappropriately sharing intimacies with strangers. But really, I was the one who had started the indiscrete behavior with my crazy question. I don't think I would have taken such liberties with a black woman. There would have been too much unspoken baggage between us, too many unexplored possibilities for me to feel the kind of comfort that would let the indiscretion slip from my lips.

I grinned goofily, wondering if Malena was flirting with me. But she seemed too uncalculating for that. Why couldn't I just accept her warmth without attaching some sexual shrewdness to it?

I heard footsteps approaching down the corridor. Already wearing an unpleasant expression, which I'm sure was plastered on for my benefit, Sheila marched toward me, dragging Laney behind her. Almost immediately Malena was forgotten—replaced by the saintly face of my daughter. My little girl was staring into all the offices she was passing, a curious little smile on her face. Slowly her head turned and finally she saw me.

"Daddy!" she squealed, breaking free from her mother's grip and sprinting toward me. I felt a giddy and familiar warmth spread from my cheeks, across my chin, and down my neck into my stomach. Surely every parent knows that drug, the soaring high from a child's joyful greeting. I craved that high on a daily basis, and suffered when it wasn't available to me. That was the pain of the part-time parent.

The little girl wrapped her arms around my waist and smashed her face into my stomach. Lane truly did love her father, it was clear to anyone watching. As I leaned over to pick her up, I saw the grin on Malena's face—which held a wide-eyed expression that any loving father would recognize. It was the look we got from the female strangers who overreacted whenever we showed our child public affection. I caught Sheila's face, too, but I couldn't quite read it. Her feelings about me and my daughter were so complicated that even she couldn't easily describe them. If I could try, they seemed to bounce from contempt for the strength of our bond to gratitude for the same, with a little jealousy and admiration thrown in there to gum things up.

"How are you doing today, my little pumpkin lumpkin?" I asked her, using an expression from one of her favorite cartoons. I picked her up so that we were face-to-face. Immediately I noticed her hair, which was neatly and artfully braided on one side, but had a funky ponytail sticking out on the other—looking like something scary I might have done.

"I didn't like the way her hair looked when I picked her up from school, but I didn't have enough time to fix it," Sheila said. She wasn't apologetic exactly, but she did apparently feel the need to explain herself to me. Or at least to explain why she was handing over a little girl who looked like she had been preyed upon by a schizophrenic hairdresser. I stared at the hairstyle again, then I looked back at Sheila. Hair issues were undoubtedly the hardest part of my caretaking with Laney. I was a thirty-four-year-old man who had learned many things in his life thus far, but how to do a five-year-old black girl's hair was not one of them. Laney had started to get wise to my cluelessness, too. The last time I tried, she wore a troubled expression and suggested that she just wear a hat until I brought her back to Mommy. These tykes are too wise for me.

"Maybe your mother could finish braiding the rest?" Sheila said hopefully. But she knew better than that.

"You know my mother can't braid hair, Sheila. She's made that quite clear."

Sheila shrugged. I could tell that she was officially handing the problem over to me—a problem she had created. I felt my face start to throb, the warmth I had felt only seconds before changing into a throbbing resentment. Things could never be simple with Sheila. Drama followed her around like a lovesick puppy, I was sure of it. Sometimes I wondered how she managed to get through each day without either killing somebody or getting killed.

"Okay, well, I have to get ready to go," she said, already moving on. She handed me the bulging overnight bag that dangled from her shoulder. She'd overpacked, as usual.

"I'll be back late Sunday night, so you'll need to bring her to school Monday morning," she said matter-of-factly. I groaned inwardly. I couldn't remember if she had told me that part on the phone the day before. Getting Laney dressed and ready for school on a Monday morning was no joke. It always made me late for homeroom. No matter how early we started, I'd find myself dashing out the door, sweating and pissed off as I dragged my daughter toward the car. Not a pleasant way to start a Monday.

Sheila leaned forward and gave Lane a kiss while the girl had her arms wrapped around my neck. Lane leaned toward her mother to make it easier. With that, Sheila turned on her heels and was gone. Lane and I watched her walk away.

" 'Bye, Mommy," Lane said softly, almost like a whisper.

"Aren't you a happy little girl with your daddy!" Malena said, drawing our attention behind the desk. Lane gave her a smile and nodded her head. With my little girl in my arms, I forced myself not to look down as I gazed back at Malena. I quickly recalled the quick and juicy communion we had shared. She leaned forward again, pressing her mountains against the top of the desk. Damn.

"I think her hair looks fine," she said, as if she were sharing a secret with me.

This time I shrugged. Lane's hair didn't look fine at all. The receptionist was either being polite or it was something a white woman just didn't have the ability to see.

"Well, we'll see what we can do about it," I offered. We headed for the door. I tried to think of something clever but not suggestive to say to Malena, but nothing came to me.

"Bye-bye," Malena said, waving. Lane and I waved as the door closed behind us. I glanced down at my watch. My basketball game was starting in less than two hours.

"What's wrong, Daddy?" Lane looked up at me, wide-eyed and apparently worried. I had to keep reminding myself how perceptive she was. She let nothing get by. A frown on Daddy's face meant trouble in her world.

"Nothing, doll face," I said, patting her head as we waited for the elevator.

Looking back now, I can point to that moment as the instant when my world started spiraling out of control. I was soon to become engulfed in a wave of stinking shit. But I was oblivious. All I knew was that I had to get this child to my mom as soon as possible so I wouldn't be late for one of our most important games of the season—the first one. We stepped into the elevator, the doors closed—and it started zooming upward. Damn, I hadn't checked which way it was headed.

"Daddy, why are we going up?" my girl asked.

I wanted to yell "Because your daddy is a fuckin' idiot!" But I didn't.

She

I had barely put my behind back in my chair good before Florence, the office secretary/gossip/hag handed me a pile of messages thick enough to fill a small phone book. "These are for you," she said, shoving them toward me. "Somebody sure is looking for you today." I didn't even bother looking at them—just kept my eyes on her, contemplating whether I was going to bother saying "thank you." I mean, I would have, under normal circumstances, been as polite as a southern belle graciously collecting her peach tea, but this woman wasn't in the least ingratiating; just nosy as shit. It pained her to have to stand there and wonder why my phone was so hot while I was off on my hour-long lunch from the Bursar's Office of Lawrence College, and I wasn't about to entertain telling her my business. The last time I did that— when she'd first started working here a few years back, I called myself being nice and took her to lunch and divulged a little too much information about my children and their father—I got burned, big time. By the time we'd said our good-byes for the day at 4 P.M., everybody in that office was looking at me cross-eyed and asking me about that fool. It didn't take me or anyone else in the office long to figure out that you don't tell anything you want to keep to yourself to Florence. "I think it's your sister—her name is Mikki, right? She sounded upset. She called several times while you were gone. I tried to tell her that you wouldn't be back until—"

"Thanks, Florence. I'll give her a call," I said, cutting her off. I didn't so much as bat an eyelash until she'd removed her fat behind from in front of my desk, even though the idea of Mikki blowing up my phone several times over the past hour was troublesome. What was wrong? Lord, I didn't need any drama today—and if there was one thing Mikki was good for, it was some drama. Just a year or so ago she'd cheated on her husband and was a stone's throw away from getting a divorce and a half second away from losing her mind after Mommy and Daddy split up, but before they could actually fit her for the straitjacket, they worked everything out. But I swear some therapist somewhere in Brooklyn got p-a-i-d in full to straighten out her little twisted behind. So help me goodness, if she was calling me at work about some madness with Randy, I made a vow right then to personally go to Brooklyn, remove my number from her speed dial, and give her several pieces of my mind.

Florence finally moved away from my desk, and within seconds, I picked up the phone and dialed the number at Mikki's bridal boutique in Brooklyn. The phone rang, and rang, and rang, but there was no answer. I hung up and dialed her home number, and got the same thing—lots of ringing and no answer. Not even an answering machine. Where was this girl? I looked down at the messages; there were six. Two had the number to the shop; the last four, which had come within five minutes of one another, had a number with which I wasn't familiar. I dialed it anyway. God, I hope she wasn't in any trouble somewhere.

"Trier Stanton, Randy Murphy's office. How may I help you?" the woman who answered the phone said in a cheery, airy tone.

"Um, this is Zaria Chance. I'm Mr. Murphy's sister-in-law. Is either he or my sister, Mikki, available?"

"Hi, Ms. Chance. Mrs. Murphy just left, but I'll put you through to Mr. Murphy. Can you hold on please?"

"Sure."

Randy picked up almost immediately. "Zaria? What's up, lady?"

"Randy—what's happening? What's wrong with Mikki?"

"Wrong? Oh—for sure, nothing's wrong. Everything is exactly right." Then he was silent.

"Um, Randy? You want to clue your sis in on what's happening? Mikki called my phone six times within less than an hour, and frankly, both of you are scaring me. What's wrong?"

"You're going to be an aunt," he said simply.

"Huh?"

"Listen to me carefully, Zaria. Mikki and I are pregnant; we're going to have a baby. Which means that you're going to be an auntie!

"Zaria? You still there?"

"I'm here—just in a state of shock," I said slowly.

"Never thought you'd see this day coming, huh?" Randy said. I couldn't see him, but I knew he had a grin a mile wide. "Well, God willing, it's going to be here in seven months."

"She's two months pregnant?"

"Yup," he said. "Two months."

"That hooker kept the news away from me for two months?"

"Zaria—I didn't find out until a few days ago. You know how Mikki is; she claims she didn't realize she was late until a few weeks ago, and that she just went to the doctor a few days ago to get it confirmed after she started throwing up for no reason. I'm her man—the first person she's going to tell is me. The second person she called to tell was you."

"Well, where is she now?"

"She just went to Manhattan, to some store to buy baby clothes."

"Baby clothes?"

"Baby clothes. Turns out little Ms. Mikki is actually excited about the prospect of being a mommy," Randy said, his voice filled with glee.

"And I know you are, too," I said back warmly. "Congratulations, sweetheart. This is truly wonderful news." And then I added, "I hope you're ready for the drama. You know how your girl is."

"I know," he said with a sigh. "It's going to be a long seven months. But it'll be worth it—well worth it."

"You know that's right. Does she have her cell phone with her?"

"Nah, she lost it. That's why she was trying to call you before she left here. She should be back at the shop in a few hours, though—call her there."

"All right then, baby. I'll talk to you later. And congratulations."

Well, I'll be damned. Mikki is pregnant. Pregnant. Can you believe it? My little sister is going to have a baby. Gosh, I thought I'd never see the day. In fact, it was she who'd told me that I wouldn't ever see the day—told me that the night I had my James. She was there in the delivery room with me, through sixteen hours, fourteen minutes, and thirty-two seconds of labor—hard labor. I was twenty, hardheaded, angry, on my own after having moved out of my parents' house—they weren't all too pleased that their firstborn was a college junior about to have a child with a no-good, trifling-ass Negro, but I was young and in love, dumb as all get-out—and alone at the hospital, save for my eighteen-year-old sister. My baby's father, Ricky Fish, hadn't bothered to show up to help me bring our son into the world, and my parents were too angry and intent on making the point that I was on my own to come see their grandchild in the hospital, so I was left with Mikki holding down the fort. And after she saw all the blood and the contractions on the monitor and this big-headed baby passing from between my legs, vowed that she would never in her life have a child. Which, at the time, sounded like a good pronouncement from my baby sister, whom I did not want to go through what I had just gone through. My parents had told me over and over again that Ricky Fish was trouble, and that he would bring me right down to the gutter with him—and by the time I was six months' pregnant and showing, that's right where I was, in the gutter. A two-bit drug dealer who wasn't very good at his day job, he was on the run from the police, who wanted to question him in the drug-related murder of a crackhead who'd been shot to death on the Newark, New Jersey, corner where Fish dealt weed and blow. I was almost sucked into the whole mess because I was his girl. My parents, intent on not losing their middle-class, South Orange, New Jersey–born and raised first child to some nigger shit, hired the best lawyer they could find to keep me out of it—and he did a good job of doing so. But because I didn't show my gratefulness to them for saving me from the wrath of the law and vowed to be with Fish, my parents cut me off. There I was, four months away from being someone's mother, a semester away from finishing my junior year and making something of myself, and I was moving out into the world on my own—into an efficiency apartment in Newark, with hardly any clue as to how to raise a child, pay my bills, or survive on my own. I mean, I could barely boil water. The closest thing I'd ever gotten to working was as a camp counselor in the summers—just for laughs, really, and some new school clothes.

But I did it. I struggled. I had that baby and, obviously not learning enough of a lesson, turned around and had another by the same man. But my struggles were the perfect birth-control elixir for my younger sister, who swore that she was going to do it the right way: graduate high school with honors, go to school on scholarship, graduate, get a career, find a boyfriend, and get married—in that order. And she swore that she wouldn't have kids until 40—2040, if she could help it. "My nephew and niece are more than enough kids for me," she'd said over and over again. In fact, her insistence to remain childless was one of the biggest reasons she and Randy had been arguing and fighting and carrying on a few years ago.

And now, here they were, about to have a baby. Lord help us all.

I get home the same time most days—4:15 P.M., unless I stop to pick up dinner or some groceries or a movie for the kids or something. And usually Jasmine is outside with Pammy, playing with their dolls, jumping rope, or doing all the other little girlie things that little girls do. They're cute enough to eat, I swear. James is usually wrapped around that Nintendo with JJ—doesn't matter where, my house, April's house, the middle of the street, wherever a television set is, they don't care.

When I stopped by April's house after work—she'd called me just before I left to ask me if I could stop by the store and buy her a gallon of milk—I saw JJ hooked up to the Nintendo, but not James. Pammy and Jasmine were over in the corner of the den, pulling and tugging at Summer's hair. I swear, I don't know how that little girl takes it; she's got three mamas—April, Pammy, and Jasmine. And sometimes, Pammy and Jasmine out-mama April on her best day. The girl was sitting there, apparently quite pleased to have those two pulling on her thick mane.

"April?" I called out. Then I turned to the girls. "Hello, my little ladies. Where's April?"

"She's in the kitchen," Pammy said.

"Mommy's in the kitchen," Summer repeated.

"Well thank you, Miss Summer," I said, cupping her little moonpie face in my hands. "Where's James?" I asked, turning my attention to JJ. "You got the Nintendo all to yourself today?"

"He said he had a lot of homework to do, so he couldn't play today," he said, not even bothering to take his eyes off the screen.

Now since when was James too tied up with homework to get in his daily Nintendo fix?

"Well, tell your mama I bought her the milk," I said back to him as

I put the grocery bag next to him on the coffee table. "Let me go check on big head."

Jasmine and Pammy let out a few giggles from their little Amen corner. JJ was still staring into the television screen and furiously pushing buttons when the door slammed behind me.

That James was holed up in his room didn't surprise me; he was probably up there trying to finish that punishment of his. But when I walked into his room, he was just kinda sitting in the middle of his bed, not really doing anything. His books and papers were strewn about the bedspread, but he was sitting in the corner, holding on to a pillow, not really moving—just staring off into space.

"Hello, James," I said after staring at him. "How are you today?"

"Fine," he said with a shrug, not even looking in my direction.

"Fine, huh?" I said, obviously not convinced.

"Yeah, fine. I'm all right, I guess." He still didn't look up.

Oookaay. Mama was about to go on yet another fishing expedition. Two days in a row. Must be my lucky week. "So, how was school today?"

"School was fine, nothing happened," he mumbled.

"Just fine?" I said. "What did you learn?"

"A lot of things."

"Like?"

He was silent.

"Can't think of anything?" I prodded. "Well, how about we go class by class. What'd you learn in math class?"

"How to convert fractions."

"Oh! Fractions! Now we're getting somewhere," I said, feigning excitement. "What'd you do in gym?"

"We swam."

"Swam, huh? That's why you're all ashy? Didn't have a chance to lotion up?" I thought for sure his little vain behind would look down at his legs, which were so ashy I could have written an entire paragraph on them, and crack up. But he didn't even budge.

"What'd you do in social studies?"

"I didn't learn anything in social studies."

"Nothing at all, huh? You mean to tell me you were in social studies class for forty minutes, and you got absolutely nothing out of what the teacher was saying, huh?"

"I learned stuff—just not stuff worth talking about."

"Maybe it *is* worth talking about— What happened? This is Mr. Roman's class, right?" Now I was getting a little anxious. What was this man doing to my son?

"Mr. Roman tried to get an attitude with me."

"An attitude about what? Why would your teacher get an attitude with you, James?"

"He said I was talking, but I wasn't."

"Well, what would have made him think you were talking if you weren't?"

"I was talking a little bit, but then I stopped—and it was about the lesson anyway."

"Well, did you try to explain that to him?"

"No, he wouldn't listen to me when I tried to explain."

"What exactly did he say?"

"He didn't say anything—he just started picking on me."

"Picking on you? What do you mean he was picking on you?"

"He was trying to make me answer questions about material we didn't go over yet, and trying to embarrass me in front of the class."

"Well, how did it end?"

"I got in trouble for something that wasn't that big of a deal."

"Not that big of a deal, huh? That's why you're sitting in your room by yourself, silent?"

"Well, I guess it is a big deal now because he made it one."

"Uh-huh. Okay. You're right: It is a big deal. Me and Mr. Roman are going to have to have a little talk."

"It was a big deal earlier, but he might be over it by now. I don't want to bring it up anymore."

"Okay, James, whatever you say. But I'll tell you this much, I'm tired of hearing all this mess with Mr. Roman, so we're going to have a little talk anyway. I'm not going to have you sitting in class getting picked on by a grown man when you're supposed to be learning social studies. So if there's anything you need to tell me before I go over to that school, I suggest you tell me now."

James simply hung his head—didn't say another word.

And with that, I turned on my heels and stomped down the hallway. I don't know who that Negro thinks he is, but I got something for that Mr. Roman. Me and the principal are going to have to have a conversation. See if he likes getting picked on by the big dogs.

He

As soon as my mother opened the door to her apartment, I knew she wasn't happy. She stared at me with clearly evil intent before she fixed her face to coo at her granddaughter.

"Hi, Grandma Boney!" Lane bellowed gleefully. My mother couldn't help but to smile. Lane called her by her lifelong nickname "Boney"—apparently, Ma used to be skinny—to differentiate her from Lane's other grandma, who was Sheila's mother and known to my daughter as, simply, "Grandma."

"And how are you, cupcake?" she said, squeezing Laney against her as the girl giggled. Again, Ma looked up at me and rolled her eyes. Damn, what had I done?

"What's up, Ma?" I asked, alarmed. I had caught the afterwork traffic on the way to my mother's apartment—tip-off was in about an hour. I followed her inside.

"Grandma Boney?" Lane said. "My mommy said you would take me to McDonald's."

No, Laney, I thought, please don't play the McDonald's card with Grandma Boney, particularly not this early in the stay—and when Grandma was already mad at something.

"Uh, Laney," I said, trying to think of a distraction, "why don't you show—"

"McDonald's?!" my mother repeated scornfully. Damn, too late.

"With all this good food I made for you up in my house, you want to go to McDonald's?"

Laney looked up at her and nodded. Five-year-olds weren't yet equipped with the sensor to detect sarcasm. She had asked a question and Lane had given her the answer.

"Well, child, I made some fried chicken and macaroni and cheese. I thought you liked macaroni and cheese?"

Laney nodded. "I do like macaroni and cheese. But I want to go to McDonald's."

I grimaced. Not for the first time I cursed that damn fast-food restaurant and the seductive power it seemed to hold over children. We were raising a nation full of cult members who had all been secreted away when we weren't looking and brainwashed into blindly following the Golden Arches.

"Uh, baby, I'll bring you to McDonald's tomorrow, okay?" I offered, though I wasn't sure when I would get the time to do that. But one of the early lessons I had learned in dealing with my daughter was to live for the moment. In other words, I just needed a way to get Laney's cooperation at this moment—the next day might as well be a year away. She wasn't likely to remember the promise—though I had noticed that this thinking was becoming more dangerous as she got older and started to develop an actual long-term memory.

I looked at my mom and saw her staring crossly at Lane's hair. I knew what would come next.

"What is going on with this child's hair?" Mom said, reaching out and turning Lane's head to the side. "Her mother let her go to school like this?"

Mom looked at me, frowning, waiting for an answer. In these situations I was put in the foreign position of defending my baby's mama, which certainly didn't come naturally to me. But it was not helpful to me in the long-term for my mother to hate Sheila or to think she was a bad mother, because Mom would in turn put more pressure on me to do something about it. There was very little I could do except try to take my child as often as I could. Besides, I didn't really think Sheila was a bad mother. She was a bit selfish and distracted at times, but she usually did the right thing.

I shook my head. "No, she didn't go to school like that. For some reason, Sheila tried to do it over after school, but she didn't have enough time to finish." I shifted on my feet, anxious to get back on the road. The tournament was taking place at St. Peter's College, the school I had graduated from, which was at least twenty minutes to a half hour from my mother's place.

"Well, you know I can't braid hair, Kenny. What am I supposed to do with this?" She ran her hand over Laney's head. Laney watched the conversation go back and forth like a spectator at a tennis match.

I wanted to ask if her neighbor, Miss Venable, was around. Miss Venable had braided Lane's hair several times in the past during hair emergencies. But I was scared to mention her neighbor. Yes, a grown-ass thirty-four-year-old man, scared of little Miss Dolores Roman. Damn right. Thus was the longlasting power of the mother over the child.

"I would ask Miss Venable downstairs, but she's about to leave. A lady at her job gave her two weekend tickets to Foxwoods. To a show and then to stay at a fancy hotel. She asked me to go with her. But of course I had to say no."

My eyes narrowed as I pondered that last sentence. Did I hear anger? I wasn't sure how to respond. Was she looking for some sort of apology from me, for asking her to spend time with her granddaughter?

"Well, uh, that's unfortunate, Ma."

"Yes, Kenny, it is unfortunate, isn't it?"

We stared at each other briefly, waiting for something more. I didn't have time for this drama with my ma. I had to get to the game.

"Okay, Ma. I'm sorry you missed the chance to go to Foxwoods. I wasn't expecting to have to keep her this weekend. But I am grateful that you could help me out. . . . Uh, I'm not sure what time the game will be over. It'll probably be after Lane is already asleep. Do you want me to still come and get her?"

My mother shrugged her shoulders. "I don't know, Kenny. That's up to you."

"Okay, well, I'll call you either way after the game is over."

My mother nodded her head and again looked down at Lane's hair.

"What are we going to do about that hair for church?" she said, this time speaking more to Lane or to herself than to me. I saw that as my cue to exit.

I practically sprinted to my car when I hit the street. I had forty-five minutes before tip-off. In another fifteen minutes, I would have to try to reach someone by cell phone to let them know I was on my way. I reached into my jacket pocket and felt emptiness. No keys. I quickly checked my pants pockets. Nothing. Oh, God, this was not the time. I felt a sinking sensation in my stomach. I must have put them into the overnight bag, or maybe on a table in my mother's apartment. Damn, what else could go wrong?

I turned around and ran back into the building. The doorman had stepped away just that fast, so I had to ring the buzzer for my mother's apartment. I pressed it several times to make sure she heard it. I looked down at my watch again, willing the minute hand to stop moving so fast. I got no response from my mother. Where had she gone? It couldn't have been even five minutes since I'd left her.

The doorman came back and looked out at me without moving to let me in. He had been working here long enough to know me by sight. We had greeted each other fairly warmly, I thought, just a little while ago when I entered the building with Lane. Now he was going to pretend he didn't know me? He was a pudgy, middle-aged Latino man with an accent. I couldn't remember his name—Carlos, Carlo, something like that.

"Uh, can you let me in?" I asked through the glass. "For some reason my mother isn't answering the buzzer."

He stared at me for a long time, still without moving. I couldn't read his facial expression at all. Come on, man! I wanted to scream at him, to curse him for putting me through this. He had just seen my mother buzz me in with my daughter less than twenty minutes ago. Now he didn't know me? Now I was some kind of threat to the building residents? I looked at him through the glass, clenching my fists to stop myself from saying something that would hurt my cause here.

Finally, he moved from behind his desk and started walking toward me, not in a hurry. He pulled the door open, staring me in the eye, like he was trying to memorize my features in case he'd have to help the police come up with a sketch. This guy was ridiculous. I looked down at his name tag. Raul. Montanez. Damn, I wasn't even close.

"Thanks a lot, Raul. I left my keys up in my mother's apartment."

He said nothing. What an asshole this guy was. I think he might have nodded, but I'm not even sure. Whatever. I ran to the elevator. When I finally got to my mother's apartment and knocked on the door, my stomach churned as I waited in vain for her to come. She clearly wasn't there. Or maybe something had happened to her, like she could have fallen and been rendered unconscious and my daughter was trapped inside, crying and afraid.

"Ma?!" I called out. "Lane?!"

I waited some more, but got no response. My mother had probably taken her to a neighbor's, to show off her granddaughter. But which neighbor? I looked down the hall, trying to recall the people my mother had introduced me to over the years. During the summer, the residents would sit on the side of the building in a little adjacent park area built for that purpose. Though the building wasn't technically for just senior citizens, many of its residents were card-carrying members of the AARP. My mother hadn't yet reached that hallowed ground. She was only fifty-nine, still vibrant, still working as a secretary for a Jersey City public high school—a job she had had since I was in junior high. In the last few years, the principal at Snyder High School had started to badger her about convincing me to coach Snyder's basketball team. She enjoyed the attention, but she told me she wouldn't want me coaching at a trifling school like Snyder if it were the last high school on Earth.

It was too chilly outside now for the residents. She had gone to somebody's apartment. I seemed to recall a nice white woman down the hall who was a pretty good friend of my mother's, but I couldn't remember her name. I walked in that direction, hoping the apartment door would leap out and trigger a memory. But as I walked down the hall, all I saw was sameness, duplicates of the cheap, nondescript metal doors favored by the modern building contractor. A wave of nerves passed over me. I looked down at my watch—thirty-five minutes to tip-off. Damn, I wasn't going to make it! The location of one of the apartments looked vaguely familiar. I think I had been in that one before. So I stepped forward and knocked. Nothing. I rang the bell and waited. Nothing. As I turned away, I heard the door swing open.

"Yes, can I help you?" It was not a white woman and she was not old at all. She was black and appeared to be quite a bit younger than me. She wore a loose-fitting robe and she looked at me quizzically, an eyebrow rising on a roundish, pleasant, but slightly weathered face—the face of a cigarette smoker.

"You didn't have an appointment, right?"

"An appointment?" I frowned. Just as I was about to ask what I'd need an appointment for, I took in the robe in the middle of the afternoon, the scent of soap and cheap perfume wafting from her, the friendly but businesslike demeanor. Prostitute? Right down the hall from my mother was a whore, working her hustle? I was stunned. I blinked rapidly, trying to think of something to say.

"Uh, no, I was looking for my mother," I said. I realized how silly that must have sounded to her. She laughed, a girlish, sweet laugh that didn't seem to go with the rest of her. It was a very appealing laugh, one I could imagine would be strong incentive to bring men back to her door.

"I think you dialed the wrong number, mister," she said, laughing at her own little joke. The voice was a little beaten, confirming my cigarette assumption. Her "mister" startled me. I wasn't *that* much older than her, was I?

"Who's your mother, sweetheart?" she asked, still grinning. I saw that she was in serious need of some dental work. The sight of missing teeth or brown teeth usually saddened me, made me think about hard days and nasty nights. She had teeth both missing and brown. She looked a lot better with her mouth closed.

"Uh, well, her name is Dolores Roman. She lives down the hall in apartment 4B."

"4B?" she repeated. "Does she have a red coat? Kinda light-skinned?"

I nodded. "Yeah, that sounds like her." I looked down at my watch, quickly remembering my hurry.

"She's not very friendly," the woman said. "I try speaking to her, but she act like she can't be bothered."

"Yeah, well, sometimes she's like that with me, and I'm her son," I said, shrugging. "Look, I gotta run. It was nice meeting you."

She smiled warmly at me, showing a missing molar and discolored bicuspids. I smiled back. "See you around," she said. She closed the door slowly, like she was waiting for me to say something else or giving me a last chance to make an appointment. After the door was closed, I wondered if maybe I was being unfair by jumping to the conclusion that she was selling her flesh. How many times had I lectured my students about too quickly jumping to conclusions or stereotyping people based on appearances? So what if she looked like a peddler of flesh and had asked if I had an appointment? People made appointments for all kinds of things. Maybe she was a therapist—with a really bad dental plan. I chuckled to myself. Yeah, right.

I looked down at my watch. I had less than a half hour to tip-off, about twenty-seven minutes. This was truly crazy. I had never been this late to a game before. One time our bus driver got lost and we were all late to a game down in South Jersey. We didn't even get a chance to warm up. We were down by twelve at halftime, but we came back real strong in the second half. I hoped the team had enough sense to start warming up without me. This was another occasion when I could have benefited from having an assistant coach. St. Paul's was so cheap that they had been fighting me on it. As they usually presented the issue to me, it was either a raise or an assistant coach. That's what they had offered me with the last two years. Of course I chose the raise. I needed to find someone willing to volunteer, but it was hard to get anything worthwhile for free.

As I walked farther down the hall, trying desperately to draw a connection with one of the plain apartment doors, I heard the unmistakable screech of my little girl. It sounded like a happy screech and it came from my left. I rushed over and knocked on 4J.

"Who is it?" It sounded like the white lady I had been looking for.

"Yes, it's Kenneth Roman. Is my mother in there?"

The door opened and I saw Mom standing behind the white lady, who was smiling warmly at me.

"Ma, I left my car keys in your apartment." I heard a screech again and saw Lane in the living room, playing with a live wire of a little gray dog, one of those cute terriers that look like they have goatees. I thought about calling out to her, but she was having so much fun that I didn't want to distract her. Without saying a word, my mother handed me her key ring, holding up the apartment key. I breathed a sigh and raced down the hall.

When I was finally in the truck and headed toward the gym, I was in such a panic that I had a difficult time negotiating the street lights and Stop signs without breaking the law. The Jersey City police weren't too kind to black men in SUVs flying through red lights. The city didn't have the reputation for rampant crime that Newark, its peer to the west, had suffered for years, but there were certainly still plenty of lawless knuckleheads crowded into the neighborhoods that hadn't yet been taken over by New York yuppies looking for real estate steals. Jersey City was a blue-collar town with a gentrified façade.

I rocked back and forth in my seat, praying that the lights would stay green as I flew across town. I wished I had a cell phone number for Jermaine's dad, a plumber who didn't miss a game if it was in or near Jersey City. I didn't have a number for the tournament director, either. This was an eight-team tournament, so to take home the trophy a team needed to win three consecutive games, on Friday, Saturday, and the championship on Sunday. The previous year we had lost in the championship to St. Anthony's, our biggest rivals in the area. I wasn't sure if the tournament directors would let the team start the game without a coach. Tariq and Jermaine would know what to do. Well, Jermaine would know what to do. They were cocaptains, but I had a lot more confidence in Jermaine's common sense than Tariq's semiconscious drifting.

When I got to the gym, I ran as fast as I could, drawing curious looks from the ticket buyers at the front door. It was 6:55. The tournament director was just inside the entrance. His face lit up when he saw me.

"Coach Roman! You made it! We were worried."

I sucked in a few monstrous gulps of air. Damn, I thought I was in better shape than that.

"Yeah, I was worried myself," I said between breaths. "It's a long story."

When we walked into the gym, I saw my team huddled together near one of the benches. From what I could see, they were surrounding Jermaine's dad. Maybe my assistant coach had just been deputized.

"Coach, you're here!" yelled Ceasar, a junior forward who had a gift for stating the obvious.

"Coach, I thought you were holding out this season for more money," Jermaine said, drawing chuckles from his teammates.

"I think maybe I should have, Jermaine," I said, still struggling to return to normal breathing. Subconsciously, I didn't want my team to see me huffing like an old man.

"Okay, guys, are we warmed up?"

Jermaine's dad, Will Bryson, answered for them. "I had them go through all their pregame drills. I told the tournament director that I was your assistant coach because he was talking about forfeit."

I patted him on the back. "Well, Mr. Bryson, how would you like to be my assistant coach?"

He took a step back and looked into my face. I clearly had caught him off-guard. I leaned in closer because the team was watching and I didn't want them to hear the rest. I looked at Jermaine as I leaned. He had a scowl on his face. That could be trouble.

"I can't pay you a real salary right now, but I can maybe talk St. Paul's into paying you before the season is up, particularly when they realize how much I need help."

Mr. Bryson rubbed his bald head. He had such a pleasant demeanor—what was going through his son's mind? I had always liked the dad, from the first moment I met him three years earlier.

"Well, I think I can manage," he said softly. "And it'll allow me to spend more time with Jermaine."

We smiled at each other and I held out my hand. We shook hands heartily. The team burst out into spontaneous applause. I looked around and everyone was grinning except Jermaine, who tried to look away so I couldn't see his face. We would have to have a talk later. The players started pounding Mr. Bryson on the back and congratulating him while he soaked it up.

"Okay, fellas, we got a game to play!" I pointed to the bench, grinning. "Coach Bryson, you can have a seat."

At once, we all turned our attention to the court. We were playing St. Peter's Prep, a school whose basketball program had improved markedly in recent years. But they were still no match for us. I might even get to relax a little in this game because they had absolutely no answer for Jermaine and Tariq.

By halftime, the score was 54–33. Tariq already had twenty-four points, while Derrick, my skilled point guard, had twelve assists. I was watching Jermaine closely and he appeared to be distracted. His father noticed, too.

"I'll have a long talk with my son tonight," he said to me as we walked back on the court to start the third quarter. "He'll come around. I think he just feels like the basketball was, you know, his thing. Now he doesn't have it to himself anymore."

"I'll talk to him, too," I said. "He's a good kid. I don't know if I would have liked it either if my father had been the assistant coach on my high school basketball team."

As soon as the words fell from my mouth, I felt like a fraud. By the time I got to high school, I didn't even remember what my father looked like. I hadn't seen him since my sixth birthday party and I spent long hours praying in my bed that the Lord would see fit to send him back home. But the Lord must have had other plans for him because he never darkened our doorway again. Nothing would have made me happier than to have my father as the assistant basketball coach of my high school team.

"Yeah, but he'll be all right," Coach Bryson repeated.

I heard a ringing noise coming from my jacket after a St. Peter's timeout early in the fourth quarter, but I was so distracted that it didn't register as my cell phone. Bryson leaned over.

"I think your phone is ringing, Coach," he said.

"Huh?"

"Your cell phone," he said.

I immediately thought of my mother and Lane. Had something happened to my child? I scrambled to grab the phone before it stopped.

"Hello? Hello?" I said into the tiny receiver. I noticed my hands were shaking.

"Kenny?" It was my mom.

"What's wrong, Ma?" I felt sweat start trickling down my forehead.

"This girl is getting sleepy. Are you gonna be picking her up tonight or should I put her to sleep here? And she said she always gets ice cream before she goes to bed. But I don't think she needs to be eating no ice cream every night. Y'all feeding this child too much junk as it is."

I exhaled deeply. This was minor mommy drama, something she was good at creating. My watch said it was close to nine. It would be well after ten before I could pick her up.

"You can put her to sleep. I'll pick her up in the morning. And of course she doesn't get no ice cream before bed every night. Maybe in her dream world."

I thought I heard annoyance in her voice as she said "Okay," but maybe it was her everyday impatience. I shook my head as I put the phone away. Was she trying to imply that my daughter was getting fat? My mother was not the master of tact. How come she couldn't be one of those warm and fuzzy grandmas you see in TV commercials?

* * *

The weekend slid downhill rapidly after Friday's game. Laney got sick on Saturday morning and we got blown out on Saturday afternoon.

I had planned on bringing the child with me to the game—in fact, my plan was to convince my mother to come along with her—but my mother called early that morning to tell me Laney was throwing up all over the place. So I spent the morning calling the doctor's office—after a frantic twenty minutes of trying to remember the name of her pediatrician—every half hour until somebody could give me some kind of diagnosis over the phone. I had my mother buzzing around telling me to bring her to the hospital, but I only wanted to do that as a last resort. A child with an upset stomach wasn't exactly an emergency-room priority. I envisioned a whole day of sitting in uncomfortable plastic chairs with a sick child moaning and trying to sleep alongside me. And, no, I had not forgotten the basketball game that afternoon.

Laney stopped heaving and finally went to sleep shortly after noon. I closed the door to my mother's apartment with her scowling face sending me off. She was not pleased to be trapped inside with a sick child. But hey, isn't that what grandparents are for?

As it turns out, I should have stayed. My team played horribly and lost to a far less skilled team from a fancy suburb in western New Jersey. The all-white team was practically a basketball stereotype—very disciplined, not very athletic, deadly from behind the three-point line. Jermaine was in an even deeper funk than the night before. It looked like he was having a childish tantrum on the basketball court. I was surprised by his immaturity, but I didn't have time to talk to him after the game—I had to run home to my child.

On Sunday, Laney woke up feeling much better, so my mother decided to take her to church—despite the condition of her hair. Rolling around in bed for an entire day had only made the hair even more painfully unkempt. But I wasn't going to argue. Church would give me a break. A listless and ailing child and a grumpy mother did not make for exciting company, or for peace of mind. When they went to church, I went back to my apartment.

I had a comfortable two-bedroom in a fairly new high-rise. The apartment was totally lacking in character—basically the rooms were four walls with a window cut out of one—and I hadn't exactly been born with a flair for decorating, so the place was about as nondescript as four rooms could get and still be considered habitable. But it was home—and I didn't have time to worry about decorating. My last girlfriend, Cynthia, had been appalled by the lack of even an attempt at palatable decor and had promised to redo the whole joint. But her promises turned out to be about as reliable as her mental stability. So she ran away and the place remained a tribute to male dullness.

I decided to make myself a big breakfast before I left for the basketball tournament. We had to play in the consolation game that afternoon. It was the ultimate humiliation—whoever had invented the whole concept of the consolation game must have been a student of the Marquis de Sade because it was cruel. A game for the losers. That's what some of the players had called it bitterly the night before. But as the coach I had to make it seem like a great idea to come back on Sunday and play a meaningless game before the winners squared off in the finals.

I grabbed a pot to make coffee and ran water into another pot for grits. But when I opened up the refrigerator door to get the eggs, the refrigerator light wasn't on and it felt warm and humid inside. What the hell? I squeezed my head behind the unit and saw that it was still plugged in. This was odd. Was the damn refrigerator broken? This building was a high-rise disaster. Cursing under my breath, I picked up my portable phone to call the super. But there was no dial tone. Huh? The phone was clearly plugged in and had been on the base, so it should be fully charged. I stood in the middle of the kitchen and looked around me. Maybe it was the electricity. There had been so much sunlight streaming into the kitchen that I hadn't even turned on the lights. I flipped the switch and nothing happened. Nada. No lights could only mean one thing. I slumped down in the kitchen chair. I had forgotten to pay the electric bill. I was supposed to have done it the previous week, but for some reason I'd forgotten. I reached over and opened my briefcase and saw the bill sitting right on top, the words SHUT-OFF NOTICE printed on top of the letter in boldface. It would cost $100 to get it turned back on, according to the letter. How could I have forgotten to pay?

The letter said it would be shut off on Thursday if I didn't pay the bill in person. But they didn't get around to it until the weekend, meaning I would have to wait until Monday to pay the bill and get it back on. I pressed my fingers into my temples, angry and annoyed at myself. Sloppy, careless, stupid. What had I been thinking? It came back to me slowly, the schedule I had worked out in my head. I was supposed to go pay the bill the morning after the parent-teacher conferences, but for some reason I had forgotten. What was it that had so distracted me? I thought back to the conferences, the other teachers, the gossip, the parents—of course, Zaria Chance. Zaria Chance. That angry, hostile, lovely woman. My thoughts went to James, her son. I was supposed to have called him or something, right? That Friday conflict with him seemed so far away. Hopefully he'd had a chance to cool off over the weekend, to realize how close he was getting to pure knucklehead status. At the beginning of the year I had predicted to myself that he was going to be a star in the class because he was bright and had a pleasant, engaging personality. But engaging had turned into annoying, which was now moving dangerously close to insubordinate. Maybe I could try to start all over with him on Monday, proclaim that we could begin anew with a clean slate. Yeah, that sounded like a good idea. I nodded my head, pleased. But then I saw the water in the pot. No grits, no eggs.

She

It was a Kodak moment—I swear. I wish you could have seen his face when he rushed in all harried. He was ten minutes late for class and, of course, even later for our little impromptu meeting in Principal Bell's office, which began about five minutes before the homeroom bell. Hate to say it, but he was ambushed. Just the way I wanted it to go down.

I had to save my fire for Mr. Roman until Monday morning, which, in hindsight, was all the better, because it gave me a whole weekend to stew on it and contemplate what I was going to say to the principal. To be honest with you, though, I didn't get around to thinking about it until Sunday. Saturday morning, the kids and I got up and cleaned the house from top to bottom—can't stand a dirty house, and a little elbow grease never hurt anybody's children—and then I took Jasmine to her dance class and, later, James to his friend Billy's birthday party (believe it or not, homeboy actually finished his writing punishment in time to make it to the party, but not Friday night's basketball game) and myself and the kids to their Auntie Mikki's house to see what all she had bought that baby a full seven months before the child will breathe his or her first gulp of Brooklyn air. I swear, she's already filled an armoire full of clothes—all pink because Miss Mikki has set it in her mind that she's carrying a girl child. I can't imagine the madness she'll put the sonogram technician through when they find a little penis peeking out at them on that television screen. She just sets her own self up. I didn't even bother to ask her if she'd lost her mind; I'm convinced she's certified.

Anyway, by the time Sunday rolled around and we got back from Sunday school and church service and cooked and ate Sunday dinner and cleaned up the kitchen, I'd almost forgotten that I was going to light up Mr. Roman's ass down at the school the next day. But when I remembered, oh, I promised myself it would be on. Question my role as a mother and then pick on my son? Don't think so.

Though I'd contemplated all the different things I could do to him—get him written up, pull his records and question whether he'd harassed any of the other students, demand he be barred from the classroom—I didn't decide on what to ask for until I had watched James trot off into school behind his friends and I pulled the car into a parking space. Principal Bell was a strong-willed black woman who, I'd decided, would not appreciate the implication of a man questioning a black woman's mothering. Sure, she'd seen some trifling heffas in her day running all through that school, but she knew quite well that I wasn't one of those. On many an occasion, I'd been the one who led the bake sales and helped decorate for this and that party and lent my services helping raise money to get the kids new sports equipment and speakers for Career Day. You name it. We weren't homies—I didn't call her at home and invite her over for Sunday dinner or anything—but she knew I had her back when it came to the kids. So it wasn't going to be hard to get her to do what I wanted to her to do—particularly if it involved my James.

We'd already exchanged formalities, small talk about the families, upcoming school events, and most of what I'd come there for in the first place—to blow the whistle on Mr. Roman's teacher/parent and teacher/student etiquette—when he bum-rushed the door.

"Mr. Roman," Principal Bell said, peering over her glasses. "Nice of you to join us."

"Good morning, Principal Bell," he said, before mumbling what sounded like an apology for being late. But it wasn't the principal he was looking at; his eyes were locked into mine, even as he fumbled his way to the seat next to me, and across from the principal's desk.

"This is Zaria Chance, James Chance's mother, but from what I understand, you two have already met," Principal Bell said. Both of us were silent, but he was still looking at me—I knew this even though I was looking dead in the principal's mouth. Had some nerve, trying to stare a hole in my head. Anyway. "Ms. Chance tells me some disturbing news about your parent-teacher meeting, and even more disturbing news about your handling of her son in your class." More silence. "She's requesting that I take her child out of your class."

"Well, that's a bit harsh, don't you think? I actually like her son and am quite pleased to have him in my class."

Oh, now he was going to ignore me—act like I'm not sitting two inches away from him. "That's not the way James tells it. He came home last week extremely upset," I said as calmly as I could. "After much prodding, he finally broke down and told me that you were picking on him in class. Now, I can take you picking on me in a parent-teacher conference, but I can't have my son coming home distracted because he thinks some teacher has it in for him."

Mr. Roman was about to say something, but Principal Bell shut him down rather quickly—and a bit harshly, even for me. "Don't say anything," she said, raising her hand and closing her eyes. She was silent for a moment, as if she was carefully trying to find the best words to lay him out. "In the past, you've been quite good at handling males in your classroom, and frankly, I'm surprised that you let things get to this point. Now, perhaps we'll have to review what exactly happened in class a little later, but I can tell you right now that James Chance has been in this school for two years now and has never once darkened my doorway. His grades are up to par," she said, shuffling around some papers on her desk, "and he participates in after-school activities, as does his mother, who has proven to be a dedicated parent to this school."

"I've never once questioned her dedication to South End, nor her son's ability to learn—" Mr. Roman said weakly, but Principal Bell didn't let him finish.

"Well, when we start questioning a mother's home situation and relating that to her child's activities in the classroom, we are questioning that child's ability to learn—and, we both know this goes directly against our school's long-standing policy of not using a child's home situation as a barometer for his academic achievements. Here, a child's home situation hasn't any relevance to what happens in our classroom."

Mr. Roman slowly closed his mouth and then said, quietly, slowly, "Yes, ma'am. You're absolutely right. And I apologize to both you and Ms. Chance for any insult I may have caused to her or her child." Then he turned to me. "Ms. Chance, please accept my apology for any hurt or harm I may have caused you or James. I only ask that you please keep James in my class; I really enjoy him as a student and I know that we can work through whatever problems we have without affecting his grades or his learning experience in my social studies program."

And damn if I didn't feel bad for that. Here he was, getting ripped a new asshole and handed his old one on a platter, and he was apologizing to me and caring about holding on to my son? I hadn't thought he was capable of forming the words "apologize" and "please." But the arrogance I'd detected in our parent-teacher meeting just wasn't there this morning. Instead, what I was seeing was what seemed to be sincerity—something I'd hardly ever seen in any man, much less one who'd come off like a bull in a china store in our first meeting. I got to thinking that perhaps I'd taken this a little too far, maybe opened my mouth a little too fast. Maybe I had also made some improper assumptions about him. Maybe.

I wasn't prepared to let him know that just now, though—not in the principal's office. How would I look having come up in here, guns blazing, and then back down from the fight? I didn't want her to think I'd wasted her time this morning, or that we didn't still have a problem that needed to be solved. I couldn't let him off that easy. "Well, I'm sure you'll understand, Mr. Roman, that this is something that I'll have to think about and talk over with my son," I said, turning to face him and stare into his eyes. Damn. April was right: He is fine. Good grief, how had I missed that? His hair was very short, obviously by choice; his face was full of a rich, shiny, dark brown hair that mixed beautifully with his light mahogany skin. He had faint freckles, and eyes that were brown/borderline hazel, and the longest eyelashes I'd ever seen on a man. His neck was thick, leading me to quickly assume that he had a muscular body—like that of an athlete. I wanted to look at his chest, to check it out, but that would have been obvious. So instead, I looked down at my lap, and then my purse on the floor, and instinctively picked it up. I turned to the principal, trying hard to shake from my mind my temporary lustful lapse and get back to the matter at hand. "How about this," I proposed, "James can stay in the class until the end of the week and, when he comes home on Thursday, I'll discuss with him how he fared in Mr. Roman's class. If I'm convinced he's had a good week and that he's happy there and the environment is conducive to learning, then he can stay. But if he's not happy, I'll inform Principal Bell on Friday, and he can start in a new social studies class next Monday."

"That sounds more than reasonable and fair," Principal Bell said as she pushed herself up from her chair. "In the meantime, Mr. Roman and I will discuss the course of action he'll need to take to make sure that we can keep your son in his class, because it really is one of the better programs and Mr. Roman is certainly one of my more astute teachers. I'm sure that we can work this out and that we'll reach a conclusion that is both amicable and satisfying. Mr. Roman? Do you have anything to add?"

"Um, yes, um," he stumbled. "That sounds like a good, fair plan. I'll be sure not to disappoint."

"Thank you," I said coldly—a little too coldly. I didn't want to be cold now. I stood up, just as Mr. Roman did, and, shockingly, he pulled my chair back. A gentleman, too, huh? "You both have a wonderful day. I'll look forward to speaking with both of you on Thursday." I gave Mr. Roman a final look, turned on my heels, walked out the door, and shut it quietly behind me without saying another word. I could see through the yellow, stained-glass door that Mr. Roman had taken his seat again, probably to get a firm lashing from Principal Bell.

But you know what? I didn't have time to worry about that this morning. I needed to get to work.

No one really ever calls my house during the day except for people trying to sell me stuff—insurance, mortgage refinancing, aluminum siding, loans. For the life of me, I can't figure out how these people get my number. First of all, it's unlisted. Second of all, I never give my number out to people who aren't family or friends I actually want to talk to—of which the latter is rare. I hate gabbing on the phone; can't stand it when it rings. I talk enough on the phone to people I don't care to converse with while I'm at work—students begging for more time to pay for classes, kids trying to track down what happened to their financial aid, others trying to pretend like they don't know why they got kicked out of class when they know good and well ain't nobody paid tuition this semester. All of them are pains in my behind, but I do my job because it's easy and it pays the bills. It's that simple.

But when I come home, I want peace, quiet, not phone calls. People who really know me know that. When the phone rings, I cringe—and I mentally cross my fingers and hope that it's one of James's little friends calling to see if he can go wherever, or Pammy calling Jasmine, asking her to ask her mom if they can have yet another slumber party. If the kids aren't here, most of the time I just let the answering machine pick up for me and screen the call, which is what I did when the phone rang as I walked through the door this afternoon. I'd just turned the lock when I heard a deep voice filling the air in the den, where the machine was. I walked a little closer to the den to hear, and was shocked by what was being said. "I just wanted to let you know that James had a good class today; we continued our discussion on apartheid in South Africa, and started a new project to tie the South African experience with the black American one. James seemed quite receptive to the class, which ended on a high note, without any problems." Then he fell silent for a moment, before he started talking again. "I just want to reiterate what I said to you in our meeting this morning," he added, his voice growing gentle. "I am truly sorry about last week's incident, and I'm fully prepared to work with you and James to ensure that his time in my class is pleasurable and enriching." He was silent again, and then he said something that made me almost drop my bag. "I was hoping perhaps we could get together for a cup of coffee sometime this coming weekend to talk—you know, in a less formal setting—so that, you know, I could explain to you my teaching philosophy. Think of it as the parent-teacher conference we never had. Give me a call at home to let me know if you'll be available either Saturday or Sunday, at 201-555-2341. Have a great evening."

Uh, no, I didn't pick up the phone because what the hell was I going to say? I mean, he was inviting me out to coffee. Off school grounds. On the weekend. Without the kids. Like a date. Okay, maybe not a date. There wasn't really anything in the message that said "date," right? He just called me to have coffee. Another parent-teacher conference. Right? His way of making up with me? Why was it so important for him to make up with me? He could have just been happy enough to send James home each afternoon without being depressed or sad, right? Without having to tell me a story about some grown man making him feel like a fool in front of his classmates, right? That would have been enough for me; I probably wasn't going to take James out of his class anyway. I was more than satisfied with how the meeting had gone this morning, and really didn't want to get Mr. Roman into any more trouble with the boss lady. Did I really need to go to have coffee with this man? Would I be giving him the wrong impression by being willing to meet him outside of the school? Would it mean anything?

I had the phone in my hand and had half dialed Mikki's number at the shop before I even realized I'd picked up the phone. She picked up after two rings. "*Mekhi's.* Mikki speaking."

"Hey."

"Hey yourself. What's up?"

"Nothin'—what's up with you?"

"Girl, I went furniture shopping today at this cute little children's boutique in SoHo. I think I might have found the perfect little crib for the baby's room—it's a sleigh crib, beautiful teak wood, shiny red finish. I didn't buy it right off because I still haven't settled on the color of the walls, but I'm probably not going to go for pink because, you know, pink is a little too girly and while I'm going to appreciate a girly girl, I don't want her to be too prissy, you know? Besides, I don't really like pink all that much—"

"Mikki?" I said, interrupting her flow. "Breathe."

"Huh?"

"Take a breath, girl. Let me get a word in edgewise, goodness."

"Well, jeez. I was just trying to tell you about my fabulous find, but if you don't want to talk about your niece then I'll shut right on up—how 'bout that?"

"Aw, Mikki—you are so very over the top, you know that?" I laughed. "I wouldn't change a thing about you though. Except for a few things—maybe your mouth, your inability to let other people talk, perhaps turn your energy down a notch or five so the rest of the world can try to keep up with you."

"Uh-huh. You know you love me just the way I am." She laughed right back. "What you doing calling me anyway? Where're my niece and nephew? Shouldn't you be in the kitchen cooking dinner by now? No, no, wait a minute—it's only 4:30. You've only put your purse down, changed your clothes, and sat down with a glass of Diet Pepsi and the *TV Guide*. At precisely 4:45, you'll be starting dinner. What you cooking?"

"Okay, you know what? I didn't call you for all this abuse, Miss Mikki," I said, only half kidding. I hesitated telling her why I was calling, because telling Mikki that I was afraid to call Mr. Roman back could go one of either two ways: She could clown me for getting so excited about a phone call from a man; even if it is my son's teacher, or she could give me a break and give me some sound advice. Mikki is good for sound advice, but sometimes it takes her a little too long to get to the point, and often, her pondering comes at the expense of your feelings. Well, my feelings. We've got our issues, you know? But I wasn't about to tell April about this, not just yet. She was a little too open over Mr. Roman, and even if there weren't anything to his invitation, she would hound me as if we were going to get married tomorrow. Nah, I needed to talk to Mikki—no matter how hard it would be to wrestle something constructive out of her mouth.

"Well, what are you calling for, Miss Zaria?"

"I need your opinion about something."

"Okay—shoot."

"Well, I had some problems with one of James's teachers last week, and it kind of turned into this big thing down at the school—"

"What? What happened with my nephew? Whose ass do I have to kick? I can't believe—"

"Mikki?" I said, interrupting her tirade.

"Huh?" she said.

"Let me finish, dear."

"Sorry. But you know I don't play that with anybody messing with my nephew."

"Uh-huh, I know, baby. Just let me tell you the story." Mikki listened quietly while I recounted what happened at the parent-teacher conference, and James's run-in with Mr. Roman, and the meeting with the principal, and, finally, the phone call. "And then he hung up, and I don't know what I should say when I call him back, or even if I should call him back."

"What do you mean, 'if you should call him back'?" Mikki said, indignant. "Why wouldn't you call him back?"

"Because this kind of meeting off school time could be misinterpreted as something more than a business meeting."

"By who? Sounds to me like he was just asking you for a second chance to talk to you about your son," Mikki said matter-of-factly. "If anyone is reading into this, it's you. I wonder why that is?"

"Mikki, what the hell are you talking about? How am I reading into this?"

"Well, from what you told me, James's teacher messed up at the parent-teacher conference—monumentally, might I add, because if he would have known your ass and how you feel about men, particularly your trifling-ass baby daddy, he would have known better. But I give the brother credit for stepping to you; I hope he's recovering from his wounds."

"Ha, ha—anyway," I said, "get to the point."

"Oh, well, he called you to get a second chance to show you that he can tell you about your son without making assumptions about his home life, which is what the principal told him he needed to do to keep out of trouble, right?" I didn't answer her, but she wasn't really look-ing for a comment anyway. She just kept right on talking. "So he's try-ing to clean up his act and get back into your good graces. It didn't sound like he was saying anything about wanting to go out on a date. Which is why I said you're the one reading into this, and, perhaps, wanting it to be a date."

"Mikki—that's a stretch. I said it reeked of impropriety because he was asking me to meet him off the school campus, on a weekend, with-out the kids. If he wanted to talk only about James and school and teaching, I could meet him at the school at his office."

"He's a schoolteacher. He doesn't have an office. And maybe he just wanted to get out of the school environment because the last time you two were there, it was pretty intense. He's probably looking for a more laid-back atmosphere so that you two can get to know each other a lit-tle better and understand the situation without all the pretense."

"I don't know about all of that," I said, still unsure.

"What does he look like?"

"Huh?"

"Huh?" Mikki said right back, mocking me. "You heard me. What does the man look like? Is he fine?"

I wasn't sure I should tell her; she'd already read right through my insecurity about the meeting and determined that I may be hoping for something more than a simple meeting with the man, which was not cool, because if Mikki and her aloof behind could read into that, then I wasn't hiding my emotions well enough. I wasn't going to tell her. "I didn't notice either way if he was handsome or not, Mikki," I said simply. "I wasn't there for a beauty shoot."

"Yeah, but you know if a man is good-looking or not," she said. "Is he good-looking?"

"Um, I guess he's all right."

"So, let me get this straight: A handsome man who has a really good job and a strong teaching relationship with your son, and, might I add, concern for his well-being, is asking you to sit down and have a cup of coffee and a simple conversation with him, and you don't know if you should go."

"Don't make it sound so simple," I said.

"Well, babe—I hate to inform you, but it is that simple," she said. "You call the man back, tell him you'll meet him for coffee on Saturday afternoon, talk to him about your son, and leave it at that. And if he remotely shows any more interest in you than a teacher/parent relationship, jump all over his ass."

"Mikki," I said, sucking my teeth and sighing. "You can be so very crass."

"Uh-huh, and you can be so very intense. Let your hair down, girl—go drink you a cup of coffee, get that man."

"It's just a cup of coffee while we discuss my child, Mikki," I said. "Nothing more."

"Uh-huh, okay. Call me when you call him, so that I can hear what you said."

"No, I have to cook my dinner now and I don't feel like talking to you anymore." And with that, I took the receiver from my ear. But I could still hear that fool yelling into the phone, "Call him, Zaria!"

I went into my kitchen, and floured my chicken. I knew the kids would be bounding in the front door hungry as hell any minute now, and I was kinda hungry myself, so I needed to get the fried chicken going. By the time I'd got my rice going, turned the fire on up under the broccoli and dropped the first piece of chicken into the frying pan, Jazzy came running into the kitchen, out of breath, disheveled, excited—like she was running from someone. The girl was panting so hard I was afraid she was going to pass out. "Mommy!" she said between breaths. "Mommy. I got something to tell you."

"Hello to you, too, Jasmine," I said, wiping the flour off my fingers and resting my hands on my hips. I hated when the kids walked in the door mid-conversation without so much as a "hello" for their mom. I mean, we hadn't seen each other since early this morning. Could I at least get a "how are you" from my own child?

"How was your day, Jasmine?" I said. "Mine was fine. I missed you today. Did you miss your mother?"

"Yes, Mommy, I missed you, too, but I got somethin' to tell you," she said, still out of breath.

"You *have* something to tell me," I corrected her. "Not 'got.'"

"I have something to tell you," she said. Then the child just stopped talking. Like she was going to keep whatever it is that she had to say to herself.

"Jazzy?" I said, widening my eyes for emphasis. "Are you going to tell me what you were going to tell me, or are you just going to make me guess?"

"Huh?"

"Jazzy!" I yelled. "What did you want to tell me?"

"JJ told Pammy and Pammy told me that James got . . . I mean, has a black eye," she rushed.

Okay, now she had my attention.

"A what?"

"He got a black eye."

"A black eye? How'd that happen?" I said, stepping a little closer to my daughter, my voice growing a little shaky. "Where is he?"

"I don't know, Mommy. JJ said he must be walking home because he missed the bus because he got into a fight with somebody," she said. "He's not at Pammy's house, yet."

My mind was racing. Who was James fighting with? Did he get hurt? Of course he got hurt; he had a black eye, dummy. Where is he? My God, he was walking all the way home? That had to be at least two miles. He'd have to cross that big, six-lane wanna-be highway to get to our part of the neighborhood. Are the crossing guards still out? Do they even have any over there? It's past five o'clock. Where is my child?

"Jasmine," I said. "Go over to April's house and ask her to come over here and watch this chicken, hear? I have to go find your brother."

"Okay, Mommy," she said, scurrying through the kitchen and out the back door.

I grabbed my keys, snatched my purse out of the den, and took off down the driveway. I was putting the car into reverse and about to pull down the driveway when, through the rearview mirror, I saw James heading up the walkway. I turned around in the car seat so fast I hurt my neck. I pushed the door open and got out of the car just in time to meet him face-to-face. "James, what happened to your face?" I yelled, placing my hand on his face and yanking his chin up toward me. "Who did this to you?"

"Nothing happened, Ma," he said as he tried to push past me.

"Wait, James—where are you going? What happened?"

"Nothing, Ma. I'm fine."

"No, dear, you are not fine. Don't stand here and tell me you're fine. Your eye looks like it's about to come out of the socket and it's as black and shiny as this car. Now tell me what happened."

"I said nothing happened!" he practically yelled.

I was so shocked that he yelled that I jumped back, making enough room for him to get past me. He disappeared into the house, letting the door slam behind him. Okay, this boy done lost his mind. I know he didn't just walk up into my house with a black eye, refuse to talk to me, physically move my body out of his way, and walk away from his mother. I know he didn't. I stood there in the driveway dumbfounded, not quite sure what, exactly, I was supposed to do. Clearly the boy had been in a fight. Clearly someone had gotten the best of him. Clearly, for the first time, I didn't know what to do. James had never been in any real trouble before, and he'd never, as far as I'd known, gotten into a fistfight with anyone. Sure, I'd witnessed him get into little boys' faces before, but he usually backed down before blows were thrown. And he certainly never behaved this way toward me. It took me a minute, but I collected myself, closed my car door, went back into the house, and sat down on the couch. I heard April walk in through the back door. I could see her from where I was sitting; she was poking at my chicken in the pan. I knew it wasn't brown enough to turn over, but she was using the tongs to flip it over anyway. She wasn't all that good of a cook; I didn't want her messing in my chicken. What the hell am I thinking about chicken for? My child needs my help. But what was I going to say? He wouldn't tell me what happened. And he was angry. I'd never seen him like this before. I had to talk to him, even if he didn't want to talk. But how was I going to reach him?

For the first time in a very long time, I began thinking that perhaps I needed to talk to a man about my son. A man would know how to deal with bullies and fighting and the kind of trouble boys get into with other boys. But whom should I call? I mean, it would have been nice to be able to pick up the phone and call his father, but our relationship had grown increasingly hostile since he'd gotten out of prison, mainly because he kept walking in and out of my children's lives, each time stealing a little bit more of their hope of having an honest, real relationship with him—one that wouldn't be filled with empty promises and lies. Still, he might be able to talk some sense into James, get him to see that this path was the wrong path to go down—the one that could lead exactly to the place his father is right now. Aw, who the hell am I kidding? That fool doesn't see anything wrong with the place he's in right now—at least I haven't seen any evidence of it. That's why I don't want his stupid behind around my children.

Randy. I'd call him. Surely he'd know what to say to James—how to reach him. I called Mikki's house, but there was no answer. Of course there wouldn't be; he's probably still at work. I didn't know the number there. I didn't want to call Mikki to get it because then I'd have to explain everything to her and she'd try to fix it herself, and I didn't need her two cents on this. I pressed the flash button on the phone and dialed Daddy's number. He would know how to handle it, wouldn't he? He could tell me what I should say to James, how I should approach this. I pressed the flash button again. No, he wouldn't be able to help; he raised two girls, one of whom wouldn't have had James in the first place if she would have listened to her father to begin with. He recognized trouble when he saw it, but actually handling it is wholly different. Besides, what did he know about kids today? Boys today?

I put the phone back in the receiver, and then I did something I would have never imagined in a million years I'd do: I dialed Mr. Roman's number. I told his answering machine that he should meet me at Café Cocoa on Saturday afternoon at 12:30, and that I looked forward to our meeting. I said it in the most businesslike tone I could conjure up, so as not to make him think I was all excited about this. This was, after all, about my son—not about him.

I went back into my kitchen and found April still poking at my chicken with those tongs. She didn't say anything to me—just instinctively knew that this wasn't a good time to talk about what was going on in my house. She handed me my tongs, gave me a hug, and went right out my back door without saying a word.

He

The shrill ring of the bedside phone snapped me awake. I looked around the room—I had fallen asleep waiting for the sports report on the 11 P.M. newscast. Who could be calling me after eleven?

"Uh, hello," I muttered into the phone.

"Kenneth, did I wake you up, baby? I'm sorry."

I sat up in my bed, the grogginess immediately washed away by the voice on the line.

"Antoinette?" I said, trying to drop my voice down a little lower, sexier. "Nah, I wasn't really asleep yet. What are you up to?"

"Well, I'm actually in your neighborhood and I was wondering if you might be interested in a little company. I haven't seen you in a while. I've been thinking about you."

I took a quick glance at the bedside alarm clock. Damn, it was 11:37 on a Tuesday night. My old friend Antoinette was making one of her unmistakable late-night booty calls. They only came about three or four times a year, and when they did I felt like a little boy who had gotten a surprise personal visit from Santa Claus, the Easter Bunny, and the Tooth Fairy all at once, each laden with little-boy gifts. Yeah, it'd take me a week to catch up on the sleep I would miss after a night with Antoinette; my teaching and coaching might suffer the consequences, but I didn't know how to say anything to Antoinette except yes. Didn't want to say anything else. I especially needed it after the week I had been having. Warnings from the principal, irate mothers, a losing basketball weekend—yeah, Antoinette was the perfect salve.

"Well, I've been thinking about you, too, babe," I lied. Responding in kind was just being polite, you know? "How long would it take you to get here?"

"Funny you should ask that," she said, chuckling sexily. Antoinette knew how to do sexy over the phone like a damn champ. More than once I had told her she could pocket big money as a phone-sex operator. "How d'ya know I don't?" she'd always answer.

"I'm sitting in my car, right below your window," she said. "Why don't you come and take a look?"

"Look out the window? All right, hold up a second." I giggled slightly as I jumped out of the bed and practically sprinted to the window. I yanked up the blinds and looked down. There she was, right underneath the streetlight, sitting behind the wheel of her late-model sports car, a sleek-looking Toyota that didn't look like anything else Toyota made. I could see her through the windshield—oh shit, was she topless? Damn, she was a stone freak.

"Antoinette? Are you showing me your titties, baby? Are you being a bad girl?"

She laughed. I could see her throw back her head as she chuckled into the celly.

"I just wanted to give you an appetizer, a visual appetizer. You like?"

I felt the familiar thickening in my crotch area pushing against the too-snug briefs I was still wearing. Antoinette always managed to take the concept of foreplay to unthought-of levels, like a musician with an innate ability to create genre-busting melodies. She turned sex into performance art. What man could resist that? What man would want to? Sometimes I had the abstract fear that when I finally did meet the so-called woman of my dreams, Antoinette would have wreaked havoc with my expectations. Sometimes she seemed to me like the sistah from another planet.

"Darling, you know what you do to me," I said, trying to drop it yet an octave lower. "Now would you please come up here before I bust through my drawers—and before you catch a cold?" I was going to add "before my neighbors see you," but I didn't want to sound like a prude. I watched Antoinette slip her coat back over her shoulders. Had she even looked around to see if perhaps any heads were poking out of windows before she had practically disrobed? The woman was virtually without shame—a definite prerequisite for top-shelf freakiness.

"I'll leave the door open for you," I said. "You know where I'll be."

With those suggestive words, I pressed the Talk button to hang up the cordless. I watched her step from the car, wearing some shiny, sexy trench coat and very high heels. We rarely actually went out on dates or appeared together in public, so I wondered not for the first time whether she looked like this every day—or if it was part of her late-night call-girl game. Was she an all-day freak or did she just enjoy dress-up? Antoinette told me she was a social worker for the state of New Jersey, but I had never tried to verify that. I had never called her at her job—didn't even have her work phone number. We'd met several years earlier when she showed up at one of my basketball games to watch the younger brother of a friend of hers play against my team. We destroyed the kid's team that day and after about ten minutes of intense post-game flirting she took my phone number. I had to admit, there must be something about watching me during a game in action in front of the bench that acted as an aphrodisiac for women. Well, maybe aphrodisiac was too presumptuous—after all, I hadn't had any wet panties tossed onto the court, a la Teddy Pendergrass, at least not yet. But surely the sight of me going through my game-time antics was a powerful attention grabber because I had received more than a few post-game phone numbers from female admirers. Antoinette, as you might guess, wasn't shy about making her intentions known. Within five minutes she had told me that she'd love for me to put my big mouth to even better use. I'm no dummy—I was putting her words into action the next night on my living room couch. That first night pretty much sketched the arc of our relationship—energetic, after-hours sex. Antoinette would not be getting an invitation to meet my mama. But apparently she was cool with that.

I heard her heels start the *clickety clack* against the pavement as she approached my building. I rushed toward the bathroom to grab my toothbrush and then out to the living room to buzz her in. I put the toothbrush to work with vigor as I waited. Once I got her ring, I reached out to let her in—and got a frightening whiff of underarm funk. Oh, I needed to handle that. I sprinted toward the bathroom, catching with my left hand a glob of toothpaste spit that was threatening to dribble down my chin. After rinsing out my mouth, I lathered up a washcloth and was about to hit the armpits when I heard the doorbell. Damn, how'd she get up here so fast? I didn't even get a chance to leave my door open. I glanced in the mirror, noting that my hair needed brushing, too. But there was no time now to get pretty. Antoinette would just be messing the hair up anyway. However, I did make her wait while I handled the armpits. Nothing like underarm funk to kill a mood. Like that time in college with that fake-bohemian mixed-race girl, Clarice—or was it Clara?—who apparently hadn't bothered to wash in the days leading up to jumping into my bed. The girl had confused bohemian with grimy. Her underarm funk scared me so much that I was afraid to slide my face southward to sample her lower regions, even after she had enthusiastically done me. Homegirl even had the nerve to complain about it. She even told some of her friends, I discovered months later. You can be sure Clara—Clarice?—never found her way to my bed again. She was lucky I was a nice guy, even in college, or I would have put her hygienic habits in bold headlines.

Once I opened my front door, Clarice/Clara was a distant memory. The presence of Antoinette didn't leave much room to think about other women. With her actions, her demeanor, her looks, she demanded every bit of your attention. Sometimes I had to struggle with an impulse to be a little intimidated by her. But the power of her ever-present sexuality and its effects on my loins overpowered any other impulses. When I saw her, smelled her, talked to her, envisioned her, all I could think about was sex.

"Hello, Kenneth," she said with a smile. The lipstick glistening on her full lips appeared to be the only makeup she was wearing. Her dark brown skin was flawless, like a burnished and shellacked slate of oak, and her heart-shaped face was the ideal frame for large brown eyes that didn't miss a thing. Her nose, a bit too wide and flat, made her approachable—without it she'd be verging too near flawlessness. She sauntered into the room, almost exaggerating the sexy strut like a stripper walking around a shiny pole. "I thought you were gonna leave the door open. What happened, you were scared I'd come in here and have my way with you?"

Without even pausing for my answer, Antoinette headed straight for my bedroom, pulling the shiny coat from her shoulders to reveal her smooth, bare back and a tiny maroon strip of a thong riding up her round, meaty ass. As usual when she arrived, Antoinette made me feel like I was starring in one of the letters in Penthouse Forum that my college buddies and I used to devour every month like it was our religion. We always swore that the letters had to be made up—but we each secretly hoped that they weren't. Maybe I should write up one of these nights with Antoinette and send it in—and then call up my boys and give them a page number. As I followed behind her, it occurred to me that maybe Antoinette was also a fan of the letters—maybe they were a source of her inspiration.

Once she hit the bedroom, Antoinette pivoted and welcomed me into her arms. As we kissed, the stickiness of her lips made me know what it would feel like to get intimate with flypaper. But I ignored that brief unpleasantness; we didn't usually do much kissing anyway. I think we only started that way because we were supposed to—otherwise it would too closely resemble a paid session. While they might arrive in shiny trench coats with nothing underneath, whores didn't kiss. Antoinette reached down and squeezed between my legs, as if she were checking the heft and thickness before putting it in her shopping cart.

"Is it ripe?" I said, mumbling into her mouth.

She pulled back and laughed. "That's funny—that's just what I was thinking!" I was always a little surprised when she exhibited a sense of humor.

Antoinette slid from my arms and walked to the bed. She was done with the kissing. Over the next hour or so, we didn't leave any body surfaces untouched by caresses or unworshiped by eager tongues. Antoinette was an extremely accommodating partner—she didn't try to direct the action and she always made it clear that she was enjoying herself immensely. Being with her was an enormous ego boost; she made me feel like I was a sexual maestro, like each of my moves was exactly what she wanted.

By her third orgasm, I decided that it was okay for me to follow her. When I was with her, I always fought the fear that I was going to come too soon. I wanted her to get plenty before I got mine. Because our encounters were so purely sexual in nature, any failure would be magnified. If I came too early, we'd be confronted with the question "now what?" Talk? No, I didn't want that. Talk was not Antoinette's reason for being—or at least her reason for being at my apartment.

After I finally came, looking down at her quivering buttocks while

I moved forcefully into her from behind, I collapsed beside her on the bed. We were both sweaty; I felt tingly all over. At that moment I wondered why we didn't do this more often—and why we usually did it only after she initiated the call, usually late at night. That's the pattern we had fallen into. Patterns were hard to break. I sat up and decided to head for the bathroom. I didn't really feel like talking.

I flushed the toilet after relieving myself and lathered up a washcloth to scrub my face. When the din of the tank finally died down, I heard a voice coming from the bedroom; it wasn't Antoinette. I put my head to the closed door—it was the message from Zaria Chance. Antoinette was listening to my messages? I felt my neck start to get hot. I was tempted to open the door and start screaming. But perhaps that would be the wrong move, I sensed. I needed to be more careful here.

"So, who is this woman, Zaria Chance, that's inviting you out on a date?" Antoinette said when I opened the door. Her voice contained a trace of tension, I thought, like she was trying to sound nonchalant but it wasn't working. I walked over to the bed and sat down next to her. Antoinette was getting jealous? That wasn't supposed to happen.

"I'd hardly call it a date. She's the mother of a kid in one of my classes. She wants to talk about her kid." I reached out to stroke Antoinette's exposed butt cheek. She was turned away from me so I couldn't really see her face. When my hand made contact with her flesh, I felt her flinch a little. I slowly took my hand back; my feelings were a bit bruised. Since when did Antoinette flinch?

"Can't you talk about her kid at school, like at a parent-teacher conference or something? And from what she said, it sounded like you invited her out first." She still wasn't looking at me, strangely. What was going through her head? I slid across the bed and leaned on my elbow so I could see her face.

"Antoinette? Why do you care?" I tensed slightly; I didn't mean for it to sound so much like a challenge.

She stared at me. I couldn't read her expression.

"I'm not supposed to care, right? That's the deal here, that we just fuck each other's brains out, but it's not supposed to go any further than that, right?"

What do you say to a question like that? I couldn't very well tell her that was a perfect description of our arrangement. No woman wants to hear that—especially after sex—even if it was 100 percent accurate.

Was a lie necessary here? Was I supposed to tell her that she meant more to me than that? I just wanted to avoid the land mines.

"Well, we've never talked about what our deal is, Antoinette. I thought that our relationship was exactly the way you wanted it."

She stared at me again. I was a little concerned about throwing the word "relationship" into the discussion. That was an open invitation for trouble. I needed to escape from this without committing myself to an unwanted entanglement with this woman—but to make sure she kept visiting me late at night.

"You mean great sex with no strings attached? That's what you want, right Kenneth?" She laughed out loud. I got the impression it was a mocking laugh.

"After all, you've never called me up and invited me out for coffee at some café. You've never even taken me out to dinner. What's this mother look like?"

I never thought I'd hear Antoinette whining about going out for coffee. She always made such an effort to present herself as uninhibited and carefree, existing on a plane way above such tired, mundane concerns like whether I called her as many times as she called me. But perhaps it was all an act. Now she was asking me girlfriend-type questions. What did Zaria Chance look like? Of course what she wanted to hear was a brutal critique and dismissal.

"Uh, well, she's—come on, what does it matter? It's not like I'm going to have a, uh—well, it's just a meeting. You know? I haven't really paid much attention to—she's all right, I guess. You'd probably say she was attractive. Probably."

I reached up and wiped the sweat from my nose. I couldn't believe I was having this conversation with Antoinette, this inquisition. And here I was sweating like a lying husband caught with his dick out. I just couldn't summon the words to give Zaria the dismissal that was called for in this situation. How easy it would have been to call her ugly.

In an instant, Antoinette popped up from the bed, as if she had been stuck with a needle. I reared back in surprise. I might have even flinched.

"I'm just messing with you, Kenneth Roman," she said. She chuckled. Or at least a close approximation.

"Look at you, all sweaty. Looking all scared and shit. You thought I was catching feelings or something, right?" She grinned at me as she headed toward the bathroom. "I scared you to death, didn't I?" She stepped into the bathroom, cackling to herself. "Kenneth Roman thought Antoinette was in love."

I heard the cackles, but I wasn't sure if I should totally believe them. No one was *that* good of an actress, not even Antoinette. What I saw was the desperation of a jealous woman. Something that she had heard in Zaria's voice had set her off. I needed to listen to that message again, maybe several more times, to search for what Antoinette had heard. I looked at the answering machine and glanced back into the bathroom, wondering when she was going to leave.

She

I had just poured a bowlful of eggs and cheese into a sizzling frying pan full of butter and poured myself a second cup of instant coffee—hazelnut, extra light, super sweet, just the way I like it—when the phone rang. Who in the hell was calling the house this early in the morning? It was barely 7 A.M.; the kids were still yawning and struggling to open their eyes wide enough to figure out where the Colgate was, and I hadn't even begun to put breakfast on the table, much less fix their lunches and get myself ready for work. A phone call this early in the morning meant only one thing: Something was wrong. With my mother. Or my father. Or, Lord, both. Or Mikki—the baby. I picked up the cordless. "Hello?" I said, the word rushing into the receiver.

"Good morning, Ms. Chance," said the man on the other end. His voice unfamiliar, but his tone said he not only knew me, he was familiar. Very familiar. Who was this? "Zaria Chance? Do I have the right number?"

"That depends on who this is on the other line," I said slowly, a hint of annoyance ringing my voice. "You want to help me out?"

"This is Kenneth," he said, this time a little less confident. I didn't say anything. "Kenneth Roman. Um, your son James's social studies teacher."

Oooh. God. Um. Goodness—it's Mr. Roman. He called me back. At seven in the morning. With a sexy voice. A super-sexy voice. Like he was making a booty call. I mean, I recognize I told him I'd go out with him for coffee, but it was to talk about my son—not make a new one with him. Good grief, is that what he's thinking, that I said yes to him because I'm interested in seeing him? Like, on a date? I mean, not like it would be a bad thing to go out on a date with Kenneth Roman. But did I come off as one of those fast mothers from the school who throws herself at the male teachers every chance she gets because that's the only man they see during the course of the day worth half of something? How many of the other mothers did he call at the crack of dawn with that voice? And what in the world was he doing calling this early, anyway? "Good morning, Mr. Roman," I said curtly. "What can I do for you this morning?"

"I was returning your phone call," he said, his voice sounding a bit more normal this time.

"Yes, I gathered," I said, just as James walked into the kitchen.

"Mom? Can I just have some Froot Loops?" he said, still rubbing his eyes. "I don't really want any of those." His finger was aimed at the stove, where the eggs I'd poured into the pan were quickly turning a perfectly nasty shade of burnt brown. I walked over to the stove, turned off the flame, and removed the pan from the red-hot burner. I really didn't want to have this conversation with Mr. Roman in front of my kid. I needed to get him off the phone. I turned my back toward James and lowered my voice just a bit.

"Is there something wrong?" I asked.

"No, no—of course not," he said. "I was just confirming our, um, appointment for this Saturday. Sorry for such an early call, but I wanted to catch you before I left for work. I didn't think I'd have a chance to call you later, and besides, I don't have your business phone number."

Appointment? Was that all it was? An appointment? Damn. "I assumed that my phone call to you last night accepting your, um, offer, was sufficient. But yes, Saturday is fine," I said, peeking over to see if James was paying any kind of attention to what I was saying into the phone. He wasn't. Completely oblivious.

"Um, great, so I'll see you at the café at 12:30 Saturday, correct?"

"Yes, Saturday, 12:30."

"Wonderful. See you then," he said. And he hung up.

I pushed the Talk button on the phone and put it back in its receiver. What exactly was that? I leaned back on the counter and looked over at James, who was hunched over a huge bowl of cereal—enough to feed two grown men. I don't know where it all goes; he's a skinny little kid—lanky and bony and not all that tall. Got that from his daddy's side of the family—the lot of them were tiny people. James went out of his way to pretend like he was actually bigger than he was, with his loud mouth and all that bravado. I caught him trying to lift weights once, and another time, he was downstairs in the laundry room, hanging from the metal clothing pole, talking about he was trying to stretch himself so that he could get a little taller. I wanted to smack him for almost breaking my line, but I had to giggle over his belief that his little body was going to somehow stretch from his hanging on to a pole. That's my James.

We were always close, me and my little man. I didn't quite understand what had been happening between us over the past few weeks—he was always quite candid about his feelings and told me everything about what was going on in his life outside this house. I always took great pride in the trust he had in sharing his feelings with me, and especially sharing all his secrets, even if they didn't mean much in the greater scheme of things. Like the time when he called himself liking some little girl in Mrs. Browning's class, and he asked me to come along with him to the CVS so that I could help him pick out a card that "wasn't too mushy, but that was nice." Most boys his age were still trying to pretend like girls were yucky pains in their behinds, but not my James. Not that I wanted him to have a girlfriend; the idea of him kissing some little girl, or, worse yet, having sex with one, was a situation with which I just couldn't deal. I definitely didn't want to be somebody's grandmother before I hit forty. Or fifty. I wanted to be in a rocking chair with a cane and an I.V. before either of my children came up into this house with a baby old enough to say my name; there was no way I was about to go through what I put my parents through when I came home knocked up. So it was important to me that James thought enough of his mother to tell her about that little girl, and I was certainly pleased to be included in the courting.

But now, here I was, being shut out. Our conversations began and ended with what he was going to eat, or what activity he had to do for the day, or where he was going to be. But details, these days, were few and far between. He still hadn't told me what had happened the day he came home with that shiner, and every time I brought it up—whether it was nicely or by demand—he kindly refused to give up the goods. Shoot, he was so tight-lipped, even Jasmine couldn't tell me what had happened. And I swear, sometimes that girl knew so much of everybody's business, you would have thought she was down with the FBI and the CIA.

At any rate, I was at my wit's end with James, and I wasn't going to sit here and pretend like I could figure this one out by myself—so Mr. Roman was about to come in handy. Just how handy was still up in the air.

Okay, clearly I'd entered the Twilight Zone, because what I'd seen made absolutely no sense whatsoever. In fact, it was a bit freaky—and I'm sure that I needed much more time than I had to actually regroup and comprehend what was happening before my eyes. I was on my way to my hot date (?) with Mr. Roman and dropping James and Jasmine off at my parents' house—well, actually, it's my mom's house now because my father stopped living there well over a year ago—so that they could visit with their grandmother while I handled this business, and who should be sitting on the porch swing, as relaxed as you please, with a glass of lemonade and a Kool-Aid smile but my father, my mother at his side with an equally pleasant look on her face. The two looked downright euphoric—laughing and carrying on, grabbing on each other's arms and talking to each other in hushed tones. They looked, well, happy.

Which is just beyond crazy to me because my parents haven't been happy—at least not with each other—since my father's illegitimate son had come knocking on my mother's door. Or, more specifically, calling on her telephone every other day for almost a month. The long and short of it is this: My father got this woman pregnant just around the time that my mother, his wife, was pregnant with me, and my mother responded to this bit of news—which she had got just last year—by telling my father to get to steppin'. She filed for divorce shortly after she had kicked him out of the house, and started dating this really handsome guy named Joe, who was just wining, dining, and romancing her like they were sixteen-year-olds in their first fling. My parents had been married for well over thirty years, so it was hard to comprehend, even at my age, the demise of their union. I just always thought they'd be together because it was natural for them to be together—the model black couple who had endured the craziness of the times by holding on to one another and their union. They were supposed to stay together because that's what old couples did—stick together. Not like us young 'uns who broke up over the slightest mess—like my sister Mikki did when Randy left her for a three-month gig in Paris. I mean, he didn't leave her for another woman for three years; he left her to make some money—and Mikki went and cheated on the boy just like that. It was just too easy—for Mikki and Randy, and all the other young couples I knew who seemed to value their own feelings and needs more than those things required to sustain a successful marriage. Walk away—that's what they did. At the first sign of trouble. Or what looked like it *might* be trouble.

But folks like my parents gave me hope—hope that marriages could work. My father? Gave me confidence that there were good men out there willing not only to be responsible and take care of family, but love their women the way they deserved to be loved—with wild abandon. Unconditionally. My mother? Well, she was the epitome of a loving wife who, while she was full of fire and never took any guff, was extremely protective of her family and the role she played in it. She wasn't ashamed to do what her mother taught her was a wife's "duties"—you know, take care of the kids, keep the house up, feed the family, all the things the officers of NOW would string up a member for even considering doing. But beyond that, she was—and still is—a terrific mother who served as a role model for me and Mikki on how to be strong, independent, black women.

I didn't truly latch on to what it really meant to be strong and independent until I had to raise my children on my own. Sure, I thought that defying my parents and dating that trifling man who had fathered my kids was the ultimate in independent, but I realize now that it was more defiance than anything. I might have loved that fool, but if his touch made me float on cloud nine, doing the opposite of what my parents wanted me to do put me clean on cloud ninety-nine. Yeah, I thought I knew everything and that nobody could tell me shit, but when my babies took their first breaths and their father took a hike, it was clear that I was going to get a crash course in what it truly means to be on my own. And I decided soon after he stepped that no man was ever going to treat me that way again. Ever. And that the next Negro who stepped into my life better well come with Mr. Perfect stamped on his forehead, and willing to work real hard to prove it if he wanted some of this.

I'll tell you this much, I haven't run across him yet.

Which is why I decided when I got up this morning that my talk with Mr. Roman this afternoon would be just that—a talk. Nothing more. I wanted to find out what was going on with my son and that was it. I wasn't going to come on to him, I wasn't going to entertain that he would come on to me, I wasn't going to daydream about what might transpire between us over coffee and crumpets. Just talk.

I decided this after about a half an hour into trying on clothes in preparation for our date—I mean talk. I swear, I must have climbed into every outfit I had in my closet—business suits (too conservative), Sunday dresses (too, um, clean), dresses I'd worn back in the day when I'd actually tried to meet men at the club (way too fast for brunch). I put on makeup, then, in a flash, washed it all off and replaced it with a simple coat of mascara and some lip gloss. That's all that was necessary because this wasn't supposed to be a love connection. He was my son's teacher, for goodness' sake. What was I supposed to do—marry him? Don't think so. Screw him and keep it moving? No time, no desire—not desperate enough to put myself out there like that. Date him and wait for what would inevitably be the end. Had my heart broken one too many times. Not trying to let it happen again with a social studies teacher who has half the PTA wanting to drop its panties for him. Got enough problems.

I settled on a pair of jeans, a T-shirt, and a funky crocheted poncho Mikki had made for me years ago. My hair was pulled back into a neat ponytail. Simple and to the point. Like this meeting was about to be.

Then I happened upon my parents, and realized that nothing is ever that easy.

"Well, don't you two look cozy," I said to my parents as I walked up the porch steps, Jasmine's hand in mine. They hadn't even bothered to look up when I pulled into the driveway, or as I was struggling up the stairs with all of James's and Jasmine's playthings. James was taking his sweet time getting out of the car, and Jasmine was too busy running for her papa's arms—she hadn't seen him in quite a while because he wasn't around and I, still a bit angry about his infidelity, wasn't really going to be all that bothered trying to go out of my way to hook him up with the kids—to actually help me carry her Barbie dolls, play cooking utensils, play makeup case, and playhouse set into the house. I dropped everything at my mom's feet and leaned in to give her a big kiss and warm embrace. I just looked at my father and said, "Hi."

"Lovely day, isn't it, Zaria," my father said, still smiling from ear to ear.

"I suppose," I said, looking up at the blue, cloudless sky. An airplane was roaring overhead.

"So, where you going on your hot date?" my mother asked, giggling.

"It's not a hot date, Mother," I said, annoyed, looking around for big-mouthed Jasmine while I talked. She didn't appear to be paying any attention, so busy was she tugging on her grandfather, but I threw my mother a look that clearly said, "watch your mouth, lady." "I'm going out for coffee with one of James's teachers to discuss his schoolwork. That's all that's going to be happening today, so get your mind out of the gutter, please."

"Oh, Zaria, calm down—I'm just kidding with you, girl," my mom said before she turned to Jasmine. "How's my little pumpkin pie?" she said to her granddaughter.

"I'm fine, Gamma," she said cheerily before hopping from her grandfather's lap to her grandmother's.

"Well, you sure seem to be," my father said, grabbing her hand and kissing it. James was standing at the bottom of the stoop, waiting for his turn to greet the folks.

"Anyway, I'm going to get down the road. I don't want to be late," I said.

"No, dear, you don't," my mother said. "First impressions are everything. You wouldn't want the good teacher to think you're irresponsible," she said.

I shot her another "daggers through your heart" look and turned on my heels, headed back for the porch steps. "My meeting shouldn't take long; I'll be back home in about an hour and a half if you need me for something," I said. "Bye-bye, James. 'Bye, Jasmine. Be good and mind your grandma. I'll see you tonight."

And with that, I got into the car and pulled out.

He

The place that Zaria had picked for our meeting, Café Cocoa, was a bit fancier than I had expected, near the heart of downtown Teaneck. The owners had obviously spent serious money on the decoration, exactly so that first-time patrons would have the reaction I did: admiration. I arrived before Zaria, so I had the chance to pick out a table. The host, a white guy who was so effeminate that he might make a woman feel insecure in her femininity, asked if I wanted a cozy booth or a table near the window. I chose the booth, then I second-guessed my decision for the entire ten minutes until Zaria arrived. I hoped she didn't think a booth was presumptuous. Why did I pick the booth anyway?

I saw Zaria approach the host and watched him daintily point to where I was sitting. She looked over at me and smiled. She was wearing slacks and a shawl thing that made her look suburban but chic at the same time—if that was possible. The woman really was very pretty. I wanted to be as formal as I could with her, particularly after what she put me through with Principal Bell, but already I was charmed by her looks. I even felt a strange grinding in my stomach, a signal my body didn't give me very often. I had been duped enough times to know that looks were just a small part of the entire package—okay, maybe "small" was underselling it a bit—but it certainly was hard to quickly get past them when a woman was as lovely as Zaria Chance. She had a smooth, confident walk, like a woman who knew that all eyes were on her—but who didn't mind.

As she slid into the booth, I reminded myself that she was the one who had extended the invitation here. I wasn't sure how meaningful that was, but the memory put me at ease a little. I tried to stand as she sat down, but the effort caused me to bang my knee on the table. I grimaced through my smile, hoping she didn't hear the loud knock. If she did, she didn't let on.

"This place is really nice," I said. "I've driven by it before, but I never knew it was this pretty on the inside."

Her face brightened even more as she looked around. "Yes, it's beautiful. I love the colors they used in the rooms. Taupe is a very soothing color, but at the same time it's not boring or bland."

"What color did you say? Taupe?" I asked with a smart-alecky grin. "And here I was thinking it was just brown."

She smiled happily. "Well, it's in the brown family. I really like interior design. I do get into my colors."

I wanted to tell her that her face looked almost like taupe, but that might sound too much like flirting. Despite appearances to the contrary, this woman was not supposed to be a friend. We were supposed to be talking about her son and his behavior in class. At least I assumed that's why we were here in this fashionable café. I was enjoying the small talk, however, so I wasn't going to mention her knucklehead until she did.

"Have you had a chance to do much interior design?" I asked her.

She shook her head. "No, not much. Not as much as I would like. Of course, I did my house. Or I should say I am doing my house because I'm always changing things around. My kids are always telling me that whenever they go stay with their grandparents, the house is all rearranged when they come home. I'm surprised when they even notice. You know how kids are—they aren't the most observant creatures in the world."

I nodded. I wanted to ask her how many kids she had—that was the obvious follow-up question. But for some reason I held back. Well, actually I know the reason—I wasn't ready yet to tell her I had a child of my own, out of wedlock. I loved Laney to no end, but her existence was still somewhat embarrassing to me. It was just too stereotypical. Another black man with kids scattered about who had never been married. I hoped one day to learn to live gracefully with the indignity of feeling like another dreadful statistic. But I wasn't there yet.

"I also designed some of the office space at the college where I work—Lawrence," she continued. "Well, I don't know if *design* is the right word. I chose the color patterns and decided where the office furniture should go."

"That sounds like design to me," I said, trying to be encouraging.

She shrugged. "I guess so. People seemed to be happy with it."

She was much easier to talk to than I had any reason to expect after our first two meetings. The tension I was feeling when she approached the table was now completely gone. It felt like I was chatting with an old friend. There aren't many human encounters as potentially awkward as a first date, especially if it's not even clear it *is* a first date. I could always quickly judge how much more time I'd want to spend with a lady by how comfortable she managed to make me feel in the beginning. A lot of females tried to make you do all the work while they just sat back and played pretty. As if the responsibility for positive social interaction was all yours. As if you'd be interested in a serious relationship with an attractive, potted plant. I hated that.

I wanted to ask her about James, about how he had gotten the black eye—since he had refused to tell me when I confronted him after class—but I didn't want to interrupt the small talk. And I was afraid the mention of James would darken her sunny mood. We ordered from the menu, light snacks and fancy coffees for us both. We joked about the growth of the fancy-coffee industry. I noted that there was even a Starbucks in Harlem now, but she grimaced when I asked if she had ever been there. I wasn't sure what the grimace was all about, but I let it go. We watched the host seat another couple near us and enjoyed a little laughter at his expense. Zaria was especially disapproving in her humor, surprising me. Women were usually more accepting of over-the-top queens, or at least I thought. Finally, after our food and drink had arrived and, I must admit, I was totally mesmerized by this woman, we got around to her son.

"I'm a little worried about James," she said. "I didn't appreciate the things you said during our meeting in your class, but I admit that he can be a handful at times. A week ago or so he came home from school with a black eye. I'm sure you must have noticed."

She paused as I nodded my head. "Well, he hasn't been willing to tell me anything about what happened. He goes to his room all the time now and keeps the door closed. We were always able to talk

about his problems before, but now he's seeming so distant from me."
She wasn't looking at me anymore as she spoke. She was swimming in
her painful reflection. "I'm at a loss for what to do."

Now she looked at me. Her eyes searched mine, sending a delicious
tremor down my spine. These were the kind of heart-pounding moments upon which some deep feelings could be built. That acknowl-
edgment scared me a little. Actually, what scared me was the
sweatiness I felt in my palms as I gazed into this lady's face, trying to
find a comfortable place in the intense, amber glow of her eyes. Her
last statement lingered, sitting conspicuously out there like Vegas neon.
I was at the edge of the cliff, staring down into a dark, thrilling abyss.
I had told myself after my last attempt at a relationship ended so badly
that I would give up on the dating for a while because it was too much
work, too much drama. As I got older, I was so rarely even meeting
women that I'd want to spend more than fifteen minutes with that a
dating moratorium hadn't been difficult at all. Of course I had a few
sex partners, women like Antoinette who for one reason or other had
moved into my bed but not my head. But the pickings out here were
starting to look scarily slim. One of my male friends had jokingly said
that when a man enters his mid-thirties and he's still not married, all
that's left to him are the "soap opera chicks." When I asked him what
he meant by that, he said they were the Young and the Crazy—either
they were clueless twenty-somethings or crazy thirty-somethings. But
Zaria felt different, at least at this early stage. She didn't appear to be
overflowing with the neuroses that I was increasingly finding in
grown-ass women. I took a deep breath and I decided to jump into
that abyss, to let go.

"Well, I could help," I said. It felt like I had put too much starch on
the I, making the statement too self-important. She didn't answer me
right away. I tried to translate her expression, but it was impenetrable.
For an instant, I reached the terrifying conclusion that I had just
supremely screwed up, that I had made the same kind of tragic presump-
tion that had started our first battle in my classroom a few weeks earlier.
She was going to grab her bag again and bolt from the table, pointing the
same long, angry finger at me for thinking she needed my help.

Then she smiled. Oh God, what a lovely vision it was! I breathed
finally and smiled right along with her, though I wasn't sure exactly
what we were so happy about.

"What are you smiling about?" she asked me, still smiling.

"I'm smiling because you're smiling," I said, not smiling as much.

"Well, why do you think I'm smiling?" she said, still smiling.

I was afraid again. Was this a little mind game, one of those female mental tests that they taught in the rows of women's magazines at the check-out counter? Should I admit to my trepidation or play it like the cool brother? I decided that Zaria had been real with me so far—this was no time to resort to mind games.

"Considering our history, I think it'd be a little dangerous for me to try to guess why you might be smiling, frankly. The last time I made any assumptions about you, you ripped me a new asshole—right here," I said, pointing to my forehead. "So I guess right now I'm a little scared."

Zaria threw back her head and laughed. It was the first time I'd seen her do that. The laugh came from deep in her belly and the sound it produced brought me back to a documentary I'd seen once on Billie Holiday—Billie's laugh was the most glorious sound I'd ever heard because it felt like a rare gift. I knew that I'd be spending a lot of time in the future trying to make this woman laugh like this again. Those feelings were especially startling because there had once been a time when I told myself I didn't want to go there with a single mom—too much drama with somebody else's kids. But over the last few years I had encountered so many single moms on the dating market that I had come to accept my fate—that unless I was going to mess with one of those young ones or crazy ones, I'd probably have to deal with somebody else's kids. Besides, who was I to talk? I was lugging my own baby drama to the table.

"Scared, huh?" she repeated, watching me with a glint. "So now I'm scary, the mean, scary, angry black woman?"

"Now I didn't say anything about mean and angry. In fact, I think you are very nice and incredibly beautiful. I just don't want to give you the wrong answer. But I'll give it a shot. Let's see—you were laughing because you find me incredibly sexy and you were overjoyed at the prospect of me wanting to help you with your son because it meant we might be spending a lot of time together. How's that?"

If Zaria's mouth wasn't attached to her face, I swear her bottom lip would have been resting on the table. Her eyes widened. But she didn't say anything right away. She looked down at her hands. She brought her eyes back up to my face.

"That's a bit much, don't you think?" she said softly.

It felt like a reprimand, a scold for moving things to a place she didn't want to go. My neck started getting hot and my stomach roiled on spin cycle. I was mortified. My gamble with truth had failed spectacularly, or so it seemed. What in the world had I been thinking?

After my screwup, Zaria withdrew a bit, retreating to a safer place. We talked in very general terms about the horrors of adolescence and how tough it is to reach teenage and preteen boys. I recounted a few stories from my teaching experiences to show her that I understood exactly what she was going through, even if I didn't have any teenagers of my own at home. But I was disappointed that what looked like the possible start of something promising turned out to be a tantalizingly false alarm.

After we finished our fancy coffees, Zaria looked down at her watch, giving me the international sign language for the blow off. I beat her to the punch.

"I gotta go to basketball practice in a little while," I said. "But I really enjoyed this talk."

She gave me a smile that looked a lot less sincere, more manufactured, than her earlier efforts. We rose from the booth at the same time. I extended my right hand for a polite shake. She looked down at it, then she surprised me by stepping toward me. As her face approached, I excitedly thought for an instant that she was going to kiss me on the lips. But her lips veered to the right at the last minute and I got them on the cheek. A soft, polite kiss on the cheek. A noncommittal kiss.

I watched her glide smoothly from the restaurant, the fullness of her round hips visible under the loose-fitting slacks. I wasn't quite sure what had just happened. Had anything been resolved? Would we ever see each other again? Did she even want me to try to work with her child? I knew none of these answers. As I made my way to my truck, I wondered how long I should wait before I tried to gauge her level of interest in me. Clearly there had been some interest there. Well, maybe it wasn't so clear.

She

I know April was about to bust, seeing as I hadn't told her a thing about my meeting with Mr. Roman, save for the basics—"coffee was good, he was nice, talked about James, trying to figure out what to do with the boy," is all I said about it. It'd been a few days since our rendezvous, and I couldn't even begin to explain for myself whether there was some kind of love connection between us that day, or if he was just a shameless flirt who tried to win me over like some difficult mother he assumed would gladly drop the drawers for him if he said just the right thing. Surely that would stop me from finding my way back to the principal's office to complain about him again.

In fact, I didn't even know if he was as attracted to me as he assumed I was to him—and boy did he do a lot of assuming that day. That I wanted to meet with him for something other than coffee and a talk about my kid. That I thought he was sexy. That I wanted to see him again—in a setting that was even more intimate.

I guess I did send some mixed signals, though, mainly because after I saw him, I didn't know in which direction I wanted to go either. April was right; the man sure as hell was good-looking. And it seemed like if I'd just made the move, he would have bit. But I wasn't sure if I was ready to reel him in.

"What?" April was incredulous. "Tell me that Zaria Chance, a woman who has not had a date since Gladys broke up with the Pips, isn't turning down a prime piece of ass for no reason in particular other than to turn it down. Just confirm that much for me."

"Well, goodness—why does he have to be a 'piece of ass'?" I said, putting a wide-eyed innocent look on my face. "You make it sound like he's a side of beef."

"Oh, I'm sorry—let me rephrase," April said, looking up at the ceiling and stroking her chin like she was thinking of something brilliant to say. As usual, what came from her mouth was nothing but complete ignorance. "Zaria, dear," she said, assuming one of those fake, "please pass the Grey Poupon" voices. "Do you mean to tell me that Mr. Roman doesn't meet your standards for a man worthy of the pleasure of your company in the boudoir?"

"You know what, April? You have issues—and every last one of them needs to be addressed."

"Yeah, yeah—don't change the subject," she said, getting back to her more sarcastic tone. "We're not talking about me right now. I'm trying to get to the bottom of why you won't go on ahead and let go of your man moratorium and get with Kenny Roman. Clearly, he's into you."

"And what makes you think that?"

"Honey, there isn't a man on this earth who is going to outright offer to help a single mother with some badass boy—not that your boy is bad, but you know what I mean," April said, clearing her throat. "They got enough problems without having to play daddy to someone else's kid just so they can get laid. Trust me, Kenny Roman doesn't have to offer to do a damn thing for a woman to convince her she should drop the drawers for him."

"Well, that's just my problem," I shot back. "Who told him that I needed him to play daddy?"

"You did when you told him over coffee that you didn't know what to do with your son," she said just as forcefully, a sign that we were about to have yet another one of our fights on our differing childrearing philosophies. She's my girl and all, but she just doesn't get the single-mother thing. Okay, yeah, she's a single mother, but it's different; she has it all laid out—money, lots of family help, uncles to help her raise her son. And there are times when she almost looks down on single motherhood, as if she's not in this by herself. We've had one too many arguments over this; I'm really not in the mood for another. I needed to steer this conversation back to Kenneth and off my kid, before she says something I'll make her regret.

"If you're recounting what the man said right, he offered to help you straighten out all this James mess and pretty much said that he couldn't wait to jump in because that would give him more time to spend with you," April continued.

"Well, he didn't exactly say that he wanted to spend more time with me," I said. "He assumed that I was looking forward to spending more time with him. There's an ocean of difference between the two, April."

Well, that is what he said, right? That *I* would be excited about his helping me because *I* found him sexy and *I'd* get to spend more time with him? A bit presumptuous, don't you think? Cocky, even. He didn't gush over my looks or tell me I was sexy. Well, at least not with words. But Kenneth sure did know how to send a message with his eyes. I don't know if he knew he was doing it, but his stare when I walked into the café made me feel like the sexiest creature alive. I had put a little extra pep in my step just to give him a show, and prayed with every second that passed by that I wouldn't trip over my size eights and mess up the whole entrance. I know, I know—I had just told my parents our meeting was strictly business, but when I saw him and was reminded just how fine he was, I flirted briefly with the idea that a romp in the sack with Mr. Roman wouldn't be such a bad thing.

But it still would have been nice if he weren't so sure of himself. "Which is why I made him feel like he was wrong in his assumptions about my wanting to get with him," I explained to April. "I'm too old to have some Negro thinking I'm sweating his little tired butt."

"Uh-huh. And just what's wrong with showing affection?" she asked.

"Well," I said, "the moment you let a man—particularly a black man—know you're attracted to him, he does what Negroes have done since the beginning of time."

"And just what is that?" April said, leaning in.

I looked her dead in the eye and added a silent beat for emphasis. "He grabs the coochie and runs. Off he goes. Never to be seen again."

"Oh, is that right?"

"Yup. That's right. And in the end, all you got is a bed full of dirty sheets and a real bitterness toward the next one who comes along."

"And so to avoid coochie jackers, you're just going to avoid all men at all costs, huh?" April said. Now it was her time to be incredulous.

"I didn't say that," I answered quickly. "I didn't blow the man off or anything. I gave him a kiss on the cheek before we left. That should have been enough to tell him that I was interested. I think."

"So you *are* interested?"

"I don't know."

"You must have been if you kissed the man."

"I said it was a tap on the cheek."

"Uh-huh. Let me ask you this: the last time you met with one of James's female teachers, did you give her a tap on the cheek?"

"Oh shut the hell up, April—I'm tired of this conversation," I said.

"Oh, don't get tired now," she said, laughing. "We're just getting started."

"No, I'm getting started out this door, because I'm tired of talking to you now," I said, pushing myself back from her kitchen table. "I have to get home and get a few things done so that I can relax and enjoy my time alone while the kids are at their grandma's house. Can I please be excused?" I whined.

"I guess," she said, sighing. "But you know what? This conversation just confused the hell out of me. You don't know if he's attracted to you, but he makes you feel sexy. You don't know if you want to get with him, but you kiss him on the cheek. You need some help with your son and you have a good man offering to help, but you're not sure if you're going to accept. I'm thinking you need to make up your mind before you lose out on a good thing, dearie. Just a thought."

"Yeah, yeah, yeah," I said, walking out the door. "You need to stop worrying so much about my vagina and get some help for your own."

"Oh, you got jokes now," April yelled just as I slammed her sliding door.

Truth of the matter is, I didn't know what the hell I wanted. The only thing I was sure of was that my child needed help, and I wasn't quite sure how to get it to him other than to reach out to someone else for a hand. I'm just not so sure that seeking help from a man to whom I'm physically attracted would be the best help I could get for James. I mean, what if we hit it off, and Mr. Roman becomes a father figure, and then things don't work out between us. Will I be digging a deeper hole for James? Am I willing to put myself out there for that kind of heartache? Should I take that chance?

I wasn't so sure.

*   *   *

Show me a child who can come into a house without waking the entire neighborhood with his loud mouth and ripping the door off its hinges, and I'll show you a child in a wheelchair, in a sling, with a muzzle on his mouth. My kids, obviously, didn't fit the bill. I was in the den, relaxing, watching television—actually, the television was watching me—when my two rugrats came storming into the house. "Bye-bye, Gamma! 'Bye, Papa," the two of them screamed through the screen door. "Thanks for the ice cream! See you soon! Love you!"

I looked over at the cable box to see what time it was—9:36 P.M., it read back. Good grief, where did the time go? "James? Jasmine? I'm in the den. How was Gamma's?" I called out to them. Jasmine came rushing into the room first. She was covered practically head-to-toe in what appeared to be ketchup and chocolate syrup. My guess was the 'rents had taken them to McDonald's and then Carvel.

"Great," she said, full of enthusiasm. "Gamma and Papa took us to McDonald's, and then we went for sundaes at Carvel. I had a chicken nuggets Happy Meal, and a hot-fudge sundae with nuts and whipped cream and Gummy Bears on top. It was gooo-oood."

"That's nice, dear. Where's your brother?"

"I'm right here," he said. I hadn't even seen him, he'd walked in so quietly.

"Did you have a good time at Gamma's?"

"Yes."

I paused, waiting for some more. Nothing came. "That's it? Just, 'yes'?"

"I had a good time, Ma," he said, annoyed.

"What'd you do?"

"Just what Jasmine said—we went to McDonald's and Carvel."

"So all you two did was eat for, what, nine hours while you were there?"

"Well, Gamma and Papa played a few games with us and we watched a coupla videos and then we went out to eat. No biggie."

"Oh. Well, thanks for the details." I smirked.

He turned on his heels and took off upstairs to his room. I heard the door close behind him. Jasmine just looked at me with this big grin on her face, completely oblivious to the tension between me and her brother. "Mommy? Can I have something to drink?"

"The refrigerator is full of water—have some," I said, knowing full well she was talking about getting some juice.

"Can I have Citrus Punch instead?"

"If you're that thirsty, you'll have water," I said.

"I guess I'm not that thirsty," she said, and trotted slowly upstairs. Kids.

I struggled out of the recliner and headed up the stairs behind her, but instead of making a beeline for my room, I stopped in front of James's room and contemplated what I was going to say. I needed to talk to this boy—get through to him that I just wanted the best for him. And I couldn't do that if he shut me out. I knocked gently on the door—something I never do. I'm a firm believer that as long as I pay the mortgage in my house, I can walk through any closed door I please without knocking—particularly if one of my kids is on the other side of it. But for some reason tonight, I knew it would go over better if I didn't just barge into the boy's room.

"Jasmine—go away!" he seethed.

"It's not Jasmine," I said softly. "It's Mommy."

"Oh—come in, Mom."

I opened the door slowly, and peered in. "Mind if I come in?"

"Is there something wrong?" he asked.

"No. Does something have to be wrong for me to want to talk to my son?"

"No," he said slowly.

"I just wanted to hear about your day, see if you had a good time."

"I told you it was all right. We didn't do much but sit around watching TV and eating."

"Did Papa stay the whole time?"

"Yes," he said. Then, after a beat, he added, "It was nice to see him back with Gamma. I missed him and I missed them together."

"Are they back together?"

"I don't know, really." James shrugged. "But they were kinda all over each other while we were over there—you know, sitting next to each other and laughing and stuff."

"Hmm," I said.

There was an awkward silence. I didn't really know what else to say, mainly because I couldn't think of anything else to say. But just as I told myself to turn around and walk away, James spoke again. "How was your lunch with Mr. Roman?"

I just looked at him. How the hell did he know I was going out with Mr. Roman? Who told him? My mother? Kenneth Roman?

"I overheard you talking to him yesterday morning while I was eating cereal."

"What were you doing listening to my telephone conversations?"

"Mom, it was pretty easy to hear you making your plans—I was sitting right there at the table eating cereal. I couldn't *not* hear you."

"Uh-huh. Well, don't you worry about how my lunch was with Mr. Roman," I said defensively, hoping that I could get out of the room before he started asking questions.

"Well, I just wanted to tell you that if you're still worried about whether I should be in his class or not, it's all good. We're getting along just fine," he said.

"No more problems, huh?"

"Nope. No more problems. Even the guys are starting to forget that I got him in trouble with the principal," he said. A grimace quickly crossed his face and disappeared, like he had made a mistake.

So was that what all the drama was about—some boys were messing with him because I had a conversation with the principal about Roman? "Hold up, wait. What do you mean, 'guys are starting to forget you got him in trouble'?"

James was quiet. He knew he'd just let me in on what he'd been holding back from me for the past week. "Did someone do something to you because of what happened between me and Mr. Roman?"

"I guess." He shrugged. He was quiet some more.

I just looked at him, gape-jawed. I honestly didn't know what to say to the boy. Obviously I'd overreacted without once thinking about how my confronting Mr. Roman would affect James. No wonder he'd shut me out. "Do you want to talk about it?" I asked, mainly because I couldn't find any other words to say to him.

"Not really," he said.

"Well, if you want to talk about it, I'm here," I said. He didn't say anything else. Just looked down at his lap, then his wall. Never at me.

"Okay, well, I'm going to go to bed now. You should probably get some rest; we're going to be going to church in the morning."

Still, no words.

"Good night," I said.

" 'Night, Mom."

I walked out of his room and shut the door quietly behind me. I walked slowly to my room and spent the next twenty minutes readying myself for bed, and thinking about my dilemma: go out with Kenneth Roman and see if this thing could work, or skip Kenneth Roman just to be sure that James wouldn't get caught up in my romance drama.

And once again, when it came to Kenneth Roman, I was stumped.

He

The basketball season settled into a comfortable rhythm, a nice tempo between practice, rest, and games. And we were winning the games quite easily, my finely crafted offense and defense working their magic. Honestly, the magic came solely from my two star players, who were having the season that everyone expected them to have. In fact, my superstitious nature had started to tell me that things were going too well. I tried to fight the fatalism, but it always crept up on me in times like this, robbing me of the pleasure that should be mine. As it turned out, once again my superstitions were on target.

I walked into the gym and immediately knew something was wrong. Trouble hung in the air like a fog, slathering worry all over my players' faces. My first thought was death—somebody must have died. My eyes quickly bounced around the gym to do a headcount. I was a practical man, so I started with Jermaine and Tariq. I saw Jermaine in a corner working on his free throws, smoothly swishing the ball through the net. But no Tariq. I didn't see him anywhere. My stomach did the same maneuvers as when I'd turned on Tariq's block weeks ago and saw all the police cars. I quickly made my way to Jermaine to inquire about his cocaptain. Jermaine was still bothered by his father's new coaching gig, so he had been somewhat cool to me of late. I had tried talking to him about it, but he still hadn't returned to his normal wisecracking self. I wanted to shake the boy and tell him to get over it, that his life should be so perfect that his major beef was his father's wanting to spend more time with him.

He stopped shooting when he realized that I was standing nearby. "What's up, Coach?" he said.

I nodded my head. "Is there something I need to know about?" I asked. "Where's Tariq?"

He looked down at the floor. "He's having some kind of trouble at home. I think they got kicked out of the projects. He told me last night that they don't have nowhere to live. He said he couldn't even afford bus fare to school. I think his mother got fired from her job. I ain't even know you could get kicked out of the projects."

I'm embarrassed to admit that my first thought went to my team, to Tariq's availability for the next night's game against a tough opponent. That might be a bit harsh, but I'm a basketball coach, you know? Not a social worker. After I moved past the game, I wondered where the family might be staying. What kind of mindset must Tariq be in right now? How was his mother holding up? How come no one from St. Paul's had alerted me?

I blew my whistle. As the team gathered around, I told them to all work on their free throws while I went to the office and made some inquiries about Tariq.

"He told me he was gonna have to quit the team," said Ceasar, the junior center. The other players immediately dropped their heads and stared at the floor. Ceasar, with his big mouth, must have spread that devastating tidbit to his teammates with the dispatch of a network anchorman.

"Nobody's quittin' the team," I said loudly. "Particularly Tariq. Y'all know how much that boy loves basketball."

That produced a few grins.

"I'm sure the school will be able to find a way to help him," said Thomas Manton, one of the three white players on the team. I nodded, but I noted to myself that it always had to be the white boy to retain such hope in the institution. Good for him that he still could. I rushed through the halls of the school, hoping that the vice principal, Father Brown, was still around. If something was amiss in the lives of one of the school's black students, Father Brown would know about it. He was one of those Jesuit priests who seemed so selfless and Christ-like that you almost wanted to convert to Catholicism to take a shot with his God. He was a tremendous help to the black males on the basketball team—he also happened to be a passionate basketball fan and a former St. Paul's star himself—providing much-needed counsel and solace during their inevitable trials at a predominantly white school that they often felt cared about them strictly for their jumpshots. Father Brown stood apart from the others; all the players had to do was see his concern etched all across his big pink face to know his care extended far beyond basketball. If Tariq Spencer was in trouble, I knew Father Brown would know.

I heard the father's booming voice before I even got to his office. He was about 6-4 and 300 pounds, and his amplified baritone seemed to go with the rest of his oversize persona. I peeked in and saw that he was on the phone. He waved me in.

The principalship of St. Paul's changed at least every three years—the church treated the job like a years-of-service prize for its aging priests—but Father Brown was a human institution at the school. He had been the vice principal for at least fifteen years and he poured himself into his job like only a priest could. He attended virtually every sporting event the school had; his voice could be heard above all others calling out encouragement at home or on the road. I had leaned on him heavily during my first coaching season. He was an assuring presence for me when I felt like I had no clue. But I had been a little annoyed with him of late because he wouldn't budge on the assistant-coach issue. He still refused to pay any salary to Jermaine's dad, Will Bryson, who was working out extremely well, though he couldn't make all of the practices.

"I got the housing authority on the phone," he said, placing his hand over the receiver. "Trying to find out what happened to Tariq and his mother. I think they—"

"Uh, yes ma'am," he said into the phone. "The name is Reverend Louis Brown. Yes, I would definitely like for him to call me back. I'll be waiting by the phone."

He hung up and shook his head sadly. "Damn city bureaucracy. They couldn't find their ass if you put it in a sandwich for them. I been on the phone with practically everybody in the damn agency today. Now they tell me the director is going to call me back. They claim that Tariq's mother hasn't paid rent in over seven months and she owes them more than four grand. Does that sound possible to you?"

I conjured up an image of his mother, trying to reconcile it with this new information. Sure, it was possible. They were living on the hard side.

I nodded. "Yeah, sure it's possible."

"Tariq told me she lost her job a couple of weeks ago. But that wouldn't explain not paying the rent for seven months, now would it? Clearly there's more going on here than meets the eye. But the problem now is that the housing authority won't let them back in, even if the back rent is paid. They've forfeited their right to a housing authority apartment. They say it's an ironclad policy. I'm going to talk to the director to see if maybe they got exceptions."

I knew Father Brown could be an extremely persuasive man—I had seen him in action many times. Sometimes I was on the receiving end of his persuasive talents.

"Where's Tariq?" I asked him. That was my key question.

"He called me this morning. They're staying with his mother's friend, in the Bronx. He said he's not even sure how to get here from the Bronx. He said it's way up in the Bronx, like somewhere near the Bronx Zoo."

"Damn, the Bronx? How's that gonna work? We gotta get them back to Jersey City."

Father Brown nodded. "Indeed. But I'd hate to think of them staying in a homeless shelter. Our church is affiliated with a facility, but that's mainly all men, and most of them are not the most appetizing fellows in the world to be around."

We sat there silently for what seemed like hours, both of us deep in thought. Father Brown stared at the wall behind me. I stared at the doodads on his desk. I had a spare bedroom, at least when it wasn't a Laney weekend, but I was having a hard time wrapping my mind around the idea of sharing space with Tariq and his mother. I wondered if she'd be amenable to letting Tariq stay with me in Jersey City while she tried to figure something out from her friend's place in the Bronx. Tariq might drive me crazy, but at least he'd be able to go to school and play basketball.

"Well, maybe Tariq could stay with me. I got a spare bedroom."

Father Brown looked up and smiled. "I knew you were going to say that," he said. "That's a true coach for you." We beamed at each other. I liked the implications of his comment.

"There's something else you should be aware of. As you know, Tariq is required to pay a very small tuition. We've had many conversations about this. Well, his mother hasn't paid anything since the boy was a sophomore. It has built up over time. Six hundred dollars a semester adds up when you haven't paid in two years."

I did the quick math in my head. "So they owe over $2,000?"

Father Brown nodded. "I've been able to keep the wolves away from them for this whole time, but the principal and the bursar are making a lot of noise about it now. They won't let him get a diploma, I know that. And the bursar was in here a few days ago talking about the boy getting kicked out of school. Of course the principal wouldn't allow that. The whole school would burn him in effigy if he did. But this issue isn't going away. Something needs to be done about it now, before we start getting close to graduation. I know Tariq is being recruited by some of the best colleges in the country. We need to nip this in the bud, so to speak."

Damn, what was wrong with his mother? Where was her money going? She certainly didn't look like a crackhead. I had never gotten wind of any alcoholism in the house. She'd never appeared drunk and he'd never complained about that. Clearly there was more there than I was seeing. I rose up from the chair.

"We'll take care of this, Father. We have no choice."

Father Brown nodded. "Good luck, Coach."

As I walked toward the door, I heard him clear his throat. "One more thing, Coach."

I turned around, waiting.

"I think we can find something in the budget for your new assistant, Mr. Bryson. Tell him to come and see me so we can work something out." My face-splitting grin must have been infectious because Father Brown matched it with one of his own. I loved this man.

I considered myself a fairly street-smart guy—after all, I grew up in a rough-and-tumble Jersey City neighborhood and had had my share of physical encounters that, years later, scare me now more than they did then. I tried to look unmoved by the way these fellows on the street were staring at me because that's the way you're supposed to do it in the 'hood. There were about seven of them, lingering in front of a row of burnt-out buildings. They had stopped their conversation when I approached and now their gazes followed me like a pack of hyenas might a tasty antelope. I held my breath as I passed the group, praying that my rusty street toughness got no tests on this frigid and gloomy night.

When I moved beyond them, I realized with a shudder that I had passed the address. 1305 was apparently one of the buildings that I had assumed was burnt out. Tariq was staying up in there, in one of those nasty-looking shells? So this time I was going to have to walk *through* the bitter stares. I braced myself. In these situations, I knew you couldn't look frightened, you had to make some sort of eye contact. Damn. The Bronx had always been a place with the mythic menace of a haunted house in my mind. I knew it had the potential to scare the starch out of me, but I never had any reason to test it up close. Now I did. What I was about to walk through was no myth.

I lifted my eyes and let them graze casually over the group as I tried to squeeze past them without actually making any physical contact—but at the same time not appearing to go too far in bodily contortions to do so. In the ghetto ballet, if you had to twist and turn too much to get past someone, they had just declared you a punk. While I had absolutely no problems admitting my punkness to these boys, I knew that once it was established I became glistening, raw meat.

"Wassup, man—can we help you?" one of them spit out from beneath his hoodie. His voice had that unmistakable tinge of a Puerto Rican who had been raised on 'hood Ebonics.

"Nah, man," I said, letting the first word flow out like an easy, uncaring drawl. "I'm aaiight."

Before I dropped my eyes back down to walk up the stoop of the building, I saw a few nods. They all went back to casting their malevolent stares outward, even resuming their banter of traded insults. I went into the building, pulling open the heavy metal door and stepping into a cloud of the foulest pee stench I had encountered since my last ride on a city subway. Right away I started praying that this was somehow the wrong place. When I spoke to Tariq on the phone—Father Brown of course had the number—he had warned me that the building was "not very nice," but that was a huge understatement. He had even tried to keep me away, but I also picked up the impression that he was pleased I was coming. I peered at the row of buzzers, looking for 3C. Only a few of them had names next to them. Just then, a wisp of a woman slipped through the inner door and drifted past me a little unsteadily. Her eyes met mine for an instant and I was looking into an empty void, a body without a soul. Crackhead. I started to lunge for the door before it closed again, but then I heard her voice.

"Don't worry. It don't lock," she said. The sound of her voice gave me a shudder. It was all fractured and bruised, like the yelping you might hear after a woman has been slammed repeatedly in the ribs with a bat. Her voice tripled my conviction to get Tariq out of this place this very night.

I practically sprinted up to the third floor, increasing my speed after I encountered a strange odor on the second floor that I assumed was the pungent stench of crack. I hadn't smelled it enough times in my life to be sure, thankfully, but I would have put money on it. I started putting together the pieces—the soldiers out front, the exiting crackhead, the stench. Apparently this place was a crack den. Of all the buildings on God's green Earth, how had my star player, one of the nation's top recruits, wound up staying in a Bronx crack den? His mother should be taken out and shot. As I approached 3C, my attitude toward Ronnie Spencer turned from pity to fury.

I knocked on the door of 3C and waited several minutes before I heard footsteps. Someone must have been looking through the peephole because I got no immediate answer.

"Coach!" It was Tariq. I heard him unlocking bolts, at least three of them, before the door swung open.

A huge, pleased grin spread across his face, already almost making the harrowing trip worthwhile. It renewed my conviction to bring Tariq back home with me. The boy had been used to living in some rough circumstances, but this was on an entirely different scale of severity. At least back in the Jersey City projects he wouldn't have been able to get a crack contact high while sitting in his living room watching *Cosby Show* reruns.

I reached out and hugged the boy to me, a spontaneous gesture that was slightly awkward at first but that he seemed to appreciate. I could feel the tension in his body and it hit me—he feels responsible for his mother's safety. He's not going to want to leave her here by herself. I would have to bring both of them back to my place if this Roman rescue was going to happen.

"I'm glad to see you, Coach," he said softly. For a second I thought he was crying, but when he pulled back I saw no evidence of tears.

"I'm even more glad to see you," I said. "Everybody is worried sick about you."

"Everybody knows what happened to me?" I could see the embarrassment, almost fear, cross his face. I could understand that, but there wasn't really anything I could do about it. He was a big dog on the St. Paul's campus—kids talked about him all the time even during the normal course of things. This particular item would be treated like the first man on the moon in its newsworthiness.

"Nah, *everybody* doesn't know," I said, probably telling the boy a lie. He could find out the truth later, when he stepped back onto the small, close-knit campus. I heard footsteps approaching. "Hello, Coach." It was Ronnie Spencer, still behind Tariq, whose oversized frame could block out the sun.

"How did you find this place?" she asked. As she stood next to her son, the resemblance between them was startling. I had noticed it before, but it was especially strong tonight as they stood there with matching sheepish expressions.

"It wasn't that hard. There's a number on the building." Of course, what she was really asking was how did I make it here in one piece, running the gauntlet of menace.

"Well, it's good to see you, Coach. Come inside. We were just sitting at the kitchen table, talking about this neighborhood." I followed them down a narrow hallway, past the living room on the left and two closed doors on the right.

"What were you saying about the neighborhood?" I asked.

"Mainly that it sucked," Tariq answered. His mother turned and shot him a look, but didn't say anything.

"Well, my friend Sandra, whose apartment this is, was giving us the lowdown on the area."

As soon as we entered the kitchen and I saw Sandra, I knew why she lived in this building—she was obviously a crackhead herself. She still had some meat on her frame, but her face had a crumpled, beaten-down look. Her eyes danced over my face, but they didn't stay there for long. Oh God, this just kept getting worse.

"Nice to meet you," she said, giving me a limp hand to shake. If she wasn't a crackhead, there were serious things wrong with her. I got no energy from her, no vibrancy.

I sat down at the kitchen table next to Tariq. I wondered how long

I needed to stay, for hospitality's sake, before I made my pitch to take the boy back to Jersey City. I hoped it wasn't long. The kitchen smelled strongly of roach spray, an odor I always associated with poverty. Those nasty little bastards didn't bother people with money, no matter how much people in the ghetto tried to convince themselves that "everybody got roaches," as I've heard it said. Sandra offered me some food and drink, but I politely declined, trying to fight the convulsion from the thought of eating on her plates.

Instead of waiting for the right opening to make my case, I decided to dive in headfirst before the roach spray started making me nauseous. Wasn't really interested in small talk with a crackhead.

"Uh, have you all thought about the basketball season, how Tariq is going to make it to the games—and to school?" I could have smacked myself for putting the games before school. But they didn't even pick up on my scary priorities.

There were glances around the room. Clearly it was something that had been discussed. Tariq shrugged.

"We don't have anywhere to stay in Jersey City, Coach. I can't go to school there if I don't have anywhere to stay." I saw his mother nodding. Well, the move was now mine. I took a deep breath.

"Uh, well, there's room at my place."

My statement was greeted with silence. I think it was stunned silence. Tariq stared at me, then looked down at the table. His mother just kept staring. Sandra picked her teeth.

"Coach Roman, that's very sweet of you, but we couldn't put you out like that," Ronnie said. Tariq shot his mother a look now. In that look was packed a catalog of meaning, of frustration, and of soaring possibilities being snuffed out like the light in Sandra's eyes. Tariq knew that he had to grab for his chance.

"Ma, I have to play ball." His voice cracked a little when he said it. I looked more closely at this man-child and saw tears welling in his eyes. There was pain in his face, in his voice. It sounded like a beg, a plea. The moment was breaking my heart. Suddenly, that quick, I felt my eyes starting to moisten. Ronnie Spencer stepped over and wrapped an arm around her son's shoulders. She leaned down her head—she didn't have to lean far—and rested it on his nearly clean-shaven dome. Tariq closed his eyes, probably to stem the tears from popping. I felt my heart slamming against its casing inside my ribs, its own suit of armor.

"I know, baby. I know," she said, murmuring into his scalp. I wondered if the mother knew how good her son was at his sport, that he had the potential to transform her life in ways she couldn't even imagine just by shooting the basketball. Apparently she didn't know these things because, if she did, she would have stayed in Jersey City even if it meant sleeping in a cardboard box.

"Coach, what about my mom?" Tariq asked, looking worriedly at me. "I can't leave her here."

I glanced at Sandra to see if she had taken offense at this barely veiled attack on her home. But her face was expressionless as she watched the scene unfold. It had been a vague thought all along, that the boy might want his mother to come along and I'd be faced with the question of whether I could bring her into my home. I should have resolved it when it occurred to me, but I had pushed it away, perhaps because none of the answers were satisfactory. So here the question was again, except now I didn't have the option of escaping. I imagined what it might feel like to have this woman in my fairly small apartment, knowing how aggressive her advances had been, knowing how much her presence would stifle romantic possibilities with the rest of the female population. It sounded way too dangerous. And what would I do when my daughter came to visit?

"Well, I got enough room for her to come, too," I said, wincing as I heard the words fall from my lips. What the fuck was I thinking? I wanted desperately to reach back out there and pull the words back, even after the smile spread across Tariq's face. His mother had a small smile of her own, though I could see her trying to find the strength probably to object.

"No, Coach, I couldn't think of disrupting your home like that," she said. Then she added with a grin, "Though you do look like you could use some of my cooking."

She was throwing the ball back into my court with a weak-ass objection. I froze, fear and uncertainty whipping through my veins. If I let her come, if I let this woman settle into my space, it would serve as powerful incentive to find them living quarters as soon as possible. But, God, it might be uncomfortable as hell. All eyes were on me. I felt like the machinery of my thought process was visible to everyone in the room, like those see-through clocks that allow you to see their guts.

"No, both of you come stay with me," I said. "I have enough room for both of you."

"Are you sure, Coach?" Ronnie said. Her eyes were dancing and her fingers were twisted together—I realized that's what the expression "wringing your hands" looked like. I knew the decision might have been terribly wrong, but my ego enjoyed the feeling that I was rescuing this family from the evil crack den. I nodded at Ronnie and smiled. Tariq smiled even wider and gazed at me thankfully. Sandra, dear Sandra, searched for her cigarettes.

After we had piled their things in my truck and headed back over the George Washington Bridge, I got an early indication of how Ronnie was going to handle this delicate situation. She tried to stick her face all up in my business.

"I hope you don't have a girlfriend," she said, laughing.

"Why do you say that?" I said, glancing over at her with a frown.

"Because if you do, she's not going to like some other woman staying up in your apartment, that's why."

As prying goes, it was a fairly clever way to get some information. I had a bare minimum of respect for this woman, this mother who could bring her child to a place like that, but perhaps she wasn't as dumb as I had been assuming all along. Should I tell her I was with someone, as a way of creating an instant buffer? It'd be like Shaq walking around wearing a fake wedding ring to keep away the gold-diggers. (When I first read that in a magazine, I had to stop and take several deep breaths because I was overcome with awe and envy, imagining how many beautiful women this man must have to fend off every day to take such an extreme step.) Would she treat such news as a deterrent? I had my doubts. But I was willing to give it a try.

"Uh, well, yeah, I am kinda seeing somebody," I said. Immediately I thought of Zaria Chance, of the way my stomach had turned when I watched her stroll into that café. Out of the corner of my eye, I saw Ronnie's body move slightly, but I couldn't tell if it was a reaction.

"Good for you!" she said, giving me a lot of fake cheer. I glanced over at her and smiled.

"Thanks," I said.

I wondered what Zaria actually would think if she came to my apartment and saw Ronnie Spencer all cozy and comfortable. I guessed the sight would not be a welcome one for Zaria—or the handful of women who made it back to my apartment on occasion. Since I had broken up with Cynthia from Queens about seven months earlier, I hadn't been on many real dates at all. But I did have a few reliable, longtime, uh, acquaintances whom I could call when I was in need of company. Women like Antoinette. The thought of Antoinette brought a warm feeling to my belly, like a shot of scotch. Damn, that was a good time I'd had last week. But then I remembered Antoinette tripping over Zaria's message on my answering machine. Antoinette would not take kindly to Ronnie's presence at all.

"Well, your girlfriend has nothing to worry about with me," Ronnie said. "I know her man is off-limits." I could see her smiling. Why was that so funny?

"And besides," she added, squirming again in her seat, "we probably only gonna be there for a few days until I can find another place."

Well, talk is one thing, but Ronnie's actions were something else entirely. After they were settled down in my spare bedroom and I assumed tucked away for the evening, I sat down at the kitchen table to quickly review my lesson plans for classes the next day. It was already past midnight; I knew my customary eight hours of sleep had been compromised by at least two hours—I usually awoke at six. I heard the door to the spare bedroom close and footsteps approached the kitchen. Ronnie Spencer walked into the kitchen wearing a tight little T-shirt that barely fell below her crotch—and nothing else. Not even a bra.

"Oh, excuse me, I didn't know you were in here," she said, acting surprised. I wanted to smirk at her obviousness. The woman was no Angela Bassett in the acting department. I tried to avert my eyes, but before I did they took in her form. She was actually more shapely than I had previously thought. She was thick, but her waist was still small enough to give the strong impression of curves. Her legs looked sturdy and not unattractive. And of course her large, bouncy breasts were hard to ignore as they pushed through the thin fabric of the shirt, oversized nipples greeting me with a midnight salute.

"I just wanted to get a little something to drink," she said as she walked slowly to the fridge, twisting her hips. She opened the wrong cabinet, looking for a glass. I got a glimpse of panty as she stood on her tiptoes to look inside the cabinet. Her large, round ass challenged the hemline of the T-shirt. "This is a kitchen for a tall person, I see," she said, giggling and looking back at me—no doubt to make sure I was enjoying the show. This was ridiculous. I could feel the erection straining under the table. How long could I torture myself like this? I absolutely could not touch this woman. It would be bad in so many ways. I would feel like I was stealing candy from a child. I was sure of that. Ronnie bent over to look in a lower cabinet. She knew damn well no one kept glasses down there. Her panties were clearly riding up her behind—the ever-present female wedgie—giving me a close-up of the underside of two fleshy, brown cheeks.

"Let me get you a glass," I said, rising quickly from the table before she got a chance to notice the bulge.

"Oh, I didn't want to interrupt you—you looked hard at work," she said, giggling again. What was so damn funny?

I handed a glass to her. She took it from me, purposely brushing her fingers against mine. Her flirting was almost laughably conspicuous— but it was still working, wasn't it? I smiled at her, though it probably looked more like a grimace. I knew I had made a huge mistake tonight. This was supposed to be about Tariq, about basketball, about helping a family. Not late-night erections and fleshy ass cheeks.

"Good night, Ronnie," I said. I turned on my heels and tried to appear casual as I snatched up the lesson plans.

"Good night, Kenneth," I heard over my shoulder. Oh, so she had graduated from "Coach" to "Kenneth"? I stepped into my bedroom, closing the door behind me. I didn't even like the door closed.

She

"**Y**ou got a booooy-friend. You gonna git some. It's 'bout tii-iime. Make sure you use a con-duuum!"

Mikki was riding shotgun in her own BMW, which she had insisted I drive because "pregnant women shouldn't drive, and you know I'm not getting on anybody's subway, girl." Mind you, she was only three months' pregnant—not even showing with her little bony self. And in all those pregnancy books she was reading—I swear, there had to be at least a dozen of them on her dresser bureau—I know they say you can drive clean up until nine months, so long as you do it with a seat belt. But not Ms. Mikki. "We could get into a car accident and the seat belt could be faulty and I could go stomach first right into the steering wheel, and if something happened to this baby, I swear I would just lay down and die. So I'm not taking any chances. You drive."

Of course, because she didn't have to concentrate on driving, she was talking—a lot. Actually, she was asking a whole lot of questions—about my meeting with Kenneth Roman. And I guess I must have divulged just a tad bit too much enthusiasm because girlfriend decided from my description of what had happened at the coffee shop—or, specifically, what he had said to me—that Mr. Roman and I were going to walk down the aisle, say "I do," and lie down and make babies on the honeymoon, all before the week was over.

"Mikki—don't be so ridiculous," I said, shaking my head, mentally kicking myself in the ass for telling her verbatim what Mr. Roman had said to me. "We had coffee to discuss James's behavior. Don't go marrying us off."

"Who said anything about marriage? I was just saying you gonna get some."

"And what, exactly, makes you think that we're going to have sex?" I asked, shifting uncomfortably on the seat and looking out the rearview mirror. We were about to make a right onto the Brooklyn Bridge, but some maniac cut me off and let another car pass in front of him, making me miss the light. I just wanted to drive to distract myself from this conversation because, clearly, we were about to enter territory I wasn't interested in visiting with my baby sister.

"Aw, come on, Zaria," Mikki said, shifting her body to face me. "Surely if you just gave that brother half an ounce of hope that he was going to get to hit it, he'd take you up on the offer. Without hesitation. Tell me he wouldn't."

I was silent for a moment. "I don't know that, Mikki."

"Well, certainly sounds like he's interested," she shot back. "Seems like all you need to do is give him the chance."

"To do what? Sleep with me? I don't need him to sleep with me. Shoot, if that's all I wanted to do, I could have Negroes lined up around the block from sunup until sundown waiting to do that. Doesn't take that much to get a man interested in screwing you. All you need is a vagina."

"Oh, really?" Mikki said, swirling her neck and feigning surprise. "Well if it's that easy, when's the last time someone other than you saw yours?"

"Saw my what?"

"Your vagina."

"Huh?" Thankfully, the light had changed—but Mikki made it clear that she wasn't going to let my concentration on the road stop her from prying into my personal business. "Mikki? What the hell are you talking about?"

"When's the last time you slept with a man?"

"Mikki, (a) That's none of your business; (b) I don't want to talk about this right now, especially with you. I'm trying to drive, here."

"It's just a simple question, Zaria: When's the last time you had the pleasure of a man's company? I'll bet you haven't seen any paaaarts of the penis in years—since ol' what's his name, um, damn. What was his name? Rendy? Rudy?"

"His name was Remy, and never you mind what he and I did."

She ignored me and kept right on talking. "Remy—right. Remy. Like the liquor. He was cute. Nice guy. Really liked his locks—had that boho/Maxwell thing happening. That was, what? Two, three years ago when you dated him? Three years without some dick? That's a long time, Zaria. I'm not a freak by any stretch of the imagination; the last thing I want to do these days, what with me praying to the porcelain god and eating crackers and sucking on ginger ale, is screw Randy. But he's my husband and the father of my child, so he knows what's up. But damn—three years without getting some? Take my left breast from me and I'd be happier."

I can't believe we're having this conversation. After all, Mikki and I aren't exactly close. I mean, we're sisters, so we do tell each other *some* things. But those things do not include with whom I'm sleeping. And I'll be damned if I'm going to be interrogated by my baby sister for the salacious details.

Anyway, Remy *was* the last so-called boyfriend I had. I call him "so-called boyfriend" because he wouldn't know the meaning of what it was to be a significant other if Mr. Webster wrote the definition in gold on his forehead. He had started out just fine; I'd met him at a singles' party a friend of Mikki's had thrown in Harlem. The idea was for all those invited to bring an ex to the party—you know, one of those, "one woman's trash is another woman's treasure" things. Well, Mikki had sent me in her stead; her being married and all, it hadn't made sense for her to be all up in a singles' party getting her swerve on. I had brought one of Mikki's colleagues, a designer who owned a clothing store just down the way from her bridal boutique—I think his name was Darryl. Honestly, I thought Darryl was swinging in the other direction, if you know what I mean—or at least had considered it on more than a few occasions. But whatever. I had to bring a man, not marry him.

Anyway, so Darryl and I went to this party in this beautiful brownstone in the Striver's Row section of Harlem, up on 137th Street. It was owned by the family of the chick who was throwing the party, and she had it all laid out—candles all over the place, a nice spread of Jamaican and Indian food, mood music, I'm talking the works. And the room was full of some of the most stunning men I'd seen in ages. Men from every background, from bank teller to high-powered stockbroker, buttoned-down in suit and tie, to super casual with jeans and Timbs, big and burly to short and pudgy. And, supposedly, they were all single—at least that's what the stipulation was for everyone who had brought a guy to the party. After he'd introduced himself and led me to a quiet corner to talk, Remy confirmed that he was girlfriend-less and wifeless.

"I'm Remy," he'd said, sweeping his locks from his eyes. I had detected a slight accent—perhaps Haitian?

"Pleasure to meet you, Remy," I'd said, staring into his eyes. "I'm Zaria Chance. Do you have a last name?"

"Marcel."

"Well, it's my pleasure to meet you, Mr. Marcel. Are you enjoying yourself?"

I was trying my hardest to be cool and sexy—to not appear like I was going to swallow my tongue any second now, which is how I felt every time I opened my mouth to talk to a guy. After two babies and moving on from dealing with their trifling-ass daddy, I'd gotten a little rusty—I'll be the first to admit. But within minutes he'd put me at ease—and our conversation was as smooth as butter. We talked about movies and books, music and its effects on our youth, classic movies, even the taboo subject: politics. Surprisingly, he was almost as conservative as I—he, too, thought that welfare needed to be reformed, didn't understand the ghetto mentality of blaming everybody but black folks for poverty and its effect on our community, agreed that there was a need for a new African-American leadership that was going to do more than suck our bank accounts dry while they stomped up and down the street, mugging for the brightest camera lights. This was, in fact, what turned me on most about him—not just the fact that he was fine as hell. He had some sense. And that was surprising, considering he was an art director for one of those urban magazines. I thought he would be one of those liberal, firebrand, poetry spouting artsy-fartsy types—and younger than me. But he wasn't. He was my age and childless, but a self-proclaimed lover of kids. Mr. Perfect, right?

Not. He was just as crazy and deranged as all these other guys out there, who, as soon as they got bored or didn't get their way, ran to someone else's arms. I thought Remy would be different, but I found out—thank God it was early in the relationship—that he simply wasn't.

We kicked it for about seven months. Our courtship was nice, but it wasn't anything out of the ordinary—dinner, movies, museum exhibits, parties. I even slept with him—but not until we'd dated about six times (personal policy; I'm no slut), and he'd never been to my house to meet my kids (I don't play that; no strange men walking naked, drinking up all the orange juice in front of my babies). But he had been growing on me—particularly his intellectual capacity. I love a smart, worldly man—and that, he was. He'd been to all kinds of places—would just take off on a whim to visit countries that most of us only read about in the magazines they keep in the doctor's waiting room. He'd been to Bali and Hong Kong, Venice and Versailles. And he'd come back with these wonderful stories about the different cultures, what the people were doing, the beauty of the world outside of the confines of the New York metropolitan area—and America.

I wasn't surprised when he told me he was going to Belize. But I was gape-jawed when he asked me to come along with him. "We'll have a blast," he said, his French patois peaking through his words as it usually did when he was excited. "We could rent a villa and a Jeep and find a remote beach where we can make love in the moonlight. How about it, eh?"

I admit, it was a tempting prospect: I could have certainly stood the break, what with the pressures of the job and all. I hadn't been on vacation to a beach in years. Hell, I hadn't been on vacation, period, in forever. The closest I'd gotten to that was when I sent James and Jasmine with their auntie and uncle to Martha's Vineyard for two weeks a few years back; while they were gone, I relaxed at the house, gave up cooking to eat fast food (well, I did that maybe only a few times, but still, that's a lot for me), went to the movies and bowling with a couple of my girlfriends and my mother, and slept in. I had a good time; it beat getting up for my 6 A.M. routine of showering, cooking breakfast for me and the kids, fixing their lunches, making plans for dinner, going to work, coming home, preparing dinner, showering again, and going to sleep, only to get up and do it again. Mostly, I really didn't have the time or the money to go on vacation—that's what young, single people with money did. I had kids. And a mortgage. And a job that I really needed to keep.

So, when Remy asked me to go to Belize with him, I was tempted to say yes, but was forced to say no. Well what did I say that for?

"What do you mean, 'No'?" he'd laughed. "You hardly even considered it. Come on—we'll have a great time. Say yes."

"I'm sorry, baby, but I just can't right now," I had said apologetically. "I have to find someone to take care of the kids and I'd have to find some time off from the job and I don't see how that could happen with summer school coming up. It's a busy time of the year for us. I just don't think I can swing it."

"Hold up—let me get this straight: You're turning down a trip to Belize because you'll be busy at work? Let me tell you something, darling: If you got hit by a bus tomorrow, they'd find someone to do your job before your body even got cold. Keep it all in perspective and come on out and have some fun with me."

"Well, I'm not anticipating being hit by a bus tomorrow, and I'm a lot more responsible than you make me out to be."

"What's irresponsible about taking a vacation?"

"Well, let's see: I have two kids who need their mother. Would you suggest I just leave them sitting in the house while I go cavorting on the beach with you? Do you suggest that I miss a few mortgage payments and start looking for a new job since I'll probably lose the paycheck I get for leaving my office in the lurch at an extremely busy time of our season so that you and I can go exploring around a country I've hardly ever heard of? Perhaps you can step in and take care of me and the kids when we get back."

"How would I be able to do that?" he'd said, incredulous. "If they walked onto my stoop right now, I wouldn't know who the hell they were. But that's a whole 'nother subject altogether."

Yup. He'd taken it there. Now, anybody who knows me knows that you don't bring up my kids in matters of relationships—especially if you're a man. That's just, like, The Rule. What I do with my kids is my business because I gave birth to them, I raised them, and I'm taking care of them by myself because the man who helped me create them isn't man enough to see to it that they grow up to be decent, well-adjusted human beings. And if their own daddy can't do right by them, then the last thing I'm expecting is that some stranger will step in and do the job the right way. So I make it a point of not bringing men around my kids. I'd long ago decided that the man who was lucky enough to meet my kids would be the man I was going to marry—and that meant that he had to have the same philosophy as me when it comes to raising kids, that he love them as much as I do, and that he understand that these are my children, not his. Which means that he's not to put his hand on them, he's not to punish them unless I say he can, and he's not to consider making any kind of decision about their lives or well-being without my okay. After all, if I don't protect them, who will?

Well, I'll tell you this much: Very few have met the challenge. And I wasn't about to introduce them to Remy just because we had a few dates, hot sex, and a couple of deep conversations. He didn't quite understand this at first—"What do you think I'm going to do, eat them?" he'd say whenever I turned down his request to come to my house. But with a little explanation, he'd get off my back and leave it alone. Later on, though, he started raising a little more of a ruckus about not being able to come to my house while the kids were there, and sometimes, it tended to get a little loud.

"Oh, so are you having visions of a happy, two-parent nuclear family? Where's my ring?" I'd joke.

"That's not funny," he'd shoot back. "I can't see how you would expect me to give you a ring when I hardly know you and I've never met your children."

"Exactly. Which is why you're not going to meet my kids. We're having fun and I'm enjoying what we have, but until I know there's more to this, you won't be meeting my kids. Sorry."

Yup—it had gotten nasty on occasion. But his bringing it up in the context of that vacation he'd wanted to take was about to make an ugly situation just ass.

"You know, you can leave my kids out of this, please. I said I'm not going to Belize and that's that."

"Well then maybe I'll just take someone else then," he'd said, just as cool as you please.

No, he didn't.

"I mean, if I can't take my lady on vacation, then I'll just find someone else to occupy my time."

"Oh, you're going to find someone else to occupy your time, huh?"

"Sure," he'd said, matter-of-factly. "It won't be hard for me to do. It's not like we're exclusive, anyway."

Aw shit. Now it's on.

"Oh, we're not, huh?" I had said, putting my hands on my hips and following him into his kitchen. "Then just what the hell are we?"

"Not exclusive," he had said, going to his refrigerator and reaching for a carton of orange juice just as calm as you please. "You didn't think that you were the only person I was seeing, did you? I mean, this has been nice and all, but if I can't get enough trust from you to be around your kids, then this must not be a real relationship. Plus, we never said we'd be exclusive."

"Oh, I'm sorry—I wasn't aware that you needed a fucking ceremony and a certificate to know that you're not supposed to get with other women while you're in a relationship with me," I'd said, getting in his face. "You have a lot of nerve."

"What? We never talked about being exclusive."

"But you think that you're going to just be able to come around my kids, even though you're seeing other women? What the hell kind of madness is that, Remy? I've been very clear from the giddy-up that I'm not going to be anybody's side dish."

"Well, I considered you a main course, but obviously, you don't feel the same way about me."

"Oh, you know what? I don't need this shit," I'd said, spinning my body toward his living room and grabbing my coat. "I'm outta here. Have fun fucking on the beach in Belize."

That was three years ago. I was twenty-nine. Haven't had a boyfriend since. Had sex a few times since then—but not with anyone worthy of sticking it out with, or even trying. There was the guy I met at church—Brian—and there was Kedar. I met him at the CVS around the corner. But I haven't been intimate with any man for about a year and a half now. And while I do miss boning—I'm not going to lie—it's just not worth the effort to try to find someone worth doing it with. I don't screw for nothing, these days. I like to think that I make love with a purpose. I've got too much to think about as it is, without adding the possibilities of diseases and unstable men and drama to my stress. Truth be told, I don't even get horny anymore. Well, not enough to really notice—or take action. Instead, I focus on matters that are important to me: my kids, my immediate family, my home, my job, and what few friends I have, in that order.

And that's exactly what I made clear to Ms. Mikki since she was so damned concerned with what I was going to do with my vagina.

"You know what?" I said to her as we pulled into the parking garage down the street from the chichi Tribeca shop where she was going to buy her baby's crib and bassinet. "You better stop worrying about my coochie and get yours ready for Armageddon. Giving birth to kids isn't easy, and neither is raising them. Be glad you have a man and don't have to worry about the bullshit the rest of us mothers without husbands have to put up with to get through the day. I guarantee you, the last thing you'd be thinking about is whether some stranger wants to have sex with you, dear."

Finally, Mikki closed her mouth.

Truth of the matter is that I'm still not so sure about the Kenneth Roman thing. I mean, yes, he's got the goods—he's a professional, independent, seemingly smart (or he wouldn't be a star teacher), and good-looking. But my experience has always been that guys who fit the bill in all those categories usually have something wrong with them—or something to hide. Could be married. Or have a gang of kids he's not taking care of. Or gay. Or all three. Who knows?

I was perfectly beat by the time I'd dropped Mikki off at her brownstone, parked her car, hopped into mine, and beat it back to Teaneck. I didn't remember being so indecisive about what to buy to prepare for my kids' arrival—probably because I didn't have much to spend on them anyway, what with their broke-ass father and the lack of support from my parents, and my being short of cash and all. But Ms. Mikki took this baby shopping thing to a whole new level: She spent well over $4,000 for furniture for the baby without blinking. She did say, at some point, that Randy was going to kill her for running up their American Express, but it didn't seem to deter her from adding more items to her shopping cart. In fact, she was in the process of being rung up twice when she noticed something else pretty, and added it to her order. Oh, my Mikki. She'll learn.

Anyway, when I got home, I went straight to April's house; I was sure both my kids would be there, eating her food, playing her Nintendo, and tearing up her house. Sure enough, that's where they were.

"Mommy!" Jasmine yelled when she heard me coming through the back door and greeting April. She came running into the kitchen and gave me a big hug.

"How's my girl?" I said, kissing her cheek and picking her up. She wrapped her legs around my waist and held on tightly. I never will get tired of that feeling.

"I'm fine, Mommy," she said. "I had a good day. Did you have a good day?"

"I sure did," I said, smiling. "Where's your brother?"

"He's playing video games."

So much for some love from my son. I walked into the living room, and there he was, his thumbs furiously hitting buttons on the joystick. So fixated by the screen was he that he didn't even notice I was standing there—and if he heard me say "Hello, James," he sure didn't acknowledge it. "I said, 'Hello, James!'" I yelled into my cupped hands.

He looked up for a slight second, said, "Hi, Mom," and kept right on staring at the game. Within seconds, though, the TV made some kind of funny noise, and the words, GAME OVER flashed across the screen. "Aw man!" he shouted.

"Don't start the game again," I said, just as he was about to reset it. "It's time to go home. It's a schoolday tomorrow."

"Aw man. Can't I just play one more?"

"James? What did I just say?"

"That it's time to go home."

"All righty then—you've answered your own question."

He frowned, handed the joystick to JJ, and pushed himself up off the floor.

"Ask her," JJ said, all at once grabbing the joystick off the floor and nudging James on his leg.

I looked at James, who looked back, but without saying a word. So I spoke for him. "Ask me what?" I said.

James didn't say anything—just sort of stared at me. So JJ spoke up for him. "He wanted to know if you could take us to the big game at St. Paul's tomorrow. It's a big one, against St. Anthony's, and everybody's going to see Tariq and Jermaine kick some butt."

"I know you didn't say 'butt' in my house," April called from the kitchen. I giggled and looked at JJ, who was red-faced.

"Booty butt," Jasmine said, giggling and wiggling hers.

"That's enough, Jazzy," I said, trying not to laugh.

"Sorry, Mom," JJ called out. "Can you take us, huh, Ms. Zaria? Please?"

"Mr. Roman is coaching," April chimed in, almost singing it. "Just before you came in, they were interviewing him on channel 11."

I didn't respond to April, but the idea of watching him in action was, indeed, intriguing. I could watch from the stands without him seeing me, and even if he did see me, I could simply make the excuse that the kids wanted to go. That way, it wouldn't be so obvious that I was going to check him out. I turned to James and asked him what time the game started.

"I think 7:30, but I'll find out for sure," he said, his eyes lighting up. "Can we go?"

"Sure," I said. "Now get your things, say good-bye, and let's go."

"Okay," James said, bounding from the living room.

Later that night, as I was spreading Noxema cold cream all over my face to clean off my makeup, I heard the sports news on channel 4 playing in my bedroom. Something about a big game in Jersey City. I peeked around the corner, anxious to see if the announcer was talking about Kenneth Roman's school. Sure enough, as I focused on the screen, there was Kenneth's fine face, leaning into a microphone, bragging about some star players he said were "going to play hard and give their all in tomorrow night's game."

James had told me he was a great coach, but I'd never given Mr. Roman's moonlighting job much thought. Now, here he was on my television, of all places—in my bedroom. Going to that game probably wouldn't be a bad thing, I thought as I went back into the bathroom and splashed warm water on my face. Not bad at all.

He

With Tariq back in the fold, the team entered the meat of our schedule with its confidence threatening to burst through the roof of our gym. We had a Friday night matchup with St. Anthony's, always our biggest rival for Hudson County supremacy. The game would be an early indication of who had the goods to go all the way to the state title. We had the state's two best players, Jermaine and Tariq, who were probably two of the top-ten players in the country—at least that's what Street and Smith's, the high school basketball bible, had said in their preseason edition. But St. Anthony's had guard Tyrell Zane, whose dribbling and penetrating skills were breathtaking. He had thoroughly embarrassed our point guard Derrick during the state championships last year, once slicing past him with a crossover dribble so wicked that Derrick fell to the floor trying to stay with him. The crowd had ooohed for a full two minutes, causing a distinctive shade of crimson to cover Derrick's light brown face. In street parlance, Tyrell had broken Derrick's ankles. I had talked to the boy constantly during practice this week to get him ready for the matchup—and I had prepared Ceasar, our center, to step up to defend the penetration whenever Zane got past Derrick. If he ran into Ceasar's big body a few times, Mr. Zane would start losing his interest in breaking anybody's ankles.

The gym exploded when we walked out onto the court. I was glad this first big, regular-season contest against a rival was at our place.

Even the New York media had helped in hyping the game. I had been interviewed by several TV stations in the last two days, though I didn't get a chance to see any of the reports on the news. We were about three or four minutes into the game when I happened to look up and see a sight that literally changed my life: Seated about six rows behind our bench was Zaria Chance. She was with her son, James. There was another boy who sat next to James, a friend who appeared to be a little bigger and who looked vaguely familiar. Startled, my mouth fell open and I'm sure I looked utterly ridiculous. Zaria smiled warmly and they both gave me quick little waves. I waved back, pleased and a little rattled. I turned back around to face the court, but for several minutes I had a difficult time concentrating on the game knowing Zaria's eyes might be boring through the back of my head. I called a time-out for no apparent reason, just so that Zaria could see me at my coaching best, pushing my team. We were up by six and seemed to be easily controlling Tyrell Zane.

"Okay, guys, you're doing a great job out there, but I just don't want you to lose your focus," I said a little louder than normal. "Focus wins ballgames. Derrick, you are doing a masterful job on Zane. I want you to be even more aggressive with him. Remember what I told you—I'll never be upset with you for being aggressive, even if he beats you from time to time."

I paused and glanced up into the stands. Zaria was watching me intently. From where I was sitting, I thought I saw fascination on her face and maybe a glint in her eye. She was liking the Pat Riley act. I stepped it up yet another notch.

"Guys!" I said, leaning closer into the players, who were staring up at me, perhaps a little surprised at my level of intensity so early in the game. "I want you to start visualizing how easily you're going to score baskets against this team. Imagine dumping the ball into Ceasar and letting him eat that center's lunch. Picture Derrick feeding the lob to Tariq on the fast break and him throwing it down with authority. See Jermaine stroking three three-pointers in a row, putting us up by twenty. It's all possible, guys. It's all within reach. And you're going to go out there and make it happen."

I had used the New Age visualization stuff on them once before and, after staring at me like I was crazy, they had gone out there and put my visions into action. Since then, frankly, I had forgotten about the technique, which I had picked up in some book a couple of seasons ago. Before I sat back down, I stole another glance at Zaria. This time she caught me looking and she smiled once again. I felt that same churning in my stomach that I had felt when she was approaching the table in the café. She was wearing a skirt; I saw plenty of her smooth, brown legs when the guy in front of her leaned forward. She truly had the whole package—looks, smarts, class, and what appeared to be a great body. I wondered how old she was. She looked younger than me, but you could never tell with black women.

"Hey, Coach!" It was her son, James, interrupting my millisecond trance, bringing me back to reality. This woman had two kids, one of whom was in my class. Did I really want to venture into a relationship and have to heft all the baggage that would come with it? I nodded at James, smiled at Zaria, and turned back to the court. Who said she was even interested in a relationship—just because she had come out to a game in Jersey City, about twenty minutes from her Teaneck home, on a Friday night, still wearing her work clothes, didn't mean she wanted to dive into bed with me. No, not necessarily. But it did mean something.

Remarkably, my players acted out my visualizations as if they were performers playing parts in a scripted movie. Derrick came down and fed Tariq with an alley-oop over the sleeping St. Anthony's defense, sending the crowd into hysterics when Tariq viciously slammed the ball into the basket.

"Man, that was nice!" Will Bryson gushed from his perch next to me on the bench.

Then Bryson's son Jermaine started stroking three-pointers, hitting an incredible four in a row.

"He didn't listen to you, Coach! You said three in a row!" Bryson said gleefully.

I was shaking my head in amazement. I couldn't remember the other things I had told them to visualize—until Derrick came down and dumped the ball into Ceasar, who gave his man a drop step and freed himself for an easy layup.

"Just like you said, Coach!" yelled Bryson, who didn't usually get this excited. But I was unusually excited, too. This kind of direct player response to my coaching didn't happen often. I would usually have to tell them things at least twenty-five times before they put it into action. This was not common.

We were up by fourteen by halftime and we proceeded to increase the gap to twenty by midway through the second half. I didn't even want to acknowledge the thoughts that started going through my head at that point because they were so selfish they were embarrassing. I actually started worrying that we were winning too easily and Zaria might decide to leave out of boredom. In fact, I called a time-out just so I could stand up and take a read on her level of interest.

But she wasn't there! In a panic, I swiveled my head around to see where she might have gone. My heart pounded as if I had just lost my child. What was wrong with me? I turned back to the players, who were eyeing me curiously. A couple of them even followed my lead and looked around the gym themselves, trying to figure out what I was searching for. I leaned in and addressed my team, hoping to push Zaria out of my mind for the moment.

Several minutes later, I swiveled in my seat—and was enormously relieved and more than a little embarrassed to find Zaria staring right at me. No man wants to be so plainly caught showing his interest, particularly when he was supposed to be in the middle of coaching a basketball game. But there'd be no chance that she'd misread my intentions at this point. It was clear that some serious sparks were soaring between us.

After the game ended, I lingered for a moment before following my joyful team into the locker room. They had beaten their archrival by twenty-two points, so they had reason to be happy. I was gleeful and excited, too, but partly for other reasons. I watched Zaria, James, and James's friend make their way down onto the court and approach me.

"Great game, Mr. Roman!" James said, jumping up to give me a high-five.

"Thanks, James. What brings you to a St. Paul's game?"

James glanced at his mother. "Well, after we saw you on TV talking about this big game coming up, I, uh, convinced my mom to bring me. And this is my friend JJ. He lives next door to us."

I extended a hand to the friend, a husky kid with a round, pleasant face. He shook it limply—it took awhile for little boys to understand the handshake protocol, I thought as I let go, particularly if they didn't have fathers in the house to provide instruction. "You guys gonna come to St. Paul's and play some basketball for me?"

They both ducked their heads shyly and grinned. "I don't think we're good enough to play for you," JJ said.

"Well, my players weren't this good when they were your age. But they practiced their behinds off." They both nodded.

"About the only practicing of basketball they're doing is on the video screen," Zaria said, embarrassing the boys thoroughly.

"Mom!" James said in protest.

"James, I'm just 'keepin' it real,'" she answered, grinning. Then she turned her attention to me. "That was a wonderful game, Coach." She grinned at the title. "I'm glad I came."

"I'm glad you came, too," I said, returning the grin. The boys had run off to shoot baskets with the other little boys who had congregated under the hoop. I welcomed their momentary disappearance.

"Do you play any basketball yourself?" I asked. "You know, I also have some serious skills coaching grown women."

Zaria smiled broadly. "Are we still talking about basketball?"

I laughed. "Uh, yeah, of course. What else would we be talking about?"

"I dunno. Maybe I might be willing to learn a few moves from you." She had stopped grinning. Her face changed into that anxious, hopeful, sexy look that women got in the middle of flirtation. They cast their eyes downward, they thrust their chests outward a little, move a bit in the man's direction. Zaria brought the whole package.

I felt my stomach turning again. My team had been gone for several minutes. They were probably wondering where I was. I had to finish this up quick, get to the point.

"Well, I'd love to show you some moves." It was clear we weren't talking about basketball anymore. "Maybe we could get together soon so I could do some coaching."

She nodded her head. "Maybe we should."

"Okay, well, I have your number. I'll call to set up a, uh, session." I laughed at the continuing word game.

"Yes. That would be nice. Maybe I'll even go and buy me some sneakers. You know a lady has to have the right equipment." She paused, probably realizing that her comment was more suggestive than anything we had said yet, then she burst out in a laugh of her own. I reached out and touched her arm, letting it linger for a minute. I gave her another broad smile, then I turned and headed for the locker room. I don't even know if my feet touched the ground.

She

This time, lip gloss, mascara, and slacks weren't going to cut it. I wanted to look extra special for Kenneth because this was no meeting—we were about to go on a date. A hot date. And I wanted to look jaw-dropping good because I was craving for him to look at me the way he looked at me at the ball game the other night, when he turned around and saw me on the bench trying desperately not to stare a hot hole in his head. I swear when he waved at me the first time, my heart tapped out a beat that a rapper would pay me good money to sample in a song. The next few times, our eye contact was so intense that Lydia, the mother of one of James's little friends from school (apparently coming to Mr. Roman's games was a popular activity at the middle school) started asking questions she shouldn't have been asking.

"Is it me, or is Coach staring up in this corner of the stands a little hard?" she said, leaning over to whisper in my ear.

"Really?" I said, trying desperately to act like I didn't know what she was talking about. I needed to change the subject. I wasn't ready to have this potential hookup be the subject of mommy gossip at the South End Middle School. "I hadn't noticed. I was just looking around this gym and admiring how nice it is. This school must have some serious cash, huh?"

"It's a Catholic high school—you know they care about their basketball," Lydia said. "And there isn't a parent in the state who doesn't want their boy to be a part of Coach Roman's basketball program. He's amazing."

"Hmm," I said. "I never really paid much attention to it. James follows this stuff; I'm just the chauffeur. You know how that—"

Lydia cut me off. "See, see? Look at him. He's all up in the stands. What's that all about? Shoot, I might have to go have a conversation with him after the game."

"Hey, guys," I said, turning my attention to James and JJ. "You want some popcorn and juice from the concession stand?"

"Yeah!" they said simultaneously.

"Okay, I'll go get it. Stay right here," I said before turning to Lydia. "Excuse me, love—I'm going to get the boys some snacks. Can I bring you back something?"

"No thanks, I brought some with me," Lydia said, reaching down to grab an overstuffed bag she'd sat next to her feet. She pulled out a greasy, brown paper bag, and, from that, a big ball of aluminum foil. It had fried chicken in it. "Want a piece?" she said, picking through it with a paper towel she'd had rolled up next to it.

"Um, no thanks—I'm in the mood for a hot dog," I said, excusing myself. The last thing I was going to do was eat anything that woman brought from her house. I'd seen how she sent her son to school—which didn't say much for her cleanliness inside the home. Anyway, I wanted to get down the bleachers before Mr. Roman looked up and saw me stumble or something.

But if the googly eyes during the game weren't enough to tell me that he was interested, the conversation afterward was. I was surprised at myself for being so sexually suggestive—but I couldn't help it. There was no denying the chemistry between us, and I wanted more.

But a few days later, when he called me to set up our date, I didn't have the balls to follow through with it. I fear I might have come off a little aloof and a lot prudish compared to game night.

"So—you ready for your coaching session?" he asked with that supersexy voice of his.

"Coaching session?" I said, acting like I hadn't a clue what he was talking about.

"Yes, you know—our get-together."

"Oh, yes, right. We were supposed to be making arrangements to see one another. Is that why you're calling?"

"Uh, yeah," he said, sounding a little less confident and sexy. "Well, how about next Friday night?"

"Let's see—Friday," I said. "That's kind of short notice. I'll have to make some phone calls to see what I can do with the kids." I knew full well that April and my mother stood at the ready to watch my children whenever I needed them to, even though I rarely did. I just didn't want him to think this was going to be that easy. "But you can pencil me in."

"All right, I'll call you later in the week to seal the details," he said. Then he took one last stab at that suggestive talk I'd so handily knocked down from the gate. "Don't let the, uh, equipment get cold."

"Don't worry—not a chance that'll happen," I said suggestively, surprised at myself and pretty embarrassed by it by the time I hung up the phone. Lord, I didn't want that man to think I was easy—that this relationship, if we had one, would be easy. Easy I am not. By any stretch of the imagination.

When he called Wednesday to give me details on where we were going—dinner and a movie; not very original, but I'd take it—I immediately made plans to take an extended lunch break to buy something to wear. It should have been a no-brainer—what? A pair of slacks, a nice shirt, some sexy shoes, a jacket?—but these days, clothes shopping doesn't come too easy for grown women, especially grown black women. I swear, I went into just about every damn store in the mall in Paramus—one of New Jersey's largest—and I couldn't find a thing that would fit past my left leg, much less over my behind. What was it about the designers and their style choices? I mean, everything was cut for prepubescent fourteen-year-olds with eating disorders—at least that's what it looked like. All the jeans and slacks were low-slung hip huggers, all the shirts cut above the navel. The dresses? Cleavage down to the belly-button, with slits up the side of the leg that would show off everything your mama gave you—whether you intended them to or not. After a while, I thought maybe I needed to readjust my price expectations and go for an outfit a little more expensive, just so that I could find something that fit—but the upscale couture shops were just as bad, if not worse. And I damn for sure wasn't about to run up my credit charging an overpriced, awkward-fitting outfit that I'd be pulling and tugging on during my whole date. Just as I'd resigned myself to putting my money back into my pocket and pulling something out of my closet, Mikki called my cell phone.

"Hey! What you doing?"

"I'm on my lunch break."

"Well I know that, or I wouldn't be calling you on your cell phone. Your nosy-ass secretary told me you were at the mall."

"Oh she did, did she?"

"Yup. You wouldn't happen to be at the mall in Paramus, would you?"

"And if I am?"

"Well, they have a Pottery Barn there, and it would be great if you could stop in there and pick up these curtain rods I saw in the catalog. They're just perfect for—"

I cut her off. "Mikki? I've been walking around this mall for well over an hour, and the last thing I want to do is go into another store. Why can't you just order it from the catalog or over the Internet?"

"Well, what were you doing in the mall so long? James need a new pair of tennis shoes? Jasmine need a new dress for church?"

"Actually," I said, making sure that she would hear the annoyance in my voice, "I was here to buy myself an outfit."

Mikki sucked in her breath in mock surprise. "What? You were actually in the mall buying—gasp—something for yourself? Whatever brought this on? It wouldn't have anything to do with that boy, would it?"

"Mikki? I'm so not in the mood for this. You and your designer people get on my nerves with all this low-waist, high-cut, scanty, over-priced mess in these stores. When you designers decide to make clothes for normal people who aren't millionaires, let me know. In the meantime, I'm heading out the door so I can make it back to work."

"Ooh—so you got a hot date with the coach, huh?" she said in a voice that made it sound like I was about to do something freakish and nasty. I knew she was going to make fun.

"Yes, I'm going on a date with Kenneth," I said, feigning annoyance and digging into my purse for my keys. "And if he can't appreciate the jeans and sweater I'm going to be wearing on our 'hot date,' then he can go find himself one of those young 'uns who can actually fit into the outfits you ridiculous designers are making."

"Hold up. Tell me you're not about to wear jeans and one of your tacky sweaters on a first date with that boy."

"What's wrong with jeans? And why my sweaters gotta be tacky?"

"I'm not going to let you go out like this," Mikki said, dismissing my question. "Let me put something together for you."

"Mikki—please," I said. "All of that drama is not necessary. We're going to the movies and dinner. Jeans and a sweater will be fine."

"Not on your first date, it won't. I'm going to need you to put a little effort into it. Damn, you ain't had a date in . . ."

"I don't need you to remind me when was the last time I went out on a date, Mikki. And I don't need you to make anything for me. I'll be fine."

"If you thought you'd be fine, you wouldn't be in the mall parking lot mad as hell that you don't have anything new to wear on your date. Let your lil' sis help you out. I'm going to whip together something really cute. I still have all your measurements on file, and it won't take me but a minute to design it—trust me. When's your date?"

I hesitated telling her; I wasn't so sure I wanted her going out of her way to do this for me—or Kenneth to think I was trying too hard. But the idea of wearing something sexy was indeed the whole reason I'd just wasted close to two hours walking up and down this oversized mall. So I said, "The date is Friday."

"Friday?! Good grief, Zaria—you couldn't have given me a little notice? It's Wednesday."

"Um, like I've been telling you for the past ten minutes, you don't have to make anything for me."

"Oh no, buddy. You're not getting off that easy. I can get it to you by Friday."

"Well, I don't want to put you out. I'll come get it after work. Maybe I can get off an hour or two earlier to come into Brooklyn to get it."

"Oh please, don't worry about it. I'll make Randy send a messenger from his agency to leave it on your back stoop. That way you won't have to do all that traveling."

I said a silent thank-you for that. I sure as hell didn't have time to trek into Brooklyn on Friday before Kenneth showed up on my doorstep.

"I'm thinking a cute skirt and top would be nice. Oh, and I'll let you borrow my jean jacket—they're hot this season—so I'll make sure that whatever I make, it goes with that. I'm going to try to find some material that complements your maroon ankle boots, so plan on wearing those," Mikki said, out of breath from talking so much.

"Um, okay," I said. I was tired of trying to talk her out of spending so much energy on it. "Please tell Randy to tell the messenger to leave the outfit with my next-door neighbor. I don't want the kids to see it or they'll start asking questions about where I'm going."

"Ooh. A secret date? What are you going to be doing on this date that you can't tell your kids about it, huh?" she asked.

"Mikki? I'm hanging up now."

"Uh-huh. Go on ahead and hang up. Sneak around on the kids with that man. Just don't do anything I wouldn't do, freak mama!"

"'Bye, Mikki," I said. I hung up the phone. I'm sure she was still talking when she heard the dial tone.

She may talk too much, but she was a sewing fool—and an absolute genius at creating clothing that makes black women's bodies look good. I'd told her a million times that she should branch out from wedding-dress designs and make some clothes that everyone could wear—but she refused, loudly and often. Said if she did that, she'd be forced to confine her talent to the same conventional fashion standards—designs that fit far fewer people than the super-tall, super-skinny women everyone was aiming their clothing at—that had stagnated the industry. Wedding dresses were special, she'd always say, because you design for people—not mannequins and hangers.

Well, I may not be a mannequin, but what Mikki pulled together for me sure made me look like a supermodel. It was a flowered wool skirt with a funky fringe that made it hit my leg midcalf. It covered my curves in all the right places, but it wasn't so tight that I felt uncomfortable. She paired it with this cool, ice blue, cap-sleeved blouse that picked up the same color in one of the flowers in the skirt, and assured me in a note that my maroon boots would work wonders with the pieces. She was right. The jean jacket was the perfect topper—particularly with the big, bouncy flower pin she'd added to the lapel. I'm telling you, this woman is a fashion genius.

After I ushered the kids over to April's house—I had them spend the night over there so they wouldn't see Kenneth picking me up; I had told them I was going to the movies with their aunt Mikki—I stepped gingerly into my outfit and then sat down at my vanity with all my makeup laid out across the counter, most of it from Bobbi Brown. I'd bought a few new colors at the mall on Wednesday, and I was hoping they worked with my outfit. Wait, who was I kidding? Bobbi Brown always worked with what I was wearing. I swear, that white woman had to have a few black women in her employ just trying on shades that look good on African-American skin. I refused to use anything else, except for maybe a little M.A.C. every once in a while. But I only messed with their lip gloss, and an occasional eye shadow or two.

Sure enough, the colors I'd picked worked wonders. I had to admit, I looked good. Surely my man's mouth was going to drop when he saw me. (Ooh! Did I just call him 'my man'? Let me stop it.) Just as I leaned into the mirror to give myself a pep talk—I wanted to tell me that I shouldn't be nervous, that this was just a man and a movie and that there wasn't any reason to be nervous and that I was a fierce creature who was worthy of having a nice time and to take it easy, like he's a girlfriend—the doorbell rang. And everything that I was going to say to me flew out the window, replaced by a bundle of nerves. Honestly, I didn't see how I was going to make it down the stairs without my knees buckling. So I went for speed instead.

I grabbed my leather coat and, when I got to the bottom of the stairs, ran right through the front door, barely saying "Hi" to Kenneth. I hadn't quite figured out what to say, actually, and plus, I needed him off my stoop just in case the kids happened to be looking out April's window or something.

"Hey to you, too," he said as I grabbed his hand and dragged him down the stoop. He opened the door of his truck for me—bonus! chivalry wasn't dead—and helped me in, waiting to close it behind me. I'm sure he was looking at my booty. Go Mikki. Go Zaria.

"So," I said as he pulled out of the driveway, "where we going, Coach?"

"First dinner, and then the cineplex," he said. "I figured we could sit in the back with the teenagers and hold hands in the dark."

He was making me hot. But I wasn't about to let him know it.

"Uh-huh. I've heard that teenagers do much more than hold hands in the back of the movie theater in the dark," I said.

"Do they really?" he said, feigning shock. "Well, just what do they do?"

"I'm not sure. But you wouldn't be trying to get me to go back there to take advantage of me, would you? Because you should know that I'm a fine, upstanding young woman and it's going to take a whole lot more than a plate of food and a movie ticket to get to know me like that," I said in a slightly joking manner, but I was dead serious.

"Me?" he said, drawing in breath for emphasis. "Never that. I'd never take advantage of you. Unless you want me to."

I didn't say anything back to him on that one, and for a few minutes, there was an awkward silence. But by the time we made it to the restaurant, we were in full conversation mode. We talked about the appalling state of music, how awful New York radio is, and both of our addictions to NPR. Whether or not Lauryn Hill is as deep as Stevie Wonder or Bob Marley (I said she was, he wasn't so sure). Who was sexier—D'Angelo or Marvin Gaye (I couldn't decide; I told him that since he's a guy, there was no way for him to know unless he swings both ways. He assured me he was no character from an E. Lynn Harris novel, living on the down low). Conversation was easy—light. I was just glad that he wasn't doing any more of the sexual talk; I wasn't quite sure how to respond to it without coming off either like a cold fish, or a tramp willing to lie down with him right after dinner and just before dessert.

The ease of our conversation came to a screeching halt, though, when we got to the movie theater window. We just couldn't agree over what the hell to watch.

"But *Against the Odds* has gotten rave reviews," Kenneth insisted. "The guy on NPR said it was the most brilliant movie about the drug trade since that movie with Benicio Del Toro—what was the name of it? Oh yeah, *Traffic*."

"I can see the drama of a drug trade watching the eleven o'clock news, Kenneth," I said, still not budging. "Movies are for fantasy—to escape the reality of a hard day and go somewhere you can't go to in real life. It's an escape. You get the popcorn, a smoothie, some bonbons, some Raisinettes, and you sit back and let someone entertain you."

"But you can be entertained and still be enlightened," he said. Hmm. As stubborn as me.

"If you want to be enlightened, read a book or become a Buddhist."

He laughed at that one—a deep, hearty laugh. It sounded like soft thunder. "Okay, I'll tell you what: Let's shoot for it."

I looked at him like he was out of his mind. "You know what? You've been hanging around children way too long. You actually want to stand here and shoot over a movie? Like, one, two, three shoot?"

"Yes," he said. "Let's shoot for it. I don't see how else we're going to solve this, and there's a whole lot of people standing in line waiting to buy their tickets, so we kind of need to make a decision now. So what do you have—evens or odds?"

"Evens," I said, holding my fist up above my right ear.

"All right. One, two, three—shoot!"

I put two fingers out; he put out one. "Ha! *Against the Odds* it is."

"Oh no you don't," I said, putting my hand back up to shoot again. "Two out of three."

"Oh—a sore loser, eh? Okay—I'm a gentleman. I'm willing to let the lady have her way with me. Get ready: one, two, three—shoot!"

He won again.

Without even looking at me, he put a crimp in his step and bopped to the ticket window. "Two for *Against the Odds,* please."

I laughed and followed him over, pulling my wallet out of my pocket as I strolled. He turned to smile at me—one of those glorious Kenneth Roman smiles. I swear, I could wake up to that every morning for the next twenty years and not get tired of it. I was trying to figure out something nice to say about it when his face went flat.

"What are you doing with your wallet out?"

"I'm about to pay for my ticket," I said matter-of-factly. Hey—my father's three cardinal rules on dating for his girls were as follows: Never leave the house without money in your pocket—enough to pay your way to wherever you're going, so that the boy you're with won't be expecting anything more than a "good night" when the date is over. Never leave home without enough taxi fare to get you back home, in case the boy you're with is expecting something more than a "good night" and refuses to take you home. And the final rule? Never do anything on a date to make a boy think that he was going to get something more than a "good night" when said date is over. I admit I hadn't listened to my dad when I was a young, hardheaded, know-it-all teenager, but damn if those rules didn't come in handy now.

"Oh you are, huh?" he said, twisting his body around to face me. "I thought I'd invited you to the movies. Usually, the person who invites, pays."

"Well, we're both on this date, and the least I can do is pay my way."

"Zaria, give me a break. Let me pay for the ticket, okay? What kind of brother would I be looking for you to pay for the movie on our first date? Please, do me this favor: Put your wallet away."

I put my wallet away, and said, "Thank you." But when we got inside and headed for the concession stand, I turned to Kenneth and insisted on paying for the snacks. "Come on, man—I like the big box of popcorn, and you'll probably try to buy the bargain size and then I'll eat it all and you'll think I'm greedy and never call me again. So, to avoid putting an end to what could be a wonderful friendship over some popcorn, why don't you just let me get it. And a frosty. And some bonbons."

He laughed and obliged, then gave me the tickets so he could carry everything to the seats. By the time we had settled into our seats, the movie was starting. It was good, but it was about as predictable as I had figured it would be. It was, in part, about a drug addict whose father refused to help her kick her habit. The whole movie, I was thinking, "What kind of parent would do that? Just sit back and let his kid spiral into the abyss of drugs and despair, and coldly do nothing to help?" By about my fourth sigh, Kenneth reached over and grabbed my hand. At first I thought he did it to silently say, "Calm down and just watch the movie." But then he started caressing it—his fingers were warm and soft. I didn't want him to stop; it was a perfectly sensual act to me for a man to touch my hand softly, without letting it wander. I looked over at him and smiled. He looked back and smiled even harder.

"So, what did you think?" he said as we walked through the parking lot and back to the car.

"It was okay—but completely unrealistic," I said.

"Unrealistic?" he said, incredulous. "I thought it was even better than *Traffic*. You couldn't get more real than that, or at least that's what I thought."

"Well, I'll tell you what bothered me: I don't know a parent on this earth that would leave their child hanging like the father did in that film. I mean, there's always horror stories about parents who refused to adopt that tough-love stance they tell you to give your loved ones in all those drug-treatment places. Why should I believe that a parent could be so coldhearted toward their own child?"

"Oh, come on, Zaria," he said. "Surely you have to understand that not all parents are going to react in that way—that human beings may have different ways of dealing with the same situations."

"Not if you're a parent," I insisted. "No matter how strict you are, no matter how intolerant you are of vices, that's still your child—and your love for that child is always going to be stronger than anything else in this world."

"I don't understand that mentality," he said.

"Well, that makes sense. You're not a parent."

He was quiet after I said that, and I immediately felt bad for being so forceful. But it was perfectly naïve for him to suggest what a parent would do in that situation, particularly since he didn't have any children. Besides, he's a man. What would he know about a mother's love? The sacrifices she's willing to make, the battles she's willing to fight, the fires she's willing to run through to save her babies. We simply put our children's needs way ahead of our own at every turn because that's our instinct—and how we're raised. To nurture. I don't care how far women have come in the new millennium compared to their mothers; the fact of the matter is that we all revert right back to the Stone Ages when we see that little round face for the first time. And while some men, I wouldn't doubt, love their children just as much as their babies' mothers do, they're just not willing to sacrifice like a woman does. It's all about him and his needs; everyone else is second. They might take care of the kid eventually, but that child will be second to their numero uno—themselves—all the same.

Most fathers with kids don't even want to admit this, let alone men who don't have babies. But that's okay; if Kenneth sticks with me, he'll learn.

He

I had another chance to tell her about Laney, but I didn't. The words were sitting right there, on my tongue, and that's where they stayed. We were arguing about the movie we had just seen, and she made a forceful point that the main character in the movie wasn't realistic because he didn't do enough to save his daughter from drug addiction. I was trying to argue that he had to let her reach bottom before she was ready for his help—something I'd often heard said about dealing with addicts of all sorts.

"Well, that makes sense—you're not a parent," she said, waving her hand dismissively in my direction.

The words rose up in my mouth, ready to be released into the fall evening chill in the front of my SUV. I turned them over a few times, held them up for inspection, considered the consequences if I let them out. But things were going so well between us; I wasn't ready yet to have the Laney discussion. It would take us down a path I wanted to avoid for the moment. I knew I would have to have the discussion soon—the sooner the better—but I wanted her to continue thinking I was "perfect" for a while longer. She had called me that over dinner, saying that she hated to sound pessimistic, but I was just too "perfect."

"Something must be wrong with you," she said, chuckling. "My luck with men has never been this good. So why don't you just 'fess up and tell me about the women buried in your backyard."

I laughed about five minutes over that line. Zaria was truly a funny lady. She had one of those unexpected senses of humor—sometimes I don't even think that she intended the comedy, but funny things just seemed to fall from her mouth. In retrospect, that was yet another opportunity to drop the Laney bomb. I didn't even see that at the time. I was too busy watching Zaria's dancing eyes as she laughed along with me.

The evening went so well that the good-bye scene wasn't even that awkward. As my truck sat in the driveway next to her darkened house—she said her kids were staying with her next-door neighbor—we both confessed how much fun we had had. I apologized for the cliché of the first date—dinner and a movie—and promised that I'd get much more creative the next time. Of course, she hadn't yet agreed to a next time, but she laughed at my apology.

"I can't believe you're apologizing for bringing me to such a wonderful restaurant," she said. "I had a great time. But I'd love to see what you come up with for the next one."

So there it was, an acceptance for a second date without me having to ask. I congratulated myself on my cleverness.

"You're a great guy, Kenneth Roman, and I had a great night. I gotta run in there and rescue April. She got five kids up in that house, poor thing."

Zaria leaned toward me, so I followed her lead and moved toward her. Our lips met in the softest, gentlest, sexiest three-second kiss I have ever experienced. After the kiss, we lingered and stared into each other's eyes. I think we were both surprised by how nice that was—and how much electricity we had suddenly created. I felt a thickening in my crotch.

"Wow," she said. "That was nice."

I nodded. I had a sudden vision of taking her smooth, naked form into my arms and how it would feel for our bodies to melt together. The crotch started throbbing. Zaria grabbed her bag and slid from the car. I shook my head at her sexiness and the excitement that was coursing through me. I watched her hips twisting in her tight, funky skirt as she glided toward her front door. The woman had a wonderful walk, like she had been taught at a finishing school or something, one of those places where they placed a book on your head and made you walk across the room. Before she pulled out her keys, she turned around and waved. It was a short, economical little wave, a lifting of the hand and fluttering of the fingers, but it sent information my way—telling me that she regretted our parting, that she would be thinking about me, that I should be imagining how glorious we would be together. I waved back, telling her the same thing.

On the way back to my apartment, I tortured myself by embracing, then rejecting, every idea for a second date that popped into my head. Like an idiot, I had placed a load of pressure on myself by announcing to her that the second date would be creative and extra special. An outing in the park? Nah, it'd probably be too cold for her—remember how cold she had gotten in the movie theater? (I had to lend her my jacket, which I hadn't minded at all.) How about a New York City museum? Nah, too pretentious. Not to mention boring. But going into the city wasn't such a bad idea. The theater? No, that wasn't much better than the movies—just a hell of a lot more expensive. Maybe a Knicks game? That was a strong possibility, particularly if she had never been to one before. But how would I find that out? I thought about asking her son, like after class. Hmmm, her son. Hadn't considered him in more than a minute, the possibly troubling reality of dating the mother of a seventh-grade knucklehead. Well, James wasn't really a knucklehead. He just acted like it sometimes. I stayed with the basketball game, telling myself that I should call a friend who worked in Knicks management to see if I could get some special seats. I'd still have to pay for them—the dude wasn't *that* good of a friend—but he could produce fabulous seats (not Spike Lee seats, but close) at a big discount. He had introduced himself after we had won a tournament at the Garden two seasons ago, destroying three vaunted New York City squads. He called me from time to time, usually finding a way to inquire about the progress of Tariq and Jermaine pretty early in the conversation. For basketball junkies, particularly those connected to the NBA or big-time college ball, following the twists and turns in the lives of precocious ballers was a religion. I ran into the flock quite regularly, eagerly scrambling for a little Tariq or Jermaine tidbit.

As soon as I hit the front door of my apartment, I could smell Ronnie's perfume and hear the television squawking in the living room. Damn, it was well past midnight—did I really have to deal with my houseguests this late? I prayed that it was Tariq and not his mother, but as I took off my jacket I heard her voice.

"How was your date?" she asked, walking slowly toward me. Her voice took on a strange tone, perhaps jealousy, maybe annoyance—or both.

I shrugged. "It was all right." I didn't want to give her *any* information about Zaria. But at the same time, I did want to encourage the thinking that me and Zaria were in the midst of something serious. I desperately needed protection to fend this woman off because she was getting out of control. The day before, I thought I caught her peeking at me through the tiny opening in the bathroom door after I stepped out of the shower. There was a slight movement I thought I saw through the crack; when I came out of the bathroom and spotted her, she looked guilty. At least as guilty as Ronnie Spencer was capable of. The woman appeared to have no shame.

"Well, if it was so good, why are you already home at 12:20?" She was right in front of me now. "Why aren't you in her bed, making her scream for her momma?" She grinned, enjoying her own nastiness.

I was extremely bothered by her familiarity. I didn't want to be having this conversation. I wanted to say something mean, like to tell her that there was nowhere for me and my special lady to be alone because I had space invaders crawling throughout my apartment.

She took a step closer to me. "I know if I was your girlfriend, I'd have you howling at the moon right now." She came closer still, so close that I could hear her breathing. Her eyelids were half closed, like she was turning herself on with this talk, and she was grinning suggestively. I was glad that she was at least dressed. I could smell her cheap perfume, which reminded me of the overpowering scent favored by strippers. I was nearly trapped in a corner near my front door. Damn, where was Tariq? "I'd make sure you put this thing to good use," she said. She reached out her right hand and gently ran it up the length of my crotch, holding her hand with palm upturned like she was lifting a curtain.

I nearly gasped, but I didn't want to overreact—I sensed that's what she wanted me to do. I stared at her, at the wicked smile crossing her face. At least it looked wicked—though in retrospect, maybe I was looking at all her actions in the worst possible light. She was literally throwing her stuff at me, daring me to turn my back on it. All I needed to do was give even the barest hint of interest, and she'd be on her knees in a heartbeat, with her mouth full. Probably right here in my hallway. This was almost laughable now, getting molested by a sexy woman in my own apartment. Lord, please keep me strong.

I smiled at Ronnie. It was intended to be a pitiful smile, meant to tell her that she had no powers with me, not even with the offer of easy pussy. I was old and wise enough to know that I would have serious regrets one day soon if I accepted the offer. So I continued to surprise myself by shooing it away.

"Ronnie, I told you, I have a girlfriend. This will not be happening."

Ronnie smiled back at me—didn't look so wicked now—and shrugged. "Okay, okay. I hear you." She started to walk away, twisting her ass in an exaggerated prance, almost like she was mocking me—or showing me quite literally what could be mine. She turned before she got to the living room. "You'll let me know when you change your mind, right?"

"I won't be changing my mind, dear. Don't you worry about that."

She

I got through the front door and, after finally allowing myself to breathe—I'd been holding it in from the time we'd kissed and said "good-bye"—congratulated myself for actually making it up the front stoop. I knew he'd been watching me walk, and it made me nervous as hell. I don't know what I was thinking letting Mikki talk me into wearing those stiletto ankle boots. I kept repeating to myself, "Don't shake it too hard, don't trip. Don't shake it too hard, don't trip." I turned around and gave him a final wave, closed the door, and, straight out of a Terry McMillan novel, exhaled. Did what just happened really happen? Did I really just go out on a date with a man and actually have a good time? And invite myself on another date with him, too?

I damn sure did—and I was glad I did it, too. Kenneth was the full package—smart, sweet, tender, full of conviction (though I figured I could only take that in doses; it's not like we agreed on everything, but okay), thoughtful. The full package—quite a catch. I started considering the possibilities—what it would be like to call him my boyfriend, how my parents would receive him if I introduced him to them, having him over for dinner to introduce him to the kids as Mommy's new man. Perhaps I was jumping a little ahead of what was going to happen; I certainly didn't want to set myself up for heartbreak. But I didn't want to throw water on this sizzler just yet; I wanted to fantasize. Because not only was Kenneth all those wonderful things we women look for in a man, he was sexy as hell, too—but not just because he looked good. Because of the way he made me feel. With him, I felt so, so beautiful. The men I'd been with before were so busy knocking me from in front of the mirror to admire their own beauty that they had never acknowledged mine. It was the way of men these days; they wear more designer clothes than we do, spend more time than we do in the hairdresser's chair, some of them even get their nails and toes done faster than some of us mothers who just don't have the time for all that extra grooming. And then they climb into their super rides and parade around town like they're God's gift to us unworthy women. And if we weren't smart enough to recognize their fabulousness, well then we could kindly step aside because there's a line of hookers and hoes standing at the ready to give them all the attention they can stand, so long as they can ride shotgun.

But not Kenneth. He made me feel like a queen. Helped me into his SUV, opened doors, paid for almost everything, and was bothered the few times I insisted on contributing to our date (trust me—it's rare for these cheap Negroes these days to tell a woman to put her wallet back into her purse), and, best of all, didn't try to store his tongue in my throat or invite himself in for a nightcap, if you get my drift. Perfect gentleman. And I have to admit that a small part of me was sorry for that. Because for the first time in a very long time, a man—this man—had me wishing he had followed me through that front door. I wanted another one of those kisses, and another one, and another still. I wanted to feel his soft hands on something other than my hand—perhaps my thigh and the small of my back, my cheek, my breast.

I actually touched my breast at the thought. I was in my room by then, and had already stepped out of my boots and skirt, pulled my shirt over my head and put my hair in a high ponytail. Now, I was standing in front of the mirror, in my black silk thong and matching bra, imagining Kenneth standing behind me, his hands softly running across my shoulders and down my arms. I imagined him turning me around toward him, his eyes taking in every inch of me, and his leaning in and kissing my lips, just like he had outside minutes ago. And before I knew it, I'd climbed into my bed and started to do what I hadn't done in about as long a time as I'd last had sex—slowly I pulled my underwear down past my ankles and let them drop to the floor, leaned back, parted my legs, and made my fingers send shivers up my own spine.

It didn't take long for me to reach a climax; it'd been so long since someone had made me come—much less myself—that almost as quickly as I had started caressing my clitoris and stroking my nipples, I'd felt the tingle begin in my toes and work its way up my thighs and into the pit of my stomach. It was so strong that I lifted my ass clean into the air, and even let out a little yell (my kids weren't there, but I still couldn't bring myself to scream out loud). I laid motionless for a moment, trying desperately to catch my breath. Then I reached over and grabbed my underwear off the floor and made it into the bathroom. I was washing my hands, but I couldn't bring myself to look in the mirror. It's weird, but I was still slightly embarrassed by what I'd done—and how I'd let what had been a nice date spiral into this. I know, I know—I didn't sleep with the man. But here I was, a grown-ass woman, getting myself off after just one date with Kenneth. I mean, it *was* one date. "He was *supposed* to be sweet and gentlemanly, you low-expectation-having dummy," I said, borrowing a line from Chris Rock. And all in an instant, I felt stupid. A relationship? With someone like Kenneth Roman? Who was I kidding? "It was one date," I said, looking into my eyes in the mirror. "Get over it."

And with that, I turned the light out, walked back to my bed, and went to sleep—intent on wiping Kenneth Roman out of my consciousness.

The phone was ringing awfully early for a Saturday, so I was sure it was one of my kids, calling from next door to ask me something dumb. I'd already been up for well over an hour—I can't help it; no matter how late I go to sleep, my body wakes me up at 5:45 A.M. every morning, without fail—so it wasn't a big deal, but still. Could I get a break maybe? And that's how I answered the phone, too—like I didn't want to be bothered. "Whoever this is, it better be good," I said, expecting it to be Jasmine, who can't seem to go a quarter of a day without talking to, seeing, or touching her mama.

"And you know that," the voice on the other line said. I didn't recognize it right away and thought that perhaps it was Kenneth, who'd displayed before that he didn't have any qualms with early morning phone calls. But this voice wasn't sexy; it was gutter. "What's happening, baby?"

No, please, not Ricky Fish. Not baby daddy, drug-dealing loser. Please. I didn't say anything.

"Za-ree," he said, singing the nickname he'd call me when he was trying to sweet talk me. "It's me, baby, Fish. How you?"

I thought hard about what I was going to say back, and then decided to say as few words as possible. I rolled my eyes. "Fine."

"How are my babies?"

"Your babies?" I asked, incredulous and smirking all at once. "James and Jasmine are fine, but they're hardly babies. But you wouldn't know that, seeing as you haven't seen them in, what, four, maybe five years?"

"Aw, come on, baby, you know what I mean. But listen, Za-ree, I didn't call to fuss with you, baby—I called for a favor and I don't have much time."

I didn't respond. Actually, I had been headed back to the base to hang up the phone the moment he said "favor," but I knew what he was about to say would just be too incredible to resist hearing, so I let him talk.

"You there, baby?"

"Oh yes," I said with mock enthusiasm. "I'm waiting with bated breath to hear what you have to say." Of course, my sarcasm went right over his head, and that fool kept talking like he was calling me at the job to ask me to stop and pick up some milk on the way home.

"Check this out, baby. I'm a need a favor from you. Next week, I'm getting out and I need you to pick me up because I don't have anyone else to come get me."

"Come get you from where?" I said.

"I'm upstate right now, but they're going to transfer me to Brooklyn next week when it's time for me to get out, so don't worry, it won't be one of those long drives. My lawyer hooked that up."

Hold up. Please tell me this Negro wasn't calling me from prison, and asking me to pick his funky behind up at the gate. After disappearing for—gosh, I can't even remember how long it's been since me and the kids heard from him last. My kids haven't had any contact with him in years. I haven't seen so much as a dime from him for child support. He has, for all intents and purposes, been on another planet somewhere, with absolutely no access to phone, stamps, tin cans and string, paper and bottles—whatever means there are to communicate with someone. And here he is, calling me at home, just after 7 A.M. on a Saturday, to ask me if I can do him a favor? I was, for a moment, speechless. But I recovered quickly.

"Um—how were you able to call me from prison without calling collect?" I asked.

"Oh—a friend of mine gave me a phone card so I wouldn't have to run up your phone bill. See, baby, I've changed. I'm not the same guy from before. Things are going to change. We're going to change."

I ignored the craziness coming from his mouth—knew better than to digest even one word. I'd heard his lies so many times I'd made a point of erasing the words "we" and "Fish and Zaria" from my lexicon. "Well, let me tell you what," I said, slowly and succinctly, "why don't you call your phone-card friend and tell her to come pick your ass up."

And with that, I gently placed the phone back on the base and went back to dusting my coffee table. The kids were going to be home soon. James needed a new coat, and Jasmine needed snow boots. I wanted to be ready to walk out the door when they arrived.

He

The visit to my basketball game had a magical effect on Zaria's son, James. He not only looked interested in my class all the time, but he actually was raising his hand now. And he usually had insightful things to say when I called on him. I asked him about the change after class one afternoon—about four days after my first date with his mother.

"What do you mean, Mr. Roman? Nothing happened to me," he said, looking about five years old as he stared at me, wide-eyed.

Ah, once again I had forgotten my audience. With preteens you can't use the vague generalities that adults favor when engaged in small talk. Adolescents were primed to uncover the real meanings underneath adult questions. They knew something like "What's been happening with you lately?" could have dozens of meanings, none readily apparent on the surface. They weren't likely to assume they knew what you meant—to make a mistake might mean unveiling information that they intended to keep hidden. In the tussle between adolescents and the adults that buzzed around them, information, particularly information about the sealed vault that is the adolescent mind, was valuable currency.

"What I mean is, you have been a much, uh, more attentive student of late. I wondered what brought about such a change—but I am definitely not complaining about it." I smiled at him, something I hadn't had much occasion to do in the classroom in a while. He smiled back shyly, turning away from me. Something, a teacher's intuition, told me he didn't know anything about me and his mother yet. What there was to *know*, I'm not sure. But there could be something soon. We were about to try date number two. That was more than a notion. If you included the café, it might even be labeled date number three. Date number three was a destination that many searching singles didn't often reach.

James shrugged. "I don't know, Mr. Roman. Nothing happened to me," he repeated. He stood in front of me uncomfortably, not knowing what to do with his arms, where to direct his eyes. Middle schoolers had to be the most awkward creatures on the planet, particularly in one-on-one situations. Parents were always complaining to me about the sudden distance of their children; I usually told them not to take it personal—often they just didn't have anything to say and tried like hell to avoid conversations with adults that revealed their cluelessness. But that didn't mean that adults should stop trying.

"Okay, James," I said. "Whatever it is, let's keep it up, all right?"

He nodded and smiled, ducking his head again. As he left the classroom, I heard the abrasive sound of his too-big jeans chafing at the pants legs. I shook my head, chuckling at the impracticality of the adolescent wardrobe. There were some boys in my classes whose pants were so large that you'd have a hard time even distinguishing the separate pant legs—they just looked like they were wading inside an enormous denim tent.

"Got a minute?"

I looked up. It was Evelyn Richie, another seventh-grade teacher, who had become a good friend over the years. Richie was a cute little white woman who could bowl me over with her sense of humor. A bit on the mousy side, she was several years older than me. I enjoyed spending time with her just to hear some of the outrageous things that came from her mouth.

"You would not believe what just happened in my class," she said in her scratchy, smoker's voice. She came in and sat in a chair in the front row. We both had a free period, which we were supposed to use to eat lunch and do "professional development" at the same time. Professional development, at least in Principal Bell's conception, meant teachers spending time together sharing notes on the youngsters in our charge. But most teachers used it to gossip, which was as natural a part of a teacher's day as chalk.

"We were talking about drugs." She saw my eyebrows rise. Richie was an English teacher. "Don't ask," she said, laughing. "We're doing the poet, Allen Ginsburg. You know that famous poem he wrote, 'Howl'? Anyway, we were talking about the drug culture in the '60s and '70s. And one of the girls told the class that her parents were drug dealers."

"Whaaaat! Drug dealers?!"

"Yes, drug dealers. You know that cute little blond girl, Sharon Nichols? It just amazes me the things these kids will say sometimes. Nothing more dangerous than a middle schooler to put all their parents' business out on the street. She said they had a lot of people working for them and they never actually sold it themselves, but they had it shipped to places like Newark and Harlem where other people sold it for them."

My eyes were about to pop from their sockets. "She said all that? Sharon Nichols told the whole class that? Wow. You believed her?"

Richie nodded. "Yeah, actually I kinda did. She had a lot of details. And she's not the kind of kid to make up crazy stories to draw attention to herself."

I thought of Sharon sitting quietly near the back of my class, not volunteering to answer very often, but not exactly shy either. What did her parents look like? I couldn't place them. But I thoroughly enjoyed the idea of these white-washed middle-class parents playing Scarface in the 'burbs.

"Excuse me." It was James, standing in the classroom doorway. "I forgot my ink pen," he said.

I waved him toward his desk. Richie and I watched, and listened, as James went to his desk, his jeans loudly matching his pace, and then left the room. "Thanks," he said over his shoulder.

After a beat, Richie said with a snort, "Now I wouldn't be surprised to hear *his* parents were drug dealers."

If we were actors in a movie, the camera would have zoomed in tight on her eyes, which widened to what seemed like twice their natural size. If we were on a television show, the laugh track would have come screeching to a halt. It was one of those moments I would likely remember for the rest of my life. What I guessed was that she forgot who she was talking to, feeling so loose and comfortable around me that I had become one of the girls—more specifically, the white female teachers she spent most of her time gossiping with.

What to do? What to say? Black people are regularly faced with such moments, a rude, racist, insulting remark tossed in our face, sitting right there in front of us, as unavoidable as getting wet in a rainstorm. And after the remark, we just as regularly kick ourselves in the behind for weeks or even months because of the inadequacy of our response. So here was my big chance, my racism response test.

"Damn, Richie," I said.

"I know, I know. I shouldn't have said that." Her eyes were still big and round, an expression lingered on her face halfway between fear and embarrassment. It was the one rule when black people and white people were going to be friends: no racist remarks, jokes, or assumptions. (At least coming from the white people.) That's all we asked—don't give me reason to think that you spewed nastiness behind my back. Didn't seem like an overly tall order in my mind. Of course, the easiest way to get obedient white people was to spend time around those who didn't harbor racist thoughts. But you could never be sure. Sometimes you even got those funky vibes to serve as a flashing red light—stay away from this one or you might get your feelings hurt. I had never gotten that vibe from Richie—she seemed to be one of those do-good liberals who would rather help a poor black child than help herself. But this science wasn't foolproof.

I had a thought, an idea of how I could make this especially embarrassing for my colleague, and throw that comment right up in her face.

"Actually, I can tell you for a fact that his mother's not a drug dealer because I'm dating her."

Richie's eyes widened again. It had to be the last thing she would have expected me to say, which is why it was so perfect.

"You're dating that kid's mother?" I could tell she was trying to keep her voice as even and emotionless as possible. But she couldn't hide her disturbance.

I nodded my head. I didn't want to give details—because there weren't that many to give. I didn't think Richie had the balls to ask any follow-up questions.

"Oh."

That's all she could come up with. I let it sit there for a long moment, making her squirm in the hard wooden chair like a seventh grader. So Richie decided to change the subject.

"Hey, have you gotten any closer to finishing your master's?" she asked brightly, overcompensating.

I shrugged. "No, not since the last time we talked about this. I told you, it's hard with basketball. The season happens to straddle both semesters, so I don't really have time. And I don't really feel like doing it during the summer."

"The money isn't enough motivation for you?"

I shrugged again. "The money would be nice. But I get another salary from coaching, so I'm doing all right."

"How's the team doing? I saw you on television the other night talking about the game against St. Anthony's. You guys won pretty easily, right?"

Usually one of the last things I wanted to do was engage in small talk about basketball with the teachers at the middle school. Even with Richie. Well, especially with Richie in this circumstance. She desperately wanted to leave the room, I'm sure, but she had to leave on a more positive note. She had to show me she wasn't racist and she did care about me. But the damage was already done. She couldn't take it back. She was going to have a cloud floating over her head for the foreseeable future. I wondered what happened in interracial marriages when the white partner got lazy and let their prejudice show. Did it irreparably damage the marriage?

I nodded my head. I purposely was showing a lack of enthusiasm, trying to make her so uncomfortable that she'd flee.

"Okay, well, I have some papers to grade," she said, bouncing up from the wooden chair.

"Okay," I said.

She hurried from the room. She stopped at the doorway and looked back at me. I knew what she was doing—she was trying to decide if she should give it one more apology.

"I'm so sorry, Kenneth," she said. The pain and sincerity in her voice was palpable, particularly when she pushed on the word "so." But I didn't want to let her down with a simple apology. I wanted her to have to think about what she had said. Damn, in effect she had insulted the hell out of my girlfriend. I should be about to punch her in the face. So I just stared at her.

She quickly got the message and scurried from the doorway like a spooked cat. I knew I wouldn't be getting any visits from her anytime soon. She might not even throw the gossip item out to her friends, as juicy as it was, because the subject would be too painful for her. Inevitably, one of the meddling teachers would ask how she knew I was dating James's mother. What could she say to that without revealing her dreadful gaffe?

I gathered up a few items I needed to read and headed for the teachers' lunchroom. I had some homemade lasagne waiting for me in the refrigerator. I didn't want Ronnie's body, but I wasn't above eating her food.

As I approached St. Paul's, I saw Tariq on the other side of the parking lot, bent over and listening to a short white man who was talking intently into his ear. I had seen the little man at a few of our games, and had assumed he was some type of college recruiter or maybe a scout for one of our rivals. There were a lot of balding white men at our games these days; it was hard to keep track of who was who. But this scene didn't feel right to me. I parked the truck and hurried over to the little parking lot confab.

The little man saw me before Tariq did. I thought I saw fear on his face—and his fear actually frightened me. What was he afraid of—and what should I be afraid of? He took a step back, away from Tariq, causing the teenager to look up. When Tariq saw me, he also looked a little embarrassed, like a little boy who had been caught stealing cookies. What was going on here?

"Hello, Tariq. Who's your friend here?"

The little man, who looked quite a bit younger up close—his loss of hair had been particularly premature—reached out a hand to me.

"Hello, Coach. My name is Donnie Nazerio. I was just telling Tariq here how wonderful a basketball player he is."

The guy was as slimy as they come, a villain in a bad, after-school special. But seventeen-year-old boys don't yet have a sensor to detect sliminess, even the over-the-top variety that stood before me. Nazerio clearly wasn't a recruiter. No college in its right mind would send this guy out into the world to woo teenagers and their parents. A scout was possible—but why would he be talking to Tariq in the parking lot? Why would he be talking to Tariq at all?

I tried to make my facial expression signal all the leeriness I was feeling. I didn't appreciate strangers coming around my guys, especially Jermaine and Tariq. It was starting to get ridiculous, all the people trying to get a piece of them. Recruiters calling me all evening long, even a couple of sneaker companies wanting to have meetings—Father Brown snuffed that one in a hurry. I was starting to regret the advice I had given them to wait until the end of the season to sign their college letters of intent. Tariq had wanted to sign before the season started to reduce the pressure on him. It had seemed like a bad idea at the time—it was too early to be making such a major decision. But maybe I was wrong. From where did Tariq get such wisdom?

"Nice to meet you, Mr. Nazerio." I squeezed his hand especially hard; it was an overtly aggressive act. It worked as well as shaking a fist in the man's face.

"Uh, well, I'll see you guys around," he said. "Great meeting you, Coach."

He scurried away, no doubt to crawl back under a rock. Tariq still looked embarrassed. He stared at the ground instead of at me.

"Are you gonna make me ask or are you gonna start explaining?" I said. I was trying to keep my voice from shaking—I didn't want Tariq to hear the fear that was causing me to shudder. I knew whatever Donnie was doing, it was bad. Real bad. And I had little confidence that I would hear the truth from the big kid in front of me.

"It's nothing, Coach," he said, shrugging.

I had been around enough teenagers to get worried when they said it was "nothing," it was usually quite the opposite.

"Nothing? If it's nothing, then why won't you look me in the eye? If it's nothing, why did the little man practically run away when I came? If it's nothing, why were the two of you hiding in the parking lot? What the fuck did he want, Tariq?!"

Tariq's eyes widened at the curse and the tone. He looked up at me and quickly back at the ground. He was wearing a blue blazer and a hideous blue-and-yellow tie, which he seemed to wear almost every other day. (St. Paul's required jackets and ties.) For about the thousandth time, I reminded myself that I needed to take the boy shopping. His body language was all wrong, shoulders slumped, turned slightly away from me, as if he needed to protect himself. But all I was doing was trying to protect him. There's irony somewhere in there.

"All he was talking about was my game, that's all. He didn't say nothing else. I wasn't hiding out here. I was walking past the parking lot and he called me over. I didn't even know his name until he told you what it was."

Just like a teenager, talk to a stranger and not even ask his name. They had so much to learn.

"He didn't mention anything about money?"

Tariq glanced up at me and quickly looked back at the ground. That told me I had poked a nerve. I prepared myself for a lie.

"Well, he did say something about me getting a lot of money to play basketball one of these days."

"He said that?" I said. I felt even more tension building in my shoulders.

"People are always saying that to me, Coach."

I looked at him hard. Money. Maybe Nazerio was one of those street scouts, employed by agents to try to suck players into their greedy webs. A few people had warned me that they would start sniffing around Tariq and Jermaine, talking to them about signing contracts or giving verbal agreements to work with the agents. Oftentimes, money was their primary lure.

"Look, Tariq. If that guy comes around you again, you tell him to get the hell away, okay? He does not have your best interests at heart, okay? And by all means don't sign anything, don't commit to anything and don't take any damn money."

He continued to look everywhere but at me. I had thought we were growing a little closer since we'd shared the same home for nearly two weeks, but he seemed far away from me right now.

"Do you hear me?" I said, sounding too much like the boy's parent. "Look at me, Tariq." He looked up, stared me in the eye. "Do you hear me?" I said it softer that time.

He was trying to be tough, but it wasn't working. He still looked like a scared little boy to me. The brow on his handsome face was furrowed. I saw the beginnings of a beard starting to form. Who was going to show him how to shave? Did that task fall to me?

"All right." I reached out and squeezed his shoulder. I wasn't expecting his response. He reached out and grabbed my arm and pulled me into a hug. He held it for several seconds. I wondered if he could hear my heart pounding. What was going through his head? When he stepped back, I tried to peer into his face, but he was turned away. Abruptly, he started walking, his long strides quickly taking him out of the parking lot. His tie whipped around in the breeze created by his pace.

I told myself to relax, to let the tension slide from my shoulders and my stomach. Not only was I his coach, but the boy was staying in my house. Surely I would be able to keep an eye on him, to protect him from all the sharks. Right? I walked toward the school, not liking the answer that was screaming back at me.

She

Every other Saturday, I take Jasmine down to Aisha's Hair Braiding Salon to get her hair done. I can do hair, mind you, but for $25 a really nice African lady named Fundimaia will wash, condition, blow dry, and braid Jazzy's hair in less than an hour and a half—which is a miracle because Jazzy has a head full of thick hair. I'm not complaining about it; it's beautiful hair—hair that I prayed long and hard for because my child didn't have any for the first three years of her life. But when she got it, boy did she get it. I used to keep it in ponytails, but just tussling with that head in the morning would make us all late for school and work. So I broke down and got someone else to do it in a style that would last.

Anyway, on this particular Saturday, my mother invited herself along for a "girls' afternoon out," which meant Jasmine was getting her hair done, we were going to lunch and, inevitably, my mother would find herself in a store somewhere, spending her money on my kids. I didn't necessarily agree with her doing it, but she loved to spoil Jazzy and James. I think it had to do with all the madness she let Daddy put me through when I first had them and he forced me to raise them by myself without any help from him. Oh, she tried to help out—would use Mikki to sneak some money and baby clothes and food over to the house every now and then—but she let me live in squalor, refusing to defy my father's order that Fish and I "figure out our own messes." So if Mommy felt like she had to go out of her way to feel a little bit better about herself as a grandmother, so be it. Hair, lunch, shopping it was.

"He actually called you what time in the morning to ask you this?" my mother asked, putting down her raggedy 1994 copy of *Ebony* magazine—I swear, this shop's reading material was so old, they could have easily auctioned some of these relics on eBay—and staring at me in horror.

"Just after seven in the morning," I said. "I didn't even realize convicts could get phone time that early in the morning."

"I actually didn't know he was in prison." She shook her head and released a deep sigh. I could feel her irritation building.

"Neither did I," I said. "I'd given up trying to find him so long ago. I knew he was in trouble and on the run for something, as usual, but I didn't know they'd actually caught him."

"If you would have filed for child support like I told you to all those years ago, you would have known," she said. We were about to traverse familiar terrain. I wasn't in the mood for a Fish lecture.

"Well, a lot of good that would have done me, with him in jail, huh? And what was he going to pay us in—cigarettes?" I laughed, but Mommy wasn't amused.

"Very funny, Zaria," my mother said. "I don't care if he's only got two nickels to rub together—both of them belong to my grand-children, and it was up to their mother to make sure they got it."

"Ma—I don't want to talk about this anymore," I said. "And keep your voice down—I don't want Jazzy hearing this conversation, if you don't mind." I knew exactly where this conversation was headed. Although the craziness surrounding my forbidden relationship with Fish had long ago passed—it'd been well over twelve years since my parents warned me not to see him—there was still bitterness over my defying their wishes, getting knocked up, getting kicked out of the house, and having to fend for myself while I raised my kids without help from their father. I really didn't want to have this conversation—fight, rather—with her. Not today. She sensed the tension rising too, and, after peering over to make sure Jasmine's big ears hadn't heard anything, Mommy changed the subject.

"So, Mikki tells me that you're quite taken by one of the teachers at James's school." I wanted a subject change, but this wasn't the one I was looking for.

"Tell me about him," she said.

I flipped nervously through the hair magazine I'd been holding, took a sip of my soda, leaned back into my chair, made sure Jasmine wasn't looking at my mouth, and tried not to look my mother in the eye. "He's a nice guy."

There was silence. Clearly, she was looking for more. "And?" she said. More silence. "Is that it? He's a nice guy?"

"Pretty much," I said. I took another sip of soda.

"Uh-huh," she said, chuckling. "Well, let me tell you what Ms. Mikki told me: She said he's James's social studies teacher, that you've said he's extremely handsome, that you even got dressed up for your first date, and that you like him a whole lot."

"Mikki told you all of that, huh?" I said, finally looking her in the eye. "Sounds like you know all there is to know, then."

"You mean I know all that you think I need to know, huh?"

I didn't say anything.

"Well, does James know you're dating his teacher?"

"Nope."

"And why, exactly, is that?"

I looked over at Jasmine again. "Mom, can you keep your voice down?" I said, making sure to tint my words with a hint of annoyance. "I haven't told him or Jasmine because my relationship with Mr. Roman is on a need-to-know basis—and right now, neither of them need to know about us because we've gone out on only one date and though I like him, we're not getting married tomorrow."

"Well, do you really think you'll be able to keep that information from James at the school? I mean, one of the mothers there is bound to find out that you're dating him, and it's only a matter of time before somebody's little nosy child comes back and starts putting it out there in the universe—James's universe."

"Well, I haven't had any problems, and no one knows that we went out on a date."

"You don't know that for sure. That's an awfully small school, and it's only a—"

"I'm fairly sure, Mother," I said sternly. "Now can we drop the subject?"

"I'm not finished talking about it," she said, laughing. "So I guess the answer to that question is 'Nope.' But let me ask you this: How long are you going to date this man before you tell your children about him?"

"Mom, what does it matter?"

"Well if it doesn't matter, then you shouldn't have a problem answering the question," she said, shifting her body to face me.

"I make it a point of not telling my children about men that I date until I know that they're worth keeping around. I don't think it's necessary to expose them to a bunch of strange men, okay? Now, you know the method to my madness. That's a long-standing policy for me, and I'm not about to change it just because the man is cute and we had a good first date."

"But if it's someone you truly like, why wait? Why not let him meet the children so that he knows what he's up against?"

"Because it's not about him—it's about my kids."

"Exactly. And you're driving men away by not letting them fully into your life, Zaria. Isn't that why the last one left, because you wouldn't let him be a part of your life? Your children are a part of you, Zaria, and no man is going to want you if he feels he's not trusted."

Oh. She done stepped in it now. "Oh," I said loudly. "So the reason you and Daddy are back together is because you've decided to trust him again? Does that trust extend to his illegitimate child?"

And with that, I'd stepped in it. My mother proceeded to launch into one of her infamous lectures about her and Daddy and their love for each other, and how even though things got hairy when she'd found out about his other child, she had to make some tough decisions, blah, blah, blah. I'd stopped listening to her when she started on how the two of them had met, how they'd fallen in love, and why they'd stayed together so long. I'd heard the story plenty, particularly when I was starting to date and especially when Fish and I got together. It was annoying then, and it was particularly annoying now, because the truth of the matter is that I was disgusted by my mother's decision to take my father back in. Oh, she'd started out on the right track by immediately kicking him out and getting her attention from somewhere else. But no one was more shocked than I when I saw the two of them hugged up on the porch swing that time, and my mouth dropped even more when I came over early one morning with the kids and Daddy was still asleep in the bed. Just like old times. My mom was in the kitchen, reading the paper, drinking coffee, with one eye on the bacon sizzling in the oven.

Plates were set out on the table, and the pancake box stood sentry over her cast-iron frying pan. She was cooking Saturday breakfast while he slept, like she'd done for him for years. And I was incredulous. Disgusted, even. Because as far as I was concerned, there was no coming back from cheating, let alone producing a child out of wedlock and then lying about it for years and years and years. My mother was strong—valiant even—for kicking him out of the house when she'd found out. And now, here she was, being sweet talked and suckered into forgetting the whole affair, and falling back into the same ol', same ol' routine for his benefit. Trust? I don't think so.

I interrupted my mother's history lesson and told her exactly what I thought about it all, and how I would have handled it if it had happened to me—much to her consternation.

"Now I just know you're not trying to climb into my business like that, Missy," my mother said, taking on the tone that I'd heard so many times when I was about to get a lecture/tongue lashing/ass whupping. "It didn't happen to you, so you don't have any business putting your worthless two cents into it. Your father and I have been married for more than thirty years now, and that doesn't even count how long we were courting. And we have our own special way of handling adversity and conflict—something you don't know anything about because the last time you were in a serious relationship was . . . oh, wait a minute, you haven't been, have you? So don't you judge me and don't you judge your father and don't you judge our decisions. When you get a husband and go through thirty years of marriage, then you can fix your mouth to tell me what you would have done in the situation, okay? Until then, refrain from getting in the middle of our personal business and understand that we are grown adults who are in control of our bodies, feelings, and lives—and we don't need your two cents to figure out how to make it through the day, okay?"

I was going to argue with her, but there's no winning with that woman. She's stubborn as all get out, and will not stop until she has the last word. Besides, Jasmine was climbing out of Fumimaia's chair, and I needed the subject to be dropped. So I just nodded and took another sip of soda. But I'll tell you this much: I would never let a man stomp on me like my father did her. A liar is a liar, and if there's one thing in the world I will not tolerate from my man, it's lying. Believe that.

Besides, I had bigger fish to fry. That fool of a father of my children was about to get out of prison, and apparently he thought there was a chance for him and I to get back together. Not that I was scared by the prospect of Fish knocking on my door; I could handle him easily. But I didn't feel like dealing with it. Things seemed to be going well for me—I had a good job, happy kids, possibly a new boyfriend—and the last thing I needed was for him to come jacking it up and, worst of all, disrupting my children's lives. They'd finally gotten used to the fact that they didn't have a daddy—that he didn't care anything about them. And I didn't even have to tell them that—I never once put their father down in front of them; he was doing a good enough job by himself letting them know he was worthless. Jasmine stopped asking for him altogether; she barely knew him anyway—she hadn't so much as seen his face since she was about three. James was simply bitter. His father had called him on several occasions, making grand promises that he never had intended to keep—like all the times he called days after the child's birthday, telling him he'd put a gift in the mail for him that never showed up, and all the times he said he would be stopping by for Christmas, only to call after James was asleep to say he got sidetracked, or his car broke down, or he ran out of gas and couldn't make it. The one that broke the camel's back was when Fish promised my boy he was going to pick him up and take him on a cross-country driving tour, and he didn't show up. For months, James was harassing me to help him map out all the states they were going to travel to, and all the different tourists attractions he could check out on the way. "Do you think the Grand Canyon is neat, Mommy?" he'd ask. "How big do you think the roller coasters are at Disney World?" He even asked me about Motown, because his dumb daddy said something about going to Detroit. "Did you know that it's right across the river from Canada? Maybe we could go over there for a day!"

Well, who do you think was wiping up those tears when his father called a week before they were supposed to leave to tell my boy he wasn't going? Like I said, I didn't have to say anything bad about James's father; his daddy did that job all by himself.

And now, here he was, thinking he was going to roll up to my doorstep, fresh out of prison, with nothing but whatever he was wearing when he went behind bars, to get "us" going again. I don't think so.

He

By halftime, as the Knicks and the Sixers trotted back through the tunnel and out of sight, I could honestly say it was about the most fun I had ever had at a basketball game. Zaria and I couldn't keep our hands off each other, stroking and squeezing arms and hands and thighs. We had even kissed a few times, making out like teenagers in the backseat at a drive-in movie. I wasn't at all embarrassed to be kissing this beautiful woman in public. I didn't care who could see us—and from some of the looks we got plenty of people were acting like we were the show. But I thought I saw jealousy on their faces.

Zaria had started it all. I wouldn't have been so presumptuous to do more than hold her hand, which is what I did midway through the first quarter. She grinned at me and made my heart flutter by pulling my hand toward her face and kissing it right on the veins that protruded from the dark side. It was an ice-breaking gesture—well, we didn't really have any ice between us from the moment we'd hopped onto the train to Manhattan. It was a Thursday night and we were both primed to have a good time. The conversation was light and easy and there were plenty of smiles all the way up to the moment I wrapped her fingers inside of mine.

I pulled her hand toward my face and planted a gentle kiss on the back of her lovely hand. She grinned at me again. I adored the way her dimples creased her smooth cheeks when she smiled. I could let that smile brighten the rest of my days. She leaned over and I saw her lips coming toward me. I mirrored her by moving mine toward her. Our lips met in the softest of kisses. We let it linger long enough for me to feel a delicious shiver travel from the base of my neck down the length of my spine, hitting each individual vertebra along the way like a pianist running the scales. When she pulled away, the look on her face matched the feeling in my soul.

I say it was the most fun I had ever had at a basketball game, but I wasn't even paying attention to most of the game. Zaria would ask me questions, questions that I would answer as expertly as I could, but really I was concentrating on the fluttering of my heart, the unbridled joy that I hadn't felt in a long time in the company of a lady. This wasn't about sex or my libido. Something deeper was there, right from the very start. And I could tell she felt it, too.

When she wasn't resting her hand on my left thigh, it was softly caressing my back, almost making me scream from the slow, sensual pleasure of her tender touch. It didn't take much stretching of my imagination to visualize the bliss we would find together in bed. But I didn't even want to linger there too long, on the sex we would one day have, because that would cheapen the joy of these early moments, when a look was enough to send me to the throes of near ecstasy. I was more than old enough to know that I could wake up one morning to find the bliss gone, drained, and in its place a chilling tolerance. It was all downhill from there—a short trip from tolerance to annoyance, leading to resentment right around the bend. The whole journey could be traveled in neck-turning haste—so fast that you were almost afraid to go down that road again. But then you look up one day and a beautiful face has found reason to offer you a smile and all the pain and upset stomachs are forgotten.

In the middle of the fourth quarter, Zaria slipped in a little tongue when we kissed. It was the first time I had gotten tongue and I was thrilled. Particularly since she was the initiator. It foretold exciting things about her possible aggression in the bedroom. When we were teenagers, guys used to think they could predict the bedroom temperament of a girl by her mannerisms and attitudes, her walk, her disposition, her spirit. It was the dumbest thing in the world, but we held on to it in our ignorance because it provided material for the all-important world of our sexual imgainations—just like the silly belief that a girl couldn't possibly be a virgin if there was a visible gap between her legs, the unmistakable triangle, when she wore tight pants. It all served a crucial purpose, to break down this inexplicable gender into digestible parts—perhaps even emboldening us to risk rejection. How ridiculously juvenile we were about it all, to think that women could be so easily gauged with formulas and theorems. The older I got, the more I realized that knowing women was to know nothing and to guess even less.

When she pulled back from the kiss—yes, she initiated its end, too—I couldn't miss the glint in her eye that told me she was just as intoxicated by all the possibilities that stretched before us. We were like a deep red, shiny apple sitting in your hand, glistening with the promise of something juicy and sweet, something that might obliterate the memory of every apple, every piece of fruit that had come before it. It was exciting stuff.

We strolled from the Garden side by side, silent but happy. The Knicks had lost but that mattered not a bit. Our fingers brushed against each other a few times as our arms swung. I took a deep breath and extended a finger on the next swing, reaching out and trying to catch her hand, imagining myself a circus trapeze artist. I could have sworn that her finger was also extended when they made contact. Our fingers, the pointers, did a little intertwining dance, joined by the middle and the ring, grasping and touching and twirling until our hands were firmly locked together, my right and her left. We swung our arms extra high, enjoying the sensation of walking as a unit, showing the world that we were joined. When we got outside, I chuckled at the sight of us. Nobody held hands on the streets of Manhattan except teenagers without a port and tourists, who announced their stranger status with their giddy I-Love-New-York smiles and peppy steps, so distinguishable from the quick but grudging pace of the worker bees.

We got on the PATH train, heading back to Jersey City. Zaria had driven to my apartment to pick me up, then parked near the PATH station so we could hop the fast and easy train to midtown. I was so enjoying her company that I was not prepared for what happened on the train. We had an argument.

It wasn't a knockdown brawl, but it was bothersome. Things had been going so smoothly that you might have convinced me to start shopping for the engagement ring. Okay, that's a bit much, but you get my point. I was thinking that she was my ideal mate, as if such a thing existed. And then she looked up at a newspaper that a man was reading across the train and commented on the headline: Welfare Numbers Start Rising Again.

"Damn, they letting all those lazy asses back on welfare again?" she said, her voice filled with contempt.

I was taken aback. Welfare reform was an emotional issue for me. My mother had been on welfare for several years before she got the secretarial job at Snyder High School. It was during those crucial elementary school years when peer ridicule was at its height and a classmate had seen us using food stamps one day in a local supermarket. The shame was enough to dampen my pillow at night from the hot tears. But I came to realize later that the welfare had, indeed, sustained us, doing exactly the job it was intended to do.

"Uh, not everybody on welfare is lazy," I said, struggling to keep my voice even.

She turned toward me with a smirk. "Yeah, yeah, I know that's what we're supposed to say."

I wanted to let it go, to rush back to our blissful harmony, but I felt an obligation to mount a stronger defense. To represent for all welfare recipients.

"Welfare has helped a lot of people, Zaria, people who were trying to support families, make ends meet. They weren't all lazy. Sometimes it's more logical to stay home and take care of your children on welfare than get a low-paying job and not even be able to afford good daycare."

It was the classic defense and I presented it with all the appropriate passion. I didn't want to make it personal; I wanted the case argued on the merits.

Zaria gave a disgusted snort. "Yeah, okay. But that doesn't mean there aren't some lazy asses out there abusing the system, getting multiple checks, saying they can't work, trying to get over. So we make everybody go find a damn job and their gravy train comes to a halt. Nothing wrong with a job."

I think my lip made a noise when it fell to the floor. Was this woman serious? Maybe she was just trying to be contrary. But she was the one who started the discussion, without even knowing how I felt. I took a deep breath.

"You can't be serious, Zaria. Just because there are a few lowlifes abusing the system doesn't mean it's not working for thousands of other needy families. We don't throw out the whole thing because of a few rotten apples. We have some corrupt politicians, but you don't see anybody saying we should trash our whole political system."

Zaria shrugged. "Well, maybe we *should* trash our whole political system. 'Cause politicians are too willing to let special interests get their way as long as they get returned to office."

"Special interests? Tell me what you mean by special interests."

She swiveled in her seat so that she was facing me. "Are you sure you want to have this conversation? We were having such a good time. Why are we messing it up by talking about stupid politics?"

She was right, of course. This was silly. Politics didn't belong here with us on this perfect evening.

"You're right," I said, smiling. "We are having a great time. Let's talk about something more pleasant."

She nodded her head and slipped her hand inside of my arm, settling back into her seat with a satisfied smile. I also settled back, feeling the tension start to ease up. But I stole another glance at Zaria. I knew I wouldn't be able to shake her comments so easily. I knew we would have to return to them at some future point. My fear? That Richard Nixon had been reincarnated as a beautiful black woman from Teaneck.

There was silence between us in the car. I think we both were still thinking about the welfare conversation. At least I know I was. But I wanted to get a little passion going in the front seat before I went upstairs, so I needed to do something, to say something sweet or sexy or funny.

"I don't think the Knicks have ever won when I've gone to a game," I said, chuckling. It was easily a lie—I had been to dozens of Knicks games in my lifetime—but I thought it might break the awkwardness.

"Awww, that's sad," Zaria said. "You're bad luck."

I chuckled again. "Yeah, I guess I am. But I feel my luck changing tonight, even if they did lose."

Zaria glanced over with her eyebrow raised. "Oh yeah, well why is that?"

I took a deep breath. This needed to be good. "Well, I have this theory. I know things are going well in a relationship if nobody has talked about the weather yet. As soon as one of us is so bored that we need to have the weather conversation, then it's not going to last much longer. When I've been with you, I haven't even noticed what the weather's been like. I think it could have been a blizzard when we came out of the Garden and I wouldn't have noticed."

"Awww, what a sweet thing to say!" she said. She took her right hand off the steering wheel and reached across the seat to stroke my leg a few times. Her touch felt like an electric charge, instantly sending a jolt to my crotch. My little speech had worked like magic.

As the car approached my building, I looked up to see my apartment beaming brightly. My, uh, "visitors" must have turned on every light in the joint. After nearly three weeks, I was more than ready to reclaim my home, but neither Ronnie nor I had been able to find alternate lodging. Well, I don't know how much Ronnie was trying. I had put their name on several lists for special, government-financed housing, but I hadn't heard anything back. I had even thought about telling Ronnie to make up a story to get into a battered women's shelter that was supposed to be fairly nice. But my conscience had made me shelve that idea—I'd be taking a legitimate slot from a woman who was getting her ass beat.

Zaria parked the car in front of the building. We were sitting close to the streetlight—nearly the same place where Antoinette had parked when she gave me the striptease show from her front seat. Zaria released a deep sigh and settled back into her seat, making herself comfortable. It was clear that she didn't plan on going anywhere soon. I knew I couldn't invite her upstairs even if I wanted to, and I silently cursed Ronnie and Tariq. I didn't expect things with Zaria to reach this point this quickly. I thought my houseguests would be gone by the time I'd get her upstairs. But then again, maybe we hadn't quite reached that point. It was hard to know. And I couldn't ask.

"Kenneth—or should I call you 'Coach'?—I had a great time," she said, laughing at her little joke. "Even if the Knicks did lose."

"Yeah, this was a wonderful night," I said. "Even if the Knicks did lose."

"The next time I want to bring *you* out on a date," she said, turning to face me. "Okay?"

"Of course. Where we going?"

"Somewhere special." She burst into laughter. "I just have to figure out where!"

She looked so lovely and inviting when she laughed, I was inspired to make my move. I reached over with my right hand and softly stroked her face. She abruptly stopped laughing and somehow seemed to melt into my touch, moving her face ever so slightly like she was stroking my hand in return. It was a terrific gesture—how to return a facial caress. Our eyes met; it felt like I was falling, losing all sense of time and place. My body was all nerve endings and fluttery sensations. Oh, the power this woman had over me. She didn't even know. Almost imperceptibly I started toward her; but she saw it because she came toward me, too. Our lips met somewhere over the drive shaft of her car. (The car was a Honda Accord, fairly old model, over 100,000 miles.) I concentrated on nothing but the softness of her kiss and the sturdiness of her shoulder as I gripped it with my right hand. I relaxed the hand and let it stroke her arm through her sweater. Her right hand was busy, too, sweeping across my chest in big, looping caresses that made me tingle. I tried to move closer but felt the emergency brake dig into my thigh. The backseat, maybe? Nah, that was too tacky for my Zaria. If we were going to do the backseat, we might as well go upstairs, at least in theory. Finally, after our tongues danced and darted for a good five minutes of serious front-seat petting, I pulled away.

"Whew!" she said, letting out an audible gush of air.

I felt a little sweaty. I knew it was time to make my exit, to not push this too much too soon. "Okay, beautiful lady, I will be waiting for your phone call with details about our fabulous date." I reached out my hand and stroked her face again. "Don't disappoint me, okay?"

She laughed and pushed my hand away. "Get out of here, Kenneth! I don't need any more pressure."

I opened the car door reluctantly and waved to my new girlfriend. I really didn't want to leave her. This was very promising. I stood in the building lobby and watched her drive away. Promising, indeed.

When I got off the elevator on my floor, I heard loud voices. Before I turned the corner, I identified one of them as Ronnie. And the other one was a male, but not Tariq. I slowed my pace to a near standstill so I could hear what they were saying.

"But I'm not working anymore, Boo," Ronnie said.

"Damn, woman, I know that. I know that's why you up in this nigger's crib. My question was when do you think you gonna be gettin' some more money? I know you ain't working. What about yo baby daddy?"

I desperately wanted to peek around the corner to see the face attached to this ghetto caricature. This man had been up in my home? I shook my head. Ronnie had to go.

"I never know when he's gonna give me money," Ronnie said. Her voice had a fearful, pleading tone.

The man snorted. "You need to go ask that nigger. He ain't gonna come handing it to you like the fuckin' mailman. I know he got it."

"Well, that's not the way it's supposed to work," Ronnie said.

"I know that, Ronnie! I told you, I ain't stupid. Damn. Anyway, I'll call you." I heard a smack that sounded like hand on flesh. "Take care of that ass. So I could take care of it for you." He chuckled maniacally, like a dastardly villain in a karate flick. I held my breath and started backing up toward the elevator. It would take him at least fifteen steps to reach the bend. After a few seconds, I casually started forward again. Finally, "Boo" turned the corner. He looked about as I expected, like an overly mature character in a rap video. He had on a black doo-rag and huge baggy black jeans, and a scruffy beard covered patches of his brown face. He wasn't a bad-looking guy, but the outfit looked ridiculous. Once a man passed age thirty, he needed to stop looking toward fifteen-year-olds for his fashion statements. Boo appeared to be startled to see me walking toward him. He tried to put a scowl on his face, but it was too late. When we passed each other, I also noticed that I was considerably bigger than him. My 6'2" frame probably had a good fifty pounds and five inches on him. He was a mini-thug.

Ronnie was just walking away from the door when I opened it. She spun around—the look on her face told a long story. Now I knew where all her money went, why she wasn't paying her bills. She was getting pimped by the lovely Boo. Again she was wearing a T-shirt with no bra. I wondered whether she even had on panties. Had they just been fucking in my apartment? Damn, what if I had returned twenty minutes earlier—if Zaria and I hadn't made out in the front seat? Where was Tariq?

"Oh, you're home already," she said, trying to be casual about it. I knew she was trying to figure out if I had seen her man. She gave me a fake smile. "How was your date?"

I nodded at her, in no mood for small talk. I wanted information—

and I wanted her out of my apartment. I was not interested in bringing any ghetto drama into my home. If I wanted to see that, I knew where to go.

"Who was the dude, Ronnie?" I said, trying to sound stern. I feared that I sounded too much like a parent.

Her eyes widened. She shifted on her bare feet and tugged at the hem of her shirt. Oh, now it was too short?

"The dude? Oh, you mean the man who was here? He wasn't nobody." She waved her hand, as if dismissing Boo. "He's just a friend of mine, that's all. I didn't feel comfortable having him in here, so I told him he had to go."

I took a few steps closer to her. I thought I smelled something slightly funky, slightly musky in the air. I leaned toward her and sniffed, as dramatically as I could.

Ronnie took a step back. I thought I heard a gasp.

"What are you doing?!" she said. She was frowning.

"Oh, nothing. Thought I smelled something."

Ronnie tried to laugh it off. "You're crazy, Kenneth!"

"Yeah, I guess I am. I guess that's not the smell of sex all up in my apartment. Ronnie, were you having sex with that dude in here?"

Her eyes widened again. I believe her face even got a little redder. She brought her left hand to her cheek and she stared at me. What was she thinking?

"I can't believe you asked me that," she said.

I shook my head. This was not the time to play games. I had no interest in her little drama scene.

"Yes, you can believe it, Ronnie. I heard part of your conversation in the hall. You were talking loud enough for me to hear you from the damn elevator. I'm sure half the building heard you. Now, I opened my home up to you because I really love your son and it pained me to see him in such trouble. You came along because a boy needs to be with his mother. If it was up to me, I might have left your ass back in the Bronx, in that fucked up neighborhood." I did hear a gasp that time. But I was on a roll.

"But I thought I was helping out you and your family by bringing you here. Now, it's been three weeks. I don't know how hard you've been looking for another place. It seems like I've been doing all the looking. But Tariq seems comfortable here and he's playing great ball, so I wasn't gonna complain. Then I come home and find some crazy scene being played out in my hallway, like from some bad thug movie. What the hell is that, Ronnie? Don't you think that's just a bit disrespectful, for you to bring some Negro up in my home like this? And did you actually have the nerve to fuck him here? In my apartment? When I could have been returning at any moment? I'm not completely believing this is happening."

Ronnie stood there for several seconds with her mouth agape. She stared at me, but I couldn't read her expression. I stared back at her, breathing a little heavily after the exertion of my big speech. Waiting.

"I'm sorry, Kenneth," she said in a little girl voice, slightly above a whisper. "I told you, I didn't want him here. And as for the sex . . ." She paused, clearly embarrassed. "He made me." She said that last so low I could barely hear her.

"He made you? You mean he raped you?"

She shook her head. "No, I wouldn't call it that. But I told him we shouldn't be doing it here. I tried to—"

"You know what, Ronnie?" I said, interrupting. "I'm not interested in any details. Okay? I think you got my point. Whatever you said to him and he said to you, the end result was that you were fucking in my apartment. If anybody should be fucking in my apartment, it should be me." I saw her change of expression and realized how that might be interpreted, so I rushed to finish. "I mean, what if I wanted to come back here with my girlfriend? And we walked in to find two grown people having sex? Damn, did you do it on my daughter's bed? Or on my couch?"

Ronnie shook her head, but she didn't say anything. I took that to mean that the doing *was* done in one of those two places.

"Well, we weren't really *on* the couch," she said softly.

Despite my best efforts, her statement created a stirring in my crotch. I certainly didn't want to get turned on here, but I quickly imagined Ronnie bent over the back of my couch with Boo giving it to her from behind, slapping against her big jiggly butt. I shook my head, disturbed.

"Ronnie, I'm going to my room now. But I'm really upset by this." I thought of something. "You know, I'm supposed to be getting my daughter this weekend. What if she had been with me?"

"Your daughter is coming here?" Ronnie asked.

I nodded. But actually I was considering having her stay with my mother again, just to keep her away from the drama and all the people in my apartment. "She might be," I said.

"I'm sorry, Kenneth. I'm so sorry." Ronnie looked sincere enough. Her eyes were a little watery, like she might start crying. I didn't want tears, just contrition—and an active interest from her in finding a place to stay. Just then I thought of something else.

"Where's Tariq?" I asked her.

She shrugged. "He said he's studying or something over Jermaine's house."

Studying with Jermaine? At almost 11 P.M.? I didn't believe that one bit. I was tempted to call over to Jermaine's house—he actually did live in a house. But Tariq was on the verge of manhood, in need of some space. I remembered when I was a high school senior. The boy was probably with some girl somewhere. He certainly got enough ass thrown at him. I had seen it with my own eyes, after nearly every game, home or away. The boy could spend a half hour collecting phone numbers if he wanted. The groupies started early—they could smell money in the water. They came after Jermaine, too, but for some reason Tariq was the more charismatic of the two. Jermaine was bright, independent, he clearly didn't need anybody. Tariq was the opposite, as needy as they come. Maybe the girls could sense that. Just as I was about to tell Ronnie that the boy certainly had lied to her, the phone rang. I stepped into the kitchen and grabbed it. I felt myself getting hot—I hadn't even removed my jacket.

"Hello."

"Hey, Coach?" It was Tariq himself.

"Yes, Tariq." I looked over at Ronnie, who smiled upon hearing her son's name.

"Uh, I'm here at Jermaine's. I just wanted to tell my mother that I'm gonna stay here tonight."

"Okay, Tariq. You got a change of clothes?"

"Huh?"

"A change of clothes. You know, for school tomorrow?"

"Oh, uh, yeah. Well, I got the clothes I wore today."

"Tariq, that's kinda nasty, don't you think? Not even clean underwear?"

"Well, I can wash out the underwear, Coach. All right?"

"Hey, that's up to you, man. I'm not going to try to convince you why you need to wear clean underwear. Oh, Tariq?"

"Yeah, Coach?"

"Why don't you put Jermaine on the phone."

There was silence on the other end. For a long time. He had to get over his shock at the question, then come up with something good. Like I said, I could remember being a senior in high school. I had gotten my share of ass on the down-low, and I wasn't even a national basketball star with groupies following me around. There were worse things than being Tariq right now.

"Uh, well, Coach, I think he's asleep."

I almost wanted to laugh. "He's asleep already, Tariq? It's not even eleven o'clock yet. Isn't this a bit early for him? Especially since he lives so close to the school. I'm quite surprised."

More silence. "Yeah, me too, Coach." Silence. "Uh, okay, Coach. I gotta go."

"You don't want to talk to your mother?" I said. I was having fun now.

"My mother? Uh, no, not really, Coach. Hey, uh, listen. I gotta go. I don't want to wake up the house, you know?" I could have sworn I heard a girl's voice in the background.

"Whose voice is that I heard, Tariq?" I wasn't going to let him off easy.

"Uh, that wasn't nobody, Coach. All right. Good night, Coach." And then the line went dead. I chuckled.

"What's so funny?" Ronnie asked.

I looked at her. I wasn't willing to share my amusement with her. I still wanted her to feel my wrath, so she would get her fat ass up out of here. "Nothing," I said. I headed for my room. "Your son is all right, Mom. He's gonna be all right."

She

The kids had been sleeping for well over two hours by the time I pulled into my driveway just before midnight. James was bunked up with JJ, Jasmine with Pammy. They'd been thoroughly worn out after a round of miniature golf at the West County Play Center and a heavy meal of burgers and fries from a nearby Checkers—places April took them to keep them preoccupied so that neither James nor Jasmine would be studying where their mother was.

And now, April was standing at the front door with a bottle of pinot grigio and two wineglasses, waiting for a blow-by-blow replay of my date with Kenneth. "A celebration," she said, raising a glass to my face as I walked through the door. "To another hot date with the hot social studies teacher." I took the glass out of her hand and took a long, deep swig, then walked toward the den without saying so much as a word. I'd already put the glass down and was climbing out of my coat and boots when April skipped around the corner. She couldn't quite read my mood, so she went with acting as if I'd had the most spectacular time of my life.

"Well? Details?" she said, pouring more wine into my glass. I'm no drinker; I can get tipsy from just a glass and a half of wine, mainly because I hardly ever have occasion to drink it. Even on holidays, the strongest drink on my table is root beer and apple cider in those fancy, wine-shaped bottles. And don't let me gulp a glass; it goes straight to my head—like it was just now.

"I don't think he likes me," I said with a frown, grabbing the wine bottle to pour myself another glass. I twirled down into my recliner, splashing a few drops of the wine on Mikki's jean jacket. She was going to kick my ass, but I didn't care.

April looked at me, and then at her watch. Then she walked over to my recliner, bent over close to my face, and peered into both my eyes. I pulled back. "You're invading my personal space," I said, laughing. "Take two steps back, dammit." April laughed and moved backward. But she kept staring. "And what the hell are you looking at, anyway?"

"Well, I'm just trying to figure out how a woman who just walked in from a date that lasted well over six hours with makeup smeared all over her face—an obvious sign that there was some lip-lock—thinks the guy she went out with doesn't like her."

"Easy. He just doesn't," I said, taking another sip before jumping out of the chair, grabbing the bottle on my way up and heading toward the kitchen. "Do we have any chips? Pretzels? I need some salt."

"Just hold on there, Missy," April said, walking closely behind me. "Details. I need details."

We sat at the kitchen table, me hording the wine, April shoving chips into her mouth, both of us enthralled by the blow-by-blow replay of my date with Kenneth—from the pickup to the train ride to the game to the romp in the car. I am, by no stretch of the imagination, a fast butt—but on this night, I really wanted to go upstairs to Kenneth's apartment. I hadn't felt that way in years, and I knew it was much more than an underactive libido screaming for attention. Kenneth was exciting—funny and engaging and, above all else, tender. Every time I convinced myself to let myself go—it took a lot of Jedi mind tricks, but I did it—he reciprocated with the sweetest of kisses, the softest of caresses. I didn't even like basketball, but I couldn't think of a place I would have rather been than Madison Square Garden with Kenneth Roman. And by the time we made it to the front of his apartment building, I had convinced myself that if he invited me up, I was going to happily accept the invitation.

"But he didn't invite me up," I told April dejectedly. "In fact, even though our lips were numb from all that kissing, he pulled away. So you see? I don't think he likes me."

I had twirled it around in my mind all the way home, but I couldn't figure out what went wrong that this grown man, with an obviously strong sexual passion, didn't take advantage of my advances and ask me up for a nightcap. Did I do something wrong? Did he not like me as much as I'd thought he did? Was he seeing someone and not willing to step out on her? Did my politics turn him off? "I don't get it. Everything seemed right."

"Wait. Let me get this straight: The only thing that stopped you guys from getting naked in the car was the stick shift, and he didn't invite you upstairs?"

"Nope," I said. "Didn't even seem to cross his mind."

"But he invited you out on another date, didn't he? That must count for something."

"I invited him out on the date. He accepted in front of my face, but what's to stop him from saying he has something better to do when I actually do call him? I don't even know if I'm going to bother."

"Hold up—you're telling me that you're not going to go out with the boy again because he didn't treat you like a whore and try to get you to screw him on the second date? Did it ever occur to you that he was being a gentleman?"

"Trust me—the way we were going at it in the car, neither of us can be accused of being polite. He doesn't like me. I think it might have been because of the argument we had on the subway."

"Argument?" April said, incredulous. "How in the hell did you get into an argument?"

I told April about the welfare conversation, and how upset Kenneth appeared to get when I suggested people on the government dole were taking advantage of the system. With each word, she frowned a little bit more. "I hate to say it, but maybe it was that mouth of yours," April said. "You know how you do."

"Well what was wrong with telling him my opinion?" I asked.

"He didn't ask for it, and he didn't agree with it," April said simply. "But you went on and on, and maybe that was a turn-off."

"I didn't go on and on," I said. "In fact, I was the one who cut the conversation short and told him to drop it because I didn't want to argue."

"Well bully for you," April said, throwing her hands in the air for emphasis. "You said something to him that might have been insulting—you don't know if he's ever been on welfare or knows someone who has, do you?—and then you cut the conversation short without letting him finish what he had to say. That's sexy."

"It wasn't that serious, April."

"Hey, I'm just trying to help you figure out what went wrong—if things did go wrong. Seems to me like you might be reading into things. I'm still thinking he was being a gentleman trying not to rush you into anything. Isn't that a possibility?"

I looked at April like she'd lost her mind. "What man do you know would turn down sex from a woman willing to come to his bed?"

"Not many, which brings me back to my original point: Maybe you just talk too much," she said. "Maybe you should stop being so full of your convictions and accept that not everybody thinks as conservatively as you."

"Maybe not, but I have a right to my opinions and any man who can't accept that I have my own mind and am not afraid to use it won't be getting any from me anytime soon."

And opinions I do have—especially about welfare.

Ricky Fish was on the run. I had two babies—neither of whom he was helping me take care of. See, he swore he couldn't have any contact with me, because if he did, I would get caught up in whatever drug mess he'd found himself in and pay for it by going to prison or having my children taken away from me or both for being associated with him. I was twenty-two years old. And my parents had disowned me. Or at least refused to give me any help. "You got yourself into this mess, you deal with it," my father had said on many an occasion when I'd brought James and Jasmine over to visit. "You're going to figure out for yourself how to get out of it—you and that, that boyfriend of yours." My mother would stand behind him, silent—in effect cosigning his decision to leave my ass swinging in the wind. Or, more specifically, a seedy, Section 8 apartment in Newark's South Ward.

I'd been placed there by a social worker that I had gone to see after Fish convinced me to get help from the government. Welfare. "I'll send you some money every now and then, but I'm out, baby. I can't stay here. A brother's on the run," Fish said, as he stuffed his clothes into an oversize leather duffel bag I'd given him for Christmas when we had first started dating. "I won't be able to send you much in the beginning, but when I get set up at my new place, I'll get something to you.

In the meantime, take this," he added, handing me a paper bag full of about $3,000 in small bills. "Tomorrow, take yourself down to the Department of Social Services and get on welfare and have them set you up in some public housing. That way, no one will suspect you and I are still together."

Ten minutes later, he climbed into his cherry red Toyota Celica and hauled ass.

I'll never forget how humiliated I was sitting on those cheap plastic chairs in that dirty, dank room, waiting for the social worker to count me among the children-laden women sitting there waiting for their turn to get what one woman called "some a dat free money."

"I mean, shit, I have all these babies and ain't nobody tryin' ta help me wit 'em, so the least they can do up in here is give me my little check, some a dat W.I.C., some stamps, something," she said to another woman sitting across from her as she cradled one baby and ordered another one—he wasn't any more than three years old—to "get up off my arm."

"I know that's right," her friend yelled out. "I'm a get me some a dat W.I.C. You can get free baby formula wit dat," she said.

I tried not to look at them—tried to make James and Jasmine sit still enough for the three of us to be invisible until the receptionist called our name, which seemed to take hours. Finally, just as Jasmine fell asleep and James was on his way, someone yelled, "Zaria Chance?" I stood up and, my kids in tow, walked over to a fiberglass door and followed the woman in to the social worker, who proceeded over the next forty minutes to ask me every intimate detail imaginable about my life and how I had ended up with two kids, no man, a lack of support from my family, and everything in between. The low was the emergency shelter, at which I was forced to stay for two weeks—even though Fish had given me money, I had to pretend I didn't have it in order to get the benefits—before they found me a one-bedroom Section 8 apartment in an eight-story building just off Petrie Street. When I moved in, I had two suitcases filled with what little bit of clothes I had for the three of us, a couple of bags of groceries I'd purchased with my food stamps, and a promise to myself that I was going to find some kind of way to get the hell out of that dive before it killed me.

I was there for seven months, and in that short amount of time, I had seen every way in which a person could take advantage of the welfare system, and had, by all accounts, figured out a few for myself. But I was using my side-hustles—I'd taken up baby-sitting and braiding hair to earn extra cash, while my mother would send Mikki over with a couple dollars every once in a while to help out—to get out of that madness. And madness it was.

There was Lah-Tischa, my next-door neighbor, who had people running in and out of her house at all hours of the day and night, playing cards, drinking, and smoking marijuana, all in front of her young son, Justin. Her baby's father would stop by to get cash and ass every other week or so; occasionally, there would be some real theater coming out of the apartment when baby daddy showed up unannounced while one of her other men was there. On one of said occasions, I heard him slapping her all the way across her living room; I'll never forget the screams—some from Justin, who witnessed the whippings, others from Lah-Tischa, whose face was connecting with various furnishings throughout her house as her man body slammed her here there and everywhere for "fucking around."

"Bitch, don't you know I'll kill you?" I'd heard him say one evening. Moments later, there was banging on my door; I didn't know if I should open it or call the police or what. "Zaria—it's me, Lah-Tischa. Open up—I need a favor."

I opened the door, but not without putting the safety lock on first. "What's wrong?"

"I need you to mind Justin for me for just a couple minutes, okay," she said, holding him up for me to see through the crack of the door. "Just a couple of minutes," she insisted.

That couple of minutes turned into two days; she'd gotten beaten so badly that she stayed overnight in the hospital, with a broken nose, a fractured cheek, and a sprained finger. She refused to press charges. "I should have offered to give him more money," she said through puffy lips when she came to retrieve Justin. "He found out about my sugar daddy, and I was holding out and all."

I did my best to stay out of her way as much as possible. I didn't want any of that.

To the right of my apartment was Ms. Elaine, a sixty-something great-grandmother who was caring for three generations of kids, including two of her own, who were well into their thirties. To hear Ms. Elaine tell it, she had no other choice but to take care of them all.

"That's just the way it is, chile," she'd tell me while I braided her seven-year-old granddaughter's hair. "That's family. You can't get rid of family, no matter how hard you try. Besides, these children here didn't ask to be born into this world—and if they mamas and daddies can't take care of them, then I guess ol' Nana will. Right, pumpkin?" she said, bending down to touch her granddaughter's face. She didn't answer back; she was a little slow.

Ms. Elaine died six months after I'd gotten there, and before I knew it, the same children who had left their children and their children's children in that apartment for her to take care of had overrun her home with all kinds of trifling shit—fighting over the Social Security checks, leaving those babies in there by themselves, sleeping in the filth that their parents refused to clean, sleeping in so late that their kids weren't making it to school. And those were just my neighbors.

The same stories played out all over that building: Women—some desperate, others just plain stupid—with children whose fathers didn't care for them, lying around, making absolutely no attempt whatsoever to change their situations, content with sitting around and letting their kids watch them get used and abused while they used and abused the system. They were, by all accounts, happy to collect their checks and their W.I.C. and their food stamps and their government-subsidized housing checks and spend it on nonsense and continue to wallow in the filth that was 346 Petrie Street—blaming everyone from the president to the white folks up the hill in South Orange for their troubles.

Well, I was the product of a family that lived up the hill in South Orange (I didn't tell any of my neighbors that), and I knew better than to continue to allow my children to live this way. So, with the $3,000 Fish left me before he skipped out on his kids, and another $2,324 I'd saved from my baby-sitting, hair braiding, and Mom cash, I got the hell out of there—found myself a slightly better apartment in the basement of a private home in East Orange, and a kind, little old church lady from St. James A.M.E., which I had started frequenting when I felt like I had no one else to turn to, to watch my children while I worked as a secretary at Seton Hall University. And because I worked there, I got to take a few classes at discount prices, which allowed me to score my job at Lawrence as a financial officer about two years later.

The bottom line is I got off welfare because I knew it was destructive for me and for my family—because I didn't want to be associated anymore with the women who used it to keep themselves in the same degradation that continued to recycle itself from generation to generation. Yes, some of the women really needed it, but a lot of them wouldn't if they bothered to change their situations.

But they didn't.

And I had no sympathy for them. None.

I hadn't actually thought about Kenneth's background, or how he might respond to what I'd said. Perhaps he had a few students who were on the dole, or maybe he was even on the dole at some point—although I never had imagined that one. But hey—if I was on it, anybody could be.

"You know, the more I think about it, the more I think that maybe you're just reading a little too much into what happened tonight," April said, interrupting my thoughts. I looked at her. I was officially high off of cheap wine and old memories, and it took me a minute to focus in on what she was talking about. "He did offer to go out with you again. I think that he was being more of a man than most and decided not to push his luck and ruin a good thing by inviting your prim and proper behind up to his place."

"Or maybe he just doesn't like me."

I was hoping that I was wrong. Maybe she was right.

I certainly was hoping so.

He

I wasn't seeking James's approval, but I did think it was important for my relationship with his mother to get his blessing. That turned out to be a big mistake. Seventh graders are starting to discover the world of sexuality and all its implications—one of the reasons I was the rare teacher who actually liked teaching the grade. To James, my admission to him probably was a declaration that I was screwing his mother. No kid wants to think about his mother doin' it with the teacher. And you especially don't want your classmates to grab hold of that information. All of this was especially unfortunate because Zaria and I still hadn't even had sex. (More on that later.)

I made my move after fifth-period social studies, when James was about to head for the lunch room. I had been thinking about it for days, so I was eager to get it over with. I hadn't told his mother we were going to have this conversation, which I knew could possibly be problematic, but I wanted to be the one to set the parameters of my relationship with James. I wanted the definitions and descriptions to come from me. And besides, I had started to think of how I could be a positive presence in the boy's life, and I was eager to get that particular ball rolling by letting him know we were going to be seeing a lot more of each other.

"What is it, Mr. Roman?" James said, looking slightly fearful as he approached my desk. At that moment, I realized lines of authority were about to get very hazy and difficult. I would want us to be friends outside of class—but I'd still want a little of that fear inside the class. Was it possible to have both at once?

"I just wanted to talk to you a minute, James. It's not about the class. It's a little personal." I saw the frown on James's face. He had no idea what was coming. I almost felt a little bad for him—his school life was about to get a lot more complicated. He stood in front of my desk, waiting. I sensed that I needed to come from behind the desk, to lessen the teacherly authority that loomed between us. I got up and walked around to his side, then sat in one of the student seats. I motioned for him to join me. The furrow in his brow deepened. Now we sat facing each other. I put on a welcoming smile, hoping James would do the same. But he just stared—and frowned.

"I don't know whether you noticed by now, but your mother and I have been dating. We like each other very much and I expect us to continue seeing each other as much as possible."

His expression didn't change. He didn't flinch, he didn't fidget, he didn't startle. He just stared. He probably had no idea what to do, what to say. I had to keep reminding myself I was talking to a child, not a grown man. An adolescent child, at that. Expressing their feelings was not exactly their greatest strength.

"Are you going to get married?" he said finally. I should have figured that's where he would take it. But I didn't figure that and the question caught me off-guard. I hoped I didn't start.

"Uh, well, I don't know, James. It's hard to say something like that this soon. We're just really getting to know each other. We enjoy each other's company very much. I don't know exactly where it'll lead." I knew that was too vague, but I couldn't bring myself to be more definitive, particularly about the M-word. I had spent most of the past decade dodging that word. I'd be damned if I was going to get cornered so easily by a seventh grader. I started to feel a gnawing dread about where this was heading—and how his mother would respond when she found out about it. Maybe this wasn't such a good idea after all.

"But it could lead to marriage?" he asked. I tried to read his expression and his tone of voice. Did he consider this a good thing or a bad thing? It was hard to say.

"Uh, well, I can't really tell that right now, James. There are so many things involved. We would be talking way down the road if something like that were to happen."

"So you're saying you might get married, even if it's way down the road?" His eyes narrowed a bit, which I didn't like. He was cutting off my escape routes, skillfully boxing me into the corner and tagging me in the ribs with body shots.

I nodded hesitantly. Why had I started this conversation in the first place? I guessed I was asking for this, to be worked over by a twelve-year-old.

"Yeah, *waaaay* down the road," I said, waving toward the horizon to demonstrate the notion of a long timeline. As I moved my hand, I could feel the sweat gathering in my armpits. Had I somehow just committed myself to a long-term relationship? How bound would I be by statements made to a twelve-year-old? I knew right then what my next task was—limit the information that would be conveyed to his mother.

James nodded as he watched the wave of my hand. Apparently he had gotten the information he needed. I still couldn't tell whether he thought this was a good thing or a bad thing. I wanted to ask a follow-up, to get his true feelings on the subject, but now I was a little paralyzed about where to go next. Clearly I should be frightened now. He had already gotten me to tell him that I might one day marry his mother. I didn't even want to imagine how that would get interpreted in his mind and regurgitated to his mother and his little sister. The danger of asking his true feelings was that he might tell me and I might not like them. What if he said he hated me and he hated the idea of me and his mother together? Where does one go from there? Kinda hard to pick yourself up off the canvas without losing a little bit of your pride and dignity. And what damage might I be doing to our relationship if I tried to make this all seem like our little secret—in other words, you better not leak a word of this to your mother, kid. How likely was that—sit a seventh grader down, tell him his teacher is now dating his mother, and not expect him to whisper a word to mom?

So I let it go. Paralyzed by indecision, I made the worst decision of all. No follow-up question, no small talk, nothing else. I told James we would talk some more, but I didn't think either one of us was especially looking forward to that. This hadn't turned out at all like I wanted.

*   *   *

When I returned home after basketball practice—with Tariq in tow—and made it to my bedroom without encountering his mother, I wasn't at all surprised to see my answering machine blinking. I'd had a hard time concentrating for the rest of the school day and at the practice because I dreaded the blinking answering machine. It became clearer to me throughout the day how big an error I had made in talking to James. Major miscalculation. So now I was going to have to pay. I just hoped the damage wasn't irreparable.

I took a deep breath and pressed the button to play my three messages. The first one was a bill collector. Damn. I had the hardest time staying on top of mundane matters like credit card bills. Didn't they know I was a busy man? The second message came on.

"Kenneth? This is Zaria. You know, James's mother." I flinched. Her voice was almost trembling. I could feel the anger—not even the sarcasm could disguise it.

"I just have one question: What the hell did you tell my son? How dare you talk to the boy about us? I can't believe you would have such disrespect for me as a parent. What nerve! Can you please call me?"

The machine unkindly picked up the sound of her slamming the phone down. Apparently she must have missed the base because there was loud fumbling, then I heard her mutter a few curse words before the message ended. I didn't even hear the third message, I was so shaken by Zaria's outrage. It was everything I was expecting and much worse. I replayed it in my mind, her claim that I had disrespected her as a parent. Of course that possibility had never even entered my mind. I hadn't been thinking about her at all.

The heft of that thought made me sit down on the edge of my bed. I really *hadn't* been thinking about her at all. It was all about me and my relationship with James. I ran my hands over my face. My head throbbed, my eyes started to sting, my stomach convulsed. If nothing else, this real physical pain told me that my feelings for this woman were special and already much more intense than I wanted to admit. I hugged myself tightly and fell over onto the bed. What I wanted to do was pull the sheets over my head and disappear into my hurt. That's what I used to do when I was a child—hide under the covers and try to wait out those sickening feelings that would overcome me, particularly when I had been nicked by some insult to my fatherlessness, real or imagined. But I had no such luxuries now. I was a grown man with a problem that I needed to confront before it killed this growing "thing" between me and Zaria. A phone call wasn't even good enough—I needed to talk to her in person, to apologize for my insensitivity, to plead for her forgiveness. That never worked as well over the phone. I'd drive to her house and call her on my celly to ask her to come out and talk to me in the car. I would be so full of sorrow and contrition that I'd melt away her anger. At least that was the plan.

I burst from my bedroom, eager to put my plan into action. I almost slammed into Ronnie, who was emerging from the other bedroom. She wore a tight-fitting knit dress that didn't miss any of her curves. Not for the first time, I wondered where she kept these outfits I kept seeing.

"Wow, very pretty dress," I said, hoping to distract her with the compliment.

She beamed and glanced downward. "Thank you!" I breezed past her, noticing Tariq sprawled out in the other bedroom, wearing headphones. Did the boy ever do homework?

"Are you leaving?" she asked, rushing behind me. She was going to ask me for a ride, I had no doubt. Ronnie was amazingly unshy when it came to asking for help—which explains how she could live in my apartment rent free for more than three weeks with no shame.

"Yes," I said. When talking to her, I tried mightily to keep all hints of annoyance out of my voice. Though I desperately wanted her to be gone, I didn't want to chase her away—because she would be taking her son with her. I had come to realize that, despite the stresses of having too many people crammed into my apartment, I had been freed of the anxiety Tariq caused me with regularity when he was living in the projects. I liked being able to keep an eye on him. I think he liked it, too, though he probably wouldn't ever tell me that.

"Can you drop me off at, uh, a friend's house?" she asked, moving closer as I slowed down. I could smell her perfume, which was suffocatingly heavy. Again I thought of strippers, eau de hootch. She came even closer; I got a whiff of the coffee on her breath. Was she drinking up all my coffee now? I wanted to take a step back—damn, why was she always up in my space? She had pretty much given up on seducing me, beaten down by so many failures. (In fact, I hated to admit this, but I was somewhat proud of myself for showing such unbending willpower. I'm not saying that I didn't enjoy the occasional little peep shows she still offered in her tight, braless T-shirts—once she had even left the door open as she stepped from the shower, feigning surprise when I walked by and caught the glimpse of her wet, shiny breasts and aureolas as big and dark as Oreo cookies—but that's where it had begun and ended.) But she still insisted on crowding my space whenever possible. It had long since ceased to be flattering—now she just annoyed me to death.

"Ronnie, I'm really in a hurry," I said. I had never turned her down before, but for each of the last couple of requests I had pledged to do so the next time she asked. On this night, she had caught me feeling particularly rushed and agitated. I saw her eyes widen in surprise. She clearly wasn't expecting rejection.

"Please, Kenneth? I don't have any money for a cab." Oh, the poverty appeal was nothing new. But instead of creating sympathy, it just pissed me off more because it reminded me of her laziness. She was out of a job and a home, yet all she did every day was watch my television, as far as I could tell. The nighttime was when she seemed to come alive—her social life was amazingly active for someone who was so consistently broke.

"I'm sorry, Ronnie, but I have something to do right now." I didn't even look back at her. I pulled open my front door and let it slam behind me. Ronnie might not like it, but so what? What duty did I have to serve as this woman's cab service, in addition to providing food and shelter to her and her child? She was probably in there cursing me under her breath, but I was determined not to care.

The ride to Teaneck seemed to take forever. I rehearsed my lines all the way there—not wanting to feel like I was memorizing them because that would create more stress, but also not wanting to sound like an idiot when confronted with her hostility. I drove through the darkened streets of the suburban town, trying to remember which one was her house. Damn, so many of them looked alike. And you couldn't hardly see any house addresses. When I pulled up in front of her house, I decided not to go into the driveway. No need to alarm the woman before I announced my presence. I pulled out my celly and nervously dialed her number. As the phone rang, I looked through the curtains upstairs for a sign of movement but saw nothing. She answered the phone on the second ring, as if she had been waiting. I said a prayer under my breath that this was a good idea.

She

I don't know what made me more angry—that Kenneth had told James about us, or that I'd been taken totally by surprise by my son's reaction to the news that his teacher and his mom were dating. It didn't matter; Kenneth was going to get my size eight in his behind, or at least the verbal version of it.

Thing was, he wasn't home when I called, so I was forced to let his answering machine have it, which wasn't at all gratifying because (a) there was only so much you could do in attack mode when your target was telephone silence and (b) after I hung up, I still wasn't sure what to say to James, who was in his room somewhere, sulking like a hulking two-year-old who'd just had his lollipop taken away. Not that he was trying to hear what I had to say anyway. He'd made that clear as a bell when I finally got him to tell me what his problem was.

I had just started cooking dinner when he came stomping into the house, which should have been my first clue because the child never came through the door any earlier than 6 P.M., and sometimes I had to call over to April's house to get him to make it home by then. His school routine had long been set: The bus would drop him off just down the road by about 3:10, he and JJ would walk together to either the pizzeria or Carvel for their afternoon snack, and by 4 P.M., they'd be knee-deep in PlayStation until either April kicked them out or I demanded James come home, eat supper, and do his homework. Today,

I hadn't even seasoned my pork chops when he walked into the kitchen, opened the refrigerator, grabbed a soda, closed the door, and leaned against it, sipping his drink and glaring at me like a hungry prizefighter waiting for the bell.

"Well hello to you, too," I said as I dropped the first chop into the hot pan of grease. "You're home early. What happened? April forget to pay the electricity bill and you guys couldn't turn on the TV?"

No answer. Just that glare.

I swear, sometimes I wonder if I should give him a shot of Midol and buy him a few tampons. Everyone told me that boys were easy when they got older and that Jazzy was the one who would PMS from the time her breasts started growing—but James was on the rag more than I ever imagined my happy-go-lucky Jazzy would ever be. But I didn't feel like entertaining his little mood today; I had had too good a morning and afternoon to let him ruin my evening. So I'd decided just for kicks to talk to him like he actually gave a damn about how my day went, seeing as the cat had his tongue. "My day was great: None of the students tried to get over on me with crazy stories about why they hadn't paid their tuition, and the crazy secretary didn't say anything to me, which is always a blessing."

Still nothing.

"And then, I had a terrific salad with all the trimmings—cubed ham, boiled egg, croutons, the works. And I ate every bit of it, and felt like a champion for getting all my veggies in," I continued. "Of course, I'm about to ruin it with these fried pork chops, but some healthy eating is better than no healthy eating, isn't it?"

Just as I was about to tell him about my trafficless commute home, James put his soda down and spoke up—but I wasn't exactly ready to hear what he had to say.

"Mr. Roman gives me a hard enough time as it is. Do you think sleeping with him is going to make me come home with an A in social studies?"

Oh my God. Did he just say what I think he said? How did he know Kenneth and I were together? My mind began to race: Did James hear me talking to Kenneth on the phone? Did he listen to the answering machine and hear Kenneth asking me out? Did April open her big mouth in front of her kids, accidentally passing the info on to mine? Did Mikki say something? My bigmouthed mom? She was arguing that I should tell them about my budding romance; would she be so bold as to tell them, even though I had forbidden her to? That must be it. My mother had told them. Everybody else knew better, and only my mother would take it upon herself to directly violate my wishes that my love life be kept secret until I was ready to reveal it to my children. She was going to get cursed out—mother or no mother.

But first, I had to clean this mess up. I wasn't exactly sure how to approach the whole conversation, but I knew that the one thing I had to do was avoid overreacting. Clearly, from the tone in his voice, my child thought he'd climbed into the driver's seat and was steering this conversation, but I couldn't have that—not when it came to my private, romantic affairs. Besides, he was still a baby in my eyes, and although he was trying his best to seem like he knew what was up, I wasn't about to let him know I wasn't in total control.

Of course, it didn't help that I had dropped my pork chop on the floor when the boy suggested that I was having sex with his teacher.

"First of all, what Mr. Roman and I are doing has absolutely nothing to do with you or your grades," I said rather sternly as I picked up the chop and ran it under water.

"Really?" he said quickly. I could tell that even though he was in the middle of what was probably the biggest, most grown-up conversation he ever had with his mother—using language he thought made him sound older than his twelve years—he was still trying to soup himself up to keep the conversation going. "Well, the last time you met with Mr. Roman, you got him in trouble with the principal, and I got my butt kicked because of it. What do you think the guys at school are going to do when they find out my mom is sleeping with Coach?"

"And just who told you that I was sleeping with Mr. Roman?" I said, turning around to face him directly. I can't believe he's concerning himself with my bed partner and standing here in my kitchen, in my house, questioning me.

"Well, are you?" he said, squaring off his shoulders—I guess to appear more brave.

"First of all, little boy, it's none of your damn business who I'm dating. I'm the mother and you're the child, and I will not have you standing in the middle of my kitchen asking me about grown-up affairs. Understand?"

My tone made him back down a bit, but I could still tell from his face that he was looking for answers—answers I surely wasn't ready to give. So I flipped it and started asking my own questions. "And just where did you get this tidbit of information from anyway?"

Silence.

"I said, who told you I was dating Mr. Roman."

More silence.

"Well, you had an awful lot to say a few minutes ago. What's the problem, you don't have anything to say now? Come on, don't clam up now that I'm asking the questions."

"Mr. Roman told me," he said quietly. "After class today." And with that, he turned on his heels and headed upstairs to his room, without saying another word.

I don't think he'd made it to the top step before I was headed for the phone. My mind was a blur; all I knew was that I needed to get Kenneth Roman on the phone. Now.

All I got was his answering machine. So I left a few choice words for him, went back into the kitchen, smothered my pork chops in gravy, and headed upstairs for my talk with James—one that I hadn't planned on having with him until the ring was on my finger. Frankly, I hadn't a clue what to say, but I had to figure it out. Quick.

He had his notebooks and textbooks spread about his bed, but James wasn't doing homework when I walked into his room. He was, instead, lying across his bedspread, his back to the door, his face toward the wall. I thought I heard sniffling when I walked in, but when he turned around and, with all the venom he could muster, said, "Get out!" he didn't have any tears in his eyes or on his cheeks. Just a fiery, angry look—the same that I would get when I was ready to light someone up. James may have had his daddy's small stature, but he had his mother's bravado—and looked just like a boy version of me when I was his age.

"Excuse you?" I said, twisting my neck for emphasis. "I'm sorry, did you pay the mortgage this month that you can tell me to get out of your room?"

"I thought you were Jasmine," he said simply, turning his body back toward the wall.

"Okay, but now you know it's me, so you can turn around now, and pay attention to what I have to say." Mind you, I still didn't know what I was going to say. But I kept talking anyway as he flipped over and cast his eyes to the floor.

"Look at me, James," I said. He looked up, but not necessarily at me. It was more like through me. I knew right then that I had to tell the boy the truth; he obviously knew what was up, and the only way I was going to get through to him was to come clean, hard, and correct. I walked over to his bed, and, while shuffling his homework into a neat pile, sat down next to him. I reached out to touch his arm, but he flinched and pulled away. I put my hand on my lap, smoothed out my skirt, and began to pick imaginary lint off of it. Where should I begin?

"Mr. Roman and I were seeing each other, but it was nothing serious," I said. "He and I went out on a couple of dates. I'm not sure what he told you, but that's as far as it went."

"He said you two were going to get married."

Okay. The boy might as well have just slapped me in the mouth. Hard. Married? Where did that come from? Kenneth Roman wanted me to marry him? And he told my kid before he told me? What in the world? "He told you we were going to get married?" I asked, all at once perplexed and giddy. I frowned and raised an eyebrow. "When did he tell you that? What exactly did he say?"

"Today," he clipped.

I waited for him to continue, but he didn't. More prodding was needed. "What exactly did he say, James?"

"He said that you were his girlfriend."

"And?"

"I asked him if you two were going to get married and he said, 'Yes.'"

More silence. "And?"

"That was it," James said, now annoyed.

I rubbed my eyes and let my forehead rest in my palm. Kenneth had messed up big-time. "Look, sweetheart, I'm going to be honest with you—okay?" I started. I paused to collect my words, knowing they had to be good and right for me to pull my son out of this funk and ease his fears. "I don't even know that Mr. Roman and I are going to continue seeing each other, but I'm sure that whatever happens, you're not going to be affected by it. The only reason you know about it is because he told you, but what's been going on between the two of us is so insignificant that I can't imagine anyone outside of this family knows that we're seeing each other. What I'm saying is that you don't have to worry about catching flak at school from the other boys."

He still didn't say anything, and his eyes were still downcast. So I continued to talk, hoping that my words were getting through to him. "I'm sorry you had to find out about it this way," I continued. "I certainly didn't want that for you."

"Why'd *he* have to tell me?" he asked, finally looking me in the eye. "Why couldn't you?"

"I didn't have anything to tell you, and he had no right to say anything to you about it because it wasn't his place," I said. "All I can hope is that you'll trust me when I tell you that everything is going to be all right, and that you don't have to worry about Mr. Roman or anyone else giving you a hard time over what your mother may or may not be doing, okay?"

James nodded. I got up and started making my way to the door.

"Mom?" he called after me. "I think it's cool that you went out with Mr. Roman."

I didn't say anything—couldn't bring myself to. Because truth of the matter was that as far as I was concerned, Mr. Roman and I were through. "Do your homework," I said. "Dinner will be ready in a few."

Days after Mikki's designs were featured in a few of the popular black magazines, all kinds of companies started calling her, offering her free samples of makeup, bath products, even sex toys to store in her shop in hopes that she would recommend the items to her clients. She kept it all in what she called her beauty closet, and was more prone to using it herself than telling any of the women who came to her for their dream dresses. So I had no problem raiding the closet for my own purposes; some of the products were really quite good, particularly the ones that were intended for the bath. There was this one that I'd lifted that was a huge vat of crystal beads that smelled like a glorious mixture of lemon and grapefruit. The directions said to pour two capfuls of the beads into a tub of boiling hot water, let them melt, then "soak in the luxurious citrus essence as all your troubles float away."

Yeah, right.

It smelled good as hell, but my troubles weren't going anywhere until I gave Kenneth Roman a piece of my mind. It was close to 11

P.M., and he still hadn't returned my phone call. Punk, chicken ass. I supposed that from my message he knew that I was pretty angry, and since he'd experienced the wrath of Zaria Chance once, I'm sure he was trying to avoid my madness this time around. But that was still no excuse to avoid me or my phone call; surely he knew he'd messed up.

I'd decided that if he didn't call me by the time I got out of the bathtub, dried off, and lotioned up, that I was going to tell his answering machine off again. Or perhaps meet him at the school and give him a piece of my mind in the parking lot. Nah, the parking lot would be a little too dramatic, wouldn't it? Then everyone would be in our business, and I wasn't trying to go there with all those nosy mothers dropping their kids off and trolling for some hot gossip. Perhaps I'd call him when I woke up in the morning. Surely, he'd be home then.

Just then, the phone rang. I answered it before it rang a second time—it was sitting next to the tub.

"Zaria."

It was Kenneth. I didn't give him a chance to say anything else besides my name. "Just who the hell do you think you are, telling James about us? Are you out of your mind? Of all the disrespectful, lowdown things you could do, you run off and tell my child about our personal business, without consulting me? Let me tell you something, Mr. Roman, that's my child. You teach him social studies for forty-five minutes during the day, but he is my son twenty-four hours a day, and I decide what he should and should not know and when he should know it. You had absolutely no right . . ."

"Zaria," Kenneth interrupted. "I'm outside. Can you come out?"

"What?" I said. "Outside where?"

"In your driveway. I need to talk to you. Can you please come outside?"

"What the hell are you doing in my driveway?"

"I wanted to talk to you about this face-to-face," he said.

"It's a fine time for you to decide you need to talk to me about it at all, but it's a little late for that, isn't it?" I asked, struggling to get out of the tub and wrap a towel around my body. Was this man really in my driveway?

"I don't think it's too late," Kenneth said. "I really want to apologize for what I've done; it was totally out of line and I need to see you to make it right."

I flew down the stairs and peeked out the window. Sure enough, the SUV was parked at the curb out front. I tried not to let him see me, but our eyes locked when he spotted me looking at him from behind the curtain. "Zaria, please baby. Just come outside. Just for a minute. Let me explain."

"Fine," I said, and hung up. If he wanted to get cursed out in person, there was no better time than the present. I was in a pair of sweatpants and a sweatshirt in no time; I was headed out my bedroom door and halfway down the stairs when I remembered that I hadn't bothered to do anything with my hair, and that I didn't have any makeup on. For a second, I debated whether I should just go on out to the car. I mean, what did it matter what I looked like? What had happened between us was no more, so there was no need to get cute to give him the boot. Seconds later, I changed my mind. I wanted to look good so that he could see what he was going to be missing. I didn't do much; just pulled my hair into a messy bun and put on a little mascara and lip gloss. I didn't want him to think I was trying too hard. "There," I said, giving myself a final once-over in the mirror. I peeked in both James's and Jazzy's rooms; sound asleep, both of them. Then I tiptoed down the stairs and out the front door.

The radio was on when I climbed into the car—Teddy Pendergast was pleading to some woman in his song, "Turn off the lights." I slammed the door, then reached over to turn the volume down. I wasn't in the mood for romantic music. Someone was about to get told. I opened my mouth to let the tongue-lashing begin, but Kenneth put his finger on my mouth and quietly asked me not to speak. Don't think so.

"What? You don't want me to say anything? I think you've done enough talking, if you ask me. What nerve do you have to tell my son anything about my personal business without consulting me first . . ."

"Zaria, baby, please . . ."

"No, don't, 'Baby, please' me, goddammit," I said, feeling my head get hot. "I'm not one of those chicken-headed mothers at the school who needs a man to rein in her son. I thought we'd already discussed this, but obviously you didn't hear me then. So let me say it loud and clear right now: I don't need you. And now, I don't want you. So you can leave me and my son alone."

There. Take that.

Kenneth looked at me, and, without responding to what I'd just said, started talking: "It was in the middle of class that I got this brilliant idea to tell James about us. I was looking into his face and seeing yours, and all of a sudden I was overwhelmed with these feelings and I needed to tell him that I had big plans for his mother—and for him. You'd asked me before to help you with him, and I want to do that—not just because he's my student, but because I really, really, really like his mother. I'm going to be in his life because I'm in yours, and I needed him to know that.

"Thing is, I was only thinking about myself—being selfish, I guess. Because you're absolutely right: It wasn't my place to tell him anything, certainly not without your permission. But I'm bullheaded like that sometimes, Zaria; I'll get it in my mind to do something and without thinking about the repercussions, I'll do it. It's worked for me in the class and on the court, but I suspect that it has no place in my relationships—at least not in the one I have with you. And for that, I sincerely apologize.

"The truth is that I haven't felt this way about a woman in a long time, and I'd hate to think that I ruined the best thing I've got going because of my insensitivity and stupidity."

Well damn. So dumbfounded was I by what he said that I, Zaria Chance, had no words. And that's rare. Particularly when I'm mad. Thing is, I wasn't mad anymore—just overwhelmed. Here was a man who had screwed up royally, admitting that he was wrong. Surely this was a first. It was for me at least. In all the relationships that I'd had, no matter how egregious their errors, the men would never, ever admit to being wrong. Somehow, they'd simply turn it back around on me. I was too domineering. I was too loud. I didn't let go enough. I was too judgmental. I was too something of everything. They, of course, were perfect. And never wrong. Ever.

But what I was hearing here was contrition, an admission—one that deserved my attention, an apology that deserved my consideration. He had sounded sincere—he really wanted to be a part of my life and my son's life—and I found it extremely seductive.

I didn't say anything. I simply reached over and gently kissed his lips. And he kissed me back. And we went on like that for several minutes before I realized we were sitting in the front of my house, sucking face like two teenagers who didn't have a basement to escape to. I didn't want to, but I pulled back and looked around the car to see if anyone was watching. April's lights were off, and I didn't see anyone peeking out of the kids' windows. Then I turned to Kenneth and invited him to the backseat. "Not that we're going to do anything in it that we weren't doing in the front seat, so don't get excited." I laughed. "But the windows are tinted back there, and I'd rather the neighbors not see me getting busy with my boyfriend in the driveway."

"Hey—backseat!" he said. He hopped out his side, ran around the car, and opened my door to help me out and back in through the rear door. He closed the door gently and then moved across the seat right next to me. Shalamar's song, "Somewhere There's a Love Just for Me," was on the radio. He was here, parked in his car, in front of my house.

He

When I sat up in the bed, my first thought was of Zaria. From what she had told me about her morning schedule, she was already deep into it. I considered calling her, just to hear her sexy voice, just to tell her I was thinking about her. As her face danced before my eyes, I felt a warmth spread all over me. I was afraid I had lost her last night after the screwup with James, but that night turned out to be one of the most exciting of my life.

"Hurry up, Tariq!" That was Ronnie, yelling to her son just barely past the crack of dawn. And this after rolling back to the apartment at 4:30 A.M.—and waking up both me and Tariq with her banging on the door. (She had forgotten her key.) No matter how hard she tried, her lack of home training kept showing up like a bad penny. I didn't need my woman to have the manners of Queen Elizabeth exactly, but just a touch of class would be nice. Ronnie cemented for me the wisdom in staying away from ghetto queens. The outside of the package might be enticing for a night, but you'd soon find yourself trapped in Pookie hell—or maybe I should say Boo hell.

I got out of the bed and still felt a tingle from the night before. Who could have imagined that I would have driven to Teaneck fearful that I had lost perhaps the woman of my dreams, and we'd wind up so overcome by passion that we would almost consummate our union right there in my backseat? Damn, when was the last time I had made out like that in the backseat of a car? I couldn't even remember. It was gloriously exciting—her lips and her skin and her smell were all as perfect as I'd imagined. I was a firm believer in the power of pheromones—it was apparent to me that some people were predestined by chemistry and biology to be attracted to each other. I had dated women who were physically attractive to me, but the taste and the touch and the smell were just all wrong. But Zaria was tastier than the most exquisite gourmet meal I had ever been served, her scent more intoxicating to me than the most expensive fragrance you could purchase. A few times when we were kissing and softly stroking each other I had buried my face into her neck just to take in strong whiffs that I would be able to bring home with me. She smelled fruity, like lemons.

"I gotta go back inside, Kenneth. My kids might wake up and won't be able to find me," she had said finally. I knew she'd be wanting to make her exit soon—in fact, I was surprised by how long she had stayed out in the car with me. We kissed a few more times before saying our good-byes. I think we both knew the backseat had been important, the scaling of a major hurdle in the relationship. No, we hadn't had sex, but we had set the groundwork for sex. The question now wasn't whether we would sleep together—the question was when.

Just when I thought I understood adolescents, they flipped the script on me and did something that had me scratching my head. After weeks of being a model student, James Chance started acting up again, talking in the back of the class, trying to make jokes like he was suddenly the class clown, and showing no fear when I tried to call him on it. The first few times it happened I tried to ignore him, but when it threatened to undermine my authority in the class I had to confront him.

"James, are you paying attention back there?" I asked. I knew the answer was "No"—I had seen him passing a note to Todd Sullivan, his former partner in mischief. The two of them had stopped their clowning of late—Todd's father had straightened him out quick after the last fateful parent-teacher conference—but they were now causing a distraction.

James looked up at me with a smirk on his face, an expression I hadn't seen from him before. I was taken aback, but I couldn't let it show. This was something new, no doubt related to me and his mother. Apparently something had changed in James's eyes and it hadn't taken him long at all to exploit it. Middle schoolers were in a constant search for weaknesses they could exploit—which is why we always had a harder time finding substitutes than the other schools in the district.

Slowly, James drew his hand back to his own desk. He eyed me warily, as if he were daring me to reprimand him. After what we had already been through, I was stunned that he would so quickly revert to knucklehead tendencies. But this was more than your run-of-the-mill obstinance—this had far deeper implications. I decided to let it go for now. No need drawing him into a battle of wills—there was no way I could really win because now I wanted the kid to *like* me. Before I was seeking respect, now I wanted respect *and* affection. It was an especially tough task for me because it grated against the most fundamental of my teaching philosophies: The teacher isn't a friend. That friendship stuff might work if you're teaching high school seniors or grad students, but seventh graders? Oh, hell no.

I went back to my lesson, but even when I wasn't watching James he stayed on my mind, distracting me with the memory of that smirk. I wondered whether I should try to talk to him again after the class, but that already was starting to feel overused. But what other recourse did I have at this point? When did James and I have an opportunity to interact outside of my classroom? I would have to wait until his mother decided to invite me into the family homestead.

To take my mind off James, I dove into the lesson with special gusto. It was one of my most favorite units to teach: the relationship between professional sports and social class. It was gratifying to watch the light bulbs come on in their heads when they started to think about professional sports like sociologists, examining how the dominance of ethnic groups in various sports was closely related to that group's place in the social pecking order in America. None of them even knew that boxing used to be ruled by Irish and Italians, or had thought about why so many Latinos were controlling major league baseball the way blacks ran basketball. It was the best of times for a teacher when you could reach into the mind of each of your students and put down an indelible stamp, making each look at the world a little differently.

I had a question that I knew James would be able to handle with ease, so I tossed it to him as a peace offering, hoping that he would oblige.

"James," I said, without looking in his direction. It was my teaching version of the no-look pass, used to catch a student daydreaming. But it was always done playfully; not intended to menace or challenge them. He looked up with wide eyes, a bit startled.

"James, tell the class who was responsible for opening up major league baseball to African-American players."

For a second, I was fearful that he wouldn't know the answer, thus embarrassing me and himself. It was one of those no-brainers for any black person old enough to know when Black History Month was. Most of the white kids in the class probably knew the answer, too. But James quickly eased my fears.

"You mean the player who was responsible? That would be Jackie Robinson. Or do you mean the guy who hired him? I think his name was Branch Rickey."

I nodded. "Yes, you're right on both counts, James. I meant Jackie Robinson, but thank you for bringing Branch Rickey into the conversation, because he showed bravery by hiring Robinson. Who knows what team we're talking about?"

A couple of the white males in the class raised their hands. James answered the question before I could call on one of them.

"The Dodgers. The Brooklyn Dodgers," he said.

I gave him a smile. I think he smiled back, but he ducked his head down before I could tell. Okay, that's much better, I thought. Maybe this juggling act wasn't going to be so hard after all, being a teacher and a father figure at the same time. I could do it—after all, who knew twelve-year-olds better than me? I glanced over at James again. He really did look a lot like his mother. As I thought about Zaria, my stomach did a quick turn. The excitement of a new relationship was delicious, the ease with which a new love could steal away your breath. However hard this tussle with James would prove to be, I was sure it was worth it.

Later that day in the teachers' lounge, as I grabbed a cup of coffee before making my usual hasty exit, I heard a familiar voice behind me.

"What's this I hear about you and one of the mommies?" It was Jerry Slavin, one of the male teachers in the school. He also happened to be my best friend in the building.

"And where are you getting this news from?" I said, turning with a smirk.

He waved his hands, gesturing all around him like a woman testifying in church. "Oh, it's in the air, Roman. Don't you hear it? Can't you feel it? I believe they call it the grapevine."

Slavin was a math teacher, but he enjoyed utilizing his colorful language in casual conversation. He was a funny guy; he could wield his dry wit like a stiletto. Though he was losing his hair, the teachers in the building still found him very attractive, primarily because of his sunny personality and wicked sense of humor. I had heard more than a few whispering about how cute he was. He was currently dating a sixth-grade English teacher whom he had been seeing since the start of the previous semester. We talked frequently about women, dating, and sex. Slavin was a divorcé with an eight-year-old son. Sometimes we talked about kids, too.

"I bet somewhere, somehow, Evelyn Richie had something to do with it," I said.

Slavin cocked his head to the side. A few other teachers had entered the room, so he took a step closer and lowered his voice. "Evelyn Richie spreading scurrilous gossip about another teacher? Nah, I don't believe that for a second. She'd never do that." He was kidding, of course. I was tempted to tell Slavin about the racist crack Richie had made about the mommy I'm dating, but I decided to keep it to myself. Sometimes it was too frustrating trying to recount a racist incident to a white person—they'd have a problem seeing the motivation behind the offense or they'd try to make excuses for the offender's actions, try to justify it, as if to say that there was a perfectly reasonable explanation that I had missed because of my blackness, my quickness to judge. I hated that.

"Seriously, are you dating the mother of one of the kids?" he asked, peering into my face a little too closely.

I looked around. A white, female teacher was nearby, a fifty-something, eighth-grade teacher whose name I couldn't remember, trying to pretend it took five minutes to pour milk into her coffee. I nodded to Slavin. "Yeah, it's true. She's a beautiful, wonderful woman. I fear I'm crazy about her."

Grinning, Slavin reached out and slapped me on the back. It was a gesture that I understood but didn't really appreciate. It was too locker roomish, too juvenile, like we were goofy ninth graders and I had just told him I had gotten head from a cheerleader.

"That's great, Roman. Take it from me, there's nothing better than sex with a single mom. They're so grateful and so desperate for the dipstick, they'll suck your damn toes if you ask them." He grinned at me again, but when he saw the look of horror on my face, the grin disappeared in an instant. He realized he had gone too far—always the clearest indication of when a guy was serious about his lady, the haste at which he took offense. Rather than apologize, Slavin decided to flee.

"All right, I gotta run, Roman. Talk to you later."

I watched him scurry from the room. It was almost funny. I wasn't going to hold the too-familiar crack against him. We had often said similarly offensive things to each other about women we had dated before, but the difference was this time it felt like more than dating. But Slavin couldn't have known that. Well, now he does.

As we headed toward Christmas, my life was proceeding at a pleasing clip. In every area, all cylinders were firing.

My students were especially responsive to my lessons and I was enjoying the hell out of teaching them—even James. It was one of those times when I was grateful to have motivated suburban students sitting in front of me rather than the ghetto knuckleheads I started my career teaching in Newark and Jersey City. I had come out of college convinced that I would rescue every black child in the 'hood, but instead they had me throwing up my hands in frustration most days. When I got recruited by the Teaneck schools in my third year of teaching, I was afraid that such a move would be tantamount to selling out. But I quickly understood the key differences between the city and the 'burbs—the teachers out here actually got an opportunity to teach rather than spending half the period wrestling with the knuckleheads. Sure, there were knuckleheads in the 'burbs, but it was a different level of wrongdoing, like comparing petty larceny to first-degree murder. They were both crimes, but you would never confuse them.

My basketball team was dominating all of its games, not just winning, but blowing away the competition. Jermaine and Tariq were having unbelievable seasons, both somehow managing to average over thirty points and close to twenty rebounds per game. I wondered if two players on the same team had ever accomplished that feat at any level for a whole season. I was still a bit concerned about Jermaine's annoyance at his father's presence. I was disappointed in him for that; we had talked about it several times and he said he was cool with it, but

I still detected a change in his demeanor. The kid just didn't appreciate how lucky he was. I tried to tell him on many occasions that if that's all he had in his life to worry about, spending too much time with his father, then he was one charmed teenager.

My relationship with Zaria was deepening, getting more serious, more intense. We had gone out several more times and we talked on the phone nearly every day. I appreciated the fact that she wasn't one of these neurotic little girls who needed to know where I was and what I was doing at every moment. When I called her she sounded happy to hear from me, but if I went two days without phoning her she wouldn't try to make me feel like I had committed a grave relationship sin. It was such an enormous relief when I discovered that about her, my feelings for her were compounded by several degrees. There was one thing that did bother me about her: her politics. We had gotten into too many heated arguments over her frighteningly conservative approach to social issues. Some of her comments deeply offended my ultra-liberal sensibilities so much that I almost thought she was joking. But the woman didn't play like that. I always naïvely assumed that most black people had the same politics as I did—sure, I knew black conservatives were out there, but I assumed it was some ploy to curry favor with white folks. Clearly Zaria had no such motivation; she couldn't care less what white people thought of her. This was all her, and it was fairly consistent across the board, whether we were talking about abortion rights, welfare, affirmative action, or immigration policy. She claimed that she didn't vote for strictly Republicans or Democrats, that it depended on the candidate more than the party. Incredulous, I'd asked her which Republicans she had voted for. She listed a couple who weren't too bad, more centrist than right wing, but then decided she wanted to talk about something else. I began to realize that her convictions were just as strong and deeply felt as mine; I wanted to know where they came from. She hadn't yet been forthcoming on that score—in fact, she'd said she was offended by the idea that she had to explain how she had become conservative, like it was some kind of disease that she had caught doing something nasty.

We still had not had sex. We had done some heavy petting in the car before good-byes, but neither one of us had yet extended the invitation to come inside. I knew why Zaria wasn't letting me up in her house—the kids. But the couple of times when we wound up at my place, the lack of an invitation was probably more glaring. I felt so bad about it that I decided to tell her about my houseguests from hell.

"I've been meaning to tell you something," I said, pulling away from her embrace. I was so turned on that I feared my erection would bust through my pants like the creature from *Alien,* screaming and looking around for something to devour. I desperately wanted to bring her up to my bed—not that she had announced she was ready for that.

She looked at me closely, her face flushed and her hair looking a little crazy. "Oh really?" she said.

"Yeah. It may be, uh, presumptuous to say this, but if maybe you were wondering whether I would ever invite you upstairs, I have a reason why I haven't."

Her brow furrowed. "I thought the reason you hadn't was because you respect me as a lady and knew I wouldn't go up there yet."

I permitted myself a brief chuckle. "Yeah, there *is* that. But I also have another reason. I—"

"You're homeless and you don't really live anywhere. You sleep in your truck," she said quickly, interrupting me.

I laughed heartily. "Yeah, that's me, another black man living in his ride 'cause his car payments are too high to pay rent. It's not so bad, actually, though using the bathroom can be a bitch."

She smiled at me. "Go ahead, baby. I'm sorry—I couldn't resist."

I cleared my throat ceremoniously. "As I was saying, the reason why I haven't invited you upstairs is because I have houseguests right now. It's one of my players, Tariq, and his mother. They got thrown out of their apartment and had no real place to stay. They were planning to live up in this crack den in the Bronx, and Tariq was prepared to quit the basketball team."

"Damn," she said, shaking her head. "Tariq is your best player, right?"

I nodded. "Yeah, him and Jermaine. I couldn't just sit by and let him stop playing basketball. The boy has a shot to go all the way."

"Yeah, the way my son and his friend JJ talk, he could be playing for the NBA right now."

"Well, I wouldn't go that far. But he is probably pretty close to that level. And after a few years in college, he'd definitely be ready."

Zaria nodded and stared through the windshield. "That's wonderful that you would be willing to help him out like that. I admire that." Then she remembered something. I knew this was coming.

"You said him and his mother are staying with you? How, uh, how old is his mother?"

I shrugged. "I don't know. She's older than me, but I never asked her age."

There was a heavy pause. I know Zaria wanted to ask what she looked like, what she acted like, whether she was attracted to me—all the obvious girlfriend questions. But she didn't want to sound like the obvious girlfriend.

"What's she, uh, like?" Zaria tried to sound nonchalant, but I could hear her concern in the question. Of course I could never tell her the truth about Ronnie Spencer. And above all else I could never let her meet Ronnie Spencer.

"Oh, I don't know. Let me see, what's she like? Well, she's not the brightest porch light on the block. She messed around and managed to get kicked out of the projects for not paying her rent. That's pretty trifling. I think she's been giving her money to some thug. We're talking major ghetto drama here. Actually, I've been trying to find some alternative housing for them for weeks now, but nothing has come through yet. I think I'm getting a little desperate. I need my space back."

Zaria nodded her head. She was silent for a moment, thinking. I prayed that she wouldn't find occasion to launch into a diatribe about ignorant ghetto mothers. I had already been accosted by that speech and I think I still had the mental scars to show for it. But I certainly didn't need her using Ronnie Spencer as her poster child for maternal irresponsibility, even if she did deserve it.

"Well, if you need any help, let me know. I could see if there's any shelters or anything up in Bergen County."

I nodded. "Okay. But remember—it has to be close enough for Tariq to continue going to St. Paul's every day. We gotta keep him close by."

"I guess right now that means your apartment," she said. She reached over and stroked the back of my neck. "I'm sorry, babe. That must be pretty awful, to have these people just up in your house, er, apartment. Especially if you're used to being alone all the time, having the place to yourself." She looked out the window again. "Boy, what I would do for just one night of peace and quiet, an empty house. That would be heaven."

"What would you do?" I asked, hoping she might hear my tone and invite me into some dirty talk.

"I'd take a nice, long, hot bath. Light candles all over the bath-room. And just soak. Maybe sleep."

"No company, huh? Just you by yourself—for the whole night?"

She finally caught my drift. "Kenneth Roman, are you being fresh with me again?"

"Yes," I said, moving my lips toward her neck, "most definitely."

She giggled. "Good," she said.

She

Florence was at it again. I could tell by the way she was leaning into her phone, and by how long she'd kept the lines hot. I swear, there must be some kind of self-help group for people like her; it made no sense that someone took such great pleasure in not only digging up gossip, but making sure that everyone in the Western Hemisphere knew what it was and that she heard it first. She was at it way before I'd walked into the office, I'm sure. I could tell because her coffee mug was already empty, and her bagel half eaten. Probably didn't get to the rest of her breakfast for all the talking she was doing on the phone. "Hold on," she said as I walked through the door. She cupped her hand conspiratorially over the receiver and practically whispered "Good morning" to me. Lord, I wasn't in the mood for this today. I was high—high from that feeling you get when someone makes you feel so special you get butterflies in your stomach just remembering what happened the last time the two of you touched. So giddy was I from my date with Kenneth Roman last night that I woke up this morning and put on a red suit and pumps. I even put a few curls in my hair and a little extra makeup than usual. Hey, I felt good—why not look good?

Besides, Mikki was coming in for a Wednesday afternoon lunch/shopping date. Christmas was practically here, and she said she still had some presents to buy. And I was always down for some shopping with Mikki because she was particularly generous with her husband's credit card—even if she was a picky pain in the behind. Even more important, though, she was coming after her ultrasound—the one that would tell her if the baby was positioned properly and if the sonogram technician knew what she was looking at, whether Mikki was having a boy or girl. I told her to drink lots of water; it made it easier for the technician to see what was between those legs. She told me to pray for her that there wasn't anything sticking out where it wasn't supposed to, because she would "just die if this is a big-headed little boy." I just laughed and hung up on her. Nut.

But Florence was about to jack up my high—I could smell it in the air. Or more specifically, I could tell by the fax machine and the printer, neither of which had paper in them. That was Florence's job—keep the paper straight. But when I went over to the printer to pick up my stories from *The New York Times*—I never bought the newspaper; why bother when you could simply read everything online?—I had to pull the paper jam out of door three, then put in new photocopy paper so that the thing would work. That wasn't my job. And if Florence didn't get her fat, c-o-n-spiracy butt up off the phone and do what she was paid to do, we were going to have to have some words—and that would surely mess up my mood.

I was hoping she was still on the phone when I made my way back to my desk. I needed just a couple of seconds to make myself look busy so that she wouldn't bother me with whatever news she was busy spreading. But just as I was tiptoeing back to my cubicle, she hung up the phone. "My, don't you look lovely today. Got a hot date?" she asked, taking a bite out of her bagel. Cream cheese was caked in the corner of her mouth, but she wasn't reaching for a napkin, which meant she was going to talk with that mess holding its own conversation just outside her lips. Nasty.

"Nope. Just got up and got dressed like any other day, Florence," I said, being careful not to give her any ammunition.

"Well, come over here because I have to tell you something," she said, lowering her voice and taking on that conspiratorial tone again. "Hurry before Rob comes back."

Dammit. I didn't want to entertain this. I said a short prayer that Rob, the college bursar, would come strolling in before she started her little story so that I could go back to my desk, read my paper, and enjoy my breakfast. No such luck, though.

"Have you heard anything about what's going on?"

"What's going on with what, Florence?" I asked, slightly rolling my eyes and making sure to sound like I wasn't interested. That didn't stop her though; Florence wasn't exactly the most attuned to when folks didn't want to be bothered with her. She just kept on going.

"With the cutbacks," she said, still whispering.

"What cutbacks, Florence?" I asked, showing just a little bit more interest.

"Well honey, go grab your coffee and pull up a chair. This one's a doozy."

"Florence, I really have a lot of work to do today, so I'm going to need the abbreviated version, if you don't mind."

"Well, just let me tell you this: The college is facing some major financial problems, and because they fear a tuition increase would set off the student body and affect the number of admissions next semester, they're considering laying off some people to find their savings. And I hear that some of those cuts are going to come out of this building, perhaps even this office."

Her words hung in the air like a thick fog. What did she mean layoffs could come from this office? How were they going to do that? We were short-staffed as it was, and could hardly keep up with the work we had. And just who was going to get the ax? Were they going by seniority? Title? Best smile? We were all necessary to this institution; we collected the money, for God's sake. Who would fire us? Who would fire me?

I could tell by the look on Florence's face that she was quite pleased that she'd stunned me with her bit of information. But I wasn't going to give her any more pleasure than she'd already gotten. So I blew off what she said with a simple, "Oh really? That's interesting," and walked back to my desk, making a mental note to go straight to Rob when he came in and ask him just what the hell was going on. I got babies to feed, a mortgage to pay, and groceries and gas to buy. I have a new niece (or nephew) on the way. I can't afford to lose this gig. Not now.

Rob was in meetings all morning and had his door closed when there wasn't anyone in his office, which I guess is normal for him, but it still worried the crap out of me. Something was in the air; I was just hoping that it wasn't what Florence was talking about. All of my other coworkers were abuzz, but it looked like they were simply buried in work. By the time I got up the nerve to go knock on Rob's door, Florence called out to me. I flinched. "You have a telephone call," she sang.

"Oh, thank you, Florence. You can put it through."

"Whoever it is sounds awfully upset," Florence said, cupping her hand over the receiver. "Is everything okay at home?"

No, she did not just sit here and try to insert herself into my damn phone call and personal business? This woman's got the balls of an elephant. "Florence," I said sternly. "Could you put whoever it is on hold so that I can answer the phone? Thank you."

She obliged, and then proceeded to stare me in my mouth as I picked up the phone. I forgot Florence was looking at me, though, when I brought it to my ear and heard sobbing on the other end of the line. "Hello?" I said tentatively. "Who is this?" There was no answer; the person just started crying louder. And in an instant, I realized who it was: Mikki. "Mikki? What's wrong? Is the baby okay?"

"It's a—it's a—it's a—booooooy!" she said, sobbing.

My mouth dropped, and then spread into a wide smile. "I'm going to have a nephew?" I said excitedly. "Oh my goodness! A boy! Congratulations, Mikki!"

"Why are you so damn happy?" Mikki said between sniffles. "Didn't you hear me? It's a boy—hello?"

"Oh—right, right," I said, deciding on the fly to make fun of her. "No boys allowed, huh? Well, I'm sorry to tell you, darling, but there's not much you can do about it now. God's decided what He's giving you and it's a boy, and you should take that for what it is—a blessing."

"Boys are not blessings; they are curses to women that God doesn't like. They're bad as hell. You can never find cute clothes for them. And you can't do all the cool things you can do with girls, like get their hair done or take them shopping, or get them used to nice things. What the hell am I going to do with a boy? A blue room? A wild-ass child?"

"Good grief, Mikki—don't you think you're taking this a little far?" I said. I was rather offended by what she was saying about boys. I mean, I had a boy, and he wasn't half bad. Certainly easier and less expensive than Jasmine when he was a baby (I'd prefer to count what we were going through now as an anomaly; he really was a nice kid). "I mean, did the sonogram technician see anything wrong with the baby?"

"Besides the penis?" she said, incredulous.

"Yes, besides the penis, Mikki. Like any problems with the kidneys or the lungs or the brain? Was his heart beating? Did he have all of his limbs? Both his eyes? Did you notice any of that? Because there are some babies who come without those things, and their mothers aren't blessed to see their faces." She didn't respond, and I could tell she was still crying. But I kept at it. "So you should count all of that as a blessing, darling. And I assure you that when you see that beautiful little face looking back at you, and feel that baby's fingers wrapped around yours, you'll love him more than anything in this world—regardless that he's a boy."

It took her a minute to respond, but she did, finally. "I guess," was all she said.

"Where are you?"

"I'm in bed, drinking hot water and lemon. I have a headache. I closed the shades to keep the sun out, but the headache won't go away."

"Where's Randy?"

"Somewhere mad," she said, annoyance tingeing her voice. "He got really upset when I started crying about the baby being a boy."

"Well, can you blame him? What'd he say?"

"He said that if he were in the bed crying over it being a girl, I probably would have slit his throat."

"You know that's right."

"Um, can I get a little sympathy here?"

"Okay—I'm sorry that it's not a girl, but I'm glad that you're having a healthy baby boy. There—that's as far as my sympathy is going to extend. Boys are wonderful, you'll see. Are you coming to lunch?"

"No. I'm going to get some rest," she said simply.

"Okey doke, go on ahead and stand me up," I said, saying a silent thank you. I didn't really want to leave for an extended lunch break, not with all that was going on in the office. "But don't call me when you have to return all those little-girl clothes you bought. You did keep the receipts didn't you?"

"Oh, forget you, Zaria," she said. And then all I heard was a dial tone.

Moments later, Florence put another phone call through to me, this time without commentary, for which I was grateful. It was the nurse at

Jasmine's school; my daughter apparently had a temperature of 101.9 and had vomited her lunch. "You're going to need to come pick her up. She needs bed rest and lots of fluids, and if it doesn't get better by tomorrow morning, you should probably take her to your pediatrician," the nurse said.

The last thing I needed right now was to call attention to myself by leaving early to attend to child-care issues—but that's my child, and I had no other choice but to go. I hung up with the nurse and immediately walked over to Rob's door. "Can I come in?" I asked, as I knocked.

"Sure," he said, a bit hurriedly. "What's up?"

"I need to go; Jasmine is sick. The school just called and told me I have to go pick her up."

Rob rubbed his hands over his eyes and then put his forehead in his hands. "Okay," he said, a mix of reluctance and annoyance ringing his words. "Um, what're the chances you'll be in tomorrow? Is she really ill?"

Well damn. It's my child. You would think that he could show a little bit more concern over her well-being. I've worked in that office for almost eight years, and I've never given him or any of my other superiors any reason to believe that I'm not a hard worker or that I don't take this job seriously. Why the attitude now? I didn't want to drop a sob story—my child really was sick—but I wasn't going to sugarcoat it either. If I needed to stay home two weeks with my child, then that's what I was going to do. Isn't that what any good mother would do? And wouldn't a boss who cared about his employees understand that?

Truthfully, I was just hoping that this didn't call attention to me, just as the college was mulling layoffs. I knew not to get too smart with Rob. "She's sick enough for the school nurse to have her go home early," I said. "I'm not sure what she has yet, but hopefully it's one of those viruses that goes away quickly." Then I added, "Are you okay? You look, I don't know, bothered."

"Just a lot going on today," he said.

"Oh. Well, I've been meaning to stop by your office to talk to you about something that's been floating around the office, but I guess I don't have the time now to discuss it."

"Well, is it something that can wait until later in the week?"

"I guess," I said, trying to read his face. I got nothing.

"Okay, then we'll schedule a meeting for then," he said. "Hope your kid is okay."

"Thanks," I said, and backed out of his doorway.

Just when I thought everything was going well, the day I woke up in a good enough mood to put on some pumps and makeup to come to this grungy office, bad news was hitting me at every turn. Maybe red wasn't my color. Maybe tomorrow I'll wear slacks, a sweater, and loafers. That way, the bad luck would pass me by.

He

It was another blowout win for St. Paul's, improving our record to 10-1 as we were about to go into the Christmas break. I was leaving the locker room, pleased that we were about to get a few days off, even allowing myself to whistle as I walked. Inevitably, my mind turned to Zaria. We hadn't made any plans to see each other for Christmas, but I still wanted to buy her the perfect gift to show her how I felt. Speaking of gifts, I still had a bit more shopping to do for Laney. I was going to have to deposit the girl at my mother's again for much of the Christmas holiday because of my houseguests, the Spencer family. Mom was starting to complain—actually, Mom was always complaining. But that was nothing new.

As I pushed open the side door to the gym and was hit by the bracing cold, I saw movement out of the corner of my eye. I took a step backward, letting the door close. I peered into the darkening gym. Sitting on the edge of the bleachers was Jermaine; his father, Will Bryson; and a small balding man who looked just like the guy who had been talking to Tariq in the parking lot. I felt a shudder race down my back—I wasn't sure if it was the bite of the cold or the unnerving sight before me. I was frozen for a moment, unsure of my next move. I desperately wanted to see what was going on over there, but clearly it was a private moment. As opposed to Tariq's situation, Jermaine had his father on hand to protect his interests. Will Bryson was a sensible man;

he wouldn't be likely to involve his son in anything silly or dangerous. Right? What was the guy's name? Don or Ron with some Italian-sounding last name. Naclerio, Nazerino, something like that. I took a step toward them, then another step. Jermaine's dad saw the movement and looked up. The gym was too dark for me to see the expression on his face. But within seconds, all three of them were looking at me. I stopped walking and stared at the trio. I hoped my stare was somewhat menacing. The little white man stood up and gave me a slight wave.

"Hi, Coach," he called out. I didn't wave back.

He scrambled down from the bleachers and quickly headed for the exit. I would say he scampered, but that would be overplaying the rodent analogy—though he did look to me like a little mole. Jermaine and Bryson walked in my direction. Both of them had the same slump-shouldered saunter, though Jermaine was about four inches taller than his father.

"Hey, Coach," Bryson said. "Great game, huh?"

I nodded. "What was that all about?" I said, motioning toward the corner they had been sitting.

Bryson looked back over at the corner. There was an uncomfortable silence. "That guy represents a sports agent," Jermaine said. "He thinks I could be a high first-round pick."

I took a step back as if I had been slapped. A tension, a tightness, gripped the muscles in my chest. I felt like I might have difficulty breathing. I took a deep drag of air.

"In the NBA?!" I said. "Right now?"

Jermaine and Bryson nodded simultaneously. But neither one of them was smiling. Bryson's face appeared to hold a grimace.

I shook my head in disbelief. I wanted to tell them they were crazy, that it was a big mistake, that Jermaine'd be swallowed whole by the NBA and spit out like a chicken fragment stuck in Shaq's teeth. But with much effort I held my tongue. I needed to think about how to handle this. It would do my player no good for me to react with emotion right now.

"We need to have a long talk about this. The three of us. So that we understand exactly what's going on right now." They nodded. I thought of something else. "You haven't taken any money from this guy?"

Jermaine looked at his father in a quick sideways glance that instantly worried me sick. But Bryson just shook his head.

"No, money has not changed hands," he said. I thought that was an odd way to phrase it. Who talks like that?

"All right, 'cause you know that money changes everything, right? You take money and you've entered a whole new realm. College isn't even an option anymore. You realize that, right, Jermaine?"

Jermaine's eyes had widened a bit. He must have been a horrible liar when he was little. He nodded his head. But I knew it wasn't the truth.

"Let's talk about this next week, after practice. We gotta get ready for that Christmas tournament in Philly. But that guy makes me uncomfortable—I don't remember his name. Can you please stay away from him until we talk again?"

Jermaine gave his father another sideways glance. "It's Don Nazerio," Jermaine said.

"Okay." I looked at Bryson. "Can you stay away from Mr. Nazerio?"

He nodded. "Sure thing, Coach. We'll talk next week." They both waved and started to walk away. I stood silently, watching them, feeling a creeping dread settle into my bones. Jermaine in the NBA? I shook my head. Six-foot-seven guards were a dime a dozen in the show now. My boy would get lost. It was absolutely the wrong move. He needed at least two years of college. Every player could use that. I had to get on the phone with my NBA people.

In the days leading up to Christmas, Zaria and I were so busy that we couldn't even squeeze a date into the mix. I was driving myself cuckoo trying to figure out what to buy the woman for the holiday. I didn't want the present to be too expensive—not that I had the kind of extra money lying around to do that anyway, especially since I did the typical part-time father thing with Laney and overindulged her on Christmas—but I wanted it to be meaningful and memorable. The couple of times we had talked on the phone, Zaria sounded especially stressed and not exactly the most engaging phone partner. She complained bitterly about the commercialization of Christmas and how her kids were driving her crazy with all their greed. Christmas was hard on parents, even more so for custodial single parents who were forced to be Santa all by themselves. I wanted to tell Zaria that I could empathize with her, since I was going through some of the same my-self—though Laney wasn't around me on a constant basis to tell me what she wanted (Sheila got to enjoy that particular experience)—but of course Zaria still hadn't been told about Lane. As she complained, I could feel the knots in my stomach tightening. I had already passed the point of no return in carrying my lie of omission forward—there was no way for it not to be ugly when I told Zaria about my child. One voice was telling me that since the anger was clearly going to be there regardless, I should just get it over with. But another voice was telling me that I needed to wait a little longer, until I was sure she was so deeply in love with me that there'd be no turning back for her after she got the news. In other words, wait until she's tightly hooked so there's less chance of losing her. Also, it was easier to wait, to avoid the un-pleasant scene—though it did give me stomachaches whenever she talked to me about parenthood in that slightly patronizing tone that parents reserve for the childless.

And I had to admit one more thing to myself—I wanted to wait until we had sex before I took the risk of chasing her away. I know that might sound too doggish, but it was the truth. We were so close to an encounter that would undoubtedly be one of the most delicious of my life—why send the whole thing crashing to the ground at this particu-lar moment? I had told Zaria that we were going to spend New Year's Eve together and I had a special evening planned. She had responded just as I had hoped, with apparent glee. I was going to get rid of my houseguests for the night—at least she now knew about them—and I was going to transform my apartment into a den of sensual celebra-tion, a dazzling lovers' nest. I had stumbled across an article in a woman's magazine at the supermarket a few weeks before that ex-plained, step-by-step "How to Turn Your Home into a Fabulous New Year's Eve Lovers' Den." I bought the magazine—even enduring the smirk of the teenage girl at the cash register who apparently enjoyed the sight of me purchasing a woman's mag. I snatched the mag from the counter and smirked back at her, knowing the best way to fight teenage girls was to throw the insolence right back at them—they took kindness as weakness.

But before I made it to my New Year's Eve, I had to get through Christmas and a tough basketball tournament in Philadelphia right after Christmas. When I thought of my team, I couldn't help thinking of Jermaine and his NBA dreams. It had occurred to me over the past two years, as their talent grew and as I watched a growing number of high schoolers declare for the draft every year, that Tariq and Jermaine might consider themselves ready to make such a move. But I had quickly dismissed such thoughts, knowing I'd be around to guide them in a different direction—namely, big-time college basketball. Of course I knew all the arguments about how these colleges exploited the players and made huge sums of money while the players got squat, but there was no denying the fact that a high schooler was still a longshot in the NBA and had so many disadvantages and difficulties that a player with just two or maybe even one year of college wouldn't have to endure. After I had spotted the Brysons talking to the little bald man, I knew I had to find the right time to gauge Tariq's mindset. The moment came a few days later, when he was sitting in my living room watching a Sunday afternoon NBA game.

I sat down in the comfortable but aging cloth chair adjacent to the couch. My living room furniture wasn't the most modern or attractive on the market, but I thought it got the job done. I really hadn't gotten around to serious decorating up here anyway. It was on my to-do list—which said something like "Go out and locate a sense of style."

"Who's winning?" I asked.

He looked up at me, probably because they had just flashed the score. But I had missed it during my musings over the furniture.

"The Lakers. Kobe and Shaq both already got over twenty and it's still five minutes until halftime."

I shook my head. "Those two are an unstoppable combination." I thought of something. "Hey, Tariq, you think you could stop Kobe?"

His head snapped around. "Huh? You mean if I was checking him in a game?"

I nodded. I watched his face closely—this was a difficult moment for a cocky high school basketball phenom who has been worshiped for his on-court prowess the past four years. He knew what the right answer was, but could he admit it to himself and to his coach?

"Well, I don't know about *stopping* him, but I tell you this—he wouldn't score no forty-five or fifty on me!" Tariq said this with a grin, but he studied my face at the same time.

"Oh, you could hold him under fifty, huh?"

Realizing that he was sounding a little too shaky, he revised his prediction, getting a little more serious now. "I could probably hold him under thirty, at least." He nodded his head, as if he were still convincing himself.

"So, you think you're ready for the NBA?" I asked. I wanted to get right to the point.

His head snapped around again to stare at me. He frowned. "Why you asking me that?"

"I think you know why, Tariq. I saw you talking to that agent rep, remember?"

He continued frowning. He fidgeted on the couch like a little kid, effectively telling me that I probably shouldn't believe whatever came out of his mouth next.

"I already told you what I talked about with him."

"Somehow I don't think I got everything. I don't even know if that's the only time you've talked to him." I paused and leaned toward him. "Is it?"

He glanced at me and turned to the screen, where Kobe was putting down an incredible dunk on some hapless defender's head. Tariq reacted to the dunk by wincing—it was the customary reaction to a Kobe move, the wince of disbelief. Tariq looked back over at me, like he was checking to see if I still wanted an answer.

"No," he said finally. "I've talked to him a few more times." He paused. Then he turned to me. "Look, Coach, all these guys keep coming up to me and telling me stuff. He's not the only one, there were two other guys just like him, telling me that I could be a high first-round pick in the NBA draft and make millions of dollars. Nazerio, the one you saw, even knew that I was living here with you. He said if I signed an agreement with his agent, then they'd give me the money right now to buy a house for me and my moms. Like a loan. You think he was lying to me, Coach?"

I sat back hard in my cloth chair. I felt the tightness in my chest again. The sensation was starting to worry me—I don't know what a heart attack felt like, but this was quite uncomfortable. Not painful, but disconcerting. Maybe I needed to get a checkup—it had been a few years since my last one. I took a deep breath. What could I tell this boy?

"There certainly is the possibility that he's lying to you, Tariq. But I can't say for sure. But let's talk about the whole picture here. We know about Kobe and Kevin Garnett and maybe one or two others, but there are a lot of guys who went straight to the NBA from high school and they're either sitting at the end of somebody's bench or not even in the league anymore. The same is true for guys who came out of college after a year or two. A lot of them weren't even dominant college players, but they had some sports agent talk them into signing on the dotted line and taking their cash, and then they couldn't go back. You are an incredible basketball player, Tariq, but you have to be thinking about the arc of your whole life. Just like you practice all these years to put yourself in the best possible position to succeed, you also go to college from high school to get the crucial experience that college will bring. And I'm not just talking about on the basketball court, either. Those guys in the NBA are grown men. They have wives and kids and adult concerns. What would you look like, an eighteen-year-old boy, who's never hardly been anywhere, coming onto a team and trying to get along with thirty-year-olds? The social and mental aspect of the league is just as important as the physical. Look at Tim Duncan. He stayed in college for four years and he was already a fully formed player when he came out. Mentally and physically. I think that has everything to do with his basketball success, the MVPs and all that. He knew how to play the game and he was prepared for the league because he had spent four years in college."

"You think I still got a lot of basketball to learn, Coach?" Tariq asked.

This was a delicate point. I couldn't damage the boy's ego, but I needed to be real with him.

"Well, I'd like to think that I've coached you well in the fundamentals, Tariq. But think about this—you've been a forward for all these years, but you're probably too small to be a forward in the NBA. So you'd have to learn the guard position. You think an NBA team will have the time or the inclination to teach you a new position when they're trying to get to the playoffs and win championships?"

He was looking at me with the wide eyes of a frightened child. I wasn't trying to give him a coaching version of *Scared Straight,* but he did need a dose of reality because he wasn't going to get it from the Don Nazerios of the world.

"I know Jermaine has been talking to these guys, too. If you'd like, I can maybe get in touch with a few NBA sources I have to see what they have to say about you and Jermaine's chances in the draft. Would you like that?"

Tariq smiled. "That would be great, Coach." Then he frowned again. "They'll tell you the truth, you think?"

I nodded. "They kinda do it every year, Tariq. They'll tell the truth because they don't want all these high school kids trying to come into the league before they're ready. That makes them look bad."

"It does?" Tariq asked.

I nodded again. As I gazed at his teenage face, the peach fuzz, a few pimples, the innocence, I knew that I had to do as much as I could to protect him. He was truly still just a boy. A big, talented, overgrown boy, yes. But a teenage boy, nonetheless.

He

Who knew that women's magazines could be so helpful to a dude? I had to tell some of my friends about my discovery, how I used the mags to turn me from a humble schoolteacher/basketball coach into the Mack Daddy Supreme. I was briefly reminded of the Bernie Casey movie *The Mack*, which my mom made the mistake of bringing me to when I was a little boy—I don't know what she was thinking. Apparently old girl didn't read any of the reviews because about twenty minutes into the flick, as Bernie is stretched out on the bed with a luscious and naked young lady, she snatches me up from my seat and drags me from the theater, cursing to herself all the way as I try to look back for a few last peeks at those big round brown buns spread across the screen. I think that might be where I first developed my uncommon interest in big round brown booty.

Using a magazine recipe for Chilean sea bass, I was in the midst of preparing what I hoped would be the perfect romantic meal. I had already transformed the apartment into a love den using the step-by-step instructions in the magazine. I felt a little stupid spreading the rose petals all over the damn floor, but what lady could resist the feeling of rose petals under her bare feet? (The mag said I had to remove her shoes—though it was intended as a guide for women to use on their men, I figured it would work even better the other way around.)

My lady Zaria was probably just beginning her treasure hunt, if I had timed it right. Thanks to yet another women's mag—I had spent one afternoon poring through a newsstand—I had gotten the idea to send her to different spots all over New Jersey, having her pick up suggestive and romantic items along the way so that she'd be tingling with anticipation by the time she got here. Just thinking about how good this night was going to be made my stomach do somersaults. I hoped I wasn't building it up too much—sometimes sex could be awkward and off-key with a new person. That didn't mean that it couldn't get better, but it didn't always start off as the epitome of synchronicity.

As I leaned over to stir the saffron rice, I looked around the apartment with a big smile, pleased at myself for unearthing a decorative flair I didn't know I had. I covered the furniture with throws and pillows I had picked up at some discount store on Route 17, and decorated a small card table I had with a funky tablecloth, candles, flowers, some glass plates, glasses, and napkins I got at the same spot. It looked like an intimate Italian bistro—really romantic and warm. When I lit the candles, it wouldn't even resemble the same apartment. I looked over at my bookshelf and almost gasped out loud—I had left out the framed picture of Lane. Damn. Were there any more Laney signs that I had missed? I rushed toward the other bedroom and opened the door. A few of her toys were stacked in the corner. As I walked toward them, with each step I felt more ashamed at the stupidity of the lie I had perpetrated. Why had I played it this way? It was now approaching two months into our relationship—what idiot keeps a child hidden from his girlfriend for two months? I vowed to tell her, maybe even tonight, after this thing had been consummated. She would be incensed, and she had every right to be, but I would feel better for getting it over with. Because the burden of carrying the secret around with me was starting to grow too heavy. I was like a poster boy for every irresponsible baby daddy on the planet, hoarding the baby secret from new women until I got to the pussy. I sat down on the edge of the bed and buried my head in my hands. I had to own up to the truth—I was now afraid to tell Zaria about my daughter. Afraid of her reaction, afraid of losing her. The fear was what had been propelling me to prolong the lie. I shook my head. Damn, that was lame.

The shrill ringing of the phone kicked me from my self-pitying daze. Was it Zaria? Had the treasure hunt gotten fouled up? I rushed toward the phone in the kitchen. As I grabbed it, I looked down at the raw fish and the raw asparagus spread across the counter and realized I still had a lot to do.

"Hello?"

"Hello, Mr. Roman. I'm glad I caught you at home." It was Antoinette. Her voice practically oozed through my phone.

"Hello, Antoinette. How have you been?" I tried to sound as noncommittal, unsexy, as possible. I hadn't heard from her in weeks. She had left a message on the answering machine in early December, but I hadn't called her back.

"I've been fine. The question is how have you been doing? You're a hard man to track down. I know you probably got a big night planned with your new girlfriend, right?"

I didn't want to answer that. How did she know I had a new girlfriend?

"I know, you don't know what to say to that, right? You don't want to lie to Antoinette. Anyway, I wonder if I could come upstairs and talk to you for a little while before you go out. I got some things I want to talk about."

Come upstairs? Oh God, was she downstairs? I rushed over to the window and tried to peek out.

"I see you up there, Kenneth. Yes, I am downstairs. Go ahead, wave."

I stepped back from the window, a little shaken. This was getting a little weird. I needed to get rid of this woman. I had work to do.

"Oh, what's wrong? Is little Kenneth scared to be seen?" she said, mocking me by sounding as if she were talking to a little boy.

"No, of course I'm not scared, Antoinette. Don't be ridiculous. How have you been doing?" I winced at that last line—Antoinette wouldn't be interested in small talk.

"How am I doing? Come on, Kenneth, you know you don't really care. I mean, *really* care," she said. She chuckled as she said it. That also felt like she was mocking me.

"Okay, enough talk. I'm going to come upstairs now. I'll see you in a second." With that, she hung up. I clutched the phone tightly in my hand. I looked up at the clock. Zaria was probably a lot closer. I did *not* need this right now. I couldn't allow this crazy woman into my home— just the sight of my decorations and food preparation would tell her the entire story, which was that someone else had been chosen. What made me believe that sex could ever be free? Free sex was the greatest contradiction in terms that the English language could manage.

I ran to the elevator, praying that I could dispose of this drama quickly before Zaria arrived. We had never talked about whether our relationship was exclusive or if I had other women in my life, but I knew she wouldn't be able to stand evidence of another relationship leering in front of her face. No woman would. When the elevator finally reached the lobby floor, I rushed to the glass doors to greet Antoinette, who was standing on the other side with her hands on her hips. She was wearing a long black coat and high-heeled black pumps. Her face was fully made up and her hair fell down to her shoulders. She looked quite lovely, but she also looked angry. I saw the scowl on her almond-colored face, but it didn't give me pause—it just made me annoyed. She was coming to my home, blowing up my spot, and I was supposed to be scared of her wrath? No, the only weapon she had against me right now was her mere presence. The scowl was to be ignored.

"Antoinette, what's the problem?" I said, opening up the glass door. The lobby separated the foyer from the more ornate sitting area with a wall of glass that had a locked glass door in its middle. You used the large panel of names and numbers to be buzzed in. I patted my pocket to make sure I had my keys, then I let the door close behind me. There was no one else around, but I felt exposed and a little vulnerable surrounded by all the glass. If Zaria arrived now, there was little I could do or say to get out of this unscathed.

"What's the problem? What's the problem?" She shook her head in apparent disgust. I saw the snarl on her face and wondered how this could possibly be the same woman who would swoop down on my apartment like a fairy-tale sex princess and then disappear with no questions—okay, maybe a few questions—asked. She hadn't made any demands on me, had made no requests. From where I stood, she didn't have the right now to catch feelings or throw anger in my face.

"I don't expect you to call me, but at least I think I deserve the courtesy of a return phone call," she said loudly. "You think you can just ignore me?"

Immediately I thought of Glenn Close in *Fatal Attraction,* the crazy rabbit-killing adulteress. Did Antoinette realize how ridiculous she sounded?

"I got your message, Antoinette, but you didn't tell me you needed to talk to me," I said. I was trying to sound as calm as possible. "All you said in the message was 'Hi.' That's not the same as, 'Please call me back because I need to talk to you.'"

I saw her eyes flash. "Man, what are you talking about? 'Hi'? I said a whole lot more than some damn 'Hi'! I said I needed to see you. That's what I said. Why are you acting like this, Kenneth? Why are you being an asshole?" She was getting louder and increasingly belligerent.

"Asshole? How am I acting like an asshole, Antoinette? You show up at my doorstep unannounced, on New Year's Eve no less, and I'm supposed to drop whatever I'm doing to, to, to entertain you?" I saw her eyebrows shoot up at the word "entertain." It was the best I could come up with, minus a thesaurus. "I'm busy, Antoinette. I got plans tonight." Before I felt guilty for blowing her off, I tried to think back on some of our conversations about the lack of strings we would attach to our liaisons. Well, I'm not sure they were actual, full-blown conversations. But there were comments made. Mostly by Antoinette (a dude wouldn't volunteer such comments, though he might be thinking them).

I heard footsteps outside. They got louder, approaching the front door of the building. I couldn't identify them as male or female. I felt a lump in my throat—please don't let this be her, I thought. Please. The footsteps stopped and the door swung open. Antoinette turned around to look. It was a white man, a little older than me. I had seen him a few times; I think he lived in the building. We were silent, waiting for him to pass through. He looked at us quizzically, but when he saw that we had stopped talking he considerately hurried past me through the glass door. Antoinette looked down at the floor. At least she had the sense to keep her ridiculousness under covers. (Ouch, that was an unfortunate double entendre.)

As soon as the man disappeared, I decided I had to make a hasty exit. This was silly.

"Antoinette, I have a lot to do right now. I'm going back upstairs. I'll talk to you, uh, another time." I turned and slipped my key in the door. I heard a harsh expelling of breath behind me. It sounded like a window had been opened in a moving car. I heard her take a step toward me. Was she going to get violent now? I slipped through the door and let it close behind me—pulling it a little to speed the process, but not enough to make it seem as if I were slamming it in her face.

"Fuck you, Kenneth Roman," she said, pointing a finger at me through the glass. Her mouth was in a nasty snarl and her hair had fallen over one of her eyes. How did we get here?

" 'Bye, Antoinette," I said, waving. I turned without another word and headed for the elevators. I had a sinking feeling in my stomach, knowing I had just done something regrettable and unpleasant. Antoinette wasn't the kind of woman to let something like this alone.

"I can't believe you are treating me like some whore!" she shouted. Her voice was a little muffled but clear. I kept walking and was relieved to see an elevator open. I stepped on—before the doors closed I got a shot of a wildly gesticulating woman with her mouth open, yelling something I couldn't hear anymore. I got a feeling that this whole scene would come back to bite me in the ass. When I got back upstairs, stepping into an apartment that smelled strongly of raw fish, I hurried to the window and looked out to see her car still parked outside. She wasn't sitting in the car either. What was she doing down there? I crossed my arms and waited for several minutes, knowing that she'd come strolling into sight any second. I looked around the apartment and tried to re-create the feeling of anticipation, the happiness, the horniness I had felt before. Antoinette had killed the mood.

I had to finish cooking so I went back into the kitchen. The potatoes had hardened so much that I had to add about a half cup of milk to get them back to mashed. The fish could be put in the oven as soon as Zaria buzzed me. I busily went back to the task of preparing a sexy, sumptuous meal, but I rushed to the window every few minutes to be greeted by the sight of Antoinette's shiny sports car, still sitting at the curb, the arrangement of the headlights and the grille giving the impression that the car was leering at me. What the hell was that crazy woman doing in my lobby? Did she somehow sense that I was about to get a visitor?

I was startled by the ring of the phone. Damn, she was calling on the celly again to yell at me? She had gone completely cuckoo. I walked toward the phone but didn't pick it up. I decided to let the answering machine handle this one.

"Hello, Kenneth?" I heard the voice coming from my bedroom. It was Zaria. I snatched up the phone.

"Hello?" The shrill cry of the feedback made me wince. "Zaria?"

"Why didn't you pick up the phone?" The feedback got louder. "Can you turn that off, Kenneth?"

I was already running into the bedroom. I hit the button. "Sorry," I said softly. I was a little out of breath from the sprint. Didn't want her to hear that though.

"Where are you?" I asked.

"I'm following your directions! You're so crazy, Kenneth! I can't believe you got me driving around half of New Jersey!"

I couldn't read the mood in her voice. Was she annoyed?

"But I'm having so much fun! I can't wait to get there!"

I let out a sigh. I knew she was not a woman who enjoyed having her time wasted, so I was a little nervous about the treasure hunt. I wasn't sure if she'd have the patience to play along and enjoy the building anticipation. Apparently she had. But how far away was she? I hurried over to the window in the bedroom.

"Where are you?" I asked, as I opened the blinds.

"I'm only a few minutes from you right now. I just picked up the champagne."

Damn, Antoinette's car was still here! What in the world was going on down there? If she had just hit Danny's Wines and Liquor, that meant she would be here in about five minutes. I could feel the tempo of my pounding heart quicken and intensify, like it was stepping into a crescendo.

"That's great. I'm glad you're enjoying it, Zaria. I was a little worried," I said, craning my neck to see if I could spot Antoinette in the front seat. I couldn't tell from the angle of the parked car. It wasn't in the same spot as the night she gave me the front-seat striptease.

"Worried about what?" Zaria asked.

I pressed my eyes shut. Please, woman, don't mess this up for me. If this relationship was going to be killed, I wanted it to at least be at my own hands. "Oh, just wasn't sure you'd want to do all the driving," I said.

"It wasn't really that much driving. I just had to make a few stops on the way here, that's all." She sounded so cheery and happy. My, how her mood would sour if she got accosted on the street by a crazy jealous woman.

"Yeah, I tried to make every stop be along the path you'd be taking anyway," I said. I saw movement in the front seat of Antoinette's car. "I'm glad you didn't mind playing along."

"Mind? Kenneth, it was a wonderful idea! You had no reason to worry."

I saw Antoinette lean forward and look up toward my window. I tried to draw back so that she couldn't see me, but I failed—I know I failed because Antoinette moved her hand toward me and lifted her middle finger. Wow, she gave me the finger! And I saw her mouth moving—she pantomimed the words "Fuck you." Nice. But I wasn't too upset because the car abruptly zoomed away. Free at last.

"Well, I'm glad, Zaria. Okay, I gotta go finish up a couple of things. I'll see you soon!"

I let out a giddy sigh and shook my head. This had the potential to be one of the most exciting nights of my life, and I almost had it ruined by a psycho-chick. But though I felt relief now, it also combined with dread because I knew Antoinette wasn't done. If she couldn't make her way back to my bed very soon, she would bring another tantrum. I had a lady now—no time for the likes of Antoinette.

I finished seasoning the fish and put it in the oven. Then I ran into my bedroom and started shedding my clothes. I had laid out my tuxedo, which I usually wore only once or twice a year. As I was putting on the shirt, I noticed some wicked ring around the collar. Why hadn't I put the shirt in the cleaners after the last time I wore it? I shook my head. I considered myself meticulous about my clothes and my personal hygiene—I couldn't stand a funky shirt. Instead of the tuxedo shirt, I decided to wear a snug, white, crewneck that would do a good job of showing off my "bumps"—muscles to the uninitiated. Just as I was admiring the fit in the full-length mirror attached to my closet door, I heard the buzzer. Zaria! I walked to the kitchen.

"Hello?" I said into the intercom.

"It's me, Kenneth." Zaria!

I let her in. I took several deep breaths, trying to calm my nerves. Why was I so nervous anyway? I looked around the room, admiring the flickering glow cast by the candles. I had much on the line here, the food, the decorations, the romance, the mood—the main course and the intercourse. I laughed at the similarity between the word for food and the word for sex. I sniffed. The aroma of the meal just added to the sensuality of the room. At least it did in my opinion. I waited.

When she reached the door, I pulled it open and gasped at the sight before me. My God, she was stunning! Her hair was pulled back off of her face, she wore a form-fitting dress that hit her in all the right places, her brown eyes sparkled like jewels, her skin was flawless—she was so beautiful I almost peed in my pants. I took her hand and pulled her into the apartment. I put both of my hands on her waist and drew her to me. She looked over my shoulders at the decorations, the candles, the works. She grinned up at me.

"Wow," she said softly. Our lips met in a light kiss that sent chills coursing down my back. Oh, this was going to be delicious.

She

Mikki had gotten over her news about having a boy long enough to whip up a spectacular gown for my hot date with Kenneth. I didn't quite understand at first why Kenneth insisted I dress formally for New Year's Eve dinner at his house, but I have to admit I became more intrigued as the day approached—the first time in years I'd actually looked forward to celebrating it. Long ago I'd written the night off as an entirely overrated affair—just an excuse for everyone to spend a ridiculous amount of money to pretend they were having a good time on an evening that was designed to isolate and punish loneliness, even more so than Valentine's Day, which was a lot easier to ignore. For sure, I'd had my fill of bad New Year's Eve experiences—paying for a baby-sitter (they always charged double, greedy bastards), new clothes (which were always uncomfortable, too skimpy for the harshly cold weather and—might I say it again?—too costly), overpriced dinners (tell me why you would think it's okay to charge somebody upwards of $60 for a plate of fried chicken, okra, potato salad, and cornbread, just because your guests are eating it on December 31?), and long lines at raggedy clubs that demand you pay $100 for entrance and really bad champagne in a tacky plastic glass at the stroke of midnight. I can't even remember the last time I'd gone out on New Year's Eve—well, I couldn't remember the year; it was some time ago. I do remember, though, that I'd gone out with April and a couple of her girlfriends, and that we had sat in traffic for almost three hours trying to make it to this club in Tribeca, talking all the way there about how much fun we were going to have and how many numbers we were going to collect, and who should be the designated driver and who was more likely to get good and drunk. By the time we got there, it was just past eleven, I was hungry as hell (we'd planned to eat at the club, but it turned out all they were serving were $20 Buffalo wings, $10 plates of fries, $15 plates of mozzarella sticks, and some really nasty $25 spinach dip), cold and already annoyed that all the old uncles in the club had somehow targeted me as their evening conquest. I was ready to go by 12:01. I'd decided right then and there that Dick Clark and I would be hot and heavy New Year's Eve dates from then on.

But then I got Kenneth's invitation. It was a beautiful, calligraphy-inscribed note inviting me to "an intimate, formal dinner for two" at his place. I eagerly accepted. (I actually had to return a reply card to his house! That's class.) And then I set to planning my evening.

When the day came, I drove the kids to the 'rents house; they never went anywhere for New Year's Eve and were usually asleep by the time the ball dropped in Times Square, but this year, James and Jasmine convinced them to let them stay up to celebrate with popcorn and noisemakers. Sorry I was going to miss that. (Not!) Then I rushed home to slip into my gown—it was a beautiful, fitted, strapless, yellow satin affair that hugged all my curves in just the right places, and hit just below the knee, striking the conservative but super sexy look I'd requested of my sister. She told me to wear it with my open-toe, strapless sandals. "You'll be inside, so don't worry about your feet being cold," she insisted. "You'll look super sexy, and he won't have to fiddle with stockings or straps when you two get naked!"

"And just what makes you think we're going to get naked?" I asked, embarrassed by her suggestion.

"Please—you don't think you're going over to his house for just dinner, do you?"

"That was the plan," I said.

"Uh-huh, okay," she said, laughing. "So, um, do you want me to sew a little pocket on the inside of your built-in bra for the condom, or are you just going to carry it in your purse?"

It was my turn to laugh now. That Mikki.

Just as I'd put the finishing touches on my makeup and was about to fill my purse with the essentials—breath mints, lip gloss, compact, cellular phone, and yes, condoms (just in case)—the doorbell rang. Who in the world was that?

I took off my shoes and eased down the staircase, stopping to quickly admire myself in the hallway mirror. I was going to knock this boy out tonight, doggone it. I peeked through my door window. It was April.

"April? What you want?" I said, mocking disgust. "Quite obviously I'm not going to be able to give you a blow-by-blow account of what happens between me and Mr. Roman until I finish the date."

She laughed. "Yeah, yeah—okay. So you *are* planning on giving me the blow-by-blow, right? Because I'm just feening to find out what's going to happen over there in Jersey City tonight. Damn the fireworks in New York; I'm betting the ball dropping is going to be going on this side of the bridge—if this envelope is any indication."

"What envelope?" I asked

"I don't know what in the world this is, but Kenneth Roman sent this package to my house by FedEx and told me in a separate letter to give it to you at 6 P.M. So here I am, 6 P.M. on the dot. Open it, dammit, I've been dying for three hours trying to figure out what's in it."

"You mean I have to read my little letter to you? I can't just enjoy it all by myself first?"

"Nope. Open it," she said, stepping in off the stoop. "Don't bother to invite me in," she added. "I know I'm always welcome."

I laughed some more and ripped open the envelope. I'll tell you this much: My feelings about New Year's Eve were quickly changing.

Dearest Zaria,

Happy New Year's Eve, darling. I plan to make this as special a day as humanly possible. To that end, I'm sending you on a love hunt that will eventually lead you back to my nest, where I plan to shower you with affection. Follow the instructions precisely to get to my waiting arms.

Kenneth

"Aw shit," April said. "What the hell did you put on that man that he's being this creative with you? You been holding out on me?"

I didn't answer her; I was too busy reading the instructions, which came on a separate sheet of paper. On it, Kenneth had ordered me to go to North Coast Video on Teaneck Boulevard, just around the corner from my house, to pick up a package he'd left for me. Instinctively I looked at my watch. My heart was racing. What in the world was it that Kenneth Roman had in store for me? I wasn't sure, but I couldn't wait to find out.

"Okay, April—beat it. I'm obviously busy."

"Oh sure, shoot the messenger," she said, backing up out the door. "But before I go, let me impart just one thread of wisdom."

"What, April?" I said.

"Have fun, and use condoms."

"That's two bits of wisdom, April," I said as I slammed the door in her face. We both heard each other laughing through the door.

Okay, okay—I know what I did next makes me a total loser, but I ran upstairs and tore my room apart, looking for something special to give him. I mean, I had manners—I'd purchased a bottle of wine to bring to his house, and even bought one of those cute wine bags from Pier 1 Imports to put it in, to make it look more special than it really was. But that wasn't going to be enough; I needed to come correct, or not come at all. I couldn't simply show up. But what could I get at this late hour? All the stores were closed except for the convenience spots; what was I going to buy him—a pack of Now and Laters? Cigarettes? A slurpie?

Mikki to the rescue. Again.

"Hello?" Randy answered the phone.

"Hey there, brother-in-law—how's my favorite dad-to-be doing?"

"Sitting here watching the game and waiting on your sister hand and foot. She's not feeling well."

"She's not feeling well, or she's taking advantage of her husband?"

"What do you think?" he said, just as Mikki picked up the phone.

"Well, hang in there, bro, it'll all be over soon," I said sympathetically. "Don't let my little sis drive you bonkers."

"Too late for that," he said.

"I heard that!" Mikki yelled into the phone.

"Good," I said. "You better leave that man alone!"

"Ain't nobody bothering him," she said. "And just what do you want? I thought you had a hot date tonight? Why you calling me? He not taking care of business over there?"

"Mikki, get your mind out of the gutter. I don't have time to go through all of this with you so listen carefully. Randy, don't hang up."

I explained to the two of them what Kenneth had done, and begged them to help me figure out a gift for him "that I didn't have to buy in the store and that would be equally creative and inspired."

"That's easy," Randy said. "Give him some."

"Well damn, Randy, she said creative!" Mikki shouted in the phone. "Just because you're hard up doesn't mean you have to try to live out your fantasies through my sister."

"A brother has to get his kicks from somewhere," he said, laughing. We both laughed with him.

"Come on, you guys—I have to go on my treasure hunt. Think of something!"

"There was this thing that Mikki did when we first started dating that was pretty cool," Randy said. "She gave me this box, and in it was a gift for each of the five senses."

"Oh yeah," Mikki said. "I gave him a picture of me when I was a little girl—that was for sight. And I gave him a tape of my favorite album, Dianne Reeves's *I Remember,* for hearing. For taste, chocolate. And for touch and smell, a naughty nightie sprayed with my favorite perfume—but you might want to pass on that one because I'm not going to sit here and advocate unsafe sex."

"Aw, the nightie and perfume was the best part," Randy chimed in. "Don't deny a brother."

We all laughed heartily again. "That's brilliant," I said. "But don't you think it would be a bit forward for me to bring a nightie? He might get some idea that he's going to get some, and that would be awfully fast."

"Precisely," Mikki said.

"Exactly," Randy said, practically at the same time.

"You two are a mess," I replied. "Thanks a bunch for your help. I might have to find something else to appeal to the touch."

"She's such a prude," Mikki said to Randy.

"No—I'm just not a slut like my sister," I said, getting a laugh out of Randy.

"Well, clearly, her sluttish tendencies are nowhere to be found. Dick Clark is my buddy for the night."

"Oh—you know what? This is too much information. I'm hanging up now."

"Yeah, hang up now," Mikki said.

"'Bye, Randy!" I shouted as I hung up the phone.

I ran upstairs and quickly assembled my gifts for Kenneth in the silk wine bag I'd purchased—wine for taste, a picture of me in a bathing suit on the beach for sight, and the copy of Stevie Wonder's "At the Close of the Century" box set I'd gotten from Mikki for Christmas (she'd understand; I'd buy a new one later). As for touch and smell, I had something much more special than a nightie and some perfume. Let's just say I was going to make Kenneth a very happy man come the stroke of midnight.

Not more than ten minutes later, I was standing in the video store, with the store manager grinning all up in my face. "Ah—you're the pretty lady your boyfriend told me to look out for," he said, coming from a back office after being called out by the clerk at the register. "He told me to give you this." The manager gave me a white gift bag. In it was a beautiful, plump red rose, a movie called *9 1/2 Weeks*, which I had heard of when I was much younger but never actually had seen, and another "Dearest Zaria" note telling me to go to Ellen's, a chocolatier not far from the video store. I smiled. "Thank you so much," I said cheerily to the manager as I skipped to the door. "And Happy New Year!"

That scene was repeated all over town—at the chocolatier, where Kenneth left chocolate-covered cherries in an identical white bag with another rose, at the 7-Eleven over on Chauncier Place, where the white bag bore yet another rose and a beautiful hair clip, which fit perfectly into my updo, and finally to a liquor store near his home, where he had left me a bottle of Moët, another red rose, and instructions to call him before I headed for his house. And I have to tell you, by the time I dialed his number, I was the most giddy woman on the East Coast. No one—and I mean no one—had ever bothered to do something as romantic as this for me. Ever. With the guys I'd been with, unsnapping my bra was the beginning and end of romance; there was never any kind of effort put into making me feel special and wanted. Needed, maybe—for a physical release, perhaps something to wear on the arm to put forth a good face. But special? Never. No, Kenneth had cornered the market on that one, and I hadn't even gotten to his apartment yet.

Kenneth sounded just as anxious as I when he answered his doorbell; when I got upstairs, he hugged and kissed me eagerly, like I was some delicious, exotic dish he'd been waiting all day to savor. I responded in kind, and walked into his apartment still in his embrace.

"You are stunning," he said, finally pushing me back to take a look at my outfit and grabbing my gift bags from my hand. "I must be the luckiest man in the world."

"No, I believe I'm the luckiest girl in the world," I said warmly, smiling. He had on a tuxedo jacket and pants with a sexy, tight, white shirt, looking quite delicious himself. I told him so, and added, "All of these beautiful presents! That was perhaps the most exciting thing I've ever done, and I'll never forget it. Everyone was so nice to me; I felt like a kid, running around trying to guess what else I was going to get. Thank you so much for making this evening so very special."

"Oh, it's just getting started," he said, grabbing my hand and twirling me like a dancer in one of those Fred Astaire movies, then directing me to a chair that was sitting by the door. "Tonight, I am your humble servant, and your every wish is my desire. And since you are royalty here in this apartment, you deserve to walk on rose petals. Let me take your shoes."

I silently said "Thank you, God," for having Mikki remind me three times to go get my toes done; had he taken my shoes off yesterday, he might have cut a finger. But I'd gotten up early this morning and sweated out an hour's wait to get a pedicure, "just in case he needs to suck on your toes or something," Mikki insisted. I had poohpoohed her, but I got that pedicure. Just in case.

And now, my feet were resting on what looked like hundreds of rose petals, which practically carpeted his floor. When he stepped aside, I got my first real look at his apartment—and Lord was it stunning. There were candles everywhere, and pillows and flowers in almost every corner of the room. And over by the window, there was a magnificent table, set just like one in a restaurant, with candles and flowers and fancy napkins. Just beyond it, the stars were twinkling against a perfectly clear night sky.

"Wow," I said, rising out of the chair. "Your apartment is beautiful. Did you do all of this for me?"

"And more," he said, stepping aside so I could walk past him to the window. "Stay here, I just need to finish up a few things in the kitchen, then we can sit down and eat."

"Something sure smells delicious. Do you need me to help you with anything?" I asked.

"I just need you to sit here and look as beautiful as you do. I'll be right back."

No more than ten minutes later, Kenneth came back into the living room with a towel draped over his arm and two plates full of salad. He directed me over to the table, placed the plates on their settings, then walked over to the stereo and turned the music up. Marvin Gaye was singing.

"Madame?" he said, pulling my chair out for me. I sat and admired the table, and my man.

"It smells delicious in here," I said. "What are you making?"

"It is a surprise, Madame," he said, incorporating a fake French accent. "Sit back and enjoy your salad. The next course will come shortly."

I did. And the salad and the Chilean sea bass and asparagus and garlic mashed potatoes were out of this world—like anything you could have tasted in one of those expensive restaurants in New York. "Are you sure you made this?" I teased, taking my last few bites. "I think you have some little Italians in the back whipping up the meal, and they're making you look good. They're awfully quiet back there."

Kenneth laughed. "Ha, Ha," he said. "I cooked it all myself, with a little help from my handy-dandy cookbook. I'm glad you're enjoying it. Are you ready for dessert?"

"Yes, but first, a gift," I said, pushing myself back from the table and walking over to where I'd put down my purse. Normally I would have been nervous and stiff, trying my best not to trip as he gazed at my body—which I instinctively knew he was doing, even though I didn't see him. What man could resist looking at a black woman with back as she walked away from him? But I was a little tipsy from the wine he'd served with dinner—we had finished the entire bottle, a rarity for me—and because of it, I was a lot looser than I'd usually be in such situations. That Kenneth was making me feel like a beauty queen certainly didn't hinder my looseness.

"I wasn't as creative for Christmas," I said (I'd given him a pair of leather gloves; no thought whatsoever), "but here's to hoping this makes up for it."

"Well, what do we have here?" he said, taking the bag from my hand. "You shouldn't have. This night is my gift to you."

"Oh man—just open it," I said, laughing.

He reached in and pulled out each of the items. "Liquor. Always a good gift," he said when he pulled out the wine. "Damn," he said when he saw the picture. "Look a there, look a there. Maybe we should move to Hawaii so you could walk around like this all day everyday," he said.

"You're a loon," I said.

He laughed, and pulled out the box set. "Aw, baby—I read about this in the *Times* awhile ago, and I'd meant to pick it up for the longest, but I never got around to it. Stevie's the man—thank you. This is great," he said as he perused the song titles on the back of the box. He got up suddenly and put the CD in his stereo, and used a remote to fast forward it. Within moments, Stevie Wonder's "Knocks Me Off My Feet," was chiming through the speakers.

"This is the best song ever written," Kenneth said, walking back over to the table and grabbing my hand. "Dance with me."

I happily obliged, relishing his embrace as he moved his hips slowly against mine. He was leading, and moving much more slowly than the music, leading me to wonder if he was one of those brothers who couldn't keep beat, or if he was simply trying to get his grind on. I wouldn't have minded either, though, for some reason, I wondered if I could teach him how to dance before our wedding reception. Damn. Wedding reception? Slow down, Zaria. Slow down. This is just one night. Enjoy it, I implored myself, but don't get to trippin'.

But I couldn't help myself; I was intoxicated—not just from the wine, but from this man.

"Wait—I didn't tell you what each gift means," I said, pulling back slightly from his embrace.

"Um, that you're trying to get me drunk and take advantage of my body while Stevie Wonder sings to us?"

"Uh, not quite," I laughed. "Each gift is meant to represent one of the five senses. The wine was for taste. The picture was for sight. The CDs are for hearing."

"That's only three," he said, tilting his head back to look in my eyes. "You're missing touch and smell."

"I didn't forget them," I said, gazing into his eyes. I leaned in slowly and kissed his lips. "They're in your bedroom." My God—did I just say that? Did I just invite this man to have sex with me?

Damn straight I did.

Kenneth simply looked at me and smiled. Then he started mouthing, then singing the words to Stevie's song, "Knocks Me Off My Feet." "Oh but I love you" he sang softly. He was off-key, but it didn't matter—only the words counted. We were both intoxicated by the moment, mesmerized by what was about to happen. Finally, after a few more kisses and a little more swaying, Kenneth took my arms from around his neck, held my hand and, never taking his gaze from mine, led me into his bedroom. "Let's go get the rest of my presents," he said.

He hadn't put as much effort into the decorating of his bedroom as he had his living room; it was neat and warm and cozy—I guess what you would expect a bachelor's room to be. The furniture was spare; he had only a bed, a bureau, and a television stand that held a DVD player and a small music box. He had no pictures that I could really make out, save for one of himself with a seemingly older women—I assume his mom, since he looked a lot like her. But it wasn't his mother I wanted to think about right now.

"Go over there and sit on your bed," I said as Kenneth hungrily kissed my neck. He looked up and smiled, then backed his way across the room and sat on the edge of his bed. I walked over to his night lamp and turned it off, then reached over and opened his shades. From his window, he had a beautiful view of some of the taller, more attractive apartment complexes in Jersey City, just at the tip of the Holland Tunnel. The light from those buildings, coupled with that of the moon, cast a wonderful glow into the room, with just enough light for me to make out his lips, his smile, his gaze. I walked over to where he was sitting; he attempted to get up, but I gently pushed him back onto the bed. "I want to give you your presents in the proper way," I said, moving in front of him. I took his hands, and slowly ran them down the sides of my dress, just past my breasts, down past my hips, my thighs. A smile slowly formed across his face. "Would that be touch?" he asked.

"Yes indeed," I said, smiling back.

"Feels nice," he said.

"Thank you," I said back. Then I slowly reached under my left arm, hooked my finger around the zipper, and pulled it south, careful to use my free hand to hold my dress up. I moved back from Kenneth, and let it fall into a heap at my feet, exposing my strapless bra and matching thong. My figure glowed in the moonlight—as did Kenneth's eyes, which, by now, were wide as saucers, though I'm sure he didn't know how astonished he looked. Surely he wasn't expecting me to initiate any of this, which is, I hoped, what made this more special for him. Usually guys were used to having to take the initiative—particularly on the first sexual encounter. I know that I had made every man that I had been with do that with me; didn't want any of them to think that having sex with me was overly easy. I needed them to work for it, more so that I could (a) feel like I hadn't disrespected myself by spreading my legs for any man moving and (b) so that the next morning, I could at least convince myself that the men I was with respected me, too.

Those silly games and mind tricks weren't necessary now, though—not with my Kenneth. Clearly I'd had his attention—and his heart. Respect had long been apparent.

"Do I get to touch again?" he asked, slowly getting up from the bed.

"Absolutely," I said, alternately kissing his lips and whispering. "And smell. And taste. And anything else you can think of," I said.

He slowly ran his hands over my breasts, giving them a slight squeeze before moving them past my stomach (I was sucking it in, but it was still somewhat flat, despite my years of exercise avoidance). He hooked his fingers in my panties, and slowly ran them around my waist, then pulled my body closer to his.

"Damn, why you been hiding all this ass from a brother?" he said, chuckling. At first I was embarrassed. I know my butt is quite large—he didn't have to tell me that. But when I saw the glee on his face, I reminded myself that, to a black man, it probably wasn't even possible for a butt to be too big.

He still had his suit on, and the fabric felt silky against my skin—fine material indeed. We both were breathing quite heavily now, our faces inches from each other's, but not kissing. And with each second that passed, the breathing got more intense, our lust unleashed. I couldn't stand it anymore; I reached up and snatched his jacket off his shoulders and then his belt and then his pants, forcing them all into a heap around his feet. He reached down and, in one stunningly quick motion, pulled his shirt over his head, exposing his chiseled chest and abs. Kenneth was in spectacular shape—had a beautiful body that wasn't quite that of a man who spent *all* his time in the gym, but of one who clearly cared enough to eat properly and put a bit of effort into keeping it trim and toned. As he stepped out of his pile of clothes, my eyes moved slowly down to his crotch; his erection made his boxers form a tent over his thighs—a nicely sized one, I might add. Taking his cue, he pulled his underwear down and stepped out of those, too; his penis bobbed at attention. It was not shy—and it was not small, either.

"Why you been hiding all of *that* from a sistah?" I said softly. I felt a rush of bashfulness—wow, did I just say that? But Kenneth laughed happily, so I laughed, too.

We embraced again, and fell onto the bed, still clinging to one another. Our lips and tongues and arms and legs intertwined. We didn't rush to the intercourse. We stretched out on the bed and slowly explored each other's bodies, our comfort and confidence growing with each new discovery, urged on by every lusty moan or sharp intake of breath. Kenneth slowly worked his mouth and tongue down and around my body, turning me so that he could spend quality time kissing my shoulders and back, which he said were beautiful, and then my ass, which he kissed and licked and worshiped like a true ass lover. I had never had a man spend so much time on my behind—it felt strange at first, but I began to really enjoy the attention when I saw how sensitive it was back there. Who knew the booty had so many nerve endings? Well, I guess Kenneth did. When he moved down even farther and started dipping his tongue into my sweetest spot from behind, I gasped. I hadn't expected him to do that from that position. Well, I didn't really have much in the way of expectations anyway. I arched my back and lifted my hips off the bed to help him out, moaning loudly as he burrowed his face in deeper. Abruptly he turned me over and continued, now with complete access to the whole organ. He ran his tongue across the entire length, up and down. Everytime he hit my clitoris I sucked air through my teeth. My God, he was quite good at this, I thought. He must have stayed down there for about ten or fifteen minutes, only stopping when I yanked his head away after an orgasm that had me unleashing an embarrassing, guttural scream that I'm sure they could hear in Manhattan. I was immobile for at least sixty seconds.

"Well, damn, Coach," I said, still sucking in gulps of air. "Your talents never end."

Kenneth grinned as he stood over me. I could make out a pleased and proud expression on his mug. My eyes wandered down his body, past the glorious pecs and abs, to the straining erection. Now it was my turn. In a quick motion that I wanted to shock him, I rolled over and took him into my mouth without even using my hands. It was a matter of aim, judging space and distance, kinda like bobbing for apples on Halloween. I almost laughed when I thought of that analogy. Boy, it had been a long time since I had performed oral sex. I hoped my skills, which I had been told at one point were quite considerable, hadn't rusted. When I was younger I had thought it was just a question of exhibiting the proper level of enthusiasm, but one night baby daddy, Ricky Fish, had stopped me in the middle of the act to give a lesson that I never forgot. Apparently enthusiasm was good, and necessary to achieve excellence, but not nearly enough. There was also technique. From Kenneth's moans and groans, I knew I hadn't forgotten much during the off years.

When Kenneth finally entered me, I had an immediate and violent orgasm, clutching his back and probably giving him permanent scars. It felt like my entire body was one giant, tingling nerve ending. But he kept going, gazing lovingly down into my eyes. Just the look was almost enough to send me over the edge again. Had I ever experienced lovemaking this good? I didn't think so—despite the oral instruction from baby daddy, we had been too young to really know what we were doing. And the few men who had come afterward were never quite as generous and considerate as my Kenneth. He inspired me to be even more giving, too. Instinctively, I knew that what was happening in his bed was special, something rare and precious that shouldn't be taken for granted. Most couples could go at it for years and never reach the level of intimacy and passion that we had found on the first time out. Biology was a peculiar thing—some bodies just didn't go together, some partners could never find the rhythm of the dance. But ours felt like the ideal match, a perfect coupling, like the parts had been designed and fitted by a team of engineers.

We'd both fallen asleep, but I woke up first. The first thing I saw was his beautiful face; he was sleeping so peacefully and soundly, I didn't want to move an inch lest I wake him. But not long after I woke up, so did he. He stretched and smiled and sat up on his elbow, letting his head rest in his palm. "Hey," he said.

"Hey," I said.

"You need anything? Something to drink?"

"No—I'm good."

"Yes, you are," he said, a sly smile crossing his lips.

I laughed. "You're not so bad yourself, Coach Roman. I think I might have learned a thing or five in apartment 8C tonight."

"Oh yeah? Like what?"

"Well, let's see," I said, then paused. "I learned that my boyfriend is a beautiful, kind, talented man who can cook his behind off."

"That's it?"

"Oh—and he has wonderful taste."

"That's it?"

"And he knows how to treat a lady."

He was silent. Then, "That's it?"

"Um. Yup. That's it!" I said.

He reached over and cracked me in the head with his pillow. I giggled and tried to hit him back, but he blocked the blow, then wrestled me back down to the mattress and tickled me in my ribs. "Stop!" I screamed, laughing as I continued to plead for him to give me some slack. After a few minutes of tussling and wrestling, we both lay back in the bed, exhausted, giddy.

"You know, you should come over to my house on Sunday for dinner with me and the kids."

Kenneth was quiet. His silence made me worry; did he not want to be around my children? Did I ask too soon? Was I unwittingly scaring him away?

"Can you cook? Because I'm not coming all the way out to Teaneck on my day off for an inadequate Sunday dinner. That would just be wrong."

"Man? Can I cook? I can put you and your mama to shame with my Sunday dinners, now—don't get it twisted."

"Oh really?" he asked. "Can you make macaroni and cheese—and I'm not talking about the kind from a box."

"Piece of cake."

"Can you make roast beef—cooked all the way through but still juicy?"

"Piece of cake."

"With homemade gravy?"

"Piece of cake."

"And speaking of cake—can you bake?"

"Don't push it, Mr. Roman," I said, giggling. "You're planning my whole menu, and you haven't even accepted my invitation."

"Oh—sorry. Hell yeah, I'll be there."

"Good," I said, lying back down on the pillow. "And yes, I can bake. My specialty is homemade South Carolina lemon pound cake. But you don't know nothin' 'bout that, Jersey boy."

He didn't say anything. Kenneth just picked up his pillow and let it fly.

He

The sun streaming through the blinds pierced through my sleep state and shook me awake as effectively as a country rooster. I had forgotten to readjust the blinds the night before after peering through them to assess the departure of the psycho-chick. I turned away from the window and saw the indentation still in the other pillow. That was where Zaria's head had rested about—I looked at the clock—about five hours earlier. She had roused herself from a deep sleep at about 3:30 A.M. and decided she had to rush home. I had protested mightily—I didn't want her on the roads at that hour on New Year's Day, when all the drunk crazies would be weaving their ways home—but she insisted that her children had to see her first thing in the morning. I let her go. I had no choice. But after she left I had moved my head next to the spot she'd lain and had fallen asleep with the faint scent of Zaria lingering on my nose.

I pushed myself out of the bed. It was early, but I had to go to my mother's to spend the day with her and Laney. At the thought of Laney, I felt that familiar sinking sensation in my stomach. No, I hadn't found the opening to tell Zaria last night. As a matter of fact, I hadn't even thought about it until after she was gone. But I now pledged to tell her during the upcoming week. She had invited me over to her house for dinner with her kids on Sunday. Maybe I'd do it after that. She wouldn't dump me after bring me home to her kids.

I walked past the edge of the bed and saw Zaria's bra crumpled on the floor. She had forgotten to put it back on in her haste. I picked it up and put it to my nose, taking a deep whiff, searching for just a tiny bit of Zaria. I caught a trace of her, the sweetly musky odor of her sweat mixed with her fruity perfume. I sniffed again. I felt a little light-headed all of a sudden and sat on the edge of the bed. Whew. The woman literally takes my breath away. Or maybe it was the bottle of wine and the champagne catching up. I looked down at the burgundy-colored bra, the fullness of the cups, and thought about the feel of her large, round breasts in my hands, the taste of her nipples in my mouth. Her breasts and her butt were much larger than I had reason to believe they'd be. Unsheathed, they had jumped out at me, making the heart thrum excitedly as I ran my hands slowly over her abundant ass. I recalled the smoothness of the flesh as I leaned forward and ran my lips and cheeks across her buns. This was undoubtedly one of the best parts of wonderful sex with a new partner—the dramatic reenactment in my head. The retracing of all the steps, the reliving of the ecstasy. I reached down and smoothed out the sheet, remembering that Zaria's knees had been pressed into the mattress at this very spot as I moved into her from behind, first slowly and sensually, then faster and faster as she yelled for me to do it "harder!" I was thrilled to oblige, so excited by her insistent commands. As I had hoped, as I suspected, she was a tigress in bed, letting me know what she wanted and not shy about letting me know how much she liked it. She told me she was a little out of practice, but the rust hadn't shown at all. I thought back on something Jerry Slavin, my teacher friend at the middle school, had said about single mothers and their eagerness and desperation in bed. I wouldn't say that Zaria had been so obviously desperate, but she did act like someone who was enjoying a good meal that didn't come often. And I was shocked by her skills at oral sex, the dexterity with which she handled and communed with the organ. I mean, she was better than Antoinette. I shuddered at the comparison—I promised myself not to make it again. But it was still true.

The lovemaking had been better than I could have prayed for. We easily moved together in a rhythm that almost felt rehearsed. I thought back to the view from above, as I moved inside of her and stared deeply into her eyes, feeling like she was gazing clean into my soul. I wanted to move us into a dozen positions at once, to twist and maneuver our bodies like we were following the Kama Sutra, but I had to keep telling myself to slow down, to fully enjoy the moment instead of leaping ahead to the next one. I stepped into the shower, reluctantly letting the hot water run over me and begin to wash away Zaria's scent. As I scrubbed my chest and my arms and my penis and my stomach, I could easily remember Zaria's hands and mouth on each of these places, kissing and stroking and worshiping my body as much as I had worshiped hers. She was a philanthropic love partner, giving me gifts without expecting anything in return, enjoying the giving even more than the receiving. At least that's what I presumed from watching her face as she gave.

I put my clothes on slowly, recalling the trembling anticipation I felt when I slowly removed Zaria's gown and then her underwear. When I got a chance to see her voluptuousness in its glory, I told her that she had cruelly been hiding all that ass from a brother, holding out on me. She had laughed lustily. Then she said something similar when she pulled my underwear down and my dick jumped out at her. That certainly helped a brother's confidence. I never had any reason for insecurity in that area, but it's nice to hear confirmation from your woman.

As I replayed the whole night in my head, I made a startling discovery—we had managed to get through the whole night without arguing or disagreeing. Maybe that's because we spent most of the night rolling around together in bed. Maybe that was the secret—the more time we could spend loving, the less time we'd spend fighting. Well, I wouldn't call what we did *fights*, exactly—more like philosophical disagreements. About everything and anything. In fact, after our last disagreement I had told her I was going to embark on a quest to find things we actually agreed on. But apparently, our bodies had found plenty of agreement. We needed to let our bodies do our talking for us, demonstrating how we felt about each other, rather than having our mouths reveal how we felt about everything else.

I walked into my living room and saw that some of the larger candles were still burning, the rose petals were all over the floor, the sink was filled with dishes and the kitchen was a mess. Damn, I can't leave the place like this—though I was tempted to let Ronnie see how we had turned the place out. But that was too spiteful. I shouldn't even be expending any mental energy on Ronnie Spencer anyway. I rolled up my sleeves and got to work, returning my apartment back to its normal, corny state.

By the time I arrived at my mother's building, it was past ten o'clock and Laney was torturing her with the morning's second viewing of *The Little Mermaid*, her favorite tape of the moment. Laney wasn't satisfied until she had seen it four times in a row. Then her day could begin. My mother looked tired, but I was pleased to see that she wasn't scowling. She had complained bitterly about my houseguests in the beginning, but by now she had resigned herself to Laney's weekend visits. I might go so far as to say she had been enjoying them. It had only been twice, anyway. I had kept Laney at my apartment one night, but after she kicked me in the head the thirtieth time I vowed that I would either throw Tariq and Mom out into the street so I could get some sleep or I would just leave the girl at Grandma's. Besides, she still was working her way through the Christmas presents, pacing herself impressively, so she didn't really care whom she stayed with, as long as the presents came with her.

"So, how was your evening?" my mother asked after I had settled on the couch next to Laney. My mother was far from the nosy type. She asked only because she thought it was polite. But I don't think she really cared. She would only get interested when I told her a wedding could possibly be in our future. After the whole Sheila and Lane affair, and reconciling herself to the reality that her son had a child but no wife, she said she couldn't get all caught up in my affairs because it was too frustrating.

"My evening was wonderful, Mother—thanks for asking!"

I saw her expression change. She clearly wasn't expecting such enthusiasm. "Wonderful, huh? What's this girl's name again?" Now Ma was getting interested.

"Her name is Zaria."

"Right, Zaria. One of those newer-sounding names."

"Newer-sounding? What do you mean by that?" I asked.

"Oh, you know, Shenequa, Tanisha, Jaquana, Zaria. As opposed to Sharon, Karen, Tina, Sheila."

I turned my head to the side. "Are you trying to imply that my girlfriend has a ghetto name, Ma?"

"I didn't use the word 'ghetto.' That's your word. I just mean it's less, uh, traditional."

I stared at her an extra few seconds. Why did she always choose to be so negative? Instead of saying she was happy for me, Ma makes fun of the woman's name. I shook my head in disgust. That was my mother; always had been, always will be.

"So, when are you going to bring her around to meet me?"

I shrugged. I certainly wasn't anxious to put Zaria through those paces. That was something I'd do purely out of necessity, when I couldn't put it off any longer.

"Has she met Laney yet?" my mother asked.

I looked over at her with an expression that must have signaled something.

"What? You *have* told her about Laney, right?" How did she so quickly figure that one out?

I shrugged again. Suddenly I was thirteen, reluctant to share any information with my mom about girls.

"Well, I, uh, I've been meaning to. Just haven't gotten the chance yet. But it shouldn't be that big a deal—she has two kids of her own."

Ma's eyes widened. Then she shook her head in disgust. There was a lot of it going around.

"Kenneth! You better tell that woman about your child. How long y'all been dating?"

"About two months," I mumbled, barely above a whisper.

She shook her head again. "You gonna have some trouble on your hands when she finds out. I don't understand why you waited so long. Men can be so silly sometimes. And it doesn't matter if she has children of her own. She's still going to be upset with you. And rightly so. She didn't try to hide her kids from you."

I felt about two inches tall. Of course my mother wasn't telling me anything I hadn't run through my own mind about two thousand times over the past few weeks. I desperately wished I could turn the clock back to the parent-teacher conference, or right after that, so I could start all over again with Zaria, telling her everything she needed to know before we even had that first meeting in the café. But it was too late now.

"Well, her son is in my class, that's how we met. So she couldn't hide him from me. But I'm going to tell her. The next time I see her."

My mother looked at me sideways with a smirk. It was the same sideways smirk I remember from my childhood when I did something stupid. I got the smirk the time I put the apple in the microwave to see what would happen—and it exploded. The cleanup had taken me two hours.

She

I burned my skillet bread, forgot to put the special sauce in my macaroni and cheese, and threatened to kill my kids all before noon. Chalk it up to nerves; Kenneth was arriving at 2 P.M. for Sunday dinner, and I was nervous as hell, hoping that he would like my home and my cooking and, above all else, that my kids wouldn't drive him crazy—and out of my life. This was a big day, much bigger than the first time we made love. That was natural. Well, kinda. As natural as sex the first time could be. But meeting the kids? The kids meeting a man? Me being in the middle of it all? What if James started being a brat, which he'd begun to be quite well of late? What if Jasmine was weirded out by this strange man in her home? She'd never been around any of the men I'd dated, and her exposure to them was limited to her grandfather and Uncle Randy. I wasn't quite sure how she'd respond to some man coming into our home and resting his feet under my table.

Which is what had me on edge that morning when I woke up and started making my cake. I had been too tired to bake the night before; I usually baked after the children went to sleep, because in my experience, that's the only time they're quiet enough not to make my cake drop. I learned that the hard way when I first started making the cake from my grandmother's special recipe. James would come bounding down the stairs, two steps at a time, and the cake would flatten. Jasmine would yell at the top of her lungs for her brother to stop whatever infraction he'd committed on her person, and the cake would flatten. I'd send the two of them outside so that the cake could bake, and they'd slam the door. You guessed it: flat cake. Over the years, though, I'd gotten them both used to the idea of being as quiet as mice when Mommy put her special cake in the oven. Mostly through threats and intimidation. But it usually worked.

That's what I had to pull this morning. I'd started baking it before they woke up, but didn't get it in the oven in enough time for it to finish cooking before they rose. So when they got into their argument and came stomping down the stairs for me to determine who had the right to wash up in Mommy's bathroom—the answer was neither of them and they knew that, but for some reason, had gotten selective amnesia and decided one of them was going to go in my boudoir and jack it up—they didn't necessarily know that the cake was baking. Even though the smell of the lemon and vanilla should have been a good tip-off. But no, not today. I put my newspaper down and tiptoed out of the kitchen and into the den, heading them off before they made it past the foyer. "If you two don't shut up, my cake is going to fall, and if my cake falls, both of you are going to take a fall—got it?" I said. I didn't mean to be that harsh, but hey—I had a cake to bake and an impressive dinner to make. I didn't need this.

By the time I'd taken the cake out, showered, ushered James and Jasmine out of the kitchen, and got around to making the macaroni and cheese, the phone rang. It was Kenneth.

"So, you're not over there in Teaneck, ordering from TJ's Soulfood Shack, are you? Because I'd hate to call you out for claiming his food."

"Ew, you eat at TJ's?"

"What's wrong with TJ's?" he asked, incredulous.

"I wouldn't drink water out of there. It just seems nasty."

"Well, thanks Zaria, for ruining my lunch spot. Now, you can just make my lunch everyday. Send it by James."

"Don't hold your breath," I said, laughing. "There'll be one hungry social studies teacher up in Teaneck if you're waiting for Zaria Chance to make your lunch every day!"

"Okay—then leave TJ's alone, dammit," he laughed back. "So we're still on for today, right?"

"Yes, we're still on. Can you be here around 2 P.M.?"

"Yup. We can eat when I get there, relax, and eat again at 5. How's that sound?"

"Like somebody is coming with an appetite."

"And I'm hoping that it's good!"

"Don't you worry your handsome little head," I said.

And with that, I hung up and put the macaroni and cheese that I'd been layering into the oven. It was 10:30 A.M., and I needed to get it moving. The roast still needed to be put in the oven, I still had to snap my fresh string beans, and my homemade skillet bread, though mixed and ready to go, had to be baked. Ten minutes later, just as I'd started the roast and the bread, I realized I hadn't put the pièce de résistance in the macaroni dish—the rue of butter, eggs, and flour. What was I thinking? I snatched it out of the oven, but it was too late; it had already started to bake together, making it impossible for me to pour in the batter. I had to start all over again. What the hell was wrong with me—I'm an excellent cook. I may have been a badass as a teenager, but I loved to eat, and I especially loved to watch my mother cook all the wonderful dishes she learned how to make from watching her mother and her mother's mother. The macaroni and cheese was a signature dish, and I'd cooked it dozens of times, to rave reviews. Now, here I was, messing up my dinner like I was some kind of culinary novice.

"Okay, Zaria—calm down," I said, leaning against the cupboard and taking in a deep breath. "There's no reason to be nervous. Everything is going to be fine."

"Who are you talking to, Mommy?" Jasmine asked as she skipped around the corner into the kitchen.

"Nobody, baby," I said, startled. "Mommy messed up the macaroni and cheese and I have a lot of work to do to keep dinner from being ruined."

"You need me to help you?"

I didn't, really, but perhaps her presence would ease my nerves. My daughter had a way with that—she is all at once a sweet, easygoing child who, when she's not arguing with her brother, spends a majority of her time smiling and finding ways to make me do the same. She loves doing girly things—a girly girl, she is, indeed, from the day she was born. At any point during the day or night, you could usually find Jasmine flitting around her mom, combing my hair or playing in my makeup or painting my fingernails. It was pretty cute, and certainly a refreshing change from having to do all of that boy stuff with James, or simply being ignored, which he had a special knack for of late.

I reached into the refrigerator and took out my bag of fresh string beans. "Here you go—how about you help me snap these beans," I said as cheerily as I could muster.

"Sure!" she said excitedly.

I was quiet for a moment, but realized that I better prep the girl for our dinner guest. I hadn't quite known how to tell her and her brother that Kenneth was coming over, so I did exactly what I shouldn't have done: I kept the information to myself. But now was as good a time as any.

"Put a little extra effort into it, sweetie—we're having company for dinner this afternoon and I'd like to make it as special as possible," I said.

"Oooh, is Auntie Mikki and Uncle Randy coming over?"

"No, love," I said. "His name is Kenneth Roman and he's Mommy's new friend. Your brother already knows him; he's his social studies teacher. And Mr. Roman can't wait to meet you."

"Cool," she said. "I'll make the beans extra special, Mommy."

Just as she said that, James rushed into the kitchen, headed, as usual, straight for the refrigerator. He grabbed a juice box and, without saying a word to either me or his little sister, headed back out of the room and for the door.

"Um, James? Where do you think you're going?"

"Me and JJ were going to go to the park to play catch for a little while."

"And how many times have I told you not to think you're grown enough to walk out of this house without telling me where you're going?"

James didn't say anything; just stood there staring at me. Then finally, "Is it okay if I go to the park, Mom?"

I looked at him, and then up at the clock, then back at him. "Actually, we're having company today, and I need you to stick around. Mr. Roman is coming over for dinner."

"Mr. Roman?" he said, crinkling up his face for emphasis. "For dinner?"

"Yes, Mr. Roman is coming over for dinner," I said, frowning my face up, too. "Is there a problem with that? You're acting like I just in-vited a world-class case of cooties to our dinner table."

James smirked, but didn't say anything.

"Well? Is there a problem?"

"No problem," he said. "Can I go to the park?"

"Yes, James, you can go to the park. But please be back by one. Where's your watch?"

"I don't know."

"Well you better figure it out, because you're not going anywhere without something to tell you what time it is."

He huffed, turned around on his heels and ran up the stairs, taking them just like he'd come down, two by two. Not more than a minute later, he ran out the door. He didn't say good-bye. I was going to call after him, but I was distracted by the smell of burning bread. "Dammit," I said, snatching the oven open. I reached for my dishtowel and pulled my skillet bread out of the oven. It wasn't burned to a crisp, but it was burned nonetheless. I turned it out into the trash can, and pulled the cornmeal out of my cupboard. This time I was going to make it perfect. I had to. Something had to go right today. Something.

There it was, 1:35 P.M., and my son was nowhere to be found. Ken-neth, if he were on time, would be here any minute now, and I was a natural-born wreck in need of not one, but two Valiums. "Get it to-gether, Zaria," I told myself several times as I got dressed. "It's just dinner." But James was turning it into something else. At least that's what I told April when I called her in a panic to ask if James was at her house.

"No, he and JJ went to the park," she said simply. "Why?"

"Because I told him to be back in this house forty-five minutes ago, and he's not here and Kenneth will be pulling into my driveway any time now and I wanted both of my children here to greet him properly."

"Um, Zaria?" April said. "Baby, calm down. James has met Coach Roman, many times in fact. He doesn't really need to be there when Coach walks through the door."

"I wanted him to be here, that's my point," I said.

"Well, he's not. And you can deal with him later," she said. "Right now, I need you to go on ahead and calm down. It's just dinner. James will be home eventually, and everything will be fine."

She was right; I was trippin'. "Okay," I said. "But as soon as you see my child, send him home, okay?"

"You got it," April said, and hung up.

Kenneth pulled into the driveway just ten minutes later. Punctual as usual. From the window I watched him climb out of his truck, grab something in a gift bag out of his backseat, and head toward the door. I smoothed down my slacks, adjusted the collar to my shirt, and opened the door before he had a chance to knock. "Welcome!" I said a little too enthusiastically.

"Good afternoon!" he said. We both started toward each other to kiss, but ended up hugging each other awkwardly. "And who is this?" he asked, looking over my shoulder into the foyer. I turned around to see Jasmine staring all up in my business.

"This is Jasmine—but you can call her Jazzy," I said. "Come say hello, sweetie."

"Hello," she said, rushing up to Kenneth and grabbing his hand with a smile as wide as the front door. "It's nice to meet you."

"Well, it's nice to meet you, too, Jazzy," he said warmly. "This is for you."

"Thanks!" Jazzy said, grabbing the bag and tearing into it.

"It's a jazzy teddy bear for a jazzy girl named Jazzy," Kenneth said. He looked at me and groaned, knowing he'd far surpassed corny with that one. But Jasmine giggled, and I suppose that's all that counts.

"Well, come on in and make yourself comfortable," I said. "Dinner will be ready in just a few minutes."

"Where's James?" Kenneth asked as he removed his coat.

"Oh, um, he's at the park with his friend JJ," I said. Didn't want to get Kenneth all worked up over the fact that my child was purposely trying to ruin dinner. "He should be back shortly. Go on into the den. Jazzy? Will you keep Mr. Roman company?"

"Sure. Come on, Mr. Roman, let's go into the den." He followed my daughter into the next room. I looked at my watch, looked back out the window for any sign of James, and headed for the kitchen. The food should be good and warm by now; it was time for me to get it on the table.

Fifteen minutes later, everything was set. I walked into the den to summon Jasmine and Kenneth to the dining room, and was quite surprised to see Jazzy practically sitting on my boyfriend's lap.

"This is when we went to the New Jersey shore last summer," Jasmine said. "Mommy bought me this bathing suit special for the boardwalk. You like it?"

"Uh, yeah," Kenneth said, barely looking at the picture. "It's very pretty."

"Thank you," she said, looking into Kenneth's eyes.

He looked back at her, but only quickly. Then he turned the page in the photo album.

"Well," I said. "Dinner's ready. Why don't you two come on in and sit down."

"Great," Kenneth said, pushing himself up from the sofa.

"You can sit next to me," Jazzy said, running for the table.

Now, I can't tell you, exactly, what was going on with Jasmine, but she was being just a little bit too, I don't know, *extra* with Kenneth. It was almost like she was going out of her way to get his attention—flirtatious even. The way she was sitting up under him and asking him to verify her beauty. Clearly, she wanted his attention, and Kenneth was doing everything within his power to give it to her, but with restraint. But Jazzy wasn't letting up, and frankly, it was making me nervous. I started doing all kinds of mental gymnastics about what this could be about, and finally settled on the fact that the girl just hasn't been around enough men to know how to act. Perhaps that was my fault, for being so incredibly protective of her, but that was my duty as her mother, wasn't it? I would be the one, after all, who would have to wipe her tears if she got attached to some man I'd introduced her to, and then he walked away—stomping on not only my heart, but hers, too. No, I couldn't have that. But I needed to figure out what to do because this was clearly inappropriate behavior for a ten-year-old—my ten-year-old. Lord, my head was hurting. I didn't want to think about it anymore. For now, though, I just needed the girl to calm it down.

Just as we were taking our seats—it was 2:30—James came strolling into the house. "Hey, Mom. Hey, Mr. Roman," he called out as he bounced up the stairs. He didn't even bother looking into the dining room.

"Excuse me," I said, pushing my chair back under the table. "I'll be right back."

I bounded up the stairs and walked into James's room without knocking on his closed door. "Where the hell have you been?"

"I was at the park," he said, not even bothering to look up at me.

"And what time is it, James?"

"I don't know, I told you I couldn't find my watch."

I raised my eyebrow. Was that a cockiness I detected in his voice? Oh, he went out there, got brain freeze in the park, and lost his damn mind. "And I do recall telling you to find it before you left here. You're an hour and a half late for dinner."

"I'm not really hungry anyway," he said, flipping his football in his hands.

"James, if you don't put that football down, I'm going to throw it out of the window, and you after it," I said, loud enough to make him snap to attention. "Now I don't know what your problem is, but you need to snap out of it, now. I want you to wash your hands and face, and bring your behind downstairs, sit at the table, eat your food, and be cordial to your teacher."

"You mean your boyfriend," he said, finally looking me in my eye.

"Yes, my boyfriend," I said evenly, looking right back at him. I wasn't going to be intimidated by a twelve-year-old. "Also your teacher. Do you have a problem with this?" James didn't say anything, just turned his eyes back down to the floor. "I said, do you have a problem with this?" I asked, more sternly than the first time.

"No," he said quietly.

"Well then get your behind into the bathroom and do as I said."

He got up and rushed passed me, without saying another word. Shortly after, he made his way downstairs and was as cordial with Kenneth as he could have gotten, considering his poked-out lip and quiet demeanor. Kenneth said "Hi," and asked him a few cursory questions about football and school. But that's where their conversation ended. James was apparently hell-bent on being a little jerk. I tried desperately not to let it ruin my dinner or put a damper on Kenneth's visit, but this wasn't going like I had wanted it to go.

Kenneth stayed long enough to eat two helpings of cake and ice cream and grab himself a doggie bag. "Well, it is Sunday, and we all have to check back in for work tomorrow, so I better get going," he said, pushing himself up from the recliner in the den.

I didn't really want him to leave, but it had been quite an awkward day. I didn't know if Jazzy was going to try to kiss the man, or if James was going to try to hit him. And I was so worried about their responses to him that I couldn't concentrate on entertaining Kenneth anyway.

Perhaps it was best that he go. But we'd have to find a way to talk about it.

"All right then," I said, getting up, too. "We really enjoyed having you."

"I had a great time, too," Kenneth said.

Jazzy picked herself up from the floor, ran over to Kenneth, and gave him a huge hug. "See ya later, Mr. Kenneth," she said.

"Bye-bye, sweetie," he said warmly. "Hopefully, I'll see you again really soon." Then he turned to James, who was in the corner pretending to be reading a book—I knew better—and said, "See you in school tomorrow, superstar."

"'Bye," James said in a tone bordering on rude.

Kenneth looked at me and gave me a short shrug, grabbed my hand, and walked me over to the front door.

"Look, Kenneth—I'm sorry that this was so . . ." I'd started to say, but he put his finger on my lips.

"I had a wonderful time. Dinner was delicious, and I enjoyed your company," he assured me, holding my hand. "I'll call you tomorrow; maybe I can take you to lunch one day this week."

"So long as it's not at TJ's," I said, laughing.

"Oh don't worry, we're going to Blimpie's, baby."

"Oooh. A sandwich. I can't wait," I laughed back.

I wanted to kiss him so badly, but Jasmine had walked into the foyer and was practically two seconds from jumping into the conversation and getting her own good-bye smooch. I didn't want to be engaged in lip lock with a man she'd just met—not in front of her, at least. I had an example to set. Kenneth did what only a man with class would do: He pulled my hand up to his lips and kissed it. Then he took Jasmine's hand and did the same. "'Bye, girls," he said with a wave, and walked out the door.

He

The phone call came on my celly during my lunch break. I was surprised—I didn't usually get cell phone calls during the day because everyone knew I was teaching. In fact, I usually turned the phone off during the day, but I had forgotten to do it on this cold, gloomy, Monday morning.

"Hello?"

I heard what sounded like sobbing on the other end.

"Hello?" I repeated. I was in the hallway, on the way back to my classroom, so I couldn't be too loud.

"Kenneth? This is Zaria." Zaria was crying? Oh God, what happened?

"What is it, baby?"

She sniffled a few times. "I'm sorry to call you crying into your phone like a little baby."

"Zaria? Tell me what happened!" I stepped into my classroom and closed the door behind me.

"I got fired," she said. Then she started sobbing again.

"Fired! Damn, how could they do that?"

She started crying even louder now. I listened to the sounds of her pain for what seemed like a very long time. I had no clue what to do.

"Where are you, Zaria? Do you want to meet me for lunch?" I had a class to teach in less than ten minutes. How could I meet her for lunch?

"No, that's okay," she said. The sobbing was beginning to die down. "My boss just called me into his office a little while ago and said they were cutting back in all the departments at the college. He said letting me go was the most difficult thing he's ever had to do. But he did it anyway. I think I made too much money and I didn't have a college degree."

She didn't have a college degree? I didn't know about that one. I guess there was a lot about Zaria that I still had to learn.

"What am I going to do, Kenneth? How am I going to support my family?" I heard the crying start again. I held the phone to my ear and listened to the wracking sobs, feeling a tightening in my chest and the beginnings of a throbbing headache. I was powerless to help ease her pain, even to comfort her.

"Well, I could help you, Zaria," I said.

"What?" she said through her sobs. "What did you say?"

"I said that I could help you."

"Help me? Help me how?"

"Well, I, uh, I have some money saved." I couldn't believe I was offering this woman my house money—the cash I had been stashing away for years toward the goal of buying a Jersey City brownstone. Damn, must be love.

"Kenneth, that's sweet of you, but I couldn't take your money."

I knew she was going to say that. I wasn't going to push it now. I'd wait a while and offer again.

"Well, if you change your mind, the offer is an open one." The classroom door swung open and students started filing in. They looked at me curiously. They had never seen me talking on the cell phone in the classroom before.

"Zaria, I, uh, my seventh-period class is about to start."

"Oh, I'm sorry. You go teach your class. I'll talk to you later." And she was gone. I hadn't meant for her to leave so abruptly. I couldn't tell from her tone whether she was upset with me. But she had so many other things to be upset about right now, my seventh-period class was likely the least of them. I was upset with myself for not being more of a comfort to her. I don't know what more I could have done, but it didn't feel like enough.

About ten minutes into a lesson on the U.S. Supreme Court, I remembered something I had heard at a recent basketball game. The community center where I spent nearly all my waking hours as a child had an opening for an administrator. Big Oak, the legendary center director, mentioned to me after the game that he now hired somebody to do all the financial and administrative stuff—he was getting too old and senile to keep up—and the last person had just quit. I wondered if Zaria would be interested in a job like that. I smiled to myself.

"Mr. Roman?" I looked up. One of the students was talking to me. It was Sharon Nichols—the daughter of the drug-dealing parents. She had quickly become my favorite student.

"Are you talking about the Chief Justice?" she asked. I saw the eyes of the class directed at me.

Wow, I couldn't even remember the question.

The community center was uptown, in a section we used to refer to fondly as "the hill." As I cruised down familiar streets, memories rushed back in a pleasant flood. I was all up and down these streets and alleys as a kid, getting into snatches of trouble, getting out of trouble, playing football on the sticky asphalt as we weaved in and out of traffic. It was one of those classic urban childhoods, where we made the streets and all of its attendant parts into our playground. We did things that would horrify the typical suburban parent nowadays—actually, they would have horrified my urban mother if she had known about them. Sometimes our fun even verged on the criminal. For instance, one of our most rewarding pastimes was to swoop down on the trucks that would barrel up the streets around a nearby park and, when they stopped at the light, one of us would hop up onto the back, break the lock and pry open the sliding door with a crowbar, reach inside and start pulling out boxes. Our booty was usually useless, like supplies for the local hospital—not much adolescent boys could do with seven boxes of cheap hospital gowns. But once, I recalled, we hit the truck-heisting jackpot—we opened up the boxes to find sparkling new sneakers, Converses in all varieties of colors. Most of us were afraid to bring home too many pairs—we knew we couldn't get a colorful assortment of new "kicks" past our mothers—but we made some serious pocket cash selling those bad boys. It was clear where I was headed.

One day, as I was running down the middle of the street to catch a long, errant football pass, I almost ran smack into a large, somewhat scary-looking man who was standing in the street watching us with his arms folded. At the last minute, I was able to dodge to the side to avoid running into him. The strange part was that he never moved, not even to flinch. As I scrambled to get the ball, I looked up into his face. "Sorry," I mumbled. He was a dark-skinned man with a long, scraggly beard, but there was a glint in his eye. "You like football, young man?" he asked in a deep, rumbling voice that perfectly matched his look. I nodded. "Well, there's a place nearby where you can play without worrying about getting hit by cars. It's called the Uptown Community Recreation Center. Right over on Communipaw, about four blocks from here. Why don't you and your friends stop by?" I nodded again.

We went looking for it the next day. Once we pushed open the doors to "the center," as we came to call it, I knew instinctively that I had found another home. It was spacious, fairly clean, with a big basketball court in the middle and evidence of sports equipment scattered about, and there were kids everywhere I looked. Gleeful, excited kids. The man from the street saw us and waved us over. He introduced himself to us as "Big Oak," and, despite his scary looks, we discovered that he was the gentlest, funniest man we had ever known. Big Oak became a surrogate father of sorts to me. He taught me how to play basketball well enough to start for my high school varsity as a freshman and eventually become a coach right after college. He made me study hard everyday in the center's well-stocked library, making use of the many volunteer and paid tutors and assistants the center used to attend to our academic needs. In fact, we couldn't hit the sports equipment until we hit the books for at least ninety minutes. If you didn't have homework that day, or you claimed to have finished it at school—a popular claim to make in urban public schools—Big Oak and the rest of the staff would make you read a book. And they weren't playing about the ninety minutes—you had to write your arrival time down on a sign-up sheet so everyone knew when you could be freed. That's where I developed the study habits that got me through college.

Even more important than the sports and the academics, Big Oak taught me how to be a man. He was one of the most principled adults I've ever been around; he had an unerring sense of right and wrong, which he would use to adjudicate the many disputes that would arise at the center. He told me to always stand up for what I believed in—

and that it was most important to believe in something. His favorite saying was, "If you don't stand for something, you'll fall for anything." He'd lure us boys into discussions about current events, trying to pull opinions out of us. If we shrugged or tried to plead ignorance, we knew he'd throw that saying at us at some point. Judging by the direction I had been going in—and where many of my friends wound up—if I hadn't run into Big Oak on the street that day, I'd probably be in prison now, or dead.

As I pushed open the heavy metal doors to the center, I kicked myself for not visiting and helping out more often. I kicked myself for the same thing everytime I saw Big Oak. When I had talked to him at the basketball game a few weeks before, I was surprised by how old he looked to me. I had never really thought about Big Oak's age until I saw him that day. He was one of those ageless living institutions that don't seem in your mind to follow the same biological imperatives as the rest of us. Like the elementary school principal who seems to be the same age when you hit thirty-five as he was when you were ten. I started trying to do some calculations. It had been twenty-two years since I had first walked into the center. Wow, that was a long time ago. Big Oak was probably at least forty then. So he had to be in his sixties. I looked around the place, marveling at how much it had changed—yet it felt the same. It had grown—another wing had been added. The sports equipment scattered about looked newer, and there was more of it. I saw a section in the corner for free weights. A few young men were over there, loudly flinging around the iron. No one was on the courts, which had glistening white nets hanging from the rims. I remembered raggedy nets from my childhood—which we had thought was a huge step up from the noisy chain-link nets or the lack of nets that we were used to. Big Oak had told me that the politicians and a few of the big local businesses had "discovered" the center, lavishing it with donations and attention, particularly whenever election time approached. But Big Oak was certainly glad to take their handouts.

I found him in his office, which overlooked the center's library. That had gotten larger, too. There were about two dozen kids hunched over books. The many shelves were stocked with books—probably more than the library at the local high school. And there was far less noise than you'd hear in the library at the South End Middle School in Teaneck, I noted. Big Oak didn't tolerate slackers. He could do more with a withering glare than most administrators could with threats and screams. I looked through his glass door and saw him talking on the telephone as he stroked his still-scraggly beard, which he did at least five hundred times a day. The beard was now mostly gray, though. He smiled when he saw me and motioned for me to come inside. I noticed that there were several offices next to his. They all looked empty—not even papers or folders on the desks.

"I understand, Councilman," he said into the phone. "Yes, I agree completely. You can count on me, sir. Okay, we'll talk soon."

He hung up the phone and stood up to embrace me tightly. He had put on a few pounds, but he still felt as strong as a young ox. I could feel the muscles bulging through his rumpled green polo shirt. Rumpled polos and sweatpants was his uniform. Like the constantly distracted professor, he had no time for details like new clothing.

"Is this the world-famous basketball coach, gracing us with his presence?" Big Oak said as he released me. His real name was Terrence Oakley. He insisted that I call him Terrence, but it just didn't feel right. "How have you been, Kenneth?"

"Oh, I've been just fine. The place looks great. Still growing. And I see you're still strong-arming the politicians."

He waved at the phone dismissively. "They keep pulling at me, trying to get me to serve on all these committees, sit on boards, all these things that amount to a big waste of time. I'm getting too tired for all of that stuff. I'd much rather be here with the kids. That's where it's at."

I smiled. God, I loved this man. "Yeah, I know what you mean. I feel the same way sometimes—the more successful I get, the less time I feel like I have to actually devote to coaching."

He nodded. "How is the team doing? I see in the papers that you're running all over everybody like a steamroller. How are Tariq and Jermaine doing? They pick colleges yet?"

I sighed. "Man, would you believe I got professional agents crawling around now, trying to convince those boys to go pro?"

Big Oak shook his head slowly, somberly. "It's gotten out of hand, Kenneth. I'm starting to feel like basketball has destroyed more little black boys than crack cocaine. When does it end? The agents are going to start recruiting them in junior high school soon." Then he nudged me in the ribs. "But I guess that's your job, huh? To get them in junior high?"

He was teasing me because he had sent several great players to me over the years, kids who showed precocious talents right down on the courts of the center. Jermaine had been one of them.

"Anyway, what brings you here today? Don't you have practice?" he asked.

"Yeah, I'm on my way to practice. But I wanted to talk to you about something. Are you still looking for an administrator to help you run this place and do the numbers?"

He nodded. "Yeah, sure am. I want to concentrate on actually running the place, rather than trying to be an accountant. I hired a fellow last year, but he went to grad school in September and things have been kinda falling apart since then. Why—you got somebody in mind?"

"As a matter of fact, I do. Her name is Zaria Chance and she has a really strong administrative and accounting background. She helped run the bursar's office at Lawrence College up in Bergen County. They're having budget problems and they let her go after like seven or eight years. She has two kids she's trying to raise by herself. She, uh, also happens to be my girlfriend."

A huge grin creased Big Oak's face. He reached down with a big paw and squeezed my hand. "Your girlfriend?! Well, why didn't you say that in the beginning? She sounds perfect. I can't imagine you'd be spending serious time with a lady who wasn't smart and talented and wonderful! Tell her to give me a call."

It was almost too easy. I almost wanted Big Oak to ask more questions about her qualifications. You didn't want any acquaintance, even your girlfriend, to get a job solely on the basis of your recommendation. You wanted the employer to at least assess her competency or something. That way, if things went bad, you weren't solely to blame. But this was Big Oak's way. He loved me, so he was convinced that he would love Zaria.

"Okay, I'll have her give you a call tomorrow. I think you'll really like her, Big Oak. She *is* a smart, talented, wonderful lady."

He eyed me more closely, raising his eyebrows. "Hmmm, you getting serious? You finally gonna settle down and stop playing?"

I shrugged. "I dunno. Maybe."

"Well, that sounds like true love to me," he said. "A *maybe* is serious business."

We laughed together. "All right, Big Oak, I gotta run. But you should be looking out for her call tomorrow. Her name is Zaria Chance. Oh, and, uh, what's the approximate, uh, salary?"

Big Oak shrugged this time. "I dunno, maybe forty or forty-five thousand. I have to look at my budget and see what I can do. The last guy got about thirty-seven or thirty-eight. Is that enough?"

"Well, I'm sure she'd be taking a pay cut from the college. But I'll talk to her about it."

He smiled and clapped his hands together. "Sounds like a bet. Zaria Chance. How could I forget it?" He sat back down in his chair with a thud. "And Kenneth?"

"Yes, sir?"

"Please call me Terrence. A grown man should be calling another man by his real name."

"Okay, Big Oak," I said.

He laughed and waved his hand dismissively at me. "Get outta here, Kenneth."

She

Here it was, almost eleven in the morning, and I was still in my night-clothes—which, today, were the T-shirt and sweatpants I'd climbed into yesterday afternoon, when I arrived home from getting the ax. Mostly, I lay on my bed with my face to the wall, bawling like a baby. I was able to pull it together long enough to order a pizza for the kids' dinner, and make sure they got to bed on time. But this morning, when my internal clock woke me up to prepare to go to a job I no longer had, it was like I'd gotten fired all over again. It was enough for me to get out of bed, much less shower and get dressed. I had nowhere to go. Nothing to do after getting the kids off to school. And I'd read through the "Help Wanted" ads so many times the paper was starting to get worn. There wasn't a single job available in the entire state of New Jersey. Not one, at least, that would pay me close to the $60,000 I'd been making at the college. Not one that would excuse the fact that I'd never gotten my college degree. What was I going to do—get a gig at the mall? McDonalds? I'm sorry, but "Hello, may I take your order?" wasn't exactly a sentence I'd ever envisioned myself saying, not even at my lowest point in Newark. There was always a better way. Except this time around, I couldn't see for the life of me what it would be. I mean, I'd grown accustomed to my lifestyle; I wasn't rich, but $60,000 wasn't anything to sneeze at for a single mother with two kids. I had a mortgage. (It wasn't nearly as high as most of my neighbors', I guessed, because I had gotten lucky five years back and found the house through a foreclosure listing. But it was substantial enough to scare an unemployed single mom.) I had a car. Good credit. My children were well taken care of. And enough cash to get what I wanted, when I wanted (though I was never frivolous) and some savings, though not a whole helluva lot. How was I going to maintain all of that on minimum wage?

The answer was, I wasn't. Which made me start crying all over again. And just then, the phone rang.

"Zaria, are you okay?" It was Mikki. "I just called you at your job and they told me you didn't work there anymore. What's going on?"

I didn't say anything; just kept right on crying.

"Zaria. What happened?"

Still nothing.

"Okay, you know what? I'm on my way over there."

And just like that, Mikki hung up. I rang her phone, but she didn't pick up. I called her shop, and she didn't pick up there, either. I dialed *69, and the service told me that the number that last called couldn't be retrieved because it was unlisted. Where in the world was she calling me from? I didn't want to see Mikki. I didn't want to see anyone.

Less than forty minutes later, though, the doorbell rang. It was my sister. I peeped out the window, and our eyes met. Slowly, reluctantly, I opened the door. She rushed in and wrapped her arms around me for a warm embrace. I didn't hug her back.

"Zaria, tell me what's going on," she said, oblivious to my lack of affection. She walked farther into the foyer and took off her coat.

"Oh, nothing much," I said, heading for the den. "My boss called me into his office yesterday and fired me and now I don't have a job or any way to pay my bills, and no prospects for a new job that will pay me anything close to what I was making, and I'm two minutes from slitting my wrists thinking about how easy it would be for me to end up right back in Newark struggling to put food on my table and support my family without government assistance. That's all that's going on."

Mikki followed me into the den, albeit slowly. She was getting big, and wasn't quite negotiating the walking very well for someone who was only six months' pregnant. I started to ask her if she was all right, but you know Mikki; she could have been exaggerating her movements for a little extra attention. She was good at that. And I wasn't in the mood to entertain it. So I sat down and waited for her barrage of questions.

"Okay, we're not going to let any of that happen," she said, flopping down onto the couch. "Start from the beginning. What happened?"

I took a deep breath, focused on a piece of lint on the carpet, and recounted the beginning of the end of life as I knew it.

It's not like I was skipping into work, anyway. Sure, I'd gotten there on time, but I was dragging, mainly because my mind was still on the fiasco that had been my Sunday dinner. After Kenneth had left, I went into my kitchen to wash my dishes and strategize on what I was going to do about James the ogre and Jasmine the flirt, and finally decided to deal with Jazzy on another occasion and focus solely on my son, who was upstairs sulking somewhere. I settled on talking—which he refused to do—and then punishment. Two weeks, no Playstation after school for showing up for dinner an hour and a half later than he was supposed to; one thousand "I will not be mean to my mother's guests," for being so incredibly rude to Kenneth. Needless to say, when boyfriend got up the next morning, he was as sour as a lemon, which made me equally sour.

With all of this on my mind, I wasn't really thinking about the buzz that had been going on around the office before Christmas vacation. In fact, I'd pushed it so far back into the recesses of my mind that I'd forgotten about the horrible rumors Florence had floated about the office, intended, my coworkers and I had decided, to try to interfere with our holiday cheer. So we ignored it and went home to our Christmas shopping and decorating and cooking and everything else we were focused on doing to get into the holiday spirit.

So when Rob called me into his office, the only thing I was annoyed about was that I hadn't had a chance to finish my cup of coffee and a story I was reading online on *The New York Times'* web site; I needed my peace—I wasn't in the mood for orders, not yet.

"Have a seat," he said. I could tell from his face—he looked grim, he was beet-red, and he wasn't looking me in the eye—that this was more than my boss handing over some student tuition casework. I sat down nervously, and crossed my legs. "I'm afraid I have a bit of bad news. I'm not going to beat around the bush: the college is in the middle of a financial crunch and all the departments are being asked to cut back, including this one. I was told to lay off two people, and you're one of the people I have to let go."

I was stunned. Let go? Fired? Fired! How did we get here?

"I don't understand," I said, after a few seconds of stunned (me), awkward (him) silence. "How can they make cutbacks in the department that collects the money? We're understaffed as it is." I thought about the silliness of my statement; here I was, asking for an explanation of how the department was going to survive, and not really getting to the heart of the matter, which was how I was going to survive. I mean, come on—"we're understaffed?" Obviously, "we" was now irrelevant. I was no longer a part of the equation. Rob interrupted my mental self-lashing.

"I'm not quite sure how we're going to handle the workload, but those were my orders."

I was quiet. Rob still wouldn't look me in the eye. "Who else was let go?" I finally asked.

"Terry."

That was the young guy they'd just hired last fall, right out of college. I guess if you had to decide to let someone go, he would have been the first on my list—you know, last one hired, first one fired. But I'd been there for eight years now, and a whole bunch of employees had been hired after me. I'd seen more than my share come and go through that office, some new graduates who figured they could get paid more money more quickly if they found their way into a different profession, some who couldn't take the intensity of the workload and the volatile students and parents who didn't take too kindly to having to hand over their hard-earned money, no matter the educational cause. But I'd been here, faithful and diligent—hardworking and good at what I did. Why not fire Lew? He was slow, a little whiney, and had been there only four years. Or Maria? She'd been there only five years. Or Jabber Jaw? All of us could answer our own phones and change the cartridge in the fax machine. We certainly didn't need her flabby ass around.

But someone had decided they didn't need my ass around. And I wanted to know why. "So, can you at least tell me why I was targeted as opposed to the other people in this office?"

"I wouldn't use the word *'target,'* " he said, wincing.

"I'm being fired, aren't I? I'd consider that a target."

"Well, the word 'target' suggests that you're being singled out—and you're not. I just had to make some very hard decisions, and one of those decisions was that you would be one of the two people who was laid off," he said. I didn't say anything, just stiffened in my seat. "The reason you're one of the two is because you are one of the highest paid in the office, and it was either you, or two others in your place. The other two make just a few thousand more combined than you do alone. Really, it was about the bottom line, nothing else."

He said that "nothing else" a little fast. Bastard. He probably thought I was trying to suggest that I was fired for my skin color. Not that that would be a stretch, considering there were only two of us there in the first place. The other black girl, Bernadette, was in support services—which basically meant she had no power, made no money, and had to answer to everyone else in the office but the loudmouthed secretary.

"You will get two weeks' severance pay, and will, of course, be eligible for unemployment, so this won't be so bad," he said with a smile, probably sincerely thinking he was easing my mind by telling me I should be happy for their pennies and the free government money.

"I don't know about where you come from, but where I come from, not having a job is as bad as it gets," I snapped. "And as for the two weeks' severance, I'll try not to spend it all in one place. Nice knowing you."

And with that, I stomped out of Rob's office and back to my desk. I didn't even bother asking when my layoff was effective; I picked up an empty box and quickly threw my things into it. I could tell people were trying not to look at me; it was quiet as all get out, save for the ringing phones. Of course, though, the tackiest of the bunch made a point of making it over to my desk to express her "sincere sorrow."

"It's so unfair, sweetie," Florence said, pouring on the syrup. "I don't feel so bad for Terry because he's young and he'll find something to do pretty quickly. But we're all worried for you. Did Rob at least tell you why you were being laid off over everyone else in the office?"

"Look, Florence," I snarled. "I'm not in the mood for your fake consolation and your gossip probe. So if you don't mind, step away from my desk so that I can get my shit and get the hell out of here."

I swear, that woman turned a shade of scarlet so unnatural a medic could have easily walked in and thought she was choking on her tongue. She didn't say anything else, just held her breath, walked back over to her desk, and answered the phone.

Speechless. It was a miracle.

Not more than ten minutes later, I had my pocketbook slung over my arm and my box of belongings in my hand. I tried not to look at the pictures of my kids resting on the top of the box; looking into their faces was going to make me break down—and I didn't want to do that. Not here.

"And that was it? You just walked out without anyone else saying anything to you?" Mikki asked, her jaw clearly dropped.

"What else were they going to say? I was fired, Mikki. Told to get to steppin'. There wasn't much else for anyone to say."

We were both quiet for a while. I was exhausted, and I didn't want to talk about it anymore. But I should have figured my sister wouldn't pick up on that.

"Well, here's what we're going to do: We'll just find you another job."

I looked at her like she was out of her natural-born mind. "Oh—my bad, I didn't know you had it like that. You just have a $60,000 job with great hours sitting around for a single mom with no college degree?"

"Come on, Zaria—it can't be that hard. We'll just look through the want ads and make some inquiries."

"And when's the last time you actually went on a job search, Mikki, that you know how easy it is to get a good-paying job like the one I just lost?" I said, venomous—maybe too much so. She didn't deserve to have a new one ripped for her, but I couldn't help it, and she wasn't making it any easier for me to back away.

"You know what? I'm going to ignore that, because I know you're upset," she said calmly, without even blinking. "Whether you want to admit it or not, you're going to need help. And I'm your sister, so it only makes sense that I help you.

"So here's what's going to happen: Randy and I are going to make a few of your mortgage payments so that you won't have to worry about that expense while you're looking for your job and waiting for unemployment to kick in. Then, I'll have Randy—"

I cut her off. "Hold up. I don't want your money, Mikki. I don't need your money. I don't need the government's money. I'm not going to go back to the days when I had to depend on someone else to figure out where me and my kids were going to eat and sleep—and I most certainly am not going to start depending on my family to do for me now what it refused to do for me when I most needed the help."

"That's foul," Mikki said. She heard loud and clear the veiled jab I had made toward my mother and father for the years they left me to collect welfare checks with two babies on my lap. "That was a long time ago, Zaria, and we've all recognized the mistakes we made and moved on. And please remember, I was only a teenager when all of that went down, so there's no need to be mad at your little sis for what our parents did to you. Just accept the help, dammit. You don't even have to say thank you."

"No, thank you," I said simply. "Now if you don't mind, I have to go shower and get dinner on the stove so that my kids will have a hot meal on the table when they come in from school."

I left her sitting in the den, mouth agape. Upstairs in the shower, hot tears mixed with the water that ran hard from the shower nozzle onto my face. "I'm going to figure this out," I said, trying to convince myself that everything was going to be all right. "I'm going to figure this out."

The phone rang just as I was getting the last of the dishes dried and put away. I wasn't really in the mood to talk, so I decided before I'd even heard a voice that I was going to be extremely short with whoever it was on the other end of the phone. But it was Kenneth, and I just didn't have the heart to be rude to him, particularly since he started the conversation by telling me he had some exciting news. Frankly, he seemed a bit more excited than I'd expect a man with a newly unemployed girlfriend to be, but whatever.

"There's a community center that's looking for a financial administrator," he said hurriedly, "and the guy who's doing the hiring is an old friend of mine. I've already talked to him about you and he really wants to meet you."

"Well, that certainly sounds promising," I said, sounding not quite as enthusiastic as I should have. "How much does it pay?"

"Somewhere between forty and forty-five thousand, but I'm sure you can negotiate with them."

"That's a pretty steep drop for me," I said. "Where is it and what are the hours like?"

"It's in Jersey City, and I'm sure their hours will be flexible. It's a community center, so it stays open through the evening, but since you'll be handling the books, there'll be no reason for you to be there past normal business hours. But I'm sure you can talk to them about that, too, if you're worried about being home in time to greet the kids."

"Where in Jersey City is it?" I asked.

"Over on Communipaw Avenue," he said.

I thought about it for a minute, trying to get a mental image of the area. I was no Jersey City expert, but that avenue sounded familiar to me—mainly because it frequently came up in newscasts as one of the places where bad things happened in Jersey City. Criminal-type things. Maybe I was mistaken, but it didn't seem like the ideal place to go every day if you didn't have to. "That's not near you, is it?" I asked, a bit of trepidation tingeing my voice.

"No, it's not. It's on the other side of town," he said.

"That's not a good area, is it?" I said.

"Why does that matter?" Kenneth asked, sounding a bit annoyed.

"Well, you probably wouldn't know anything about this, but there are some neighborhoods that are a little, uh, scary for a single woman. Of course I need to get more information. And I'm really grateful that you were looking out for me. But I don't know, Kenneth. . . ." My voice trailed off. This wasn't sounding right. I took a breath and tried again. "I just have to be careful, that's all. I think that's not the greatest neighborhood and, well, I don't know if I'd want to work every day around those kinds of people."

Kenneth was quiet for a moment. "That's where I grew up," he said softly. "And those kinds of people at the community center happened to take pretty good care of me while I was growing up. In fact, some of those kinds of people are still some of my very good friends."

All righty then. Open mouth, insert foot, leg, and most of thigh. But my bluntness didn't change the fact that it *was* a jacked-up neighborhood—and the last thing I wanted to do was to deal with the kinds of people I'd dealt with during my "low" days. I really didn't have any options to be picky, though. And I didn't have to live there; I could lock myself into my office, leave by 3:30 P.M., and bring my paycheck back to Teaneck. "I don't want you to think I don't appreciate this, Kenneth, I really do," I said. "I would very much like to talk to your friend about the position. Who should I call?"

"Don't worry, I'll set it up," he said, still sounding a little disgusted. "Are you free this week?"

"As free as free can be," I said.

"All right. I'll give you a call tomorrow with a time and date."

"That would be great, Kenneth," I said. "And thanks again."

"Yup," he said, and hung up.

He

My students were filing out of the class at the end of seventh period when my cell phone rang. I was startled—once again I had forgotten to turn it off and someone had called me during school hours. This was not going to be good. I reached into my bag and grabbed it.

"Kenneth, I'm on my way there. I have Laney with me." Sheila was on the line, sounding pissed as usual.

"Sheila? Why are you bringing Laney here? I thought I was supposed to be picking her up later."

"Well, these days I can't be sure when you're picking her up."

"What's that supposed to mean? I only missed one weekend, Sheila. Like in the last year, that was it."

I heard a disgusted snort through the phone. "Whatever, Kenneth. Laney's not feeling well and I had to go pick her up. I have something to do now, so she's yours." It sounded especially harsh to be talking about handing over our daughter like she was a book that had been borrowed. I didn't appreciate the tone at all.

"Okay, Sheila. I'm just finishing up here. I'll meet you out in front of the school."

She hung up without another word. It was my suspicion that Laney had told her mother about my new girlfriend. I hadn't really even told Laney, but little kids pick things up by osmosis, just by breathing the same air as their parents. Even though she tried to pretend otherwise,

Sheila clearly still cared. That was interesting because I had no interest or concern whatsoever about who was sliding into Sheila's bed—as long as it was out of Laney's sight.

Quickly I gathered my things and rushed out of the building. It was a Friday afternoon, so the atmosphere was a bit more rambunctious than a regular weekday. The kids had the gleeful air of inmates on a weekend furlough. I could still remember the hopeful excitement I had felt on a Friday afternoon when I was in school—even in college. I saw Principal Bell standing near the school's front entrance, directing students toward their buses like an air traffic controller in a bright blue dress. She waved when she spotted me. I moved away from the buses so that Sheila would be able to see me. A small part of my conscious brain wondered where James Chance was—certainly couldn't have him seeing the handoff. Maybe I should have told her the parking lot. I prayed that the handoff would be smooth; it sounded on the phone like Sheila was in one of her moods. Sometimes she tried to make things a little difficult for me when she was in a mood, do something mean just to tick me off. My job was to ignore any attempts to lure me into confrontation.

I saw Sheila's Toyota creep slowly around the school buses. I really should have told her to meet me by the teachers' parking lot, but that would have been too complicated. As her car approached, I received an image from years ago, when I'd be waiting in almost this identical spot with great anticipation for Sheila to pick me up after school—usually in my car—so that we could do something fun and exciting together. But those sunny days for us hadn't lasted long. By the time she was six months' pregnant, things had thoroughly soured—probably helped immensely by my suggestion that she get an abortion. I sighed—it seemed like a good idea at the time. Our relationship was clearly headed for the dustbin and I was passionate about not wanting to be responsible for another fatherless child. But you can't always get what you want.

Sheila pulled up; I saw Laney in the backseat, her face lighting up when she spotted me at the curb. That moment was one of the things I lived for, to see her face transform like someone had flipped a switch. I stepped toward the car, but the door burst open before I could get any farther and Laney sprinted toward me. Since when had she learned to open the door by herself? I felt a taste of mental anguish—she made so many strides out of my sight every day, sometimes it was like I was picking up a different child.

"Daaaaddddyyyy!" she squealed at a mighty decibel. She ran toward me and lifted off just before she reached me. I caught her in the air and spun her around. It was one of her favorite things. She once told me that she liked me more than Mommy because I could catch her and spin her around.

"Is that your daughter, Mr. Roman?" The voice was a familiar one and, as soon as I heard it, my body went so limp that I almost dropped her.

I turned around to see James and his friend JJ, standing together in their usual slouch and watching me and Laney with somewhat startled expressions. Right away I knew this was one of those pivotal moments in a life, when your fate could abruptly do a 180-degree turn and send you hurtling in another direction. I couldn't lie to the boy, not that I would want to do that anyway. Basically, it was time for me to step up, admit to my child and beg and plead to his mother for forgiveness for not telling her sooner. But how bad it would be if she found out from her son rather than me. It was past 3 P.M. She was supposed to be meeting with Big Oak at two. She might not be done yet.

"Yes, James, this is my daughter, Lane. Say hello to James and JJ, baby." But Laney ducked her head and buried it in my shoulder. She wasn't going to cooperate right now. I could sense her mood—she was looking forward to hours of uninterrupted Daddy time. Who were these strangers with the interruption?

Sheila stepped onto the curb to kiss Laney good-bye. "Okay, Laney, I'm going now." Sheila gave the boys a cursory glance, but she had no interest in slowing down to talk to any students. She had done that enough years ago—she'd say she felt like an artifact in a museum whenever she came to the school because of the stares she'd get from the students and the other teachers. Particularly the other teachers. I glanced at James's face as he watched Sheila. I wondered what he was thinking, getting this instant picture of Mr. Roman as the family man, with a child and the beautiful woman who clearly was the mother of the child. I wondered sorrowfully how this would be described to his mother. Sheila placed Laney's bag on the ground next to me, kissed Laney, and hopped back into her car, taking off without another word. So I was left with the boys.

"Okay, see ya later, Mr. Roman," James said. I thought I saw a smirk on his face. He and JJ gave me the adolescent boy wave—just barely the tiniest movement of the hand, like it was the most painful thing in the world to lift it and acknowledge another person. I watched their departing backs, hearing the swishing sound of their vastly oversized jeans rubbing at the legs. The limpness I felt at first was now gone, replaced by an eerie calm. But I knew it wasn't really calm at all—it was more like a momentary state of shock, like the way pain disappears altogether after a catastrophic injury, just before you black out.

I didn't feel like bringing Laney over to my mother's. I was too edgy to be around my mother anyway. As we made our way to my place, I truly was at a loss over what to do. Would it be best to just drive back to Teaneck and make the Laney-Zaria introductions right now? Or should I call her on the telephone right now and fess up before James got to her? Maybe James wouldn't even tell her—hadn't he and his mother been having communication problems of late anyway? Maybe he'd go home, head to his room, and close the door like usual, content to keep his little secret to himself. That would give me the chance to do the deed. But remembering the smirk on James's face, I wouldn't bet on that scenario. He looked like a kid who was going to use this news as a bat to smash over his mother's head.

When Laney entered the apartment, she immediately headed for her room, which was not really her room right now. Ronnie had claimed that they would be moving out in a matter of days because she had found a place in Jersey City. I think Boo might have had something to do with it, but I had no interest in the details at this point. As long as they were going to be close enough for Tariq to go to school everyday and attend to his basketball responsibilities, I wasn't going to turn into a social worker.

"Laney, don't go in that room right now, okay? Remember, I have friends who are staying with me?"

She gave me a look I couldn't quite read. I think it was annoyance—like, how could you let these strangers stay in my space so long, Dad? But she didn't say anything. She turned away from the room and headed for the TV in the living room.

"Can I watch a movie? Can I watch *Snow White and the Seven Drawers*?"

"It's 'Dwarfs.' *Snow White and the Seven Dwarfs.* Remember we went through this before? Dwarfs are short people."

Laney gave me a grin so big that I could see her missing tooth on the bottom. "Yeah, like midgets. You said they're men, but they're small like me." She giggled, her deep dimples creasing her cheeks. For some reason, the mental image of that made her giddy. I wondered if she would still be amused if she saw a midget in real life. Something told me she'd want to run in the other direction.

The door to the second bedroom opened and Ronnie Spencer appeared with a ready smile for Laney. On the couple of occasions when they had been together, Laney had been drawn to the woman, even sitting on her lap about five minutes into their first meeting. Ronnie had a warm, gentle way with young kids. As a matter of fact, she had recently gotten a job at a daycare center. At least that's what she told me.

"Hey, baby!" Ronnie said, holding her arms open for Laney. My daughter rushed up and gave her a hug. Ronnie was more affectionate toward the girl than her own mother was. Okay, maybe that was a bit harsh. I take that back.

"How's the job going?" I asked.

"It's good," Ronnie said, releasing Laney. "I have the early shift, so I get off at three. Eight to three." She understood that my question was really asking why she was home if she was supposed to have a new job. Though she might sometimes appear otherwise, Ronnie was not a dummy. She walked into the kitchen, brushing by me in skintight jeans. I caught a whiff of her scent. It smelled like my Yardley's oatmeal soap mixed in with a bit of her female musk. It was not unpleasant. But Ronnie had given up on trying to seduce me. I still got plenty of glimpses of her lush flesh, but it wasn't nearly as insistent now. She still didn't go out of her way to cover up when she stepped from the shower or sat on the couch wearing nothing but T-shirt and panties. But I got no more deep bends in my face with panties riding far up her ass. Actually, her new demeanor was far sexier to me than when she threw it at me every five minutes.

"Daddy, can I watch the movie?" Laney asked again. I looked down at my watch. We had to leave in an hour for a basketball game. A home game at St. Paul's against a weak opponent. They were almost all weak opponents this year. A movie would be a good distraction for an hour while I pondered my fate with Zaria. Or wallowed in self-pity over what might happen to me when she found out.

"Okay, Laney, I'll put the movie in."

"Yay!" she said, jumping up and down.

After setting Laney up, I went into my bedroom and sat on the edge of the bed with my head in my hands. My stomach was churning, reflecting my emotions at the moment. The calm that I had felt earlier was long gone now. I was actually afraid. For about the two thousandth time, I beat myself up for not revealing Laney right away. What a cliché I had turned into. I just prayed she gave me a shot at forgiveness. Zaria seemed like she could be a hard woman when she wanted. All I had to do was to think back on our first meeting at the parent-teacher conference. How would my right-wing girlfriend react to the news that I had a child? Was there any way to predict, based on her off-the-wall political views? I wondered if she had gotten the job with Big Oak—actually, there was no doubt he'd offer; the question was if she'd take it, if she'd be able to overcome her apparent contempt for poor people to take a job that would put her around them all day. I had never asked, but I bet she was a registered Republican. I shook my head—boy, if my friends from college could see me now, crying over the possibility of getting dumped by a conservative Republican. The same guy who once refused to sleep with the finest girl on campus because she said she didn't believe in affirmative action. She had the smoothest brown skin any of us had ever seen, plus a tiny waist with a big ol' heart-shaped booty that she paraded around campus like a prize. Even her name made us horny—Lorna Savage. But I said "No" and left her room in a rage after she had sucked me into a political debate. Damn, I was young and naïve then. Throw that same woman in front of me thirteen years later and I'd pop that behind all night. As a matter of fact, Zaria had told me that she thought affirmative action did more harm than good. I hadn't even reacted to her—probably because I had just watched her walk across the room in a tight skirt and wasn't in possession of all of my faculties. You can call it maturity.

Besides our mutual attraction to beauty, we appeared to have a completely different way of seeing the world, of investing hope (me) or misery (Zaria) in our fellow man. I wondered at first if this could possibly work, if we could breathe the same air and not suffocate each other with our contrariness. But soon I began to realize that there was a reason for us. We not only made sense, we were necessary. We mediated each other, softened each other's edges, scaled back our extreme and dangerous impulses. Without each other we risked the emotional isolation of the extreme, the irrelevancy of the radical. It was the same messy prudence that defined the American political system, the id and the ego of Democrat and Republican, the left and the right. Taken together, we were the practical centrist, the middle-of-the-road conformist. We were the voting bloc that carried elections, the powerful American conscience. We were America. Okay, okay, that's taking it quite a bit too far. She was fine, the sex was great, and she made me like myself. What more explanation was needed?

But I knew it was time now. I had to face the music, as the saying goes. Meet my maker. Step to the plate. Pay the piper. I took a deep breath and walked over to the phone. I heard Laney giggling in the other room, probably over something funny the "drawers" had done. I took another breath and dialed Zaria's number. She answered on the second ring.

"Hello, Zaria?"

There was a long silence. Uh-oh.

"Please, don't ever call my house again!" she hissed into the phone. Her voice wasn't raised at all, but she might as well have been screaming in my ear at the top of her lungs. The venom was palpable, seeping through the phone line like a toxic fog. I was momentarily dazed.

"Please, Zaria, let me—"

"Just leave me the fuck alone!" she said, at an even lower register this time. I almost had a hard time hearing. "I knew you were too good to be true. I let myself be fooled. Never again." The line went dead. I clutched the phone in my hand long enough to hear the dial tone, then that awful honking noise telling me to give it up. She was gone.

She

I'm a mother, okay? And there is nothing more important to me than my two hearts—James and Jasmine. I've been through it with these kids; got kicked out of my parents' house over them, got forced into and climbed out of the ridiculously oppressive cycle of poverty and government dependency to feed, clothe, and care for them, got rid of their emotionally abusive father to save them from heartbreak from a man who obviously didn't care enough about them to be so bothered to come see them, much less help me raise them. I did it because I love them. Because the very thought of losing them makes me want to reach into my chest and pull out my heart with my bare hands. I'm sure that's what I would do if anything were to ever happen to them—unless someone was able to put me in a straitjacket and throw me into a rubber room somewhere before the deed was done. Shouldn't all parents feel that way about their kids? How can you deny someone you love that much?

The answer is, you don't. I mean I have never, ever, never ever, hidden the fact that I'm a single mother. It's practically the first thing out of my mouth after I tell a man my name: "Hi, I'm Zaria Chance, and I have two kids." Repercussions, stereotypes, assumptions be damned. That's the kind of person I am. Which means that Kenneth Roman isn't who I thought he was. He can't be. Because if he were truly a person capable of loving and being loved back, he wouldn't have hidden the fact that he had a child, and he wouldn't have lied all these months to me. And he certainly wouldn't have let me find out the way he did—by exposing my child to his lies.

Not that I was in the greatest of moods the day I found out my boyfriend was a liar anyway. I'd fought my way through a ridiculous amount of traffic on the New Jersey Turnpike—there was an accident and the entire world was slowing down to five miles per hour to see what looked like a minor fender bender—to be at the community center for my interview by 2 P.M., and what did I get for my trouble? A chance to sit around watching mostly grown, dusty men who should have been somewhere earning a decent living running up and down a basketball court, acting like they were in the NBA playoffs. The director, who was supposed to be interviewing me for the comptroller's position, was nowhere to be found, and the attitudinal receptionist, Evilene, who'd acted as if I'd ruined her millennium by asking her when her boss would be back, was absolutely no help whatsoever. "If he said he was going to meet you here, then he'll be here," she said, not even bothering to take her eyes off the hair magazine she was flipping through.

"Well, can you tell me if he can be reached? Does he have a cell phone or a pager? Because we were supposed to meet fifteen minutes ago, and if he's not going to make it to the interview, then perhaps I can reschedule."

"Like I said, he'll be here when he gets here," she said, finally looking me in the eye. "You can have a seat over in the gym, or wait here in the lobby."

And so I waited. I'd stood in the lobby for what seemed like an eternity, then took Evilene's advice and went into the gym. It was fairly nice in there—nice enough, considering how run-down the outside of the center looked. Nestled in a stretch of brownstones, the building hardly looked like the center of anyone's community. A tattered awning weakly announced its name; the paint on the doors struggled against unreadable graffiti that seemed to cover almost every inch of the huge, metal doors that stood guard over the lobby. The brownstone to the right of the building was burned out; the one to the left looked as if it was abandoned, but a closer look revealed that someone did indeed occupy a few of the top floors. I'd assumed when I went into the center that it would look like an extension of the neighborhood, but it was surprisingly well maintained. Just past the gym was what appeared to be a library, where a roomful of kids sat hunched over books—a scene I definitely didn't expect to see. Kids? Studying? Here? I could have been foul and assumed that the only reason they were in there was because the men balling on the court were hogging it from the little ones, but I'm not that ridiculous. I was actually pleased to see that the children were willingly doing something constructive—or that someone at least made them. I started to sneak upstairs to see what the rest of the place looked like, but I thought better of it. Mr. Oakley was late, but I didn't want to look like I wasn't waiting, so I went back to the lobby and waited. Until exactly 3:14. I'd just written a note explaining that I had other commitments and would contact him to reschedule when this big, hulking man strolled in through the front door, a cup of coffee in his hand, without a care in the world. "Good afternoon, Janiece," he said to the receptionist. "What's going on?"

"There's a woman over there looking for you—says she's here for an interview," she said, nodding her head over in my direction. Unbelievable. She didn't even bother cracking a smile for the man who pays her bills, much less conduct herself in a professional manner. What the hell ever happened to professionalism? It's like a whole generation of black girls skipped etiquette and landed in a course on how to show the public the meanest, rudest, nastiest face possible. My, how things had changed in such a short time. I refused to deal with it in department and grocery stores, and even dropped a few doctors because of rude receptionists—but damn, did I have to work with them now? Then I remembered Florence, the nosy, infuriating, two-faced receptionist at Lawrence. Let me shut up. Maybe Janiece wasn't so bad.

Anyway, the director, Mr. Oakley, looked over in my direction and strolled his large body toward me. "Ms. Chance?" he said, switching his coffee from his right to his left hand, and then using his right to pump my hand up and down. "It sure is nice to meet you. Come on in to my office."

"Nice to meet you, too, Mr. Oakley," I said. "I was worried that we wouldn't get to speak today," I said, fishing for an explanation or at least an apology for his lateness. It didn't come.

"So," he said, taking a seat behind his desk and extending his hand to direct me to a chair before him, "Kenneth tells me that you'd be terrific for the job. Let me tell you a bit about it: The comptroller here is responsible for payroll, paying the center's bills, and keeping our financial books in order. If someone gets hired, you'll let me know how much money I have to pay him. If folks get fired, you'll be responsible for working out the details on what they're entitled to and whether they'll be eligible to collect unemployment and things of that nature. You'll also be responsible for preparing the work schedules for all employees and ordering supplies and equipment. Occasionally, I may ask you to help me write grants for the continued effort to fund-raise for this institution. That's about it. This is a nice community center and we're a close-knit group of individuals who work hard to create an open, comfortable environment for the kids and the adults who come here, so it would be great if you did participate in keeping that environment intact. Any questions?"

"Well, that sounds enticing," I said, lying through my teeth. He had me going until he suggested I'd have to actually be around the community center people. I think I needed extra for that. "Would you like to see my résumé?" I asked, reaching down into my briefcase to grab my portfolio.

"Oh, there's no need for that. If Kenneth Roman sent you, I know you must be more than all right. In fact, the way he puts it, you're much more than all right."

Gosh, was Kenneth up in this community center telling my potential boss all about our relationship? How much did he know? I made a mental note to tell Kenneth that whatever happened between us needed to stay between us if I was going to take this job; the last thing I needed was for my boss to know all my personal business. I pretended I hadn't heard his last comment and moved on to the money. Mr. Oakley was a big man, his face was a bit rough around the edges, and he had a voice like rumbling thunder; if I'd have been sitting across from him eight years ago, when I was a single mom desperate to get any job that would keep a roof over my head and a bit intimidated by head Negroes in charge, I might not have raised it. But I didn't have time to beat around the bush today; I needed this job, but I also needed to be paid. He needed to know that. "Mr. Roman said that the position paid up to forty-five thousand. Is that negotiable? And what kind of hours are you talking about?"

"Yes, the position pays forty-five thousand, but Kenneth did tell me that you might want a little more than that. I can go up to fifty thousand, but that would be under a grant that lasts only two years. After that, we'll have to figure out how to keep paying you, or I'll have to go back to doing the books myself. As for your hours, I'd like you to be here by 9 A.M., and you can leave by 3 P.M.—unless there is an event that you're required to attend, then it'll be as long as the event lasts. But I expect that won't be too often, and you will certainly have plenty of advance notice before those events come."

Yeah, right.

"Well, that sounds fine," I said. I better stop acting crazy and take this gig; no telling where I was going to get a $50,000 job where they didn't even look at my résumé, let alone sweat me over my lack of college education. I had a mortgage to pay. I could get over the low-budget way of doing business. I guess. "If you're offering, I'm taking," I said as cheerily as I could muster.

"Now, that's what I wanted to hear," he said, standing up and reaching over his desk to shake my hand. And just like that, the interview was over. I was no longer unemployed.

I wasn't going to throw a party to celebrate, but I was in a bit of a better mood by the time I'd gotten home, knowing that I had a new job. It was going to be tough taking the pay cut, and the commute was going to be a killer, and working in that kind of environment wasn't what I'd had in mind—I don't care what Kenneth says or where he grew up, Communipaw Avenue was a mess, and I was making a mental note to be out of there every day before the streetlights came on—I'd still be pulling a decent wage and decent hours. I guess that was worth half of a "yeah!"

At least that's what I'd convinced myself before James walked in with his bombshell. "Did you know that Mr. Roman has a kid?" he asked me just as easily as one would say "pass the salt." Actually, his question came somewhere between "Hi, Mom," and asking if he could have some chips before dinner.

"Huh?" I said.

"Can I have some chips?" he asked.

"What did you say before that?"

"I said did you know that Mr. Roman has a kid—a daughter. This lady who looked just like the little girl dropped her off at our school today, and Mr. Roman took her home."

"James, what in the world are you talking about?" I searched his face for any telltale signs that he was making this up, and, for a minute, I thought I saw a smirk cross his lips—something that quickly said he was pleased with my shock. It disappeared, though, as quickly as it had come.

"I think he said her name is Lane," he said, continuing the story as if I understood every word he was saying. "She looked like she was young, like Summer's age, maybe a little older."

"Is that right?" I said. "You talked to him and he said it was his daughter?" I didn't wait to hear James's answer; I'd heard him correctly the first time. He said my boyfriend, whom I had dated now for more than two months, had a daughter, and that she was about four or five, and that Kenneth was up at that school parading that child, whom he had not told me about, for all the world to see. Including my son. What the hell?

"Uh-huh. Can I have some potato chips?"

There was that smirk again. I don't know if it was because I was instantly angry about James's revelation that I decided to get on my son, or if it was because he was acting like a little jerk and playing this "gotcha" game with me, but he caught the wrath. I wasted no time ripping into his little behind.

"James?"

"Yes, Mother?"

"What exactly do you think you're doing?"

"What do you mean, Mom?" he asked, trying to act all innocent. Pretending I didn't know he was meddling in my business and taking pleasure in telling me something I didn't know about my boyfriend, knowing exactly what it would lead to.

"You know exactly what I mean," I said. "You tripped out at dinner the other night when Kenneth was here—acted like you have absolutely no home training in front of my company, and now you're standing here taking pleasure in telling me this bit of information, knowing that it's upsetting? Obviously, I didn't know about this little girl, but you can wipe the smirk off your face right now. I don't know what you have against Kenneth Roman, but I won't tolerate your disrespecting me in my house because you have issues with our dating."

He didn't say anything at first, just looked at me like I was an alien who had dropped out of the sky into the middle of his kitchen. I didn't believe this boy: Did he think he was smarter than me? More clever, perhaps? What was it with the cockiness of teenagers? It was like puberty hormones made them think they were slicker than any grownup who ever dared cross their path; all they had to do was make their eyes as wide as saucers, drop information in an innocent voice, then step aside and act as if they didn't know what kind of impact their statements and actions would have on their elders. Little dummies.

"I have a problem," he said finally, "with you dating my social studies teacher, knowing that my father is home and wants to see me and you won't let him."

Now, I was speechless. Almost. His father? When did he ever get the impression that his daddy was looking to see him? Did he hear me on the phone with Ricky when he called looking for his ride from prison? I couldn't remember, but I swore the kids weren't home that day, or they were sleep or something. How would he know about that conversation? "James, back up and tell me what's going on, please."

James took a deep breath and told me a fantastic tale about how his father had called here Saturday while I was out grocery shopping for Sunday dinner, and how his daddy told him that he wanted to come see him but I wouldn't allow it, so he was going to stay away a while, "until your mama comes around."

"I want to see my dad," James said, whining like a little boy. Tears welled up in his eyes; I caught them before he had the chance to turn his head away to hide his crying from me. I wanted to scream—to cry out over the turmoil that these men were putting me and my family through. I didn't want this—didn't need it. A liar for a boyfriend and a fresh-out-of-prison baby daddy hell-bent on tearing my life apart and turning my kids against me. Here I was, thinking I was protecting my children from all the adult drama that had found its way into my life, only to find out that my world was crumbling from beneath me and there wasn't a damn thing I could do to stop it.

Instinctively, though, I knew that no matter how I felt right now, I had to put on my game face for my child. "James," I said, walking over to the kitchen table. "Come sit down, will you please, sweetheart?" I pulled his chair close to me and cupped his chin in my hands. "I love you more than anything in this world," I said, looking into his eyes. "And I need you to know that. I also need you to know that the things that Mommy does are for your protection, because I love you so very much. I've never talked badly about your father in front of you, I've never done anything or said anything to make you think badly of him—he managed that all by himself." James squirmed in his chair; perhaps I didn't need to add that last part, but it was true. "But I need you to know that I would never knowingly keep you away from your daddy. I've talked to him maybe three times in the last six years, and the last time was a few weeks ago, when he asked me to come pick him up from prison. I told him that I didn't want to have anything to do with that and that if he needed a ride, he would have to call someone else. But I never once told him that he couldn't see you or your sister.

"As for Mr. Roman," I continued, "he has nothing to do with your father. Your father and I are history; we're not ever going to get back together, and it's important that you understand that, baby. He may tell you that he wants to be your father and eventually step to the plate and do that, but he will never be the kind of man your mother needs. I thought Mr. Roman might have been that man, but now I'm not so sure. But it's important to me that you understand that the two of them are not linked; I wasn't dating Mr. Roman to hire him as a replacement for your daddy; I was dating him because I liked him."

James didn't say anything—just broke down and cried in my arms like the child that he was. "It's okay, baby," I said over and over again, rocking him. "It's okay."

Just then the phone rang. Reluctantly, I went into the den and picked up the receiver. It was Kenneth. I felt my heart pounding. In an instant, at least ten different ways to handle him ran through my mind—wait and see if he was going to confess and then curse him out, tell him calmly to lose my number, or just curse him out without preliminaries and rudely give him dial tone. Number three was most logical—it'd eliminate the need for conversation and also satisfy my need to inflict maximum pain.

One thing was sure: I wasn't going to cry.

I didn't have time for it.

I've got to think about my kids.

Fuck these men.

That's all I have to say about that.

He

Okay, I knew it would be bad when she found out, I knew there'd be hell to pay, but I didn't really expect the end. I figured I'd be able to wait a few days, enough time for her to consider me having suffered, then I could send a bunch of flowers, maybe a deeply affecting letter, and stroll back into her life. Turns out I couldn't have been more wrong.

Zaria Chance struck me from her life so thoroughly that it made my head spin. She was one of those women who could turn off her emotions like a faucet, at least to the outside world. It was almost impressive in its efficiency, how she could effectively isolate a portion of her heart and wall it off, building enough barriers around it that she could pretend it never was.

Big Oak was supposed to be my secret weapon, my inside spy. She was working at the center now, right there under his nose, and I expected that to pay major dividends. But I was wrong—I got nothing, nowhere. After waiting a sufficient period, nearly one week of some of the most painful second-guessing and self-flagellation a brother has ever endured, I played my gambit: three dozen long-stemmed red roses. From a real florist, not a cheap little bodega, delivered to her desk at the Uptown Community Recreation Center, with a heartfelt apology attached:

Dear Zaria,

    Words cannot fully express my regret over my lie of omission. I knew it was wrong, but I wanted you to like me so much that I made a stupid mistake. Zaria, I never got a chance to tell you this to your face, but it's true: I Love You. I'm sure I always will. I pray you will give me another chance.

When I had finished the note at the florist, I almost wanted to cry. How could an admission of love fail to move her? Assisted by three dozen beautiful flowers? When I handed my credit card over to the cashier, I just knew I'd be getting a phone call from my lady, probably on my celly before I got home for the night. I raced back to Teaneck— I had driven to Jersey City during my lunch break like a crazed person—to catch my seventh-period class, feeling pleased with myself. Later, during basketball practice, I kept expecting my cell phone to ring. I took it from my bag and placed it in my pocket. An hour passed—nothing. I removed the phone from the pocket and held it in my hand. I wanted to give her the best possible chance of reaching me. I didn't even put it down when I instructed the guys on a new back-court trapping defense I was trying to teach them to use against teams with weak point guards. The phone wasn't leaving my grasp—I tucked it under my chin when I took a piss.

Finally, at about 7 P.M.—okay, exactly 7 P.M.—as the guys hit the showers, I ran to my office to call the community center and find out what had happened.

"She didn't even read the note?" I asked Big Oak incredulously.

"Nah, man, she threw it in the garbage," he said. I thought I heard a chuckle in his voice.

My God, I had told her I love her and she didn't even see it? I was stunned. Wasn't she even curious what it said? I was dealing with some breed of female here that I had never encountered, one who wouldn't even read the damn note.

"She personally handed out the flowers? Like, she held them in her hands?"

"Nah, man, she had one of the boys do it. She told Brandon, he's a teenager, not a bad student, to give one to every girl or woman in the building. We had almost exactly thirty-six females in the center at the time—not including Zaria. So it was perfect. You should have seen the smiles on their faces."

I cursed under my breath. I had no interest in their smiles. Those smiles cost me over $150—about $5 for each one of them. I thought of something else I had been wanting to ask Big Oak.

"Big Oak, has she mentioned me or talked about me?"

"No, she hasn't said a word about you. Of course, I talked about you on her first couple of days. Told her how proud I was of you and all, even showed her where you used to sit in the library—remember your corner over there? I thought her reaction was kinda cold. I started wondering if this was the same woman that you had told me about. But then at the end of her second day of work, she told me y'all had broke up. She didn't say it mean, or with any bitterness. She said it like she was telling me the weather outside, to be honest. She's a pretty tough one, Kenneth. Good luck trying to get back in her graces. I don't know what you did, but it must have really hurt her."

There was a long silence. I was speechless, letting his words wash over me like acid, searing holes into my skin. Was it really over? Or was this just a long-term punishment? How could I win her back if she wouldn't even read my love note?

Over the next few weeks I passed through all the stages of a well-known disorder—post breakup stress. First there's Self-Pity. Then there's Self-Determination. Finally there's Self-Righteousness. Each one has its own distinct character and rhythm—and own special form of pain.

Self-Pity

This was the worst, the one that brought the suffering to the surface so that I could wallow in it. I beat myself up at some point at least every hour, horrified by what I had done through sheer idiocy. I wished I could teach a seminar for all the baby daddies out there so that my heartache wouldn't have been in vain. It would have one overarching theme: Come clean—and early. If you wait too long, she'll give your flowers away.

When I was deep in the throes of the condition, I couldn't even be cheered up by something I had been waiting more than a month to see: the departure of Ronnie Spencer. She finally moved her family out one afternoon while I was at school. Tariq told me they were moving in with Boo, and that he planned on spending a lot of time out of the house to avoid his mother's thug boyfriend. That was his description. When a seventeen-year-old calls you a thug, you're a serious thug. I was on the verge of telling him he could stay with me, but I held myself back. I wanted him to leave so that I could mourn my loss in private. It's harder to wallow in grief when you have people around you, wanting to talk and make jokes—and, in his mother's case, offer you sex. I was especially glad that Ronnie wouldn't be around to throw booty in my face during my self-pity. I just might have taken it. After all, as one of my college buddies used to say, the best way to get over the loss of a woman was women.

It's one thing to feel sorry for yourself when you can hide away and escape all memories of your loved one—it's quite a different level of pity when you have to go to work every day and see the living embodiment of your heartbreak, sitting near the back during fifth period, casting an assortment of sneers and smirks in your direction on an almost daily basis. After James had given me an especially smart-ass answer to a question, I was tempted to yank his little behind out of the seat and explain to him that since his mother was no longer even talking to me, his protection was gone, disappeared—so there was nothing (except the law, my nonbelief in corporal punishment, and my desire to keep my job) keeping me from smacking him hard upside his head. But of course all I had at my disposal was my usual arsenal—hard stares, public ridicule, and threats. I employed them all, with varying degrees of success. After a couple of weeks, I resigned myself to the likelihood that James and I would just have to find some way to get to June without any (his) bones getting broken and with my heavy heart unlifted.

My self-pitying was so effective that my mother even felt sorry for me, and came over to my place to cook me a fabulous Sunday dinner. I hadn't eaten a real dinner in four days and, worse, hadn't even noticed. My mother sat across the table—the same place that Zaria had sat on that glorious New Year's Eve night just weeks earlier—and watched me devour her roast chicken, macaroni and cheese, collard greens, and homemade biscuits. Nobody made roast chicken as good as my mom. While most people just put it in the oven and let it cook, my mother continued basting like she was cooking Thanksgiving turkey. The result was meat so succulent and juicy that you needed a napkin to wipe your mouth after every bite.

"I told you you should have told her," she said. But she said it softly, not with the attitude she usually had. Still, that was the last thing I needed.

"Ma, please," I said, putting down my fork. "Can we not do this?"

She nodded her head slowly and went back to watching me. Every once in a while she decided to be motherly. It wasn't that my mother lacked the maternal instinct—she was just a selfish person, one who had always been intent on living her own life, not living mine. In some ways it was an admirable trait for mothers to have—the ability to keep seeking pleasure, even after you gave birth. But it didn't always make for a warm and fuzzy, TV-type childhood.

After dinner was over, Dolores Roman said a few choice words to me, trying to cheer me up. Shockingly, it actually worked.

"I know it hurts, but why does it have to be over, Kenneth? What you did was awful, but it's not the end of the world. I think you still probably have a chance. But you're not going to win her back sitting here feeling sorry."

I looked at her for a long time without speaking. That was a pretty effective speech—maybe I needed to bring her into the locker room to talk to my boys during halftime. I nodded. She was right. So just like that, Mom had shoved me from Self-Pity to the next stage, Self-Determination.

Self-Determination

It had occurred to me that I should try to claw my way back into Zaria's good graces, but in the Self-Pitying stage you don't ever locate the energy to actually do something about it. But Self-Determination is another matter. As if I had swallowed a libraryful of self-help manuals, I became Mr. Positive Thinking, sketching a plan of action that would have my lady back in my arms in weeks, if not days. In retrospect, my confidence was completely manufactured, not at all related to reality—which probably intensified the level of my Self-Righteousness at the next stage, once Self-Determination had failed so spectacularly.

First, I started out with a daily bouquet of flowers—not as expensive as a dozen red roses, but still sending out a strong message—delivered to her at the community center every day for an entire week. I called Big Oak the first day and he told me she had thrown them in the garbage. That was disappointing, but not unexpected. (In fact, the only message I had told them to put on the card was "I'm Sorry!" because I knew she probably wouldn't even read it.) On the second day she threw away the bouquet again. Already, that was about $80 in the community center garbage can—though Big Oak said a few of the teenage girls had gone into Zaria's garbage after she had gone home and rescued the bouquets on both nights. I told him I wasn't going to call the rest of the week—he should just call me if she didn't throw the flowers away.

I got a call on my celly on Thursday, after basketball practice. When I heard Big Oak's deep rumble, my heart skipped a few beats. Was I back in there?

"Uh, not exactly," he answered, chuckling. "She walked the flowers over to the teenage girls and gave them away instead of dumping them in the garbage."

"Well, that's something, isn't it?"

"Uh, I wouldn't say that," he said. "She found out that the girls had been rescuing the flowers. But she did have a talk with the girls about you. I don't know exactly what they said, but I heard the girls over there with her, hootin' and hollerin'. I think the girls were trying to convince her to take you back."

I let out a sigh. If there was one thing I might be able to count on, it was the untarnished romanticism of teenage girls. Unfortunately, Zaria seemed immune to romanticism.

"Oak, you think I should give it up?"

"Kenneth, she's a tough cookie, but you know what I'm going to say."

"Yeah, I know, I know. You're gonna say anything worth having is worth fighting for. How could I forget that one?"

He chuckled. "That's my boy."

After the failure of the bouquets, $200 later, I moved on to a cheaper strategy—love letters. Well, they were more like notes. I sat down at my dining room table one night after a basketball game—we had won, of course, so I was feeling blessed—and penned about eight or nine one- or two-paragraph-long love notes, expressing my extreme feelings and extreme sorrow to have lost her. They weren't poetry, but I believed they would get the job done—if only she read them. I was sending them to her home, so I wouldn't have Big Oak and any other spies to tell me what she did with the letters. I would just have to wait for the phone call. . . .

Which never came. Over the course of two weeks, she should have received nearly a letter a day—I forgot to send them out on a couple of days, kicking myself when I'd come home to see the stamped envelope still sticking out of my bag. I would have paid several weeks' salary—teaching AND coaching salary—to find out what she was doing with the letters. Could she really be tossing them in the garbage? Wouldn't there be just an iota of curiosity at this point, nearly a month after she had dumped me? It wouldn't be betraying her anger to just take a peek at the letters, right?

One day I got so desperate that I almost asked James to do some spying for me to see what had happened to the love notes. As he was walking past me heading for the doorway, I opened my mouth and even allowed a noise to come out. It sounded something like "Ja—." But I shut it up before I had completed his name. What a monumentally bad idea that would be. What would Zaria do if she found out I had put James up to some spying—and had even paid him, as I had considered in a moment of desperate delirium? I shuddered at the thought of how royally I had almost screwed up. James turned around to see if I had said his name. He looked at me quizzically, but he said nothing. He disappeared through the doorway. I ran my hand across my sweaty forehead.

After a while, I even stopped waiting for her phone call. That wasn't an admission of failure, really—just the hard shove of reality getting my attention. When I came home at night, I stopped looking at the phone like a mortal enemy, punishing me with its silence. Instead, I just went about my business, grading papers, writing out lesson plans, drawing up new ways to get Jermaine and Tariq good shots despite the double-teams. But I did have one last plot brewing in my head, something she couldn't possibly ignore.

I had been noticing the empty billboard for weeks, musing as I drove by why such a prime spot off the turnpike would go unused for so long. It was near the exit I got off for school, before the worst of the George Washington Bridge traffic started clotting a little farther down the road. One morning as I did my usual commute, I wondered what Zaria thought about when she came this same way after getting out of the community center. I knew this was the route she took because I had sketched it out for her. We had the reverse commute, but we took the same roads. Like me, did she also look up at the billboard and wonder about its emptiness?

As I steered the truck down the ramp one morning, I got a flash of inspiration—how much did an ad on that billboard cost? I had no idea about such things, but I was willing to find out. What a brilliant ploy it would be to put some impassioned message on that billboard, direct from my heart to Zaria's eyes. That would be a note she very well couldn't ignore. Maybe some of her friends would see it, too.

I pulled over and scribbled down the number of the company that owned the billboard space. As soon as I had the chance, I would find out how much my genius plan would cost me.

"A thousand dollars a day?" I said, making sure the woman on the phone heard my outrage. "But I only had a few words I was going to put up there. No pictures or anything. The spot has been blank for weeks. Where's your sense of romance? You're just losing money right now anyway."

"I appreciate that, sir. But I'm not authorized to lower the rates. I could talk to my boss and see what he says." She had the unemotional, automaton tones of a phone company operator. I knew I wouldn't get anywhere with her.

"Well, can I talk to the boss?"

"No, that wouldn't be possible, sir, because he's not here right now. Someone will get back to you by the end of the day."

I waited and waited for the return call. By 4:30 P.M., I couldn't take it anymore. I went into a hidden, dusty corner of the St. Paul's gym just before practice and whipped out my phone. As I was beginning to dial, I saw some movement underneath the bleachers. My first instinct was to jump back—I thought it was a rat or something equally unpleasant. But I looked closer and saw people, two bodies writhing against each other, apparently having sex.

"Who the hell is that?" At the sound of my voice, I heard a noise, almost like a yelp, come from one of them. It sounded like a female. I peered underneath and saw two figures in the dark, up against the wall, hurriedly trying to pull their clothes back on. "What are y'all doing down there?" Though it was clear what they were doing. Or at least had been doing.

They emerged very slowly. Leading the way was Jermaine Bryson, with his eyes cast downward, avoiding my glare. I was pissed, but it was almost funny how pitiful he looked. I waited to see who the girl was. But she had stopped, as if she were going to stay down there forever.

"Come on out, honey," I said. "Get it over with."

She creeped at a snail's pace, her face still obscured by the shadows. I saw Jermaine trying to get away. "Jermaine! Where you think you're going?" He halted in his tracks. I turned back and finally saw the girl's face. It was Sondra Whitfield, the beautiful and talented star of the girls' team. With her eyes stretched as wide as they could go and her light complexion devoid of color, the blood having fled her face, she was so full of fright and embarrassment that I don't think I'll ever forget that look. I almost gasped, I was so shocked. Female athletes were supposed to stay out of this kind of trouble, particularly star female athletes. At least that's what the statistics said. I knew a big lecture was in order at this moment, one of those sit-downs about safe sex and the need for them to treasure their bodies, et cetera. But I really, *really* didn't feel like it. I needed to make my phone call. I could lecture later.

"Y'all should be ashamed of yourselves," I started. "I'm shocked and disgusted."

They stood next to each other, their eyes cast downward like two misbehaving children. Damn, raging hormones will be getting teenagers in trouble from now until the end of time. I set my face in a disapproving snarl.

"We're gonna talk about this later," I hissed. "Now get the hell out of here and get ready for practice."

As they scampered away, I thought about maybe getting Coach Clark of the girls' team to handle Sondra. I had no idea what to say to that girl. But I was going to smack Jermaine upside his head. I glanced back under the bleachers and shook my head. Were they even using a condom?

Finally, I made my phone call to the billboard company. The supervisor said he could give me the billboard for a fee of $100 a day, but I had to use it for a minimum of fourteen days. And there was a $500 printing and installation fee if I was going to be getting my board from them. I did the quick math—$1,900 total. Ouch.

"Okay, I'll take it," I said, feeling pained by each of those words. I had put aside more than $12,000 thus far toward the purchase of a house, primarily thanks to my coaching salary. But I was starting to wipe out my savings with this Zaria quest. I had no way of knowing whether the $1,900 was worth it, but in my typically single-minded fashion once I got the idea in my head it was hard for me to divert myself.

The next day I phoned in my billboard order, explaining exactly what I wanted to say and what I wanted it to look like. I was told that they would put a rush on the installation and it should be up in five to seven business days. I tried mightily to put Zaria out of my mind after the order was placed. We were entering the toughest part of our basketball schedule as we got closer to the state playoffs, so that distraction proved to be a big help.

I never got around to talking to Coach Clark about Sondra Whitfield. Jermaine told me that they had been dating ever since the three-point shooting contest and they were serious about each other. He swore that she was the only girl he was messing around with and he gushed for several minutes about how sweet and smart she was—not to mention talented on the court.

"She's, like, perfect, Coach—you know what I'm saying?" Jermaine said, his face covered in earnestness.

It sounded to me like Jermaine was in love. Listening to him and seeing the joy on his face, I started getting wistful about my own raggedy love life. For a brief moment in time, I had felt the same way about Zaria. But apparently that moment had passed—or at least I was trying to will it past.

She

I won't go so far as to say I actually love working at the community center—"love" is such a strong word. But I will say this much: The people who work there and especially the kids who come to the center looking for help with their homework or a friendly game of ball or some adult attention from the counselors aren't as bad as I had thought they'd be. In fact, they're not anything like I expected them to be. These weren't the ghetto queens and the children of ghetto queens that I had come to know in my previous life—get-over artists who worked the system from their raggedy couches in their raggedy living rooms in their raggedy Section 8 apartments in their raggedy neighborhoods. No, these were kids from homes where, even though things weren't perfect, somebody was trying their hardest to make sure that their kids did better than they had. I saw single mothers rushing from the PATH train into the center with their business suits and sneakers to pick up their little boys, and perhaps squeeze in a conversation with the counselors and after-school teachers to make sure their knuckleheads were doing what they were supposed to. I saw fathers drop their little girls off for Girl Scout meetings, and little brothers challenging their older siblings to basketball duels.

Don't get me wrong: There were plenty of kids whose home situations were desperate and seemingly beyond repair—teenagers with one and two babies to feed, kids with parents who were caught up in domestic abuse or on the crack pipe. But so many of them proved to me day in and day out that they were so much more than victims—so much more than tragedies. And I'd actually come to like the place.

Took me a minute, though. That and some gentle coaxing from Mr. Oakley, who, in my first days of working there, would regularly pound on my office door and beg me to come down and meet the kids. "Come on, Lady Zaria—I know I pay you to work hard, but I want you to come on down and meet some of the people you're working hard for," he'd say before dragging me to watch the kids study or talk with the counselors or meet some of the parents. I was reluctant at first—would come up with a billion reasons why I just didn't have the time. But Mr. Oakley wasn't one to take "No" very often. Once or twice, maybe, but that was it. And on nearly each occasion he would tell me something about Kenneth—tall, impressive stories about how good a basketball player he was and how smart he was and how he'd light up the gym the moment 3:30 P.M. came around and he would come "strolling into the center, always with that basketball bouncing from his fingertips," Mr. Oakley would say. "His mother didn't have much, but she took good care of that boy and made sure he turned into something," he'd add. "I've seen many a child get caught up in the welfare system, but you can see for yourself that his mother knew better than to stay in it. Yessir, your Kenneth Roman is a good guy."

"He's not my Kenneth Roman," I said to him finally. "We broke up."

Mr. Oakley looked genuinely surprised, which surprised me. The way he talked about Kenneth, I'd just assumed that they talked all the time. I mean, Kenneth did put in just one phone call and got me a $50,000 gig, so they were obviously still close. Maybe Kenneth didn't talk to him about us all that much after all.

Though they didn't come as often, Mr. Oakley didn't stop with the Kenneth Roman stories after I broke the news. I think the flowers had something to do with it. Out of the blue, I just started getting bouquets at the office, spectacular bunches of roses and daisies, lilacs and peonies. I knew instinctively that they were from Kenneth—I wasn't involved with anyone else who would bother, none of my friends or family was that thoughtful (well, Mikki was, but she would have called me from the florist to tell me she'd sent them), and my kids didn't have enough money to put that kind of smile on my face. So

Kenneth it was. And since I wasn't interested in his apologies and his silly romantic gestures, I decided pretty quickly to simply chuck them in the garbage. It was going to take a lot more, after all, than a bunch of cheap bouquets from a no-name florist to get me to forgive him. Besides, flowers weren't a very creative way to get back into a lady's graces anyway; I mean, it was such an easy way out—and men clung to it like a child does an inner tube in the eight-foot end of the pool. Flowers. Candy. Jewelry. That was the extent of their romanticism, the beginning and end of their apologies. The person who writes a book explaining to men how to actually be creative when they're saying "I'm sorry," or "Happy Mother's Day," or "Thanks for having my baby," or "Thanks for putting up with my sorry ass," would make women a lot happier, let me tell you. Unfortunately, we'd cornered the market on that, and it didn't look like anyone was trying to teach the fellas how to follow suit.

Yeah, yeah, Kenneth's New Year's Eve celebration was pretty creative. But I needed him to be a truthful person, not a romantic. Every time I thought about him, which was often, I couldn't help but to wonder what kind of daddy he was—whether he was as trifling a dad as he had thought I was a mother the first time we met at that parent-teacher conference and he claimed that my son was a mess because there was no man in the house. Obviously, his daughter—what was her name? Lane?—didn't have her daddy in the house either; the times I actually made it up to his apartment, there wasn't any sign of a child living there. Of course, I didn't actually get to see all the other rooms, so I can't be so sure. But then, if he was going to invite me up, he would have to hide all of her things, and her, to keep me from knowing about her. Which brought me back to the reason why I was mad in the first place: He never told me that he had a kid. Was he ashamed of her? Of the kind of father he is? How could I possibly trust him with my kids if he couldn't even tell me about his?

So in the circular file the flowers went. Well, the first bunch I gave to all the women in the office; I figured something so beautiful should be shared. But when they started showing up every day, my first inclination was to not bother reading the cards—I knew who they were from anyway, and I wasn't interested in reading anything he had to say—to just throw them in the trash. Until one of the little girls in the center made it clear she had noticed what was going on.

"Ms. Chance," Missy said, surrounded by two of her homegirls, "can I have your flowers when they come today? Because yesterday, when I picked them out of the garbage, they had coffee on them."

"What were you doing picking anything out of my garbage?" I asked, putting my hand on my hip. "That's nasty."

"I know, but the flowers were so pretty and they were still alive and I love flowers," she said. "I took the others home and put them in my room so that I would have something nice to look at when I wake up in the morning."

One of her friends, Jonetta, looked at Missy, rolled her eyes and threw her head back in mock disgust. "You're so corny," she said. The third girl, Meeka, laughed.

"Well, if I get more today, they're yours," I said with a smile.

"Thanks!" Missy said excitedly. "But can I ask you a question? Why you throwing away your flowers? They're so pretty."

I thought about it for a moment, and then answered simply, "Because the person who's sending them isn't sending them because he really cares."

"Hold up," Jonetta said, incredulous. "So what? He's giving you presents. Who cares if he cares or not? At least you're getting something."

"Well, Jonetta, honey, just because somebody gives you something doesn't mean they care," I said, frowning a bit. "It simply means they had the money to buy you something."

"Exactly," she said quickly. "And that's what I want my man to have."

"Honey, if that's all you want from a man, then you're in for a lot of lonely nights," I responded. Missy and Meeka laughed. Jonetta rolled her eyes at them; I realized quickly that she'd taken what I said as a diss, which certainly wasn't my intention. But this little girl needed to know that life wasn't a rap video, where her only role was to be dissected into body parts with nothing but a bunch of cheap trinkets to show for her troubles. So I stood there and told her and Missy and Meeka about where I came from—how I was living after I had my two children out of wedlock, barely a grown-up myself, and how I collected checks from the government while I got myself together. "See, the same man who had given me money and jewelry and all those beautiful presents when I was a teenager didn't give me anything when it counted," I said. "What I needed most from him was to be a daddy to his kids, and he didn't do that. So I learned pretty quickly that someone sending you flowers or giving you a necklace or some other bauble doesn't mean anything. It's all in his actions."

Jonetta sucked her teeth again, but the other two were clinging to my every word. Finally, Missy spoke. "Wow," she said. "I didn't know you were living like that. I thought because you came from Teaneck you didn't know anything about living in the 'hood. You're all right."

Now ain't that some shit? Here I was making assumptions about all of them, and all the while, they were making assumptions about me. Funny how things work like that. Now I was all right because I had established my ghetto papers—I had my 'hood authenticity. I looked Missy in the eye and said, "You're pretty all right yourself."

One day, the flowers stopped. I can't tell you who was more upset—me or Missy. I'd started getting used to them, comforted in the idea that this man, though he had messed up royally, was still thinking about me and was committed to putting things right. And, I have to admit, it felt good to have a man sweating me. Missy had started getting used to them, too—she'd hop around excitedly when the deliveryman made his grand entrance with a new bouquet. When they stopped coming, I was disappointed, wondering if that was it from Kenneth, and Missy stopped cheesing in the afternoons, finding other things to do besides sit in my office jabbering about nothing.

But when I got home that evening, there was a letter in my mailbox—from Kenneth. In a beautiful envelope that was obviously a special purchase from a stationery store. For a fleeting moment, my heart beat a little extra, but it subsided just as quickly as it had started. It was a letter from Kenneth. So what? I chucked it into the garbage. I didn't really care what he had to say.

After dinner, though, I fished it back out of the can. Suppose James saw it when he took out the garbage? And, God forbid, read it? No, I couldn't let that happen; he'd been through enough as it was. So I put the damn thing in my dresser drawer, and tried to forget it was there—the same thing I did with the rest of the letters that came each day for six days after that.

"Well, aren't you curious?" asked Mikki, who'd come over that Saturday for lunch. She was dining on fresh tuna fish salad with arugula on croissants when I told her about the flowers and the letters, which I'd avoided mentioning to her all this time for this specific reason. But I couldn't take it anymore; I had to tell somebody about what was going on, and even though I loved April, I wasn't ready to tell her any more than I already had—I told her that Kenneth and I had cooled off our relationship—because I'd found out that she'd accidentally slipped and told one of the parents, a mutual friend, that Kenneth and I had a thing going on. Luckily, it was a man, so he didn't waste too much of his time gossiping to the other parents about my business, but when April told me she accidentally told him (she's messing around with the guy and it came up in innocent conversation, she insists), I decided right then and there not to divulge any more details to her. So Mikki was it. Besides, I owed her an apology for ripping into her that afternoon after I'd lost my job. She was right; she didn't have anything to do with my parents' decision to banish me from the family when I had had my children, and, after I had calmed down I called her and told her so. She forgives easily. Well, me at least. That's what I love about her most.

"What's there to be curious about?" I asked Mikki as I poured her mimosa. I could hear the kids playing in the backyard outside. It was blistering cold, but that never stopped them from running around like little banshees when the sun was shining. "It probably says, 'I'm sorry, please forgive me, blah, blah, blah.' Whatever."

"Blah, blah, blah, hell—if you don't want to read them, at least I do. Where are they?"

I was reluctant to show them to her, but dammit, curiosity was getting the best of me, too. "They're upstairs in my drawer," I said.

"Well, let's go take a look at them, shall we?" Mikki said, pushing herself back from the table and practically racing for the stairs. I stood up slowly, grabbed my mimosa, took a swig, and followed her on up the stairs. Just as Mikki had pulled the stack of letters out of my top drawer and I'd fallen back on my bed, the phone rang.

"Hello?" I said, half giggling at Mikki zealously pulling the envelope apart to get to the letter.

"Hey, baby."

It was Ricky Fish. Talk about killing a natural high. What could he want? I thought. And what should I do? Hang up? Curse him out? Humiliate him? Yeah—humiliate. "I'm sorry," I said, "but I could have sworn I told you that I wasn't going to pick you up from the Big

House. If you start walking now, you might make it to Newark some-time next week."

"Zaria—I didn't call to ask for a ride from prison. I'm not in prison. I'm home. And I didn't call to argue with you, either. I called hoping we could talk about our kids."

I sat up and put my drink on my nightstand. No, this Negro was not calling my house in the middle of a sunny Saturday afternoon to talk about *my* kids. Not today, he wasn't. "What do you mean 'our' kids?" I asked. "What exactly is there to talk about today that you couldn't in the last ten years, Fish?"

Mikki heard his name and put Kenneth's letter down.

"Look, Zaria," Fish said with a sigh. "I didn't call to argue. I called to ask if I could come and get the kids sometime in the next few weeks, so that I can spend some time with them."

My mouth dropped open. "You wanna do what? Take my kids away somewhere? Man, have you lost your damn mind?"

"Why would that be such a stretch, Zaria? I want to see my kids."

I was incredulous. "Well, let's see. You haven't seen them in years. The last time I talked to you, you were getting out of prison. The time I talked to you before that, you were on the run from the police for selling drugs. You haven't paid a dime in child support since you gave me that paper bag full of money—let's see, what was that, a decade ago? I don't know where you live. I don't know how you're living. I don't know anything about you, Fish. So tell me again why I would remotely entertain leaving my children—and yes, that's an emphasis on *my* children—with the likes of you."

He was quiet; I was tempted to hang up. But I wanted to hear this madness. "You know, Zaria, I've changed."

"Oh really, Fish? I don't count getting out of prison a sincere change. That's something the law is required to do—set criminals free after they've served their time. Rehabilitation isn't exactly a part of the equation."

"Well that's just it, Zaria," he said, still calm. "I served my time. And I've changed. I've changed a lot. I got my GED, I got a little job as a counselor at a drug treatment facility for teenagers, I got my own apartment. It's not much, but it's mine. And now I want to have my kids back in my life. I was a criminal before, but now I'm ready to be a father. Thinking about my children was the only thing that got me through that stretch in the house, and I want them to know that they have a father."

"I don't know, Fish. You could always talk a sweet game—Lord knows I know that much. I've never purposely tried to keep my kids away from you—despite what you told my son the last time you called here. You were just never interested. But it's too late now. I'm not with leaving them with you," I said.

I saw Mikki looking me dead in the mouth.

"I know, I know—that was wrong. I shouldn't have told James that and I apologize," he said. "I just wanted to see him so badly and I didn't want him to be mad at me. So I slipped and said it, and the moment it came out of my mouth, I was sorry. It won't happen again."

"You're right. It won't. Because he knows all about your bullshit and your lies. But the beauty of it is that I didn't have to tell him anything; he knows you're full of it without me having to say a word, Fish. But I'll tell you what: Give me your phone number, and you can make the arrangements with James and Jasmine directly. That way, if your ass doesn't show up, they can know that I had nothing to do with their trifling daddy being, well, trifling."

He sighed, but complied with my request and gave up the digits. "I've really changed," he said after he finished.

"Uh-huh. Right."

And with that, I hung up. And then I freaked out.

"Wow," Mikki said, still holding Kenneth's letter in her hand. "What the hell does he want?"

"He's talking about coming over here and taking them out or something. But I'm not trippin' because he won't show. As usual."

"Well, you're not going to tell the kids he called, are you?"

"Oh yeah. And they can call him, too. So that when he doesn't do what he says he's going to do, they can get mad at him, not me. He already had James thinking I was keeping him away from his daddy. I'm not going to have a repeat of that."

"I guess," was all Mikki could muster up to say. She put Kenneth's letter down. Just like that neither of us felt like reading anything he'd written.

He

I was thinking about the day's lesson on the different branches of federal government when I approached the billboard, so I didn't even have a chance to prepare myself. When I looked up and saw my simple and stark message spread across the side of the highway, I was so startled I almost lost control of the truck. I couldn't help but break out into a big grin. It looked even more dramatic and attention-grabbing than I had thought it would. What would she make of it?

ZARIA,

Every day can be New Year's Eve.

LOVE, *Kenneth*

The background was black and all the letters were white, except for her name and the *Love, Kenneth*, which were bloodred. My name was written in script. It was simple, yet quite beautiful. I was tickled. I slowed down to almost a stop. I wanted to stay on the highway and stare at my billboard for the rest of the day. How could Zaria not be moved by this?

Later that night, I lay awake in my bed, staring at the telephone, begging it to ring. She would have passed the billboard hours ago. Why hadn't she called yet? A thousand reasons occurred to me, like maybe she had started taking a different route home, or maybe it was too dark for her to see it. But the billboards were illuminated at night—in some ways they were even more attention-grabbing when the darkness was pierced by this loud message brightly displayed in the klieg lights. And it was unlikely that Zaria, who had a hard enough time following the same route every day, would have switched up to a different commute so soon.

After day five of my billboard, as my desperation grew, my friend Jerry Slavin approached me in the teachers' lounge. I didn't feel like chitchat, but I knew there was no deterring Jerry when he wanted to talk.

"Roman, we got a little betting pool going here among the teachers. I've been sent to get the correct answer. All these women are scared to ask you—even Richie. What did you do to frighten all the women, my friend? Anyway, the question is this: Do you have anything to do with that billboard out by the highway near the GW Bridge approach? It says something about New Year's Eve and it's to a Zaria, signed by a Kenneth. Is that you?"

I turned and looked Slavin in the eye. What did I want to do here? Did I really want all my business in the street? Of course I knew a billboard wasn't exactly the best way of keeping my business secret, but I had a chance here to slip away from the gossipmongers. So I took it. I shook my head.

"Nah, that's not me. I saw that billboard, too."

"I knew it!" Slavin exclaimed. "Ha. I told them that's not your style." He started walking away. "Thanks, man," he said over his shoulder.

The next week, on day twelve of my billboard—by now my depression had grown so thick that I was barely able to push myself from the bed in the morning—Slavin approached me in the hallway, clutching a copy of a local paper, *The Register*.

"I know you said you had nothing to do with that billboard, but I wondered if you saw this," he said, thrusting the paper into my face. I looked down and saw a picture of my billboard underneath the headline ROMANTIC MESSAGE HAS THE PUBLIC GUESSING—AND SWOONING. I wanted to race through the story eagerly, but I saw Slavin watching me closely. Apparently he hadn't really believed my denial.

"One of the teachers said that a kid in your class, James Chance, has a mother named Zaria," he said, peering into my face. I looked up at him and shrugged. I handed the paper back.

"Must be a coincidence," I said. I kept walking down the hall, leaving him standing there with the paper in his hand and a doubtful look on his face. Inside, however, I was quaking. The newspaper had written an article? What did it say? I was excited and a little scared at once. I didn't expect this thing to explode into some kind of local urban myth. And what must Zaria be thinking at this point? How could she have gone this long without calling me? I decided at that moment to call her tonight and every night until she talked to me. I desperately needed to hear her voice. But first I had to find that newspaper.

I tracked down a copy of *The Register* in the teachers' lounge and quickly found the story on the cover of the features section.

ROMANTIC MESSAGE HAS THE PUBLIC GUESSING—AND SWOONING
By Chandler Harding

Who are Zaria and Kenneth, and exactly what did they do on New Year's Eve?

That's the question local residents and commuters all across New Jersey are asking themselves after seeing a mysterious love message blasted on a billboard on Route 17 in Teaneck. The words are simple and the message is clearly romantic: "Zaria, Every day can be New Year's Eve. Love, Kenneth." But what do the words mean?

In downtown Teaneck at Café Cocoa, a tableful of ladies at lunch couldn't stop talking about the billboard. Apparently it touched some kind of dreamy nerve, sending these women on flights of romantic fancy.

"I wish my husband was still romantic like that," said Ellie Rothfield, a resident of Tenafly. "About the most romantic thing he ever wrote to me was, Happy Mother's Day. Maybe he can drive past that billboard and get some ideas."

Each of the ladies said they had made special trips on the highway over the past two weeks just so they could get another glimpse of the billboard before it gets taken down.

Joe Trumbull, president of the Infinity Company, which owns the billboard site, refused to divulge the identity of the man who rented the space. He said he had never met the man and the entire transaction was done over the phone. Trumbull said the billboard is scheduled to be changed Saturday unless the romantic Mr. Kenneth pays for more time.

"It just serves as a reminder that we should not take our mates and our relationships for granted," said Julie Harmon, a Teaneck resident who has been married for 11 years. "I don't mind saying that everytime I see it, I want to rush home and jump into bed with my husband."

Could the billboard possibly be responsible for juicing up the sex lives of couples all over Bergen County? The women at Café Cocoa all nodded enthusiastically.

"I think it should never be taken down," said Jamie Rumson of Teaneck, a married mother of two. "They should keep it there as a—what do you call it?—public service announcement. I don't know who Kenneth is, but I want to thank him for being so romantic. And I hope this Zaria woman, wherever she is, appreciates what she has."

"But I think Zaria has dumped him, Jamie," Rothfield said. "He's trying to win her back."

Barbara Sloman, a divorced mother of two from Englewood, said that if this indeed were true, that Kenneth had been dumped, she had her own message to send out to him: "Call me."

I didn't know whether to laugh or cry. How bizarre that all these strangers were sitting around speculating about my love life, coming up with their own scenarios about my motivations. It was thrilling but somehow discomforting. Funny, I had never considered the larger consequences of the billboard. All I had been thinking about was Zaria.

Though my plan was to call Zaria later that night, it was after eleven by the time I got home. We had a game, another easy win. After the game, I saw Jermaine and his dad huddled in the bleachers with Don Nazerio and another gentleman, a good-looking white man in an expensive suit. Must be the agent himself. I didn't even bother to approach them this time. I left the gym with a queasy feeling in my stomach.

I changed my mind about calling Zaria. I passed by the billboard the next morning, a Friday, and was startled to see a car dealership ad. Wasn't it a day early? I felt the heat start concentrating around my neck and spread through my head like helium in a balloon. I had spent $1,900 and never even got a phone call? The love billboard had become a celebrity, had people making special highway trips just to see it, and I got no acknowledgment from the woman it was intended to reach? That was outrageous.

Self-Righteousness

By the time I headed to practice later that afternoon, I was in a foul mood. My teaching lessons had not gone well at all—the kids barely paid attention. It was late February and the kids had gotten distracted by the snow that had started falling by the end of third period. In their minds, there was nothing better than a heavy, Friday afternoon snow-fall that would give them the whole weekend for snow play—well, except for a Sunday night snowfall heavy enough to close school on Monday. I hated the snow, so the white stuff didn't help my mood. I was glad for my four-wheel drive as I saw cars slipping and sliding around me, but I wasn't exactly comfortable with the driving conditions. The snow had stopped, but there were several inches of accumulation on the ground, meaning anyone who slid behind a steering wheel was vulnerable to the legions of incompetent drivers populating Jersey roads.

Why didn't she call?

The question encircled my head like a skullcap, always there, gripping my scalp. The nerve. The gall. Did she hate me that much? Damn, I had intended to tell her about Laney; she never gave me a chance. Wasn't like we had been dating for ten months. We were just starting to learn things about each other. She had never even told me anything about the father of her children—not even whether they had the same father. One can't assume these days. That may sound foul, but I'm just keeping it real.

As soon as I stepped into the gym, nearly a half hour late because of the slow-moving commute to Jersey City, immediately I knew something was up. The players were congregated in a corner, apparently talking to Jermaine and his dad. I knocked the snow off my shoes—I hadn't listened to the weather reports so I hadn't worn boots—hoping they weren't going to be ruined by the salt that had been scattered all around the grounds of South End and St. Paul's. I walked over to the group. Normally the players dispersed when I approached, but not this time.

"What's up?" I asked.

Jermaine shifted on his feet. But his father had a big smile on his face.

"Coach, can we talk to you privately for a minute?" Will Bryson said.

"Sure." I headed into the tunnel toward my office with them on my heels. I sensed what this might be about. It had something to do with that agent I'd seen after the game. I did *not* need any more drama on this day. My nostrils flared—the tunnel leading to our lockers and my office was permanently funky, decades of boy and girl sweat clinging to the walls. But it was especially pungent on this day. Needed to talk to Mr. Turley the janitor. A lone, uncovered lightbulb unsuccessfully tried to add cheer to the corridor.

"Coach, we have decided to declare for the NBA draft," Jermaine's dad said as soon as we entered my office. "I know you have advised the boys against it, but we felt it was the right thing for us. We have been told that Jermaine will be a high, first-round choice. We think he's ready."

Bryson evidently had his speech all prepared. I sat down in my chair with a loud thud. I wasn't completely surprised, but it was still overwhelming to actually hear him say the words. I looked up at the teenager, who was watching me like a frightened little boy. I knew my approval was important to him. We had had a rough time of it this season, ever since I had hired his dad, but we were still quite close. And I think I had earned some points when I didn't report him after catching him and Sondra screwing under the bleachers. It was important for me to not discourage him at this moment. But I still had to let them know I strongly disagreed.

"I figured this was coming when I kept seeing these agents crawling around," I began. "You know, sometimes I wish the whole system hadn't gotten so out of hand, so good players could just enjoy their years in high school without getting pulled at in so many different directions. High school is the last time you can be so carefree, no worries, no bills. Even in college you have to worry a lot more about money and responsibilities. But when these guys start coming around so early forcing you to think about cash and commerce and endorsements and all that stuff way too soon, kids can lose perspective."

I paused, looking at Jermaine and back at his father. I knew there was virtually no chance of changing their minds. I might have had a shot if I was just dealing with the seventeen-year-old, but he had the approval of his dad to fortify the decision. That was irreversible. I kicked myself for never getting around to calling my guy from the Knicks. This was my punishment.

"Jermaine, you are a wonderful basketball player and I'm sure you have the talent to play in the NBA. But it's about so much more than just basketball talent up there. It's about maturity, about psychological toughness. I'm not saying you don't have those things, but you really have no way of knowing until you're tested. And that's what college does—it provides you with those crucial tests that you can call on when you do move up later on. Sure, there are a few players who came out of high school who are doing well, but the vast majority of them kinda drift for quite a while. The ones who get at least a couple years of college do much better."

Will Bryson was nodding. "Yes, we've talked about all that, Coach. We've weighed all the pros and cons. Georgetown is a great school and they have a great program. But Jermaine wanted to give the pros a shot, so I don't see anything wrong with that. As I always tell him, you only live once. College isn't going anywhere. The rest of us work our whole lives, getting up every morning mainly to work for somebody else, to make somebody else rich. But my boy has a chance here to have his entire destiny in his own hands. He is completely responsible for his success or failure and he has a chance to become a rich man in just a few months. How can you turn that down, guaranteed millions? It would be like handing back the lottery ticket and saying you didn't want to cash in."

I nodded. Of course the money argument was a strong one. And of course a parent was going to be a little too interested in the windfall. There was no getting around that reality. I thought of something in a panic—what about Tariq?

"Do you know what Tariq is doing?" I asked, looking at Jermaine.

He shrugged. "He said he was going to college. He said you told him he'd be better off if he got a year or two of college under his belt. He listens to everything you say, Coach."

Jermaine said this last line with a hint of a smirk, as if Tariq's loyalty were amusing to him. That annoyed me more than a little. This smart-ass teenager was going to have his head handed to him on a paper plate in a few months when he went up against grown men who would have no mercy. Bet that smirk would be gone real quick. Shockingly, Tariq was the one who turned out to have some sense. The boy was headed to Duke. It didn't get any better than that.

I reached my hand across the desk in Jermaine's direction. I was tired of talking to these two. Time to give them my blessing and be done with it.

"I wish you the best of luck, young man," I said. Jermaine stepped forward and shook my hand. "Thanks, Coach," he said. He appeared to sigh deeply, as if he had just gotten some welcomed news. It pleased me to know he had been nervous about telling me.

When we emerged from the tunnel, I got another shock—television crews were milling about the gym, and a red-faced Father Brown was standing in the midst of it all, not looking happy. He spotted me and approached quickly. "Did you know anything about this?" he said. He sounded a little too accusatory. I was tempted to snap at him, but I held my tongue. Father Brown didn't like surprises. That was something I had learned years ago. So his irritation here was understandable and completely predictable. I shouldn't take it personally.

"No, I didn't," I said, shaking my head. "I just found out about it. Somebody must have called them. Probably that agent."

Father Brown eyed me closely. "Agent?" he repeated.

"Yeah. There's been a scout for an agent snooping around them for weeks, Tariq and Jermaine. I had talks with them and didn't think it would come to this. Tariq didn't bite, but I think Jermaine's dad wanted him to do this. You know, it's a lot of money."

Father Brown nodded slowly, sadly. We stood together and watched the two television cameramen arrange themselves in front of Jermaine and his dad. This was about to become a press conference. I also saw a reporter I recognized from another local newspaper, *The Jersey Journal*, pointing a tape recorder in their direction. The other players stood away from the gathering, watching it all in wide-eyed wonder. I zeroed in on Tariq, who had a big smile on his face—I had no idea why. Father Brown and I moved closer so we could hear.

A pretty blond woman with a layer of makeup caked on her face asked most of the questions. She was a little too aggressive, trying to play the story like Jermaine was making a big mistake.

"The NBA executives I talked to said you were taking a risk because you might not go high enough in the first round to justify this decision," she said loudly. Why did they always talk so loudly?

Jermaine appeared to be taken aback. He clearly wasn't expecting an ambush. This was supposed to be a celebratory day for him. He shrugged. "Uh, well, that's not what I've been told," he said. "I, uh, I feel confident." But he didn't look confident at all. I was torn—a part of me wanted to step in there and defend my player, but I also wanted him to feel some of the heat that would become a regular part of his life in the NBA—belligerent reporters, difficult questions, uncomfortable moments.

The cameraman whispered something in the woman's ear and she swung her gaze toward me. "You're his coach, right?" she said. Not even waiting for my answer, she continued. "Can you step over here and tell us your feelings about this?"

I felt a knot tightening in my stomach. This I hadn't expected. I took a deep breath and stepped into the fray.

"Jermaine is obviously one of the best high school players in the nation, maybe *the* best." I caught Tariq's eye beyond the cameras. I gave him a tiny wink. Another grin spread across his face. He knew he was not being dissed. "Jermaine is also an extremely mature player. He has shown that maturity night after night this season. So if any high school player were ready for the pros, it would be Jermaine." I reached over and grabbed Jermaine's shoulder as I was talking. I felt tense muscles bunched up under my fingers. Maybe he knew I was lying, particularly about the maturity. I didn't look at him, but I felt him slowly starting to relax under my touch. "If he goes high in the first round or low in the first round, he will still become a valuable member of some lucky NBA team. But if any team gets a chance to watch his tapes and to work him out, they'll quickly see that he has one of the deadliest jump shots that you'll find on a 6-8 swingman, in high school *or* college. That's very rare for a player of his age. He's deadly from beyond the NBA three-point line. If you guys stick around with your cameras and watch us practice, you'll see for yourself."

Jermaine grinned and nodded. He liked that line.

"Wow, you are *very* encouraging," the blond reporter said. "Did you encourage him to make this decision?"

I didn't like this woman at all. She was approaching this story like she was on the trail of the Watergate break-in. She needed to ease the fuck up.

I shook my head. "I'm not going to get into the details of our private conversations," I said. "Those are between me and Jermaine." I glared at her, daring her to pursue this line of questioning. But she backed off.

The reporters were done with me—the rest of the questions were directed at Jermaine and his dad and they were much friendlier in tone. I saw a bunch of students in the corner of the gym, watching the proceedings. The word must have gotten out. I could see Sondra Whitfield among them. I wondered what she was thinking. She must have known she was about to lose her boyfriend.

The cameras did stick around long enough to get shots of Jermaine shooting with his teammates. He stood out beyond the three-point line, boldly taking on the challenge I had presented, and calmly stroked three-pointers, at one point hitting seven in a row from different spots. It was an impressive display and it had everyone in the gym wearing broad grins—even Father Brown, who looked at me and shook his head in admiration. I decided at that moment that the boy was going to be all right. He had a feel for the stage, for the big moment, and he didn't shy away from it. He *wanted* all eyes on him. He could deliver.

She

I haven't a clue how I missed it; it's not like I don't travel down that same stretch of highway every day twice a day to and from Jersey City. A couple times over the past few weeks, after some super-brutal traffic on the world's largest parking lot, I tried a different route and got lost—which completely freaked me out because all three times, I ended up traveling through some pretty shady territories on the way to the community center. So I eventually made my way back to using the route that Kenneth had mapped out for me along the turnpike.

Still, for some reason, I never noticed the billboard. Probably because I never paid much attention to billboards anyway. It's not like they spoke to people like me; they either appealed to the smokers and the drinkers of the world (as if they needed a billboard to tell them to drink cheap cognac and inhale cancer into their lungs), or ordered grown people to do things they probably already knew they shouldn't be doing anyway, like smoking and drinking. So, like, what was the point? There wasn't, so I didn't bother looking up— just kept my eyes trained on the road, which was best because I wasn't the greatest driver in the world anyway. I'll admit that much. I'm a child of the suburbs, so I learned how to drive quite early; you could climb behind the wheel as early as age sixteen where I grew up, so long as you had adult supervision. My adult supervision was

Ricky Fish, who would regularly coax me behind the wheels of cars he and his boys would steal from unfortunate fools who happened into Newark with nice rides that stuck out like sore thumbs. But I would be so nervous that I was going to get caught driving a stolen vehicle, and, on top of that, Fish wasn't the most gentle driving coach in the world, so I gave up trying to learn rather quickly. Daddy never bothered; he was too busy being mad at me all the time. And my mother? Well, let's just say that despite the fact that she had fooled somebody into giving her a license at some point in her life, my dad does all the driving in the house. They both like it that way. So I never got any official driving lessons until about eight years ago, when I got my job at the college and had to find an easier, cheaper way to commute across town to the school, then to each of my kids' schools, and then to my house. I learned enough to get me through my private lessons and pass the driving test, but I wouldn't say that I've mastered it yet. In fact, I'd say it's still a little scary for me to drive on the highway, seeing as up until now, I really didn't have a reason to get on it in the first place, except when I was making my big journeys to Mikki's in Brooklyn, or my parents' house in South Orange.

So when I drive, I've got both my hands on the wheel, and both my eyes on the road. Billboards don't factor anywhere into the equation.

But one specific one was about to.

When I walked into the community center, Janiece had a crooked smile on her face and actually said "Hello" to me. A first. As I walked through the center, across the basketball court, past the library and up the stairs, my coworkers (the few who bothered to be on time everyday) were staring at me and whispering to one another. One woman, Lindey, actually broke out into applause and slapped me on my back as I walked by. "You better work it, girl," she said.

I stopped in my tracks and looked at her as if she were high. "What?" I said simply.

"Whatever you put on that boy on New Year's Eve, more power to you," she said. "You better go in the library and write up a manual on how to get a nigga sprung so the rest of us can take notes."

"Lindey, what the hell are you talking about?" I said, laughing because everyone else was laughing, but still not sure why. Was she referring to Kenneth's flowers? They'd stopped coming weeks ago; why was she talking about this now?

"You didn't see the billboard?"

All right, that's it. "When you stop talking in code, let me know, okay?" I said, getting annoyed at her taking me around in circles and the insider jokes. "Tell me in English what the hell you're talking about."

"Oh shit—she never saw the billboard," Lindey said, turning to the others. "Damn. How the hell you miss a billboard with your name on it?" After a few more giggles, she turned her attention back to me. "You need to read today's paper."

"What paper—*The Times*?"

"Huh? The what? No, baby, *The Register*."

"I don't read *The Register*." I sniffed.

"Figures," she said, sucking her teeth, another gesture that got another round of giggles out of her girls. "Tell you what: Go on up to your office. I'll be up there in a minute with a story from *The Register* that should make your day."

"All righty then," I said, turning on my heels, still reeling from her suggestion that somehow I thought I was better than somebody because I didn't read that little raggedy-ass paper. "I'll be upstairs in my office, drinking my coffee and reading *The Times*." I wanted to add "silly ass," but I resisted. They weren't worth it. I swear, some of the grownups needed to take some lessons in tact and civility from the kids around here.

But by the time I'd gotten up to my office, someone had already slid the article under my door. There it was, in bold letters for the entire world—at least the entire state of New Jersey—to see: "ZARIA, EVERY DAY CAN BE NEW YEAR'S EVE, LOVE, KENNETH."

My God. Kenneth had paid someone to put a billboard up. Right off the turnpike. Saying, essentially, that he wanted to make me feel like the happiest, luckiest girl in the world. My Kenneth. For me. In an instant, all the feelings that I had for him that evening—the most wonderful, romantic evening I'd ever spent with any man ever—rushed into my chest, all at once making each and every part of my body tingle. Love. He had ended the message with "Love, Kenneth." He loved me? He must. The flowers, the letters . . . the letters. If he had gone that far with a billboard for all the world to see—off the New Jersey Turnpike, no less—what could he have said in those letters? How idiotic could I have been to have just shoved them into my dresser drawer without even considering opening them and at least hearing the boy out? Well, I did try to read them once, but I was rudely distracted by my kids' father—more on him later—and never went back to them.

Being too evil.

As usual.

I'm such an ass.

I didn't even give the boy a chance to explain. For all I knew, James may have been mistaken and that wasn't his daughter. Aw hell, it was his daughter—no man would have gone through what Kenneth Roman had to apologize if he hadn't done anything wrong. But he'd gone through the trouble to apologize. For going on a month now. And in very public ways, without any regard for anyone else getting into his business. What man would concern himself with such things? None I'd ever been with. They'd have long ago moved on to the next hootchie—or three—and forgot about my behind in a heartbeat.

Kenneth deserved my ear. Yes, I was going to call him.

I looked at my watch; it was only 10 A.M. He'd be in class now; I didn't want to call his cell phone and disturb his lesson. I'd have to wait until he had lunch break, which was right around the time that I took mine. But wait—I wanted to see the billboard. Didn't the article say they'd be taking it down tomorrow?

Just as I was deciding whether I should zoom over to the turnpike to see it now or wait until lunchtime, my extension rang. "Good morning, Zaria Chance speaking," I practically sang into the phone.

"Okay, hooker—how come you didn't tell me?" It was April. "I have to pick up the morning paper and read all about Kenneth and Zaria's big adventures? I thought we were girls."

"I didn't know!" I screamed into the phone, giggling.

"What do you mean you didn't know? How the hell does one go driving down the turnpike every morning and miss a billboard with her name plain as day in bold letters twenty feet high? Apparently, the rest of the world saw it."

"You saw the story?"

"Yes—me and half the world. I dropped the kids off at school this morning and everybody was talking about it," she said, then added quickly, "I didn't give up any details, don't worry. But plenty of people were asking."

"Well damn."

"So, what did you do to Mr. Kenneth that he's spent thousands of dollars to express his gratitude for your freaky New Year's Eve?"

"Long story," I said, not really wanting to tell April anything about what was going on between me and Kenneth just yet. "Listen, I have to go. I'll stop by tonight and tell you all about it."

"Damn. You just gonna leave a sistah hanging, huh?"

"Girl—in case you didn't realize, some of us work for a living."

She laughed. "You know you're wrong. But whatever. Don't even bother going home tonight; come straight here. I want details, bitch. Holding out on me? Oh no—I don't think so."

"Good-bye, April," I laughed, and hung up.

Long story short: I didn't get a chance to go see the billboard during lunch because I was swamped at work. Ended up eating pizza at my desk, anxious to get what I had to do done so that I could get on the road and see Kenneth's mea culpa. Then, I decided that I would check it out on the way home. And I tried, I really did. But I got all turned around on the turnpike, and got lost somewhere in Ridgewood (don't ask). By the time I untangled myself from the streets of this and several other unfamiliar towns and had made it back to the highway, I just kept driving to Teaneck.

Of course, I'd forgotten to call Kenneth when I knew he'd be commuting to Jersey City, and by the time I remembered, I was sure he'd left Teaneck and was knee-deep in basketball practice. I debated stopping by St. Paul's, but talked myself out of it. He was at work; I didn't want to disturb him—I knew how seriously he took his coaching job, and I wasn't ready to bring that kind of drama to the court. So I decided to call him in the evening, after the kids had gone to sleep, and after I'd read his letters.

The first one was simple and elegant—a heartfelt apology straight out of the annals of Hallmark, with a little Maya Angelou kicked in for good measure. It was on this beautiful white stationery, with a simple red heart at the top of it. By his own hand—his penmanship was sorely lacking, and I had to go over the sentences a few times, but so what—he made the case why we should be together.

> *My dearest Zaria,*
>
> *Baby, there is no explanation, no apology, no words in all of Webster's dictionary that I can pen in this letter that will adequately say how sorry I am for what's happened to us. And I have nothing to blame but my own stupidity. I should have told you about Laney, but I didn't want you to think of me differently for being a single father. The truth is, I love my daughter more than anything in this world; she's my five-year-old princess, the sweetest thing you ever could imagine. I'd give my left arm to make her happy.*
>
> *I'd give my right arm to make you happy. Because you are my queen. And the truth is, I need you in my life, Zaria. These past few months have been nothing short of magic, and I want to feel that high again. Won't you let me make it up to you?*
>
> *Love, Kenneth.*

The second and third letters said more of the same; the fourth had a picture of Laney in it. She was a beautiful little girl, with great big ol' ponytails and an infectious smile. What a lovely little girl. She didn't really look anything like Kenneth, save for his complexion. She had his ears; they were big and stuck out at the top—just like her daddy's. The letter simply said, "This is my Lane. I'll love her till the dolphins fly and parrots swim the sea," a line he borrowed from a Stevie Wonder song, though I couldn't remember the name of it.

The last letter simply said, "I love you."

I had tears in my eyes when I turned over to pick up the phone and call Kenneth, but just as my hand touched the receiver, it rang. "Kenneth?" I said.

"Wrong one. This is Fish."

It was that fool father of my children, calling me with his sorry apologies for not showing up last weekend to take the kids out for dinner like he'd promised them. "I got tied up in a few things and couldn't make it," he mumbled. "But I want to make it up to them and take them out this weekend."

"First of all, you need to give your apologies to your children yourself—I'm not your messenger girl, Fish," I said, annoyed. I didn't even know why I was wasting my breath on this fool; he wasn't ready to do right, and I wasn't about to sit here and hold his hand while he fucked up and disappointed my kids. "I told you I'm not getting into the middle of all your crap. If you want to apologize to the kids, you better do it your damn self."

"Why you so angry, Zaria, damn!" he said, exasperated. He's got the nerve to be annoyed? Negroes.

"Listen," he said, "I didn't call to get into a fight with you. I just want to pick my kids up and let them spend the weekend with me."

"I don't think so."

"And why not? They're just as much mine as they are yours."

I ignored that. "Exactly where are you trying to take my kids for an entire weekend, Fish? Where will they be sleeping? How will they eat? Who are they going to be around?"

"I'm staying by my girlfriend's house in Newark. We're going to stay over there."

"*We* ain't staying nowhere, Fish," I said simply. "If you want to take the kids out to McDonald's or Carvel, be my guest. But they're not going to be sitting up in some stranger's house with you all weekend, watching you do God knows what."

"She's not a stranger. I told you she's my girlfriend."

"Whatever, Fish—they're not going over there. And if you want to apologize to my children, then you should try calling here when they're not sleeping."

"Whatever, Zaria," he said mockingly. "How about I just stop calling?"

"Now there's an idea," I said, and hung up the phone. I was so angry I was shaking.

I wasn't in any condition to call Kenneth.

I gathered up his letters into a neat pile, and put them under my pillow. Yes, Kenneth Roman would hear from me tomorrow.

We had pizza for dinner, our usual Friday fare. I'd just balled the box up and stuffed it into the garbage can and poured myself another glass of Coca-Cola when I heard a familiar voice on the television: It sounded like Kenneth. I ran to the den, grabbed the remote, and turned the television's volume up a notch. There he was, on the 6 P.M. news, talking about something having to do with one of his players. Lord, one of them was going pro. From high school. And Kenneth was standing up there in front of a camera defending it? What the hell was wrong with that man?

Without giving it a second's thought, I picked up the phone and dialed his cell phone number. He answered on the first ring.

"Tell me that I did not just see you on television, trying to convince the world that a child who barely has chin hair should go to the NBA and play with a bunch of old men," I said, talking to Kenneth like we'd just had a conversation five minutes ago.

"Zaria?"

"As many times as you told me that you would never let that snaky agent guy get at those boys, here you are defending the very thing you didn't want him to convince them to do? Explain yourself, Kenneth."

"Zaria," he said. He sounded excited, but hushed. "How are you?"

"I was just fine until I saw that craziness on my television," I said. "Now, you know you should know better. And so should that boy's parents. Oh wait—they're probably the ones who told him to do it, huh? Everybody's going to be living large off that boy's misfortune. Wait until he has to slam that body against Shaq. He'll be sorry. I hope you're happy—"

"Zaria!" he said, interrupting my diatribe. "I'm not that boy's father, so I can't tell him what to do. It's up to him and his family to decide his future, not his coach."

"Well, you certainly weren't helping matters any, telling the entire world he's good enough to battle with the big boys."

"Come on, Zaria—I couldn't dime the boy out on television. I never said I agreed with his decision. Or did you miss that?"

"Yeah, yeah, yeah—I must have missed that."

"I've missed you," he said, lowering his voice.

"I've missed you back."

I wanted him back.

He

So in the end, it turned out to be the oldest story ever told—I got the girl, I acted stupid and lost the girl, then the girl finally came to her senses and I got the girl back. Hearing her voice yelling at me into the phone was the most wonderful sound ever to hit my ears. Being on the receiving end of a Zaria Chance attack was where I belonged. The only place I wanted to be. No, ours wasn't a pairing conceived by screen-writers to fit neatly in a ninety-minute Hollywood tale. We had our is-sues—she was the most aggressively conservative black woman in the Northern Hemisphere, I was a proud descendant of Huey P. Newton. Water and oil, right? I think Joseph and Mary had fewer problems. But luckily these things didn't have to make sense. All they had to do was work. And we both knew this was right. We were back in love. And war.

Only thirty-three minutes separated their emergence into the world, one thousand nine hundred and eighty seconds of elder wisdom that Nina would lord over Aaron for the next three decades. Already mocha brown with a thick thatch of jet black hair, a brand-new Aaron greeted his audience with an endearing whimper, eliciting a joyful noise from his exhausted mother, his exuberant father, and even the slightly indifferent resident who had stepped in when it became apparent that Mom's obstetrician wasn't showing up for the big event. Eighteen miles away from Aaron's well-received entrance in Brooklyn, Nina was already swaddled tightly in the nursery in Queens, discovering the addictive taste of her own wrinkly knuckles. Nina's audience— even Mom—had been all too happy with her banishment to the nursery because the delivery room was still pulsing from the startling decibels reached by her maiden voice. The girl was loud, insistent, and to all who observed, apparently angry about this new development. Nina, for years to come, would never live down the fuss she raised. Her mother would remind anyone who listened, whenever she had reason to note her daughter's aggressive volume, that "the girl been screaming ever since she got here."

Aaron was brought home to a small Brooklyn apartment whose rhythms were hardly altered by his arrival—though the space was instantly squeezed to a maximum, which wasn't a pleasant change in late

July's summer swelter. His mother, Josefina Simmons, was still the same patient soul who could go months without ever raising her voice—even when challenged by the everyday outlandishness of her firstborn son, Carney, who seemed intent upon waking every morning to find a new way to ruffle all feathers in sight. Josefina's patience combined with her husband, Ray's, gentle humor to create a household that could easily rival the idyllic domestication of Josefina's favorite show, *The Brady Bunch*. Josefina was twenty-eight, born in postwar Harlem, so it didn't escape her notice that the world of Carol and Mike Brady was glaringly bereft of colored people. But she tried not to let tiring demands of racial consciousness intrude on her television viewing. After all, she thought, if you got worked up over things like that, you'd never have any peace. Peace was the goal in the Simmons residence, even in the early 1970s, when there wasn't much of it around them. Their goal was to achieve that airless, settled calm that one would normally associate with senior citizens—certainly not a home with two young kids. Pictureless walls, plastic sofa covers, dark beige carpet worn thin not by footfalls but by excessive vacuuming. It was a place that could be lifted whole and deposited in the Smithsonian or the Museum of Natural History, in a wing called "Americana Living Quarters: 1970s." Aaron's father was a Manhattan doorman. His whole day was defined by adhering to decorum, overreacting—or not reacting, period—to nothing. Years later, after he left his parents' house, Aaron escorted a grieving friend to a funeral home and was startled by how comfortable he felt in the company of the dead—or at least in their sitting room.

Nina was carted home by a family who couldn't have been more different from the Simmonses. The home in Jamaica, Queens, was a cluttered mess, throbbing with so much intense energy and filled with so much stuff that the place always seemed about to explode in a shower of militant black outrage. The family's central theme, in fact, told much of the story. Nina's father, Willy, was a Black Panther who had spent the last two years in hiding. The NYPD believed, with good reason, that Willy Carruthers—also known as "Baby Ruth" by party loyalists—had played a key role in the botched robbery of a Department of Transportation parking meter collector. The idea, hatched a week after an unpopular fare and toll hike, was to take back the public's money and stage a very public redistribution—even giving some to white people—thus attracting attention and thousands of converts to their cause. But Baby Ruth and three accomplices wound up breaking the man's arm—for about $35 in quarters and a permanent APB with their names on it. Willy was just the driver—but unfortunately he was using a car registered in his name. The public redistribution idea was shelved. Didn't take the police long to get to his momma's apartment in Harlem. Consequently, Nina's birth certificate read NINA ANDREWS. It would take her twelve years to discover that the name really wasn't hers.

Willy Andrews—née Carruthers—spent most of his days poring over outdated, yellowing Panther literature, harassing his wife, and claiming to look for work as a freelance auto mechanic. He wore a brooding scowl as his morning greeting and rarely found the time—or the inclination—to offer anyone a smile, including his wife, Angelique. As a defense, she had long ago gone on the offensive, berating him for his many faults whenever she got the chance. But still they clung to each other with passionate desperation. And they seemed to find many opportunities to display that passion. It was a union that confounded all who knew them.

But as far as unions go, none was as surpassing as Nina and Aaron's. From the first meeting, they became nearly the same person. It was no surprise to friends and family when eventually their powerful friendship turned into something more. Everyone just wondered what took them so long.

It took twenty-six years to build it up, fine little pieces of selflessness, layered on top of one another like the strongest brick mansion in the neighborhood. Twenty-six years of empathetic embraces, three-hour-long phone calls in the gloom of the night, bold and dramatic acts of courage with no thoughts of one's own well-being, jokes—oh, so many jokes—of such brutal wit that their bellyaching laughs would rumble into the next century; twenty-six years of plenty, of so much love and affection that they could smear jealousy over all who observed them like toddlers spreading a cold virus; two decades plus six years of a friendship for the ages.

And it was all over in exactly thirty-three seconds. Splintered by the same demons that had damned all of their individual attempts to forge meaningful love relationships with the opposite sex: the haunting presence of another woman, a creeping lack of trust, and the nasty drama